THE MASTER AND MARGARITA—

the Moscow epic in which a great Russian novelist lampoons the orthodoxy of his society. Bulgakov combines Walpurgian revel and demonic satire with a vividly realistic record of everyday life as it is lived in the Russian capital.

BANNED BY THE SOVIETS,

the reputation of The Master and Margarita continued to grow underground, until its recent publication in the U.S.S.R. in a censored edition. This Signet edition however, one of two American translations, is the only complete and unexpurgated paperback text, exactly as it was originally written by Mikhail Bulgakov.

THE MASTER AND MARGARITA, which critics knew existed but had never seen in print, is [Bulgakov's] most daring work. Its publication for the first time in Russia is part of a literary rebellion that is sweeping through Soviet letters."
—*Time Magazine*

"The Soviet Encyclopedia charges him with 'slandering Soviet reality.' If mordant, penetrating satire is slander the Encyclopedia is right."
—*The London Sunday Times*

Other Outstanding Novels in SIGNET Editions

Doctor Zhivago *by Boris Pasternak*
This celebrated novel—a bestseller and center of political controversy—has been hailed as a literary masterpiece throughout the world. By the great Russian writer and Nobel Prize winner. (#Q2014—95¢)

Death on the Installment Plan *by Louis-Ferdinand Céline. New translation by Ralph Manheim*
The first complete and unexpurgated English version of a novel that shocked the literary underground in Europe and revolutionized contemporary fiction. The father of black humor fiction, Céline's novel is rich in characterizations drawn from the French countryside and the Parisian marketplaces. (#Y3000—$1.25)

Under the Volcano *by Malcolm Lowry*
The story of a man's efforts to defeat the sinister forces within himself. "One of the towering novels of this century."—*The New York Times* (#Q2902—95¢)

Hopscotch *by Julio Cortázar*
From love in a Paris flat to a madhouse in Buenos Aires, a novel that gets to the core of life, love, and death. "The most brilliant novel in years," commented *New Republic*. By the author of *Blow-Up*.
(#Q3329—95¢)

To Our Readers: If your dealer does not have the SIGNET and MENTOR books you want, you may order them by mail enclosing the list price plus 10¢ a copy to cover mailing. (New York City residents add 5% Sales Tax. Other New York State residents add 2% plus any local sales or use taxes.) Please order books by book number and title. If you would like our free catalog, please request it by postcard only. The New American Library, Inc., P. O. Box 2310, Grand Central Station, New York, N. Y. 10017.

MIKHAIL BULGAKOV

THE
MASTER
AND
MARGARITA

Translated from the Russian
by MICHAEL GLENNY

A SIGNET BOOK

Published by
THE NEW AMERICAN LIBRARY

SIGNET TRADEMARK REG. U.S. PAT. OFF. AND FOREIGN COUNTRIES
REGISTERED TRADEMARK—MARCA REGISTRADA
HECHO EN CHICAGO, U.S.A.

*SIGNET BOOKS are published by
The New American Library, Inc.,
1301 Avenue of the Americas, New York, New York 10019*

PRINTED IN THE UNITED STATES OF AMERICA

CONTENTS

BOOK TWO

BOOK ONE

"Say at last—who art thou?

"That Power I serve
Which wills forever evil
Yet does forever good."

—GOETHE, *Faust*

CHAPTER 1

NEVER TALK TO STRANGERS

At the sunset hour of one warm spring day two men were to be seen at Patriarch's Ponds. The first of them—aged about forty, dressed in a grayish summer suit—was short, dark-haired, well-fed and bald. He carried his decorous hat by the brim as though it were a cake, and his neatly shaven face was embellished by black horn-rimmed spectacles of preternatural dimensions. The other, a broad-shouldered young man with curly reddish hair and a check cap pushed back to the nape of his neck, was wearing a tartan shirt, wrinkled white trousers and black sneakers.

The first was none other than Mikhail Alexandrovich Berlioz, editor of a highbrow literary magazine and chairman of the management committee of one of the biggest Moscow literary clubs, known by its abbreviation as MASSOLIT; his young companion was the poet Ivan Nikolayich Poniryov, who wrote under the pseudonym of Bezdomny.

Reaching the shade of the budding lime trees, the two writers went straight to a gaily painted kiosk labeled "Beer and Soft Drinks."

There was an oddness about that terrible day in May which is worth recording: not only at the kiosk but along the whole avenue parallel to Malaya Bronnaya Street there was not a person to be seen. It was the hour of the day when people feel too exhausted to breathe, when Moscow glows in a dry haze as the sun disappears behind Sadovaya Street—yet no one had come out for a walk under the limes, no one was sitting on a bench, the avenue was empty.

"A glass of lemonade, please," said Berlioz.

"There isn't any," replied the woman in the kiosk. For some reason the request seemed to offend her.

"Got any beer?" inquired Bezdomny in a hoarse voice.

"Beer's being delivered later this evening," said the woman.

"Well what have you got?" asked Berlioz.

"Apricot juice, only it's warm," was the answer.

"All right, let's have some."

The apricot juice produced a rich yellow froth, making the air smell like a hairdresser's. After drinking it the two writers immediately began to hiccup. They paid and sat down on a bench facing the pond, their backs to Bronnaya Street.

Then occurred the second oddness, which affected Berlioz alone. He suddenly stopped hiccuping, his heart thumped and for a moment ceased, then started beating again but with a blunt needle sticking into it. In addition Berlioz was seized by a fear that was groundless but so powerful that he had an immediate impulse to run away from Patriarch's Ponds without looking back.

Berlioz gazed miserably about him, unable to say what had frightened him. He went pale, wiped his forehead with his handkerchief and thought, "What's the matter with me? This has never happened before. Heart playing tricks . . . I'm overstrained . . . I think it's time to chuck everything up and go and take the waters at Kislovodsk."

Just then the sultry air coagulated and wove itself into the shape of a man—a transparent man of the strangest appearance. On his small head was a jockey cap, and he wore a short check jacket fabricated of air. The man was seven feet tall but narrow in the shoulders, incredibly thin and with a face made for derision.

Berlioz' life was so arranged that he was not accustomed to seeing unusual phenomena. Paling even more, he stared and thought in consternation, "It can't be!"

But alas it was, and the tall, transparent gentleman was swaying from left to right in front of him without touching the ground.

Berlioz was so overcome with horror that he shut his eyes. When he opened them he saw that it was all over, the mirage had dissolved, the checkered figure had vanished and the blunt needle had simultaneously removed itself from his heart.

"The devil!" exclaimed the editor. "D'you know, Ivan, the heat nearly gave me a stroke just then! I even saw something like a hallucination. . . ." He tried to smile, but his eyes were still blinking with fear and his hands trembled. However, he gradually calmed down, flapped his handkerchief and with a brave enough "Well, now . . ." picked up the conversation that had been interrupted by their drink of apricot juice.

They had been talking, it seemed, about Jesus Christ. The fact was that the editor had commissioned the poet to write a long antireligious poem for one of the regular issues of his magazine. Ivan Nikolayich had written this poem in record time, but unfortunately the editor did not care for it at all. Bezdomny had drawn the chief figure in his poem, Jesus, in very somber colors, and in the editor's opinion the whole poem had to be written again. And now he was reading Bezdomny a lecture on Jesus in order to stress the poet's fundamental error.

It was hard to say exactly what had made Bezdomny write as he had—whether it was his great talent for graphic description or complete ignorance of his subject, but his Jesus had come out . . . well, completely alive, a Jesus who had really existed, although admittedly a Jesus who had every possible fault.

Berlioz, however, wanted to prove to the poet that the main object was not who Jesus was, whether he was bad or good, but that as a person Jesus had never existed at all and that all the stories about him were mere invention, pure myth.

The editor was a well-read man and able to make skillful reference to the ancient historians, such as the renowned Philo of Alexandria and the brilliantly educated Josephus Flavius, neither of whom mentioned a word of Jesus' existence. With a display of solid erudition, Mikhail Alexandrovich informed the poet that, incidentally, the passage in Chapter 44 of the fifteenth book of Tacitus' *Annales,* in which he describes the execution of Jesus, was nothing but a later forgery.

The poet, for whom everything the editor was saying was a novelty, listened attentively, fixing Mikhail Alexandrovich with his bold green eyes, occasionally hiccuping and cursing the apricot juice under his breath.

"There is not one oriental religion," said Berlioz, "in which an immaculate virgin does not bring a god into the world. And the Christians, lacking any originality, invented their Jesus in exactly the same way. In fact, he never lived at all. That's where the emphasis has got to be placed."

Berlioz' high tenor resounded along the empty avenue, and as Mikhail Alexandrovich picked his way around the sort of historical pitfalls that can only be negotiated safely by a highly educated man, the poet learned more and more useful and instructive facts about the Egyptian god Osiris, son of Earth and Heaven, about the Phoenician god Tammuz, about Marduk and even about the fierce little-known god Vitzli-Putzli, who had once been held in great veneration by the Aztecs of Mexico. At the very moment when Mikhail Alexandrovich was telling the poet how the Aztecs used to model figurines of Vitzli-Putzli out of dough, the first man appeared in the avenue.

Afterward, when it was frankly too late, various persons collected their data and issued descriptions of this man. As to his teeth, he had platinum crowns on the left side and gold ones on the right. He wore an expensive gray suit and foreign shoes of the same color as his suit. His gray beret was stuck jauntily over one ear and under his arm he carried a walking stick with a knob in the shape of a poodle's head. He looked slightly over forty. Crooked sort of mouth. Clean-shaven. Dark hair. Right eye black, left eye for some reason green. Eyebrows black, but one higher than the other. In short—a foreigner.

As he passed the bench occupied by the editor and the poet, the foreigner gave them a sidelong glance, stopped and suddenly sat down on the next bench a couple of paces away from the two friends.

"A German," thought Berlioz. "An Englishman," thought Bezdomny. "Phew, he must be hot in those gloves!"

The stranger glanced over the tall houses that formed a square around the pond, from which it was obvious that he was seeing this locality for the first time and that it interested him. His gaze halted on the upper stories, whose panes threw back a blinding, fragmented reflection of the sun which was setting on Mikhail Alexandrovich forever; he then looked downward to where the windows were turning darker in the early-evening twilight, smiled patronizingly at something, frowned, placed his hands on the knob of his cane and laid his chin on his hands.

"You see, Ivan," said Berlioz, "you have written a marvelously satirical description of the birth of Jesus, the Son of God, but the whole joke lies in the fact that there had already been a whole series of sons of God before Jesus, such as the Phoenician Adonis, the Phrygian Attis, the Persian Mithras. Of course not one of these ever existed, including Jesus, and instead of the nativity or the arrival of the Magi you should have described the absurd rumors about their arrival. But according to your story the nativity really took place!"

Here Bezdomny made an effort to stop his torturing hiccups and held his breath, but it only made him hiccup more loudly and painfully. At that moment Berlioz interrupted his speech because the foreigner suddenly rose and approached the two writers. They stared at him in astonishment.

"Excuse me, please," said the stranger with a foreign accent, although in correct Russian, "for permitting myself, without an introduction . . . but the subject of your learned conversation was so interesting that . . ."

Here he politely took off his beret and the two friends had no alternative but to rise and bow.

"No, probably a Frenchman," thought Berlioz.

"A Pole," thought Bezdomny.

I should add that the poet had found the stranger repulsive from first sight, although Berlioz had liked the look of him, or rather not exactly liked him but . . . well, been interested by him.

"May I join you?" inquired the foreigner, politely and as the two friends moved somewhat unwillingly apart he adroitly placed himself between them and at once joined the conversation. "If I'm not mistaken, you were saying that Jesus never existed, were you not?" he asked, turning his green left eye on Berlioz.

"No, you were not mistaken," replied Berlioz courteously. "I did indeed say that."

"Ah, how interesting!" exclaimed the foreigner.

"What the hell does he want?" though Bezdomny and frowned.

"And do you agree with your friend?" inquired the unknown man, turning to Bezdomny on his right.

"A hundred percent!" affirmed the poet, who loved to use pretentious numerical expressions.

"Astounding!" cried their unbidden companion. Glancing furtively around and lowering his voice, he said, "Forgive me for being so rude, but am I right in thinking that you do not believe in God either?" He gave a horrified look and said, "I swear not to tell anyone!"

"Yes, neither of us believes in God," answered Berlioz with a faint smile at this foreign tourist's apprehension. "But we can talk about it with absolute freedom."

The foreigner leaned against the back rest of the bench and asked, in a voice positively squeaking with curiosity, "Are you . . . atheists?"

"Yes, we're atheists," replied Berlioz, smiling, and Bezdomny thought angrily, "Trying to pick an argument, damn foreigner!"

"Oh, how delightful!" exclaimed the astonishing foreigner and swiveled his head from side to side, staring at each of them in turn.

"In our country there's nothing surprising about atheism," said Berlioz with diplomatic politeness. "Most of us have long ago and quite consciously given up believing in all those fairy tales about God."

At this the foreigner did an extraordinary thing—he stood up and shook the astonished editor by the hand, saying as he did so, "Allow me to thank you with all my heart!"

"What are you thanking him for?" asked Bezdomny, blinking.

"For some very valuable information, which as a traveler I find extremely interesting," said the eccentric foreigner, raising his forefinger meaningfully.

This valuable piece of information had obviously made a powerful impression on the traveler, as he gave a frightened glance at the houses as though afraid of seeing an atheist at every window.

"No, he's not an Englishman," thought Berlioz. Bezdomny thought, "What I'd like to know is, where did he manage to pick up such good Russian?" and frowned again.

"But might I inquire," began the visitor from abroad after some worried reflection, "how you account for the proofs of the existence of God, of which there are, as you know, five?"

"Alas!" replied Berlioz regretfully. "Not one of these proofs is valid, and mankind has long since relegated them to the archives. You must agree that rationally there can be no proof of the existence of God."

"Bravo!" exclaimed the stranger. "Bravo! You have exactly repeated the views of the immortal Immanuel on that subject. But here's the oddity of it: he completely demolished all five proofs and then, as though to deride his own efforts, he formulated a sixth proof of his own."

"Kant's proof," objected the learned editor with a thin smile, "is also unconvincing. Not for nothing did Schiller say that Kant's reasoning on this question would only satisfy slaves, and Strauss simply laughed at his proof."

As Berlioz spoke he thought to himself, "But who on earth *is* he? And how does he speak such good Russian?"

"Kant ought to have been arrested and given three years in Solovki asylum for that 'proof' of his!" Ivan Nikolayich burst out completely unexpectedly.

"Ivan!" whispered Berlioz, embarrassed.

But the suggestion to pack Kant off to an asylum not only did not surprise the stranger but actually delighted him. "Exactly, exactly!" he cried, and his green left eye, turned on Berlioz, glittered. "That's exactly the place for him! I said to him myself that morning at breakfast, 'If you'll forgive me, Professor, your theory is no good. It may be clever but it's dreadfully incomprehensible. People will think you're mad.' "

Berlioz' eyes bulged. "At breakfast . . . to Kant? What is he rambling on about?" he thought.

"But," went on the foreigner, unperturbed by Berlioz' amazement and turning to the poet, "sending him to Solovki is out of the question because for over a hundred years now he has been somewhere far away from Solovki, and I assure you that it is totally impossible to bring him back."

"What a pity!" said the impetuous poet.

"It is a pity," agreed the unknown man with a glint in his eye, and went on: "But this is the question that disturbs me—if there is no God, then who, one wonders, rules the life of man and keeps the world in order?"

"Man rules himself," said Bezdomny angrily in answer to such an obviously absurd question.

"I beg your pardon," retorted the stranger quietly, "but to rule, one must have a precise plan worked out for some reasonable period in the future. Allow me to inquire how man can control his own affairs when he is not only incapable of compiling a plan for some laughably short term, such as, say, a thousand years, but cannot even predict what will happen to him tomorrow?

"In fact—" here the stranger turned to Berlioz—"imagine what would happen if you, for instance, were to start organizing others and yourself, and you developed a taste for it—then suddenly you got . . . he, he . . . a slight heart attack." At this the foreigner smiled sweetly, as though the thought of a heart attack gave him pleasure. "Yes, a heart attack," he repeated the word sonorously, grinning like a cat, "and that's the end of you as an organizer! No one's fate except your own interests you any longer. Your relations start lying to you. Sensing that something is amiss, you rush to a specialist, then to a charlatan, and even perhaps to a fortuneteller. Each of them is as useless as the other, as you know perfectly well. And it all ends in tragedy: the man who thought he was in charge is suddenly reduced to lying supine and motionless in a wooden box, and his fellow men, realizing that there is no more sense to be had of him, incinerate him.

"Sometimes it can be even worse: a man decides to go to Kislovodsk—" here the stranger stared at Berlioz—"a trivial matter you may think, but he cannot because for no good reason he suddenly jumps up and falls under a streetcar. You're not going to tell me that he arranged to do that himself? Wouldn't it be nearer the truth to say that someone quite different was directing his fate?" The stranger gave an eerie peal of laughter.

Berlioz had been following the unpleasant story about the heart attack and the streetcar with great attention, and some uncomfortable thoughts had begun to worry him. "He's not a foreigner . . . he's not a foreigner," he thought. "He's a very peculiar character . . . but I ask you, *who* is he?"

"I see you'd like to smoke," said the stranger unexpectedly, turning to Bezdomny. "What kind do you prefer?"

"Do you mean you've got different kinds?" glumly asked the poet, who had run out of cigarettes.

"Which do you prefer?" repeated the mysterious stranger.

"Well, then, Our Brand," replied Bezdomny, irritated.

The unknown man immediately pulled a cigarette case out of his pocket and offered it to Bezdomny.

"Our Brand."

The editor and the poet were not so much surprised by the fact that the cigarette case actually contained Our Brand as by the cigarette case itself. It was of enormous dimensions, made of solid gold, and on the inside of the cover a triangle of diamonds flashed with blue and white fire.

Their reactions were different. Berlioz thought, "No, he's a foreigner." Bezdomny thought, "What the hell is he?"

The poet and the owner of the case lit their cigarettes, and Berlioz, who did not smoke, refused.

"I shall refute his argument by saying," Berlioz decided to himself, "that of course man is mortal, no one will argue with that. But the fact is that—"

However, he was not able to pronounce the words before the stranger spoke: "Of course man is mortal, but that's only half the problem. The trouble is that mortality sometimes comes to him so suddenly! And he cannot even say what he will be doing this evening."

"What a stupid way of putting the question," thought Berlioz and objected: "Now there you exaggerate. I know more or less exactly what I'm going to be doing this evening. Provided, of course, that a brick doesn't fall on my head in the street."

"A brick is neither here nor there," the stranger interrupted persuasively. "A brick never falls on anyone's head. You in particular, I assure you, are in no danger from that. Your death will be different."

"Perhaps you know exactly how I am going to die?" inquired Berlioz with understandable sarcasm at the ridiculous turn that the conversation seemed to be taking. "Would you like to tell me?"

"Certainly," rejoined the stranger. He looked Berlioz up and down as though he were measuring him for a suit and muttered through his teeth something that sounded like: "One, two . . . Mercury in the second house . . . the moon waning . . . six— accident . . . evening—seven," then announced loudly and cheerfully, "Your head will be cut off!"

Bezdomny turned to the stranger with a wild, furious stare, and Berlioz asked with a sardonic grin, "By whom? Enemies? Foreign spies?"

"No," replied their companion, "by a Russian woman, a member of the Komsomol."

"H'm," grunted Berlioz, upset by the foreigner's little joke. "That, if you don't mind my saying so, is most improbable."

"I beg your pardon," replied the foreigner, "but it is so. Oh, yes, I was going to ask you—what are you doing this evening, if it's not a secret?"

"It's no secret. From here I'm going home, and then at ten o'clock this evening there's a meeting at the MASSOLIT and I shall be in the chair."

"No, that is absolutely impossible," said the stranger firmly. "Why?"

"Because," replied the foreigner and frowned up at the sky where, sensing the oncoming cool of the evening, the birds were flying to roost, "Anna has already bought the sunflower oil; in fact, she has not only bought it but has already spilled it. So that meeting will not take place."

With this, as one might imagine, there was silence beneath the lime trees.

"Excuse me," said Berlioz after a pause, with a glance at the stranger's jaunty beret, "but what on earth has sunflower-seed oil got to do with it . . . and who is Anna?"

"I'll tell you what sunflower oil's got to do with it," said Bezdomny suddenly, having obviously decided to declare war on their uninvited companion. "Have you, comrade, ever had to spend any time in a mental hospital?"

"Ivan!" hissed Mikhail Alexandrovich.

But the stranger was not in the least offended and gave a cheerful laugh. "Yes, I have, I have, and more than once!" he exclaimed laughing, though the stare that he gave the poet was mirthless. "Where haven't I been! My only regret is that I didn't stay long enough to ask the professor what schizophrenia was. But you are going to find that out from him yourself, Ivan Nikolayich!"

"How do you know my name?"

"My dear fellow, who doesn't know you?" With this the foreigner pulled the previous day's issue of *The Literary Gazette* out of his pocket, and Ivan Nikolayich saw his own picture on the front page above some of his own verse. Suddenly what had delighted him yesterday as proof of his fame and popularity no longer gave the poet any pleasure at all.

"I beg your pardon," he said, his face darkening. "Would you excuse us for a minute? I should like a word or two with my friend."

"Oh, with pleasure!" exclaimed the stranger. "It's so delightful sitting here under the trees and I'm not in a hurry to go anywhere, as it happens."

"Look here, Misha," whispered the poet when he had drawn Berlioz aside. "He's not just a foreign tourist, he's a spy. He's a Russian *émigré*, and he's trying to trip us up. Ask him for his papers and then he'll go away."

"Do you think we should?" whispered Berlioz anxiously, thinking to himself, "He's right, of course."

"Mark my words," the poet whispered to him. "He's pretending to be an idiot so that he can trap us with some compromising question. You can hear how he speaks Russian," said the poet, glancing sideways to see that the stranger was not eavesdropping. "Come on, let's arrest him and then we'll get rid of him."

The poet led Berlioz by the arm back to the bench.

The unknown man was no longer sitting on it but standing beside it, holding a booklet in a dark gray binding, a fat envelope made of good paper and a visiting card.

"Forgive me, but in the heat of our argument I forgot to introduce myself. Here is my card, my passport and a letter inviting me to come to Moscow for consultations," said the stranger gravely, giving both writers a piercing stare.

The two men were embarrassed. "Hell, he overheard us," thought Berlioz, indicating with a polite gesture that there was no need for this show of documents. While the stranger was offering them to the editor, the poet managed to catch a glimpse of the visiting card. On it in foreign lettering was the word "Professor" and the initial letter of a surname which began with a "W."

"Delighted," muttered the editor awkwardly as the foreigner put his papers back into his pocket.

Good relations having been re-established, all three sat down again on the bench.

"So you've been invited here as a consultant, have you, Professor?" asked Berlioz.

"Yes, I have."

"Are you German?" inquired Bezdomny.

"I?" rejoined the professor and thought for a moment. "Yes, I suppose I am German," he said.

"You speak excellent Russian," remarked Bezdomny.

"Oh, I'm something of a polyglot. I know a great number of languages," replied the professor.

"And what is your particular field of work?" asked Berlioz.

"I specialize in black magic."

"Like hell you do!" thought Mikhail Alexandrovich. "And . . . and you've been invited here to give advice on *that?*" he asked with a gulp.

"Yes," the professor assured him, and went on: "Apparently your National Library has unearthed some original manuscripts of the ninth-century necromancer Herbert Aurilachs. I have been asked to decipher them. I am the only specialist in the world."

"Aha! So you're a historian?" asked Berlioz in a tone of considerable relief and respect.

"Yes, I am a historian," adding with apparently complete inconsequence, "this evening a historic event is going to take place here at Patriarch's Ponds."

Again the editor and the poet showed signs of utter amazement, but the professor beckoned to them and when both had bent their heads toward him he whispered, "Jesus did exist, you know."

"Look, Professor," said Berlioz, with a forced smile, "with all respect to you as a scholar, we take a different attitude on that point."

"It's not a question of having an attitude," replied the strange professor. "He existed, that's all there is to it."

"But one must have some proof . . ." began Berlioz.

"There's no need for any proof," answered the professor. In a low voice, his foreign accent vanishing altogether, he began: "It's very simple: early in the morning on the fourteenth of the spring month of Nisan the Procurator of Judea, Pontius Pilate, in a white cloak lined with blood red . . ."

CHAPTER 2

Pontius Pilate

Early in the morning on the fourteenth of the spring month of Nisan the Procurator of Judea, Pontius Pilate, in a white cloak lined with blood red, emerged with his shuffling cavalry-man's walk into the arcade connecting the two wings of the palace of Herod the Great.

More than anything else in the world the Procurator hated the smell of attar of roses. The omens for the day were bad, as this scent had been haunting him since dawn.

It seemed to the Procurator that the very cypresses and palms in the garden were exuding the smell of roses, that this damned stench of roses was even mingling with the smell of leather tackle and sweat from his mounted bodyguard.

A haze of smoke was drifting toward the arcade across the upper courtyard of the garden, coming from the wing at the rear of the palace, the quarters of the first cohort of the XII Legion; known as the "Lightning," it had been stationed in Jerusalem since the Procurator's arrival. The same oily perfume of roses was mixed with the acrid smoke that showed that the centuries' cooks had started to prepare breakfast.

"Oh, gods, what are you punishing me for? . . . No, there's no doubt, I have it again, this terrible incurable pain . . . hemicrania, when half the head aches. . . . There's no cure for it, nothing helps. . . . I must try not to move my head. . . ."

A chair had already been placed on the mosaic floor by the fountain; without a glance around, the Procurator sat in it and stretched out his hand to one side. His secretary deferentially laid a piece of parchment in his hand. Unable to restrain a grimace of agony, the Procurator gave a fleeting sideways look at its contents, returned the parchment to his secretary and said painfully, "The accused comes from Galilee, does he? Was the case sent to the tetrarch?"

"Yes, Procurator," replied the secretary. "He declined to confirm the finding of the court and passed the Sanhedrin's sentence of death to you for confirmation."

The Procurator's cheek twitched, and he said quietly, "Bring in the accused."

At once two legionaires escorted a man of about twenty-seven from the courtyard, under the arcade and up to the balcony, where they placed him before the Procurator's chair. The man was dressed in a shabby, torn, blue chiton. His head was covered with a white bandage fastened round his forehead, his hands tied behind his back. There was a large bruise under the man's left eye and a scab of dried blood in one corner of his mouth. The prisoner stared at the Procurator with anxious curiosity.

The Procurator was silent at first, then asked quietly in Aramaic, "So you have been inciting the people to destroy the temple of Jerusalem?"

The Procurator sat as though carved in stone, his lips barely moving as he pronounced the words. The Procurator was like stone from fear of shaking his fiendishly aching head.

The man with bound hands made a slight move forward and began speaking: "Good man! Believe me——"

But the Procurator, immobile as before and without raising his voice, at once interrupted him: "You call me 'good man'? You are making a mistake. The rumor about me in Jerusalem is that I am a raving monster, and that is absolutely correct," and he added in the same monotone, "Send centurion Muribellum to me."

The balcony seemed to darken when the centurion of the first century, Mark surnamed Muribellum, appeared before the Procurator. Muribellum was a head taller than the tallest soldier in the legion and so broad in the shoulders that he completely obscured the rising sun.

The Procurator said to the centurion in Latin, "This criminal calls me 'good man.' Take him away for a minute and show him the proper way to address me. But do not mutilate him."

All except the motionless Procurator watched Mark Muribellum as he gestured to the prisoner to follow him. Because of his height people always watched Muribellum wherever he went. Those who saw him for the first time were inevitably fascinated by his disfigured face: his nose had once been smashed by a blow from a German club.

Mark's heavy boots resounded on the mosaic, the bound man followed him noiselessly. There was complete silence under the arcade except for the cooing of doves in the garden below and the water singing its seductive tune in the fountain.

The Procurator had a sudden urge to get up and put his temples under the stream of water until they were numb. But he knew that even that would not help.

Having led the prisoner out of the arcade into the garden, Muribellum took a whip from the hands of a legionary standing by the base of a bronze statue and with a gentle swing struck the prisoner across the shoulders. The centurion's movement was slight, almost negligent, but the bound man collapsed instantly as though his legs had been struck from under him and he gasped for air. The color fled from his face and his eyes clouded.

With his left hand alone Mark lifted the fallen man into the air as lightly as an empty sack, set him on his feet and said in broken, nasal Aramaic, "You call a Roman Procurator 'hegemon.' Don't say anything else. Stand at attention. Do you understand or must I hit you again?"

The prisoner staggered helplessly, his color returned. He gulped and answered hoarsely, "I understand you. Don't beat me."

A minute later he was again standing in front of the Procurator.

The harsh, suffering voice rang out: "Name?"

"Mine?" inquired the prisoner hurriedly, his whole being expressing readiness to answer sensibly and to forestall any further anger.

The Procurator said quietly, "I know my own name. Don't pretend to be stupider than you are. Your name."

"Yeshua," replied the prisoner hastily.

"Surname?"

"Ha-Notsri."

"Where are you from?"

"From the town of Gamala," replied the prisoner, nodding

his head to show that far over there to his right, in the north, was the town of Gamala.

"Who are you by birth?"

"I don't know exactly," promptly answered the prisoner, "I don't remember my parents. I was told that my father was a Syrian. . . ."

"Where is your fixed abode?"

"I have no home," said the prisoner shamefacedly. "I move from town to town."

"There is a shorter way of saying that—in a word you are a vagrant," said the Procurator and asked, "Have you any relations?"

"No, none. Not one in the world."

"Can you read and write?"

"Yes."

"Do you know any language besides Aramaic?"

"Yes. Greek."

One swollen eyelid was raised and a pain-clouded eye stared at the prisoner. The other eye remained closed.

Pilate said in Greek, "So you intended to destroy the temple building and incited the people to do so?"

"Never, goo—" Terror flashed across the prisoner's face for having so nearly said the wrong word. "Never in my life, hegemon, have I intended to destroy the temple. Nor have I ever tried to persuade anyone to do such a senseless thing."

A look of amazement came over the secretary's face as he bent over a low table recording the evidence. He raised his head but immediately lowered it again over his parchment.

"People of all kinds are streaming into the city for the feast day. Among them there are magicians, astrologers, seers and murderers," said the Procurator in a monotone. "There are also liars. You, for instance, are a liar. It is clearly written down: 'He incited people to destroy the temple.' Witnesses have said so."

"These good people," the prisoner began, and hastily adding, "hegemon," he went on, "are unlearned and have confused everything I said. I am beginning to fear that this confusion will last for a very long time. And all because he untruthfully wrote down what I said."

There was silence. Now both pain-filled eyes stared heavily at the prisoner.

"I repeat, but for the last time: stop pretending to be mad, scoundrel," said Pilate softly and evenly. "What has been written down about you is little enough, but it is sufficient to hang you."

"No, no, hegemon," said the prisoner, straining with the desire to convince. "This man follows me everywhere with nothing but his goatskin parchment and writes incessantly. But I once caught a glimpse of that parchment and I was horrified. I had not said a word of what was written there. I begged him, 'Please burn this parchment of yours!' But he tore it out of my hands and ran away."

"Who was he?" inquired Pilate in a strained voice and put his hand to his temple.

"Matthew the Levite," said the prisoner eagerly. "He was a tax collector. I first met him on the road to Bethphagy at the corner where the road skirts a fig orchard and I started talking to him. At first he was rude and even insulted me, or rather he thought he was insulting me by calling me a dog." The prisoner laughed. "Personally I see nothing wrong with that animal so I was not offended by the word."

The secretary stopped taking notes and glanced surreptitiously not at the prisoner but at the Procurator.

"However, when he had heard me out he grew milder," went on Yeshua, "and in the end he threw his money into the road and said that he would go traveling with me."

Pilate laughed with one cheek. Baring his yellow teeth and turning fully round to his secretary, he said, "Oh, city of Jerusalem! What tales you have to tell! A tax collector, did you hear, throwing away his money!"

Not knowing what reply was expected of him, the secretary chose to return Pilate's smile.

"And he said that henceforth he loathed his money," said Yeshua in explanation of Matthew the Levite's strange action, adding, "And since then he has been my companion."

His teeth still bared in a grin, the Procurator glanced at the prisoner, then at the sun rising inexorably over the equestrian statues of the hippodrome far below to his left, and suddenly in a moment of agonizing nausea it occurred to him that the simplest thing would be to dismiss this curious rascal from his balcony with no more than two words: "Hang him." Dismiss the bodyguard too, leave the arcade and go indoors, order the room to be darkened, fall onto his couch, send for cold water, call for his dog Banga in a pitiful voice and complain to the dog about his hemicrania. Suddenly the tempting thought of poison flashed through the Procurator's mind.

He stared dully at the prisoner for a while, trying painfully to recall why this man with the bruised face was standing in front of him in the pitiless Jerusalem morning sunshine and what further useless questions he should put to him.

"Matthew the Levite?" asked the suffering man in a hoarse voice, closing his eyes.

"Yes, Matthew the Levite," came the grating, high-pitched reply.

"So you did make a speech about the temple to the crowd in the temple forecourt?"

The voice that answered seemed to strike Pilate on the forehead, causing him inexpressible torture, and it said, "I spoke, hegemon, of how the temple of the old beliefs would fall down and the new temple of truth would be built up. I used those words to make my meaning easier to understand."

"Why should a tramp like you upset the crowd in the bazaar by talking about truth, something of which you have no conception? What is truth?"

At this the Procurator thought, "Ye gods! This is a court of law and I am asking him an irrelevant question . . . my mind no longer obeys me." Once more he had a vision of a goblet of dark liquid. "Poison, I need poison. . . ."

And again he heard the voice:

"At this moment the truth is chiefly that your head is aching and aching so hard that you are having cowardly thoughts about death. Not only are you in no condition to talk to me, but it even hurts you to look at me. This makes me seem to be your torturer, which distresses me. You cannot even think and you can only long for your dog, who is clearly the only creature for whom you have any affection. But the pain will stop soon and your headache will go."

The secretary stared at the prisoner, his note-taking abandoned.

Pilate raised his martyred eyes to the prisoner and saw how high the sun now stood above the hippodrome, how a ray had penetrated the arcade, had crept toward Yeshua's patched sandals and how the man moved aside from the sunlight. The Procurator stood up and clasped his head in his hands. Horror came over his yellowish, clean-shaven face. With an effort of will he controlled his expression and sank back into his chair.

Meanwhile the prisoner continued talking, but the secretary had stopped writing, craning his neck like a goose in the effort not to miss a single word.

"There, it has gone," said the prisoner, with a kindly glance at Pilate. "I am so glad. I would advise you, hegemon, to leave the palace for a while and take a walk somewhere nearby, perhaps in the gardens or on Mount Eleona. There will be thunder—" the prisoner turned and squinted into the sun— "later, toward evening. A walk would do you a great deal of good and I should be happy to go with you. Some new thoughts have just come into my head which you might, I think, find interesting, and I should like to discuss them with you, the more so as you strike me as a man with great intelligence." The secretary turned mortally pale and dropped his scroll to the ground. "Your trouble is," went on the unstoppable prisoner, "that your mind is too closed and you have finally lost your faith in human beings. You must admit that no one ought to lavish all his devotion on a dog. Your life is a cramped one, hegemon." Here the speaker allowed himself to smile.

The only thought in the secretary's mind now was whether he could believe his ears. He had to believe them. He then tried to guess in what strange form the Procurator's fiery temper might break out at the prisoner's unheard-of insolence. Although he knew the Procurator well, the secretary's imagination failed him.

Then the hoarse, broken voice of the Procurator barked out in Latin, "Untie his hands."

One of the legionary escorts tapped the ground with his lance, gave it to his neighbor, approached and removed the prisoner's bonds. The secretary picked up his scroll, decided to take no more notes for a while and to be astonished at nothing he might hear.

"Tell me," said Pilate softly in Latin, "are you a great physician?"

"No, Procurator, I am no physician," replied the prisoner, gratefully rubbing his twisted, swollen, purpling wrist.

Staring from beneath his eyelids, Pilate's eyes bored into the prisoner, and those eyes were no longer dull. They now flashed with their familiar sparkle.

"I did not ask you," said Pilate. "Do you know Latin too?"

"Yes, I do," replied the prisoner.

The color flowed back into Pilate's yellowed cheeks and he asked in Latin, "How did you know that I wanted to call my dog?"

"Quite simple," the prisoner answered in Latin. "You moved

your hand through the air—" the prisoner repeated Pilate's gesture—"as though to stroke something, and your lips . . ."

"Yes," said Pilate.

There was silence. Then Pilate put a question in Greek: "So you are a physician?"

"No, no," was the prisoner's eager reply. "Believe me I am not."

"Very well, if you wish to keep it a secret, do so. It has no direct bearing on the case. So you maintain that you never incited people to tear down . . . or burn . . . or by any means destroy the temple?"

"I repeat, hegemon, that I have never tried to persuade anyone to attempt any such thing. Do I look weak in the head?"

"Oh, no, you do not," replied the Procurator quietly and smiled an ominous smile. "Very well, swear that it is not so."

"What would you have me swear by?" inquired the unbound prisoner with great urgency.

"Well, by your life," replied the Procurator. "It is high time to swear by it because you should know that it is hanging by a thread."

"You do not believe, do you, hegemon, that it is you who have strung it up?" asked the prisoner. "If you do, you are mistaken."

Pilate shuddered and answered through clenched teeth, "I can cut that thread."

"You are mistaken there, too," objected the prisoner, beaming and shading himself from the sun with his hand. "You must agree, I think, that the thread can only be cut by the one who has suspended it?"

"Yes, yes?" said Pilate, smiling. "I now have no doubt that the idle gapers of Jerusalem have been pursuing you. I do not know who strung up your tongue, but he strung it well. By the way, tell me, is it true that you entered Jerusalem by the Susim Gate mounted on a donkey, accompanied by a rabble who greeted you as though you were a prophet?" Here the Procurator pointed to a scroll of parchment.

The prisoner stared dubiously at the Procurator.

"I have no donkey, hegemon," he said. "I certainly came into Jerusalem through the Susim Gate, but I came on foot alone except for Matthew the Levite, and nobody shouted a word to me as no one in Jerusalem knew me then."

"Do you happen to know," went on Pilate without taking

his eyes off the prisoner, "anyone called Dismas? Or Hestus? Or a third—Bar-Abba?"

"I do not know these good men," replied the prisoner.

"Is that the truth?"

"It is."

"And now tell me why you always use that expression "good men?" Is that what you call everybody?"

"Yes, everybody," answered the prisoner. "There are no evil people on earth."

"That is news to me," said Pilate with a laugh. "But perhaps I am too ignorant of life. You need take no further notes," he said to the secretary, although the man had taken none for some time. Pilate turned back to the prisoner.

"Did you read about that in some Greek book?"

"No, I reached that conclusion in my own mind."

"And is that what you preach?"

"Yes."

"Centurion Mark Muribellum, for instance—is he good?"

"Yes," replied the prisoner. "He is, it is true, an unhappy man. Since the good people disfigured him he has become harsh and callous. It would be interesting to know who mutilated him."

"That I will gladly tell you," rejoined Pilate, "because I was a witness to it. These good men threw themselves at him like dogs at a bear. The Germans clung to his neck, his arms, his legs. An infantry maniple had been ambushed, and had it not been for a troop of cavalry breaking through from the flank— a troop commanded by me—you, philosopher, would not have been talking to Muribellum just now. It happened at the battle of Idistavizo in the Valley of the Virgins."

"If I were to talk to him," the prisoner suddenly said in a reflective voice, "I am sure that he would change greatly."

"I suspect," said Pilate, "that the Legate of the Legion would not be best pleased if you took it into your head to talk to one of his officers or soldiers. Fortunately for us all, any such thing is forbidden and the first person to insure that it cannot occur would be myself."

At that moment a swallow darted into the arcade, circled under the gilded ceiling, flew lower, almost brushed its pointed wing tip over the face of a bronze statue in a niche and disappeared behind the capital of a column, perhaps with the thought of nesting there.

As it flew, an idea formed itself in the Procurator's mind,

which was now bright and clear. It was this: the hegemon had examined the case of the vagrant philosopher Yeshua, sur-named Ha-Notsri, and could not substantiate the criminal charge made against him. In particular he could not find the slightest connection between Yeshua's actions and the recent disorders in Jerusalem. The vagrant philosopher was mentally ill, as a result of which the sentence of death pronounced on Ha-Notsri by the Lesser Sanhedrin would not be confirmed. But in view of the danger of unrest liable to be caused by Yeshua's mad, utopian preaching, the Procurator would re-move the man from Jerusalem and sentence him to imprison-ment in Caesarea Stratonova on the Mediterranean—the place of the Procurator's own residence.

It only remained to dictate this to the secretary.

The swallow's wings fluttered over the hegemon's head, the bird flew toward the fountain and out into freedom. The Pro-curator raised his eyes to the prisoner and saw that a column of dust had swirled up beside him.

"Is that all there is on this man?" Pilate asked the secretary.

"No, unfortunately," replied the secretary unexpectedly, and handed Pilate another parchment.

"What else is there?" inquired Pilate and frowned.

When he had read the further evidence, a change came over his expression. Whether it was blood flowing back into his neck and face or from something else that had occurred, his skin changed from yellow to red-brown and his eyes appeared to collapse. Probably caused by the increased blood pressure in his temples, something happened to the Procurator's sight. He seemed to see the prisoner's head vanish and another appear in its place, bald and crowned with a spiked golden diadem. The skin of the forehead was split by a round, livid scar smeared with ointment. A sunken, toothless mouth with a capricious, pendulous lower lip. Pilate had the sensation that the pink columns of his balcony and the roofscape of Jeru-salem below and beyond the garden had all vanished, drowned in the thick foliage of cypress groves. His hearing, too, was strangely affected—there was a sound of distant trumpets, muted and threatening, and a nasal voice could clearly be heard haughtily intoning the words, "The law pertaining to high treason . . ."

Strange, rapid, disconnected thoughts passed through his mind. "Dead!" Then: "They have killed him!" And an absurd notion about immortality, the thought of which aroused a sense of unbearable grief.

Pilate straightened up, banished the vision, turned his gaze back to the balcony, and again the prisoner's eyes met his.

"Listen, Ha-Notsri," began the Procurator, giving Yeshua a strange look. His expression was grim, but his eyes betrayed anxiety. "Have you ever said anything about great Caesar? Answer! Did you say anything of the sort? Or did you . . . not?" Pilate gave the word "not" more emphasis than was proper in a court of law, and his look seemed to be trying to project a particular thought into the prisoner's mind.

"Telling the truth is easy and pleasant," remarked the prisoner.

"I do not want to know," rejoined Pilate in a voice of suppressed anger, "whether you enjoy telling the truth or not. You are obliged to tell me the truth. But when you speak, weigh every word, if you wish to avoid a painful death."

No one knows what passed through the mind of the Procurator of Judea, but he permitted himself to raise his hand as though shading himself from a ray of sunlight and, shielded by that hand, to throw the prisoner a glance that conveyed a hint.

"So," he said, "answer this question: do you know a certain Judas of Karioth, and if you have ever spoken to him what did you say to him about Caesar?"

"It happened thus," began the prisoner readily. "The day before yesterday, in the evening, I met a young man near the temple who called himself Judas, from the town of Karioth. He invited me to his home in the Lower City and gave me supper."

"Is he a good man?" asked Pilate, a diabolical glitter in his eyes.

"A very good man and eager to learn," affirmed the prisoner. "He expressed the greatest interest in my ideas and welcomed me joyfully."

"Lit the candles . . . " said Pilate through clenched teeth to the prisoner, his eyes glittering.

"Yes," said Yeshua, slightly astonished that the Procurator should be so well informed, and went on: "He asked me for my views on the government. The question interested him very much."

"And so what did you say?" asked Pilate. "Or are you going

to reply that you have forgotten what you said?" But there was already a note of hopelessness in Pilate's voice.

"Among other things I said," continued the prisoner, "that all power is a form of violence exercised over people, and that the time will come when there will be no rule by Caesar nor any other form of rule. Man will pass into the kingdom of truth and justice where no sort of power will be needed."

"Go on!"

"There is no more to tell," said the prisoner. "After that some men came running in, tied me up and took me to prison."

The secretary, straining not to miss a word, rapidly scribbled the statement on his parchment.

"There never has been, nor yet shall be, a greater and more perfect government in this world than the rule of the Emperor Tiberius!" Pilate's voice rang out harshly and painfully. The Procurator stared at his secretary and at the bodyguard with what seemed like hatred. "And what business have you, a criminal lunatic, to discuss such matters!" Pilate shouted. "Remove the guards from the balcony!" And turning to his secretary he added, "Leave me alone with this criminal. This is a case of treason."

The bodyguards raised their lances and with the measured tread of their iron-shod caligae marched from the balcony toward the garden followed by the secretary.

For a while the silence on the balcony was only disturbed by the splashing of the fountain. Pilate watched the water splay out at the apex of the jet and drip downward.

The prisoner was the first to speak: "I see that there has been some trouble as a result of my conversation with that young man from Karioth. I have a presentiment, hegemon, that some misfortune will befall him and I feel very sorry for him."

"I think," replied the Procurator with a strange smile, "that there is someone else in this world for whom you should feel sorrier than for Judas of Karioth and who is destined for a fate much worse than Judas'! ... So Mark Muribellum, a cold-blooded killer, the people who I see—" the Procurator pointed to Yeshua's disfigured face—"beat you for what you preached, the robbers Dismas and Hestas who with their confederates killed four soldiers, and finally this dirty informer Judas—are they all good men?"

"Yes," answered the prisoner.

"And will the kingdom of truth come?"

"It will, hegemon," replied Yeshua with conviction.

"It will never come!" Pilate suddenly shouted in a voice so terrible that Yeshua staggered back. Many years ago in the Valley of the Virgins Pilate had shouted in that same voice to his horsemen: "Cut them down! Cut them down! They have caught the giant Muribellum!" And again he raised his parade-ground voice, barking out the words so that they would be heard in the garden: "Criminal! Criminal! Criminal!" Then lowering his voice he asked, "Yeshua Ha-Notsri, do you believe in any gods?"

"God is one," answered Yeshua. "I believe in Him."

"Then pray to Him! Pray hard! However—" at this Pilate's voice fell again— "it will do no good. Have you a wife?" asked Pilate with a sudden inexplicable access of depression.

"No, I am alone."

"I hate this city," the Procurator suddenly mumbled, hunching his shoulders as though from cold and wiping his hands as though washing them. "If they had murdered you before your meeting with Judas of Karioth, I really believe it would have been better."

"You should let me go, hegemon," was the prisoner's unexpected request, his voice full of anxiety. "I see now that they want to kill me."

A spasm distorted Pilate's face as he turned his bloodshot eyes on Yeshua and said, "Do you imagine, you miserable creature, that a Roman Procurator could release a man who has said what you have said to me? O gods, oh gods! Or do you think I'm prepared to take your place? I don't believe in your ideas! And listen to me: if from this moment onward you say so much as a word or try to talk to anybody, beware! I repeat—beware!"

"Hegemon—"

"Be quiet!" shouted Pilate, his infuriated stare following the swallow which had flown onto the balcony again. "Here!" shouted Pilate.

The secretary and the guards returned to their places, and Pilate announced that he confirmed the sentence of death pronounced by the Lesser Sanhedrin on the accused Yeshua Ha-Notsri and the secretary recorded Pilate's words.

A minute later centurion Mark Muribellum stood before the Procurator. He was ordered by the Procurator to hand the felon over to the captain of the secret service and in doing so to transmit the Procurator's directive that Yeshua Ha-Notsri

was to be segregated from the other convicts, also that the
captain of the secret service was forbidden on pain of severe
punishment to talk to Yeshua or to answer any questions he
might ask.

At a signal from Mark the guard closed ranks around
Yeshua and escorted him from the balcony.

Later the Procurator received a call from a handsome man
with a blond beard, eagles' feathers in the crest of his helmet,
glittering lions' muzzles on his breastplate, a gold-studded
sword belt, triple-soled boots laced to the knee and a purple
cloak thrown over his left shoulder. He was the commanding
officer, the Legate of the Legion.

The Procurator asked him where the Sebastian cohort was
stationed. The Legate reported that the Sebastian was on
cordon duty in the square in front of the hippodrome, where
the sentences on the prisoners would be announced to the
crowd.

Then the Procurator instructed the Legate to detach two
centuries from the Roman cohort. One of them, under the
command of Muribellum, was to escort the convicts, the carts
transporting the executioners' equipment and the executioners
themselves to Mount Golgotha and on arrival to cordon off the
summit area. The other was to proceed at once to Mount
Golgotha and to form a cordon immediately on arrival. To
assist in the task of guarding the hill, the Procurator asked the
Legate to dispatch an auxiliary cavalry regiment, the Syrian
ala.

When the Legate had left the balcony, the Procurator
ordered his secretary to summon to the palace the president of
the Sanhedrin, two of its members and the captain of the Jerusalem temple guard, but added that he wished arrangements
to be made which would allow him, before conferring with all
these people, to have a private meeting with the president of
the Sanhedrin.

The Procurator's orders were carried out rapidly and precisely, and the sun, which had lately seemed to scorch Jerusalem with such particular vehemence, had not yet reached its
zenith when the meeting took place between the Procurator
and the president of the Sanhedrin, the High Priest of Judea,
Joseph Caiaphas. They met on the upper terrace of the garden
between two white marble lions guarding the staircase.

It was quiet in the garden. But as he emerged from the arcade onto the sun-drenched upper terrace of the garden with

its palms on their monstrous elephantine legs, the terrace from which the whole of Pilate's detested city of Jerusalem lay spread out before the Procurator with its suspension bridges, its fortresses and over it all that indescribable lump of marble with a golden dragon's scale instead of a roof—the temple of Jerusalem—the Procurator's sharp hearing detected far below, down there where a stone wall divided the lower terraces of the palace garden from the city square, a low rumbling broken now and again by faint sounds, half groans, half cries.

The Procurator realized that already there was assembling in the square a numberless crowd of the inhabitants of Jerusalem, excited by the recent disorders; that this crowd was waiting impatiently for the pronouncement of sentence and that the water-sellers were busily shouting their wares.

The Procurator began by inviting the High Priest on to the balcony to find some shade from the pitiless heat, but Caiaphas politely excused himself, explaining that he could not do that on the eve of a feast day.

Pilate pulled his cowl over his slightly balding head and began the conversation, which was conducted in Greek.

Pilate remarked that he had considered the case of Yeshua Ha-Notsri and had confirmed the sentence of death. Consequently those due for execution that day were the three robbers —Hestas, Dismas and Bar-Abba—and now this other man, Yeshua Ha-Notsri. The first two, who had tried to incite the people to rebel against Caesar, had been forcibly apprehended by the Roman authorities; they were therefore the Procurator's responsibility and there was no reason to discuss their case. The last two, however, Bar-Abba and Ha-Notsri, had been arrested by the local authorities and tried before the Sanhedrin. In accordance with law and custom, one of these two criminals should be released in honor of the imminent great feast of Passover. The Procurator therefore wished to know which of these two felons the Sanhedrin proposed to discharge—Bar-Abba or Ha-Notsri?

Caiaphas inclined his head as a sign that he understood the question and replied, "The Sanhedrin requests the release of Bar-Abba."

The Procurator well knew that this would be the High Priest's reply; his problem was to show that the request aroused his astonishment.

This Pilate did with great skill. The eyebrows rose on his

proud forehead, and the Procurator looked the High Priest straight in the eye with amazement.

"I confess that your reply surprises me," began the Procurator softly. "I fear there may have been some misunderstanding here."

Pilate stressed that the Roman government wished to make no inroads into the prerogatives of the local priestly authority, the High Priest was well aware of that, but in this particular case an obvious error seemed to have occurred. And the Roman government naturally had an interest in correcting such an error. The crimes of Bar-Abba and Ha-Notsri were after all not comparable in gravity. If the latter, a man who was clearly insane, was guilty of making some absurd speeches in Jerusalem and various other localities, the former stood convicted of offenses that were infinitely more serious. Not only had he permitted himself to make direct appeals to rebellion, but he had killed a sentry while resisting arrest. Bar-Abba was immeasurably more dangerous than Ha-Notsri. In view of all these facts, the Procurator requested the High Priest to reconsider his decision and to discharge the least dangerous of the two convicts and that one was undoubtedly Ha-Notsri. . . . Therefore?

Caiaphas said in a quiet but firm voice that the Sanhedrin had taken due cognizance of the case and repeated its intention to release Bar-Abba.

"What? Even after my intervention? The intervention of the representative of the Roman government? High Priest, say it for the third time."

"And for the third time I say that we shall release Bar-Abba," said Caiaphas softly.

It was over and there was no more to be discussed. Ha-Notsri had gone forever and there was no one to heal the Procurator's terrible, savage pains; there was no cure for them now except death. But this thought did not strike Pilate immediately. At first his whole being was seized with the same incomprehensible sense of grief that had come to him on the balcony. He at once sought for its explanation, and its cause was a strange one: the Procurator was obscurely aware that he still had something to say to the prisoner and that perhaps, too, he had more to learn from him.

Pilate banished the thought and it passed as quickly as it had come. It passed, yet that grievous ache remained a mystery, for it could not be explained by another thought that had flashed in and out of his mind like lightning: "Immortality . . . immortality has come." Whose immortality had come? The Procurator could not understand it, but that puzzling thought of immortality sent a chill over him despite the sun's heat.

"Very well," said Pilate. "So be it."

With that he looked around. The visible world vanished from his sight and an astonishing change occurred. The flower-laden rosebush disappeared, the cypresses fringing the upper terrace disappeared, as did the pomegranate tree, the white statue among the foliage and the foliage itself. In their place came a kind of dense purple mass in which seaweed waved and swayed and Pilate himself was swaying with it. He was seized, suffocating and burning, by the most terrible rage of all rage—the rage of impotence.

"I am suffocating," said Pilate. "Suffocating!"

With a cold damp hand he tore the buckle from the collar of his cloak and it fell onto the sand.

"It is stifling today, there is a thunderstorm brewing," said Caiaphas, his gaze fixed on the Procurator's reddening face, foreseeing all the discomfort that the weather was yet to bring. "The month of Nisan has been terrible this year!"

"No," said Pilate. "That is not why I am suffocating. I feel stifled by your presence, Caiaphas." Narrowing his eyes, Pilate added, "Beware, High Priest!"

The High Priest's dark eyes flashed and—no less cunningly than the Procurator's—his face showed astonishment.

"What do I hear, Procurator?" Caiaphas answered proudly and calmly. "Are you threatening me—when sentence has been duly pronounced and confirmed by yourself? Can this be so? We are accustomed to the Roman Procurator choosing his words carefully before saying anything. I trust no one can have overheard us, hegemon?"

With lifeless eyes Pilate gazed at the High Priest and manufactured a smile.

"Come now, High Priest! Who can overhear us here? Do you take me for a fool, like that crazy young vagrant who is to be executed today? Am I a child, Caiaphas? I know what I'm saying and where I'm saying it. This garden, this whole palace, is so well cordoned that there's not a crack for a mouse to slip through. Not a mouse—and not even that man—what's his name?—that man from Karioth. You do know him, don't you, High Priest? Yes . . . if someone like that were to get in here, he would bitterly regret it. You believe me when I say that, don't you? I tell you, High Priest, that henceforth you shall have no peace! Neither you nor your people." Pilate pointed to the right where the pinnacle of the temple flashed in the distance. "I, Pontius Pilate, Knight of the Golden Lance, tell you so!"

"I know it!" fearlessly replied the bearded Caiaphas. His eyes flashed as he raised his hand to the sky and went on: "The Jewish people know that you hate it with a terrible hatred and that you have brought it much suffering, but you will never destroy it! God will protect it. And *he* shall hear us—mighty Caesar shall hear us and protect us from Pilate the oppressor!"

"Oh, no!" rejoined Pilate, feeling more and more relieved with every word that he spoke; there was no longer any need to dissemble, no need to pick his words. "You have complained of me to Caesar too often and now my hour has come, Caiaphas! Now I shall send word—but not to the viceroy in Antioch, not even to Rome but straight to Capraia, to the Emperor himself, word of how you in Jerusalem are saving convicted rebels from death. And then it will not be water from Solomon's pool, as I once intended for your benefit, that I shall give Jerusalem to drink—no, it will not be water! Remember how, thanks to you, I was made to remove the shields with the imperial cipher from the walls, to transfer troops, to come and take charge here myself! Remember my words, High Priest: you are going to see more than one cohort here in Jerusalem! Under the city walls you are going to see the Fulminata Legion at full strength and Arab cavalry too. Then the weeping and lamentation will be bitter! Then you will remember that you saved Bar-Abba and you will regret that you sent that preacher of peace to his death!"

Flecks of color spread over the High Priest's face, his eyes burned. Like the Procurator, he grinned mirthlessly and replied, "Do you really believe what you have just said, Procurator? No, you do not! It was not peace that this rabble-rouser brought to Jerusalem, and of that, hegemon, you are well aware. You wanted to release him so that he could stir up the people, curse our faith and deliver the people to your Roman swords! But as long as I, the High Priest of Judea, am alive I shall not allow the faith to be defamed and I shall protect the people! Do you hear, Pilate!" With this Caiaphas raised his arm threateningly. "Take heed, Procurator!"

Caiaphas was silent, and again the Procurator heard a murmuring as of the sea, rolling up to the very walls of Herod the

Great's Garden. The sound flowed upward from below until it seemed to swirl around the Procurator's legs and into his face. Behind his back, from beyond the wings of the palace, came urgent trumpet calls, the heavy crunch of hundreds of feet, the clank of metal. It told the Procurator that the Roman infantry was marching out, on his orders, to the execution parade that was to strike terror into the hearts of all thieves and rebels.

"Do you hear, Procurator?" the High Priest quietly repeated his words. "Surely you are not trying to tell me that all this—" here the High Priest raised both arms and his dark cowl slipped from his head—"can have been evoked by that miserable thief Bar-Abba?"

With the back of his wrist the Procurator wiped his damp, cold forehead, stared at the ground, then frowning skyward he saw that the incandescent ball was nearly overhead, that Caiaphas' shadow had shrunk to almost nothing, and he said in a calm, expressionless voice, "The execution will be at noon. We have enjoyed this conversation, but matters must proceed."

Excusing himself to the High Priest in a few artificial phrases, he invited him to sit down on a bench in the shade of a magnolia and to wait while he summoned the others necessary for the final short consultation and to give one more order concerning the execution.

Caiaphas bowed politely, placing his hand on his heart, and remained in the garden while Pilate returned to the balcony. There he ordered his waiting secretary to call the Legate of the Legion and the Tribune of the Cohort into the garden, also the two members of the Sanhedrin and the captain of the temple guard, who were standing grouped around the fountain on the lower terrace awaiting his call. Pilate added that he would himself shortly return to join them in the garden and disappeared inside the palace.

While the secretary convened the meeting, inside his darkened, shuttered room the Procurator spoke to a man whose face, despite the complete absence of sunlight from the room, remained half-covered by a hood. The interview was very short. The Procurator whispered a few words to the man, who immediately departed. Pilate passed through the arcade into the garden.

There in the presence of all the men he had asked to see, the Procurator solemnly and curtly repeated that he confirmed the sentence of death on Yeshua Ha-Notsri and inquired officially of the Sanhedrin members as to which of the prisoners it had

pleased them to release. On being told that it was Bar-Abba,
the Procurator said, "Very well," and ordered the secretary to
enter it in the minutes. He clutched the buckle which the
secretary had picked up from the sand and announced solemnly, "It is time!"

At this all present set off down the broad marble staircase
between the lines of rosebushes, exuding their stupefying
aroma, down toward the palace wall, to a gate leading to the
smoothly paved square at whose end could be seen the columns
and statues of the Jerusalem hippodrome.

As soon as the group entered the square and began climbing
up to the broad temporary wooden platform raised high above
the square, Pilate assessed the situation through narrowed eyelids.

The cleared passage that he had just crossed between the
palace walls and the scaffolding platform was empty, but in
front of Pilate the square could no longer be seen—it had been
devoured by the crowd. The mob would have poured onto the
platform and the passage too if there had not been two triple
rows of soldiers, one from the Sebastian cohort on Pilate's left
and on his right another from the Ituraean auxiliary cohort, to
keep it clear.

Pilate climbed the platform, mechanically clenching and un-
clenching his fist on the useless buckle and frowning hard. The
Procurator was not frowning because the sun was blinding him
but somehow to avoid seeing the group of prisoners which,
as he well knew, would shortly be led out on the platform
behind him.

The moment the white cloak with the purple lining appeared
atop the stone block at the edge of the human sea a wave of
sound—"Aaahh"—struck the unseeing Pilate's ears. It began
softly, far away at the hippodrome end of the square, then grew
to thunderous volume and, after a few seconds, began to di-
minish again. "They have seen me," thought the Procurator.
The wave of sound did not recede altogether and began unexpectedly to grow again and rose waveringly to a higher
pitch, and on top of the second surge of noise, like foam on
the crest of a wave at sea, could be heard whistles and the
shrieks of several women audible above the roar. "That means
they have led them out onto the platform," thought Pilate,
"and those screams are from women who were crushed when
the crowd surged forward."

He waited a while, knowing that nothing could silence the

crowd until it had let loose its pent-up feelings and quieted of its own accord.

When that moment came, the Procurator threw up his right hand and the last murmurings of the crowd expired. Then Pilate took as deep a breath of the hot air as he could, and his cracked voice rang out over the thousands of heads: "In the name of imperial Caesar!"

At once his ears were struck by a clipped, metallic chorus as the cohorts, raising lances and standards, roared out their fearful response: "Hail, Caesar!"

Pilate jerked his head up straight at the sun. He had a sensation of green fire piercing his eyelids, his brain seemed to burn. In hoarse Aramaic he flung his words out over the crowd:

"Four criminals, arrested in Jerusalem for murder, incitement to rebellion, contempt of the law and blasphemy, have been condemned to the most shameful form of execution—crucifixion! Their execution will be carried out shortly on Mount Golgotha! The names of these felons are Dismas, Hestas, Bar-Abba and Ha-Notsri, and there they stand before you!"

Pilate pointed to the right, unable to see the prisoners but knowing that they were standing where they should be.

The crowd responded with a long rumble that could have been surprise or relief. When it had subsided, Pilate went on:

"But only three of them are to be executed for, in accordance with law and custom, in honor of the great feast of Passover the Emperor Caesar in his magnanimity will, at the choice of the Lesser Sanhedrin and with the approval of the Roman government, render back to one of these convicted men his contemptible life!"

As Pilate rasped out his words, he noticed that the rumbling had given way to a great silence. Now not a sigh, not a rustle reached his ears, and there even came a moment when it seemed to Pilate that the people around him had vanished altogether. The city he so hated might have died and only he alone stood there, scorched by the vertical rays of the sun, his face craning skyward. Pilate allowed the silence to continue and then began to shout again: "The name of the man who is about to be released before you . . ."

He paused once more, holding back the name, mentally confirming that he had said everything, because he knew that as soon as he pronounced the name of the fortunate man the lifeless city would awaken and nothing more that he might say would be audible.

"Is that everything?" Pilate whispered soundlessly to himself. "Yes, it is. Now the name!" And rolling the "r" over the heads of the silent populace he roared: "Bar-Abba!"

It was as though the sun detonated above him and drowned his ears in fire, a fire that roared, shrieked, groaned, laughed and whistled.

Pilate turned and walked back along the platform toward the steps, glancing only at the particolored wooden blocks of the steps beneath his feet to save himself from stumbling. He knew that behind his back a hail of bronze coins and dates was showering the platform, that people in the whooping crowd, elbowing each other aside, were climbing onto shoulders to see a miracle with their own eyes—a man already in the arms of death and torn from their grasp! They watched the legionaries as they untied his bonds, involuntarily causing him searing pain in his swollen arms, watched as grimacing and complaining he nevertheless smiled an insane, senseless smile.

Pilate knew that the escort was now marching the three bound prisoners to the side steps of the platform to lead them off on the road westward, out of the city, toward Mount Golgotha. Only when he stood beneath and behind the platform did Pilate open his eyes, knowing that he was now safe—he could no longer see the convicted men.

As the roar of the crowd began to die down, the separate, piercing voices of the heralds could be heard repeating, one in Aramaic, the other in Greek, the announcement that the Procurator had just made from the platform. Besides that his ears caught the approaching irregular clatter of horses' hoofs and the sharp, bright call of a trumpet. This sound was echoed by the piercing whistles of boys from the rooftops and by shouts of "Look out!"

A lone soldier, standing in the space cleared in the square, waved his standard in warning, at which the Procurator, the Legate of the Legion and their escort halted.

A squadron of cavalry entered the square at a fast trot, cutting across it diagonally past a knot of people, then down a sidestreet along a vine-covered stone wall in order to gallop on to Mount Golgotha by the shortest route.

As the squadron commander, a Syrian as small as a boy and as dark as a mulatto, trotted past Pilate, he gave a high-pitched cry and drew his sword from its scabbard. His sweating, ugly-tempered, black horse snorted and reared up on its hind legs. Sheathing his sword, the commander struck the horse's neck with his whip, brought its forelegs down and moved off down the side street, breaking into a gallop. Behind him in a column of threes galloped the horsemen in a haze of dust, the tips of their bamboo lances bobbing rhythmically. They swept past the Procurator, their faces unnaturally dark in contrast with their white turbans, grinning cheerfully, teeth flashing.

Raising a cloud of dust, the squadron surged down the street, the last trooper to pass Pilate carrying a glinting trumpet slung across his back.

Shielding his face from the dust with his hand and frowning with annoyance, Pilate walked on, hurrying toward the gate of the palace garden followed by the Legate, the secretary and the escort.

It was about ten o'clock in the morning.

CHAPTER 3

THE SEVENTH PROOF

Yes, it was about ten o'clock in the morning, my dear Ivan Nikolayich," said the professor.

The poet drew his hand across his face like a man who had just waked up and noticed that it is now evening. The water in the pond had turned black, a little boat was gliding across it, and he could hear the splash of an oar and a girl's laughter in the boat. People were beginning to appear in the avenues and were sitting on the benches, although on all sides of the square except the side where our friends were talking.

Over Moscow it was as if the sky had blossomed: a clear, full moon had risen, still white and not yet golden. It was much less stuffy, and the voices under the lime trees now had an eventide softness.

"Why didn't I notice what a long story he's been telling us?" thought Bezdomny in amazement. "It's evening already! Perhaps he hasn't told it at all, but I simply fell asleep and dreamed it."

But if the professor had not told the story, Berlioz must have been having the identical dream because he said, gazing attentively into the stranger's face, "Your story is extremely interesting, Professor, but it differs completely from the accounts in the gospels."

"But surely," replied the professor with a condescending

smile, "you of all people must realize that absolutely nothing written in the gospels actually happened. If you want to regard the gospels as a proper historical source . . ." He smiled again and Berlioz was silenced. He had just been saying exactly the same thing to Bezdomny on their walk from Bronnaya Street to Patriarch's Ponds.

"I agree," answered Berlioz, "but I'm afraid that no one is in a position to prove the authenticity of your version either."

"Oh, yes! I can easily confirm it!" rejoined the professor with great confidence, lapsing into his foreign accent and mysteriously beckoning the two friends closer. They bent toward him from both sides, and he began, this time without a trace of his accent which seemed to come and go without rhyme or reason: "The fact is—" here the professor glanced round nervously and dropped his voice to a whisper—"I was there myself. On the balcony with Pontius Pilate, in the garden when he talked to Caiaphas and on the platform, but secretly, incognito so to speak, so don't breathe a word of it to anyone and please keep it an absolute secret, shhh . . ."

There was silence. Berlioz went pale.

"How . . . how long did you say you'd been in Moscow?" he asked in a shaky voice.

"I have just this minute arrived in Moscow," replied the professor, slightly disconcerted. Only then did it occur to the two friends to look him properly in the eyes. They saw that his green left eye was completely mad, his right eye black, expressionless and dead.

"That explains it all," thought Berlioz perplexedly. "He's some mad German who's just arrived or else he's suddenly gone out of his mind here at Patriarch's. What an extraordinary business!" This really seemed to account for everything—the mysterious breakfast with the philosopher Kant, the idiotic ramblings about sunflower-seed oil and Anna, the prediction about Berlioz's head being cut off and all the rest: the professor was a lunatic.

Berlioz at once started to think what they ought to do. Leaning back on the bench, he winked at Bezdomny behind the professor's back, meaning "Humor him!" But the poet, now thoroughly confused, failed to understand the signal.

"Yes, yes, yes," said Berlioz with great animation. "It's quite possible, of course. Even probable—Pontius Pilate, the balcony, and so on . . . Have you come here alone or with your wife?"

"Alone, alone, I am always alone," replied the professor bitterly.

"But where is your luggage, Professor?" asked Berlioz cunningly. "At the Metropole? Where are you staying?"

"Where am I staying? Nowhere," answered the mad German, staring moodily around Patriarch's Ponds with his green eye.

"What? . . . But . . . where are you going to live?"

"In your apartment," the lunatic suddenly replied casually and winked.

"I'm . . . I should be delighted," stuttered Berlioz, "but I'm afraid you wouldn't be very comfortable at my place. . . . The rooms at the Metropole are excellent, it's a first-class hotel."

"And the devil doesn't exist either, I suppose?" the madman suddenly inquired cheerfully of Ivan Nikolayich.

"And the devil—"

"Don't contradict him," mouthed Berlioz silently, leaning back and grimacing behind the professor's back.

"There's no such thing as the devil!" Ivan Nikolayich burst out, hopelessly muddled by all this dumb show, ruining all Berlioz' plans by shouting, "And stop playing the amateur psychologist!"

At this the lunatic gave such a laugh that it startled the sparrows out of the tree above them.

"Well now, that is interesting," said the professor, quaking with laughter. "Whatever I ask you about—it doesn't exist!" He suddenly stopped laughing, and with a typical madman's reaction he immediately went to the other extreme, shouting angrily and harshly, "So you think the devil doesn't exist?"

"Calm down, calm down, calm down, Professor," stammered Berlioz, afraid of exciting this lunatic. "You stay here a minute with comrade Bezdomny while I run around the corner and make a phone call and then we'll take you where you want to go. You don't know your way around town, after all."

Berlioz' plan was obviously right—to run to the nearest telephone box and tell the Aliens Bureau that there was a foreign professor sitting at Patriarch's Ponds who was clearly insane. Something had to be done or there might be a nasty scene.

"Telephone? Of course, go and telephone if you want to," agreed the lunatic sadly and then suddenly begged with passion, "But please—as a farewell request—at least say you believe in the devil! I won't ask anything more of you. Don't forget that there's still the seventh proof—the soundest! And it's just about to be demonstrated to you!"

"All right, all right," said Berlioz, pretending to agree. With a wink to the wretched Bezdomny, who by no means relished the thought of keeping watch on this crazy German, he rushed toward the park gates at the corner of Bronnaya and Yermolayevsky streets.

At once the professor seemed to recover his reason and good spirits.

"Mikhail Alexandrovich!" he shouted after Berlioz, who shuddered as he turned round and then remembered that the professor could have learned his name from a newspaper.

The professor, cupping his hands into a trumpet, shouted, "Wouldn't you like me to send a telegram to your uncle in Kiev?"

Another shock—how did this madman know that he had an uncle in Kiev? Nobody had ever put *that* in any newspaper. Could Bezdomny be right about him after all? And what about those phony-looking documents of his? Definitely a weird character . . . ring up, ring up the Bureau at once . . . they'll come and sort it all out in no time.

Without waiting to hear any more, Berlioz ran on.

At the park gates leading into Bronnaya Street, the same man whom a short while ago the editor had seen materialize out of a mirage got up from a bench and walked toward him. This time, however, he was not made of air but of flesh and blood. In the early twilight Berlioz could clearly distinguish his feathery little mustache, his little eyes, mocking and half drunk, his check trousers pulled up so tight that his dirty white socks were showing.

Mikhail Alexandrovich stopped, but dismissed it as a ridiculous coincidence. He had in any case no time to stop and puzzle it out now.

"Are you looking for the turnstile, sir?" inquired the check-clad man in a quavering tenor. "This way, please! Straight ahead for the exit. How about the price of a drink for showing you the way, sir? Church choirmaster out of work, sir . . . Need a helping hand, sir?" Bending double, the weird creature pulled off his jockey cap in a sweeping gesture.

Without stopping to listen to the choirmaster's begging and whining, Berlioz ran to the turnstile and pushed it. Having passed through, he was just about to step off the pavement and cross the trolley tracks when a white and red light flashed in his face and the pedestrian signal lit up with the words "Stop! Trolley!" A streetcar rolled into view, rocking slightly along the newly laid track that ran down Yermolayevsky Street and into Bronnaya. As it turned to join the main line, it suddenly switched its inside lights on, hooted and accelerated.

Although he was standing in safety, the cautious Berlioz decided to retreat behind the railing. He put his hand on the turnstile and took a step backward. He missed his grip and his foot slipped on the cobbles as inexorably as though on ice. As it slid toward the trolley tracks, his other leg gave way and Berlioz was thrown across the track. Grabbing wildly, Berlioz fell prone. He struck his head violently on the cobblestones and the gilded moon flashed hazily across his vision. He had just time to turn on his back, drawing his legs up to his stomach with a frenzied movement, and as he turned over he saw the woman trolley driver's face, white with horror above her red necktie, as she bore down on him with irresistible force and speed. Berlioz made no sound, but all around him the street rang with the desperate shrieks of women's voices. The driver grabbed the electric brake, the car pitched forward, jumping the rails, and with a tinkling crash the glass broke in all its windows. At this moment Berlioz heard a despairing voice: "Oh, no . . .!" Once more and for the last time the moon flashed before his eyes, but it split into fragments and then went black.

Berlioz vanished from sight under the streetcar, and a round, dark object rolled across the cobbles, over the curbstone and bounced along the sidewalk.

It was a severed head.

CHAPTER 4

THE PURSUIT

The women's hysterical shrieks and the sound of police whistles died away. Two ambulances drove off, one bearing the body and the decapitated head to the morgue, the other carrying the beautiful streetcar driver who had been wounded by slivers of glass. Street sweepers in white overalls swept up the broken glass and poured sand on the pools of blood. Ivan Nikolayich, who had failed to reach the turnstile in time, collapsed on a bench and remained there. Several times he tried to get up, but his legs refused to obey him, stricken by a kind of paralysis.

The moment he had heard the first cry the poet had rushed toward the turnstile and seen the head bouncing on the sidewalk. The sight so unnerved him that he bit his hand until he drew blood. He had naturally forgotten all about the mad German and could do nothing but wonder how one minute he could have been talking to Berlioz and the next . . . his head . . .

Excited people were running along the avenue past the poet shouting something, but Ivan Nikolayich did not hear them. Suddenly two women collided alongside him, and one of them, with a pointed nose and straight hair, shouted to the other woman just above his ear, ". . . Anna, it was our Anna! She was coming from Sadovaya! It's her job, you see

. . . she was carrying a quart of sunflower-seed oil to the grocery and she broke her jug on the turnstile! It went all over her skirt and ruined it, and she swore and swore! And that poor man must have slipped on the oil and fallen under the car. . . ."

One word stuck in Ivan Nikolayich's brain—"Anna." "Anna? . . . Anna?" muttered the poet, looking round in alarm. "Hey, what was that you said?"

The name "Anna" evoked the words "sunflower-seed oil" and "Pontius Pilate." Bezdomny rejected "Pilate" and began linking together a chain of associations starting with "Anna." Very soon the chain was complete, and it led straight back to the mad professor.

"Of course! He said the meeting wouldn't take place because Anna had spilled the oil. And, by God, it won't take place now! And what's more he said Berlioz would have his head cut off by a woman!! Yes—and the streetcar driver was a woman!!! Who the hell is he?"

There was no longer a grain of doubt that the mysterious professor had forseen every detail of Berlioz' death before it had occurred. Two thoughts struck the poet: first, "He's no madman," and second, "Did he arrange the whole thing himself?"

"But how on earth could he? We've got to look into this!"

With a tremendous effort Ivan Nikolayich got up from the bench and ran back to where he had been talking to the professor, who fortunately was still there.

The lights were already lit on Bronnaya Street and a golden moon was shining over Patriarch's Ponds. By the light of the moon, deceptive as it always is, it seemed to Ivan Nikolayich that the thing under the professor's arm was not a stick but a sword.

The ex-choirmaster was sitting on the seat occupied a short while before by Ivan Nikolayich himself. The choirmaster had now clipped onto his nose an obviously useless pince-nez. One lens was missing and the other rattled in its frame. It made the check-suited man look even more repulsive than when he had shown Berlioz the way to the trolley lines. With a chill of fear Ivan walked up to the professor. A glance at his face convinced him that there was not a trace of insanity in it.

"Confess—who are you?" asked Ivan grimly.

The stranger frowned, looked at the poet as if seeing him

for the first time and answered disagreeably. "No understand . . . no speak Russian . . ."

"He doesn't understand," put in the choirmaster from his bench, although no one had asked him.

"Stop pretending!" said Ivan threateningly, a cold sensation growing in the pit of his stomach. "Just now you spoke Russian perfectly well. You're no German and you're not a professor! You're a spy and a murderer! Show me your papers!" cried Ivan angrily.

The enigmatic professor gave his already crooked mouth a further twist and shrugged his shoulders.

"Look here, comrade," put in the disgusting choirmaster again. "What do you mean by upsetting this foreign tourist? You'll have the police after you!"

The dubious professor assumed a haughty look, then turned and walked away from Ivan, who felt himself beginning to lose his head. Gasping, he turned to the choirmaster.

"Hey, you, help me arrest this criminal! It's your duty!"

The choirmaster leaped eagerly to his feet and bawled, "What criminal? Where is he? A foreign criminal?" His eyes lit up joyfully. "That man? If he's a criminal, the first thing to do is to shout 'Stop thief!' Otherwise he'll get away. Come on, let's shout together!" And the choirmaster opened his mouth wide.

The stupefied Ivan obeyed and shouted "Stop thief!" but the choirmaster fooled him by not making a sound.

Ivan's lonely, hoarse cry was worse than useless. A couple of girls dodged him, and he heard them say ". . . drunk."

"So you're in league with him, are you?" shouted Ivan, helpless with anger. "Make fun of me, would you? Out of my way!"

Ivan set off to his right and the choirmaster did the opposite, blocking his way. Ivan moved left, the other to his right, and the same thing happened.

"Are you trying to get in my way on purpose?" screamed Ivan, infuriated. *"You're* the one I'm going to report to the police!"

Ivan tried to grab the choirmaster by the sleeve, missed and found himself grasping nothing—it was as if the choirmaster had been swallowed up by the ground.

With a groan Ivan looked ahead and saw the hated stranger. He had already reached the exit leading into Patriarch's Street, and he was no longer alone. The weird choirmaster had managed to join him. But that was not all. There was a third member in the company—a cat the size of a pig, black as soot and with luxuriant cavalry officer's whiskers. The threesome was walking toward Patriarch's Street, the cat trotting along on its hind legs.

As he set off after the villains, Ivan realized at once that it was going to be very hard to catch up with them. In a flash the three of them were across the street and on the Spiridonovka. Ivan quickened his pace, but the distance between him and his quarry grew no less. Before the poet had realized it they had left the quiet Spiridonovka and were approaching Nikita Gate, where his difficulties increased. There was a crowd there, and to make matters worse the evil band had decided to use the favorite trick of bandits on the run and split up.

With great dexterity the choirmaster jumped on board a moving bus bound for Arbat Square and vanished. Having lost one of them, Ivan concentrated his attention on the cat and saw how the strange animal walked up to the platform of an "A" car waiting at a stop, brazenly pushed off a screaming woman, grasped the handrail and offered the conductress a ten-kopeck piece.

Ivan was so amazed by the cat's behavior that he was frozen into immobility beside a street corner grocery. He was struck with even greater amazement as he watched the reaction of the conductress. Seeing the cat board her car, she yelled, shaking with anger, "No cats allowed! I'm not moving with a cat on board! Go on—shoo! Get off or I'll call the police!"

Both conductress and passengers seemed completely oblivious of the most extraordinary thing of all: not that a cat had boarded a streetcar—that was after all possible—but the fact that the animal was offering to pay its fare!

The cat proved to be not only a fare-paying but a law-abiding animal. At the first shriek from the conductress it retreated, stepped off the platform and sat down at the streetcar stop, stroking its whiskers with the ten-kopeck piece. But no sooner had the conductress yanked the bell rope and the car begun to move off, than the cat acted like anyone else who has been pushed off a car and is still determined to get to his destination. Letting all three cars draw past it, the cat jumped onto the coupling hook of the last car, latched its paw around a pipe sticking out of one of the windows and sailed away, having saved itself ten kopecks.

Fascinated by the odious cat, Ivan almost lost sight of the most important of the three—the professor. Luckily he had not managed to slip away. Ivan spotted his gray beret in the crowd at the top of Herzen Street. In a flash Ivan was there too, but in vain. The poet speeded up to a run and shoved people aside, but it brought him not an inch nearer the professor.

Confused though Ivan was, he was nevertheless astounded by the supernatural speed of the pursuit. Less than twenty seconds after leaving Nikita Gate Ivan Nikolayich was dazzled by the lights of Arbat Square. A few more seconds and he was in a dark alleyway with an uneven pavement where he tripped and hurt his knee. Again a well-lit main road— Kropotkin Street—another side street, then Ostozhenka Street, then another grim, dirty and badly lit alley. It was here that Ivan Nikolayich finally lost sight of his quarry. The professor had disappeared.

Disconcerted, but not for long, for no apparent reason Ivan Nikolayich had a sudden intuition that the professor was in house No. 13, apartment 47.

Bursting through the front door, Ivan Nikolayich flew up the stairs, found the right apartment and impatiently rang the bell. He did not have to wait long. The door was opened by a little girl of about five, who silently disappeared inside again. The entrance hall was a vast, incredibly neglected room feebly lit by a tiny electric light that dangled in one corner from a ceiling black with dirt. On the wall hung a bicycle without any tires, beneath it a huge iron-banded trunk. On the shelf over the coat rack was a winter fur cap, its long ear flaps untied and hanging down. From behind one of the doors a man's voice could be heard booming from the radio, angrily declaiming poetry.

Not in the least put out by these unfamiliar surroundings, Ivan Nikolayich made straight for the hall, thinking to himself, "He's obviously hiding in the bathroom." The passage was dark. Bumping into the walls, Ivan saw a faint streak of light under a doorway. He groped for the handle and gave it a gentle turn. The door opened and Ivan found himself in luck—it was the bathroom.

However, it wasn't quite the sort of luck he had hoped for. Amid the damp steam and by the light of the coals smoldering in the water heater, he made out a large basin attached to the wall and a bath streaked with black where the enamel had chipped off. There in the bath stood a naked woman, covered with soapsuds and holding a sponge. She peered near-sightedly at Ivan as he came in, and obviously mistaking him for someone else in the hellish light she whispered gaily, "Kiryushka! Do stop fooling! You must be crazy. . . . Fyodor Ivanovich will be back any minute now. Go on—out you go!" And she waved her sponge at Ivan.

The mistake was plain, and it was, of course, Ivan Niko-layich's fault, but rather than admit it he gave a shocked cry of "Brazen hussy!" and suddenly found himself in the kitchen. It was empty. In the gloom a silent row of ten or so alcohol burners stood on a marble slab. A single ray of moonlight, struggling through a dirty window that had not been cleaned for years, cast a dim light into one corner where there hung a forgotten icon, the stubs of two candles still stuck in its frame. Beneath the big icon was another made of paper and fastened to the wall with thumbtacks.

Nobody knows what came over Ivan, but before letting himself out by the back staircase he stole one of the candles and the little paper icon. Clutching these objects, he left the strange apartment, muttering, embarrassed by his recent experience in the bathroom. He could not help wondering who the shameless Kiryushka might be and whether he was the owner of the nasty fur cap with dangling ear flaps.

In the deserted, cheerless alleyway Bezdomny looked round for the fugitive, but there was no sign of him. Ivan said firmly to himself, "Of course! He's on the Moscow River! Come on!"

Somebody should of course have asked Ivan Nikolayich why he imagined the professor would be on the Moscow River of all places, but unfortunately there was no one to ask him —the filthy little alley was completely empty.

In no time at all Ivan Nikolayich was to be seen on the granite steps of the Moscow quay. Taking off his clothes, Ivan entrusted them to a kindly old man with a beard dressed in a torn white Russian blouse and patched, unlaced boots. Waving him aside, Ivan took a swan dive into the water. The water was so cold that it took his breath away, and for a moment he doubted whether he would ever reach the surface again. But reach it he did, and puffing and snorting, his eyes round with terror, Ivan Nikolayich began swimming in the black, oily-smelling water toward the shimmering zigzags of the embankment lights reflected in the water.

When Ivan clambered damply up the steps at the place where he had left his clothes in the care of the bearded man, not only his clothes but their venerable guardian had apparently been spirited away. On the very spot where the heap of clothes had been there was now a pair of check undershorts, a torn Russian blouse, a candle, a paper icon and a box of matches. Shaking his fist into space with impotent rage, Ivan clambered into the available garments.

As he did so two thoughts worried him. To begin with, he had now lost his MASSOLIT membership card; normally he never went anywhere without it. Second, it occurred to him that he might be arrested for walking around Moscow in this state. After all, he had practically nothing on but a pair of undershorts.

Ivan tore the buttons off the underwear where it was fastened at the legs, hoping that people might think they were a pair of lightweight summer shorts. He then picked up the icon, the candle and matches and set off, saying to himself, "I must go to Griboyedov! He's bound to be there."

Ivan Nikolayich's fears were completely justified—passers-by noticed him and turned round to stare, so he decided to leave the main streets and make his way through the side streets where people were not so inquisitive, where there was less chance of them stopping a barefoot man and badgering him with questions about his underwear—which obstinately refused to look like summer shorts.

Ivan plunged into a maze of side streets around the Arbat and began to sidle along the walls, blinking fearfully, glancing this way and that, occasionally hiding in doorways, avoiding intersections with traffic lights and the elegant porticoes of embassy mansions.

CHAPTER 5

THE AFFAIR AT GRIBOYEDOV

It was an old two-storied house, painted cream, that stood on the ring boulevard behind a ragged garden fenced off from the pavement by a wrought-iron railing. In winter the paved front courtyard was usually full of shoveled snow, while in summer, shaded by a canvas awning, it became a delightful outdoor extension of the club restaurant.

The house was called Griboyedov House because it might once have belonged to an aunt of the famous playwright Alexander Sergeyevich Griboyedov. Nobody really knows for sure whether she ever owned it or not. People even say that Griboyedov never had an aunt who owned any such property. . . . Still, that was its name. What is more, a dubious tale used to circulate in Moscow of how in the round, colonnaded salon on the second floor the famous writer had once read excerpts from *Woe from Wit* to that same aunt as she reclined on a sofa. Perhaps he did; in any case it doesn't matter.

It matters much more that this house now belonged to MASSOLIT, which until his excursion to Patriarch's Ponds was headed by the unfortunate Mikhail Alexandrovich Berlioz. No one, least of all the members of MASSOLIT, called the place Griboyedov House. Everyone simply called it Griboyedov:

56

"I spent a couple of hours lobbying at Griboyedov yesterday."

"Well?"

"Wangled myself a month in Yalta."

"Good for you!"

Or: "Go to Berlioz—he's seeing people from four to five
this afternoon at Griboyedov." And so on.

MASSOLIT had installed itself in Griboyedov very comfortably indeed. As you entered you were first confronted with
a bulletin board full of announcements by the various sports
clubs, then with the photographs of every individual member of MASSOLIT, who were strung up (their photographs,
of course) along the walls of the staircase leading to the second floor.

On the door of the first room on the upper story was a
large notice: "Angling and Weekend Cottages," with a picture of a carp caught on a hook.

On the door of the second room was a slightly confusing
notice: "Writers' One-Day Train Excursions. Apply to M.V.
Podlozhnaya."

The next door bore a brief and completely incomprehensible legend: "Perelygino." From there the chance visitor's eye
would be caught by countless more notices pinned to the
aunt's walnut doors: "Waiting List for Paper—Apply to Pok-
levkina,"; "Cashier's Office"; "Sketch Writers: Personal Accounts."

At the head of the longest waiting line, which started downstairs at the porter's desk, was a door under constant siege
labeled "Housing Problems."

Past the housing problems hung a gorgeous poster showing
a cliff, along whose summit rode a man on a chestnut horse
with a rifle slung over his shoulder. Below were some palm
trees and a balcony. On it sat a shock-haired young man gazing upward with a bold, urgent look and holding a fountain
pen in his hands. The legend read: "All-Inclusive Writing
Holidays, from two weeks (short story, novella) to one year
(novel, trilogy): Yalta, Suksun, Borovoye, Tsikhidziri, Mak-
hinjauri, Leningrad (Winter Palace)." There was a line at
this door too, but not an excessively long one—only about
a hundred and fifty people.

Following the erratic twists, the steps up and steps down,
of Griboyedov's corridors, one found other notices: "MAS-
SOLIT—Management," "Cashiers Nos. 2, 3, 4, 5," "Editorial

Board," "MASSOLIT—Chairman." "Billiard Room," then
various subsidiary organizations, and finally that colonnaded
salon where the aunt had listened with such delight to the
readings of his comedy by her brilliant nephew.

Every visitor to Griboyedov, unless of course he was completely insensitive, was made immediately aware of how good
life was for the lucky members of MASSOLIT, and he would
at once be consumed with black envy. At once, too, he would
curse heaven for having failed to endow him at birth with
literary talent, without which, of course, no one could so
much as dream of acquiring a MASSOLIT membership card
—that brown card known to all Moscow, smelling of expensive leather and embellished with a wide gold border.

Who is prepared to say a word in defense of envy? It is a
despicable emotion, but put yourself in the visitor's place: what
he had seen on the upper floor was by no means all. The entire ground floor of the aunt's house was occupied by a restaurant—and what a restaurant! It was rightly considered
the best in Moscow. Not only because it occupied two large
rooms with vaulted ceilings and lilac-painted horses with flowing manes, not only because every table had a lamp shaded
with lace, not only because it was barred to *hoi polloi,* but
above all for the quality of its food. Griboyedov could beat
any restaurant in Moscow you cared to name, and its prices
were extremely moderate.

There is therefore nothing odd in the conversation which
the author of these lines actually overheard once outside the
iron fence of Griboyedov:

"Where are you dining today, Ambrose?"

"What a question! Here, of course, Vanya! Archibald Archibaldovich whispered to me this morning that there's *filets de
perche au naturel* on the menu tonight. Sheer virtuosity!"

"You do know how to live, Ambrose!" sighed Vanya, a thin,
pinched man with a carbuncle on his neck, to Ambrose, a
strapping, red-lipped, golden-haired, ruddy-cheeked poet.

"It's no special talent," countered Ambrose. "Just a perfectly normal desire to live a decent, human existence. Now
I suppose you're going to say that you can get perch at the
Coliseum. So you can. But a helping of perch at the Coliseum costs thirty rubles fifty kopecks, and here it costs five
fifty! Apart from that the perch at the Coliseum are three
days old, and what's more if you go to the Coliseum there's
no guarantee you won't get a bunch of grapes thrown in your

face by the first young man to burst in from Theater Street. No, I loathe the Coliseum," shouted Ambrose the gastronome at the top of his voice. "Don't try to talk me into liking it, Vanya!"

"I'm not trying to talk you into it, Ambrose," squeaked Vanya. "You might have been dining at home."

"Thank you very much," trumpeted Ambrose. "Just imagine your wife trying to cook *filets de perche au naturel* in a saucepan, in the kitchen you share with half a dozen other people! He, he, he! . . . *Au revoir,* Vanya!" And humming to himself Ambrose hurried off to the veranda under the awning.

Ha, ha, ha! . . . Yes, that's how it used to be! Some of us old inhabitants of Moscow still remember the famous Griboyedov. But boiled fillets of perch was nothing, my dear Ambrose! What about the sturgeon, sturgeon in a silver-plated pan, sturgeon filleted and served between lobsters' tails and fresh caviar? And *oeufs en cocotte* with mushroom purée in little bowls? And didn't you like the thrushes' breasts? With truffles? The quails *alla Genovese?* Nine rubles fifty! And oh, the band, the polite waiters! And in July when the whole family's in the country and pressing literary business is keeping you in town—out on the veranda, in the shade of a climbing vine, a plate of *potage printanière* looking like a golden stain on the snow-white tablecloth? Do you remember, Ambrose? But of course you do—I can see from your lips you remember. Not just your salmon or your perch either—what about the snipe, the woodcock in season, the quail, the grouse? And the sparkling wines! But I digress, reader.

At half-past ten on the evening that Berlioz died at Patriarch's Ponds, only one upstairs room at Griboyedov was lit. In it sat twelve weary authors, gathered for a meeting and still waiting for Mikhail Alexandrovich. Sitting on chairs, on tables and even on the two window ledges, the management committee of MASSOLIT was suffering badly from the heat and stuffiness. Not a single fresh breeze penetrated the open window. Moscow was exuding the heat of the day accumulated in its asphalt, and it was obvious that the night was not going to bring any relief. There was a smell of onion coming from the restaurant kitchen in the cellar, everybody wanted a drink, everybody was nervous and irritable.

Beskudnikov, a quiet, well-dressed essayist with eyes that were at once attentive yet shifty, took out his watch. The hands were just creeping up to eleven. Beskudnikov tapped the watch face with his finger and showed it to his neighbor, the poet Dvubratsky, who was sitting on the table, bored and swinging his feet shod in yellow rubber-soled slippers.

"Well, really . . ." muttered Dvubratsky.

"I suppose the lad's got stuck out at Klyazma," said Nastasya Lukinishna Nepremenova, orphaned daughter of a Moscow businessman, who had turned writer and wrote naval war stories under the pseudonym of "Bosun George."

"Look here!" burst out Zagrivov, a writer of popular short stories. "I don't know about you, but I'd rather be drinking tea out on the balcony right now instead of stewing in here. Was this meeting called for ten o'clock or wasn't it?"

"It must be nice out at Klyazma now," said Bosun George in a tone of calculated innocence, knowing that the writers' summer colony out at Perelygino near Klyazma was a sore point. "I expect the nightingales are singing there now. Somehow I always seem to work better out of town, especially in the spring."

"I've been paying my contributions for three years now to send my sick wife to that paradise, but somehow nothing ever appears on the horizon," said Hieronymus Poprikhin the novelist with bitter venom.

"Some people are lucky and others aren't, that's all," boomed the critic Ababkov from the window ledge.

Bosun George's little eyes lit up, and softening her contralto rasp she said, "We mustn't be jealous, comrades. There are only twenty-two dachas, only seven more are being built and there are three thousand of us in MASSOLIT."

"Three thousand one hundred and eleven," put in someone from a corner.

"Well, there you are," the Bosun went on. "What can one do? Naturally the dachas are allocated to those with the most talent."

"They're allocated to the people at the top!" barked Glukharyov, a script writer.

Beskudnikov, yawning artificially, left the room.

"One of them has five rooms to himself at Perelygino," Glukharyov shouted after him.

"Lavrovich has six rooms to himself," shouted Deniskin, "and the dining room's paneled in oak!"

"Well, at the moment that's not the point," boomed Ababkov. "The point is that it's half-past eleven."

A noise began, heralding mutiny. Somebody rang up the hated Perelygino but got through to the wrong dacha, which turned out to belong to Lavrovich, where they were told that Lavrovich was out on the river. This produced utter confusion. Somebody made a wild telephone call to the Fine Arts and Literature Commission, where of course there was no reply.

"He might have rung up!" shouted Deniskin, Glukharyov and Quant.

Alas, they shouted in vain. Mikhail Alexandrovich was in no state to telephone anyone. Far, far from Griboyedov, in a vast hall lit by thousand-candle-power lamps, what had recently been Mikhail Alexandrovich was lying on three zinc-topped tables. On the first was the naked, blood-caked body with a fractured arm and smashed rib cage, on the second the head, its front teeth knocked in, its vacant open eyes undisturbed by the blinding light, and on the third a heap of mangled rags. Round the decapitated corpse stood the professor of forensic medicine, the pathology anatomist and his dissector, a few detectives and Mikhail Alexandrovich's deputy as chairman of MASSOLIT, the writer Zheldybin, summoned by telephone from the bedside of his sick wife.

A car was sent for Zheldybin and first took him and the detectives (it was about midnight) to the dead man's apartment, where his papers were placed under seal, after which they all drove to the morgue.

The group around the remains of the deceased were conferring on the best course to take: should they sew the severed head back onto the neck or allow the body to lie in state in the main hall of Griboyedov covered by a black cloth down to the chin?

Yes, Mikhail Alexandrovich was quite incapable of telephoning, and Deniskin, Glukharyov, Quant and Beskudnikov were exciting themselves for nothing. On the stroke of midnight all twelve writers left the upper story and went down to the restaurant. There they said more unkind things about Mikhail Alexandrovich; all the tables on the veranda were full, and they were obliged to dine in the beautiful but stifling indoor rooms.

On the stroke of midnight the first of these rooms suddenly woke up and leaped into life with a crash and a roar. A thin male voice gave a desperate shriek of "Alleluia!" Music. It was the famous Griboyedov jazz band striking up. Sweat-covered faces lit up, the painted horses on the ceiling came to life, the lamps seemed to shine brighter. Suddenly, as though bursting their chains, everybody in the two rooms started dancing, followed by everybody on the veranda.

Glukharyov danced away with the poetess Tamara Polumesyatz, Quant danced, Zhukopov the novelist seized a film actress in a yellow dress and danced. They all danced—Dragunsky and Cherdakchi danced, little Deniskin danced with the gigantic Bosun George, and the beautiful girl architect Semeikin-Hall was grabbed by a stranger in white raffia trousers. Members and guests, from Moscow and from out of town, they all danced—the writer Johann from Kronstadt, a producer called Vitya Kuftik from Rostov with lilac-colored eczema all over his face, the leading lights of the poetry section of MASSOLIT—Pavianov, Bogohulsky, Sladky, Shpichkin and Adelfina Buzdyak, young men of unknown occupation with cropped hair and shoulders padded with cotton wool —an old, old man with a chive sticking out of his beard danced with a thin, anemic girl in an orange silk dress.

Pouring sweat, the waiters carried dripping mugs of beer over the dancers' heads, yelling hoarsely and venomously "Sorry, sir!" Somewhere a man bellowed through a megaphone: "One chops! Two kebab! Chicken à la king!" The vocalist was no longer singing—he was howling. Now and again the crash of cymbals in the band drowned the noise of dirty dishes flung down a sloping chute to the scullery. In short—hell.

At midnight there appeared a vision in this hell. Onto the veranda strode a handsome, black-eyed man with a pointed beard and wearing a tail coat. With regal gaze he surveyed his domain. According to some romantics there had once been a time when this noble figure had worn not tails but a broad leather belt around his waist stuck with pistol butts, when his raven-black hair had been tied up in a scarlet kerchief and his brig had sailed the Caribbean under the Jolly Roger.

But that, of course, is pure fantasy—the Caribbean doesn't exist, no desperate buccaneers sail it, no corvette ever chases them, no puffs of cannon smoke ever roll across the waves. Pure invention. Look at that scraggy tree, look at the iron railings, the boulevard. . . . And the ice is floating in the wine bucket, and at the next table there's a man with oxlike, bloodshot eyes and it's pandemonium. . . . Oh, gods—poison, I need poison! . . .

Suddenly from one of the tables the word "Berlioz!" rose and exploded in the air. Suddenly the band collapsed and stopped, as though someone had punched it. "What, what, what—*what?*"

"Berlioz!!!"

Everybody began rushing about and screaming.

A wave of grief surged up at the terrible news about Mikhail Alexandrovich. Someone fussed around shouting that they must all immediately, here and now, without delay compose a collective telegram and send it off.

But what telegram, you may ask? And why send it? Send it where? And what use is a telegram to the man whose battered skull is being mauled by the rubber hands of a dissector, whose neck is being pierced by the professor's crooked needles? He's dead, he doesn't want a telegram. It's all over, let's not overload the post office.

Yes, he's dead . . . but we are still alive!

The wave of grief rose, lasted for a while and then began to recede. Somebody went back to his table and—furtively to begin with, then openly—drank a glass of vodka and took a bite to eat. After all, what's the point of wasting the *côtelettes de volaille?* What good are we going to do Mikhail Alexandrovich by going hungry? We're still alive, aren't we?

Naturally the piano was shut and locked, the band went home and a few journalists left for their newspaper offices to write obituaries. The news spread that Zheldybin was back from the morgue. He moved into Berlioz' upstairs office, and at once a rumor started that he was going to take over from Berlioz. Zheldybin summoned all twelve members of the management committee from the restaurant, and in an emergency session they began discussing such urgent questions as the preparation of the colonnaded hall, the transfer of the body from the morgue, the times at which members could attend the lying-in-state and other matters connected with the tragic event.

Downstairs in the restaurant life had returned to normal and would have continued on its usual nocturnal course until closing time at four had not something quite abnormal occurred which shocked the diners considerably more than the news of Berlioz' death.

The first to be alarmed were the cab drivers waiting outside the gates of Griboyedov. Jerking up with a start, one of them shouted, "Hey! Look at that!"

A little glimmer flared up near the iron railing and started to bob toward the veranda. Some of the diners stood up, stared and saw that the flickering light was accompanied by a white apparition. As it approached the veranda trellis, every diner froze, eyes bulging, sturgeon-laden forks motionless in mid-air. The club doorman, who at that moment had just left the restaurant cloakroom to go outside for a smoke, stubbed out his cigarette and was just going to advance on the apparition with the aim of barring its way into the restaurant when for some reason he changed his mind, stopped and grinned stupidly.

The apparition, passing through an opening in the trellis, mounted the veranda unhindered. As it did so, everyone saw that this was no apparition but the distinguished poet Ivan Nikolayich Bezdomny.

He was barefoot and wearing a torn, dirty white Russian blouse. To its front was safety-pinned a paper icon with a picture of some unknown saint. He was wearing white under-shorts with a lighted candle in his hand and his right cheek bore a fresh scratch. It would be hard to fathom the depth of the silence which reigned on the veranda. Beer poured onto the floor from a mug held sideways by one of the waiters.

The poet raised the candle above his head and said in a loud voice, "Greetings, friends!" He then looked under the nearest table and exclaimed with disappointment, "No, he's not there."

Two voices were heard. A bass voice said pitilessly, "An obvious case of DTs."

The second, a frightened woman's voice, inquired nervously, "How did the police let him onto the streets in that state?"

Ivan Nikolayich heard this and replied, "They tried to arrest me twice, once in Skatertny Street and once here on Bronnaya, but I climbed over the fence and that's how I scratched my cheek!" Ivan Nikolayich lifted up his candle and shouted, "Fellow artists!" (His squeaky voice grew stronger and more urgent.) "Listen to me, all of you! He's come! Catch him at once or he'll do untold harm!"

"What's that? What? What did he say? Who's come?" came the questions from all sides.

"A professor," answered Ivan, "and it was this professor who killed Misha Berlioz this evening at Patriarch's."

By now people were streaming onto the veranda from the indoor rooms, and a crowd began milling around Ivan.

"I beg your pardon, would you say that again more clearly?" said a low, courteous voice right beside Ivan Nikolayich's ear. "Tell me, how was he killed? Who killed him?"

"A foreigner—he's a professor and a spy," replied Ivan, looking round.

"What's his name?" said the voice again into his ear.

"That's just the trouble!" cried Ivan in frustration. "If only I knew his name! I couldn't read it properly on his visiting card. I only remember the letter 'W'—the name began with a 'W.' What could it have been?" Ivan asked himself aloud, clutching his forehead with his hand. "We, wi, wa . . . wo . . . Walter? Wagner? Weiner? Wegner? Winter?" The hairs on Ivan's head started to stand on end from the effort.

"Wolff?" shouted a woman, trying to help him.

Ivan lost his temper.

"You fool!" he shouted, looking for the woman in the crowd. "What's Wolff got to do with it? He didn't do it. . . . Wo, wa . . . No, I'll never remember it like this. Now look, everybody—ring up the police at once and tell them to send five motorcycles and sidecars with machine guns to catch the professor. And don't forget to say that there are two others with him—a tall fellow in checks with a wobbly pince-nez and a great black cat. . . . Meanwhile I'm going to search Griboyedov—I can sense that he's here!"

Ivan was by now in a state of some excitement. Pushing the bystanders aside, he began waving his candle about, pouring wax on himself, and started to look under the tables. Then somebody said "Doctor!" and a fat, kindly face, clean-shaven, smelling of drink and with horn-rimmed spectacles, appeared in front of Ivan.

"Comrade Bezdomny," said the face solemnly, "calm down! You're upset by the death of our beloved Mikhail Alexandrovich—no, I mean plain Misha Berlioz. We all realize how you feel. You need rest. You'll be taken home to bed in a moment and then you can relax and forget all about it—"

"Don't you realize," Ivan interrupted, scowling, "that we've got to catch the professor? And all you can do is come creeping up to me talking all this rubbish! Cretin!"

"Excuse *me*, Comrade Bezdomny!" replied the face, blushing, retreating and already wishing it had never let itself get involved in this affair.

"No, I don't care who you are—I won't excuse you," said Ivan Nikolayich with quiet hatred.

A spasm distorted his face, he rapidly switched the candle from his right to his left hand, swung his arm and punched the sympathetic face on the ear.

Several people reached the same conclusion at once and hurled themselves at Ivan. The candle went out, the horn-rims fell off the face and were instantly smashed underfoot. Ivan let out a dreadful war whoop, audible, to everybody's embarrassment, as far as the boulevard, and began to defend himself. There came a tinkle of breaking crockery, women screamed.

While the waiters tied up the poet with dishcloths, a conversation was in progress in the cloakroom betwen the doorman and the maître d'hôtel.

"Didn't you see that he was wearing undershorts?" asked the pirate coldly.

"But, Archibald Archibaldovich, I'm a coward," replied the doorman. "How could I stop him from coming in? He's a member!"

"Didn't you see that he was wearing undershorts?" repeated the pirate.

"Please, Archibald Archibaldovich," said the doorman, turning purple, "what could I do? I know there are ladies on the veranda, but—"

"The ladies don't matter. They don't mind," replied the pirate, roasting the doorman with his glare. "But the police mind! There's only one way a man can walk round Moscow in his underwear—when he's being escorted by the police on the way to a police station! And you, if you call yourself a doorman, ought to know that if you see a man in that state it's your duty not to waste a moment but to start blowing your whistle! Do you hear? Can't you hear what's happening on the veranda?"

The wretched doorman could hear the sounds of smashing crockery, groans and women's screams from the veranda only too well.

"Now what do you propose to do about it?" inquired the buccaneer.

The skin on the doorman's face took on a leprous shade and his eyes went blank. It seemed to him that the other man's black hair, now neatly parted, was covered by a fiery silk kerchief. Starched shirt front and tail coat vanished, a pistol was sticking out of his leather belt. The doorman saw himself dangling from the foretop yardarm, his tongue protruding from his lifeless, drooping head. He could even hear the waves lapping against the ship's side. The doorman's knees trembled. But the buccaneer took pity on him and switched off his terrifying glare.

"All right, Nikolai—but mind it never happens again! We can't have porters like you in a restaurant—you'd better go and be a janitor in a church." Having said this, the captain gave a few rapid, crisp, clear orders: "Send the barman. Police. Statement. Car. Mental hospital." And he added: "Whistle!"

A quarter of an hour later, to the astonishment of the people in the restaurant, on the boulevard and at the windows of the surrounding houses, the barman, the doorman, a policeman, a waiter and the poet Ryukhin were to be seen emerging from the gates of Griboyedov dragging a young man trussed up like a mummy, who was weeping, spitting, lashing out at Ryukhin and shouting for the whole street to hear, "You bastard! . . . You bastard! . . ."

A buzzing crowd collected, discussing the incredible scene. It was of course an abominable, disgusting, thrilling, revolting scandal which only ended when a truck drove away from the gates of Griboyedov carrying the unfortunate Ivan Nikolayich, the policeman, the barman and Ryukhin.

CHAPTER **6**

SCHIZOPHRENIA

At half-past one in the morning a man with a pointed beard and wearing a white coverall entered the reception hall of a famous psychiatric clinic recently completed in the suburbs of Moscow. Three orderlies and the poet Ryukhin stood nervously watching Ivan Nikolayich as he sat on a divan. The dishcloths that had been used to pinion him now lay in a heap on the same divan, leaving his arms and legs free.

As the man came in, Ryukhin turned pale, coughed and said timidly, "Good morning, Doctor."

The doctor bowed to Ryukhin but looked at Ivan Nikolayich, who was sitting completely immobile and scowling furiously. He did not even move when the doctor appeared.

"This, Doctor," began Ryukhin in a mysterious whisper, glancing anxiously at Ivan Nikolayich, "is the famous poet Ivan Bezdomny. We're afraid he may have the DTs."

'Has he been drinking heavily?" inquired the doctor through clenched teeth.

"No, he's had a few drinks, but not enough—"

"Has he been trying to catch spiders, rats, little devils or dogs?"

"No," replied Ryukhin, shuddering. "I saw him yesterday and this morning—he was perfectly well then."

"Why is he in his undershorts? Did you have to pull him out of bed?"

"He came into a restaurant like this, Doctor."

"Aha, aha," said the doctor in a tone of great satisfaction. "And why the scratches? Has he been fighting?"

"He fell off the fence and then he hit someone in the restaurant . . . and someone else, too."

"I see, I see, I see," said the doctor and added, turning to Ivan, "Good morning!"

"Hello, you quack!" said Ivan, loudly and viciously.

Ryukhin was so embarrassed that he dared not raise his eyes. The courteous doctor, however, showed no signs of offense and with a practiced gesture took off his glasses, lifted the skirt of his coverall, put them in his hip pocket and then asked Ivan, "How old are you?"

"Go to hell!" shouted Ivan rudely and turned away.

"Why are you being so disagreeable? Have I said anything to upset you?"

"I'm twenty-three," said Ivan excitedly, "and I'm going to lodge a complaint against all of you—and you in particular, you louse!" He spat at Ryukhin.

"What will your complaint be?"

"That you arrested me, a perfectly healthy man, and forcibly dragged me off to the madhouse!" answered Ivan in fury.

At this Ryukhin took a close look at Ivan and felt a chill down his spine: (there was not a trace of insanity in the man's eyes.) They had been slightly clouded at Griboyedov, but now they were as clear as before.

"Godfathers!" thought Ryukhin in terror. "He really is perfectly normal! What a ghastly business! Why *have* we brought him here? There's nothing the matter with him except a few scratches on his face."

"You are not," said the doctor calmly, sitting down on a stool on a single chromium-plated stalk, "in a madhouse but in a clinic, where nobody is going to keep you if it isn't necessary."

Ivan gave him a suspicious scowl, but muttered, "Thank God for that! At last I've found one normal person among all these idiots, and the worst idiot of the lot is that incompetent fraud Sasha!"

"Who is this incompetent Sasha?" inquired the doctor.

"That's him, Ryukhin," replied Ivan, jabbing a dirty finger in Ryukhin's direction, who spluttered in protest. "That's all the thanks I get," he thought bitterly, "for showing him some sympathy! What a miserable louse he is!"

"A typical peasant mentality," said Ivan Nikolayich, who obviously felt a sudden urge to attack Ryukhin. "And what's more he's a peasant masquerading as a proletarian. Look at his mean face and compare it with all that pompous verse he writes for May Day—all that stuff about 'upwards and on-wards' and 'banners waving'! . . . If you could look inside him and see what he's thinking, it would make you sick!" And Ivan Nikolayich gave a hoot of malicious laughter.

Ryukhin, breathing heavily, turned red. There was only one thought in his mind—that he had nourished a serpent in his bosom, that he had tried to help someone who when it came to the showdown had treacherously turned on him. The worst of it was that he could not answer back—one just didn't swear at a lunatic!

"Exactly why have they brought you here?" asked the doctor, who had listened to Bezdomny's outburst with great attention.

"God knows, the blockheads! They grabbed me, tied me up with some filthy rags and dumped me in a truck!"

"May I ask why you came into the restaurant in nothing but your underwear?"

"There's nothing odd about it," answered Ivan. "I went for a swim in the Moscow River and someone pinched my clothes and left me this junk instead! I couldn't walk around Moscow naked, could I? I had to put on what there was, because I was in a hurry to get to the Griboyedov restaurant."

The doctor glanced questioningly at Ryukhin, who mumbled sulkily, "Yes, that's the name of the restaurant."

"Aha," said the doctor, "but why were you in such a hurry? Did you have an appointment there?"

"I had to catch the professor," replied Ivan Nikolayich, glancing nervously round.

"What professor?"

"Do you know Berlioz?" asked Ivan with a meaningful look.

"You mean . . . the composer?"

Ivan looked puzzled. "What composer? Oh, yes . . . no, no. The composer just happens to have the same name as Misha Berlioz."

Ryukhin was still feeling too offended to speak, but he had to explain: "Berlioz, the chairman of MASSOLIT, was run over by a streetcar this evening at Patriarch's."

"Don't lie, you—you don't know anything about it," Ivan

burst out at Ryukhin. "I was there, not you! He made him fall under that car on purpose!"

"Did he push him?"

"What are you talking about?" exclaimed Ivan, irritated by his listener's failure to grasp the situation. "He didn't have to push him! He can do things you'd never believe! He knew in advance that Berlioz was going to fall under a streetcar!"

"Did anybody see this professor apart from you?"

"No, that's the trouble. Only Berlioz and myself."

"I see. What steps did you take to arrest this murderer?" At this point the doctor turned and threw a glance at a woman in a white coverall seated behind a desk.

"This is what I did: I took this candle from the kitchen—"

"This one?" asked the doctor, pointing to a broken candle lying on the desk beside the icon.

"Yes, that's the one, and—"

"Why the icon?"

"Well, er, the icon . . ." Ivan blushed. "You see an icon frightens them more than anything else." He again pointed at Ryukhin. "But the fact is that the professor is . . . well, let's be frank . . . he's in league with the powers of evil . . . and it's not so easy to catch someone like him."

The orderlies ran their hands down their trouser seams and stared even harder at Ivan.

"Yes," went on Ivan. "He's in league with them. There's no arguing about it. He once talked to Pontius Pilate. It's no good looking at me like that, I'm telling you the truth! He saw it all—the balcony, the palm trees. He was actually with Pontius Pilate. I'll swear it."

"Well, now . . ."

"So, as I was saying. I pinned the icon to my chest and ran—"

Here the clock struck twice.

"Oh, my God!" exclaimed Ivan and rose from the couch. "It's two o'clock and here am I wasting time talking to you! Would you mind—where's the telephone?"

"Show him the telephone," the doctor said to the orderlies.

As Ivan grasped the receiver the woman quietly asked Ryukhin, "Is he married?"

"No, he's a bachelor," replied Ryukhin, startled.

"Is he a union member?"

"Yes."

"Police?" shouted Ivan into the mouthpiece. "Police? Is that

the duty officer? Sergeant, please arrange to send five motorcycles with sidecars, armed with machine guns to arrest the
foreign professor. What? Take me with you, I'll show you
where to go. . . . This is Bezdomny, I'm a poet, and I'm
speaking from the lunatic asylum. . . . What's your address?"
Bezdomny whispered to the doctor, covering the mouthpiece
with his palm, and then yelled back into the receiver, "Are
you listening? Hello! . . . Fools!" Ivan suddenly roared, hurl-
ing the receiver at the wall. Then he turned round to the doctor,
offered him his hand, said a curt good-bye and started to go.

"Excuse me, but where are you proposing to go?" said the
doctor, looking Ivan in the eye. "At this hour of night, in your
underwear . . . You're not well, stay with us."

"Come on, let me through," said Ivan to the orderlies who
had lined up to block the doorway. "Are you going to let me
go or not?" shouted the poet in a terrible voice.

Ryukhin shuddered. The woman pressed a button on the
desk; a glittering metal box and a sealed ampoule popped out
onto its glass surface.

"Ah, so that's your game, is it?" said Ivan with a wild,
hunted glance around. "All right then . . . good-bye!" And
he threw himself head first at the shuttered window.

There was a loud crash, but the glass did not even crack, and
a moment later Ivan Nikolayich was struggling in the arms of
the orderlies. He screamed, tried to bite, then shouted, "Fine
sort of glass you put in your windows! Let me go! Let me go!"

A hypodermic syringe glittered in the doctor's hand, with one
sweep the woman pushed back the tattered sleeve of Ivan's
blouse and clamped his arm in a most unfeminine grip. There
was a smell of ether, Ivan weakened slightly in the grasp of the
four men, and the doctor skillfully seized the moment to jab
the needle into Ivan's arm. Ivan kept up the struggle for a few
more seconds, then collapsed onto the divan.

"Thugs!" cried Ivan and leaped up, only to be pushed back.
As soon as they let him go, he jumped up again, but sat down
of his own accord. He said nothing, staring wildly about him,
then gave a sudden unexpected yawn and smiled malevolently.

"So you're going to lock me up after all," he said, yawned
again, lay down with his head on the cushion, his fist under his
cheek like a child and muttered in a sleepy voice but without
malice, "All right, then . . . but you'll pay for it. . . . I
warned you, but if you want to . . . What interests me most

now is Pontius Pilate . . . Pilate . . ." And with that he closed his eyes.

"Vanna, put him in No. 117 by himself and with someone to watch him." The doctor gave his instructions and replaced his glasses. Then Ryukhin shuddered again: a pair of white doors opened without a sound and beyond them stretched a corridor lit by a row of blue night bulbs. Out of the corridor rolled a couch on rubber wheels. The sleeping Ivan was lifted onto it, he was pushed off down the corridor and the doors closed after him.

"Doctor," asked the shaken Ryukhin in a whisper, "is he really ill?"

"Oh, yes," replied the doctor.

"Then what's the matter with him?" inquired Ryukhin timidly.

The exhausted doctor looked at Ryukhin and answered wearily, "Overstimulation of the motor nerves and speech centers . . . delirious illusions . . . obviously a complicated case. Schizophrenia, I should think . . . touch of alcoholism, too."

Ryukhin understood nothing of this, except that Ivan Nikolayich was obviously in poor shape. He sighed and asked, "What was that he said about some professor?"

"I expect he saw someone who gave a shock to his disturbed imagination. Or maybe it was a hallucination."

A few minutes later a truck was taking Ryukhin back into Moscow. Dawn was breaking, and the still lit street lamps seemed superfluous and unpleasant. The driver, annoyed at missing a night's sleep, pushed his truck as hard as it would go, making it skid round the corners.

The woods fell away in the distance and the river wandered off in another direction. As the truck drove on, the scenery slowly changed: fences, a watchman's hut, piles of logs, dried and split telegraph poles with bobbins strung on the wires between them, heaps of stones, ditches—in short, a feeling that Moscow was about to appear around the next corner and would rise up and engulf them at any moment.

The log of wood on which Ryukhin was sitting kept wobbling and slithering about, and now and again it tried to slide away from under him altogether. The restaurant dishcloths, which the policeman and the barman had thrown into the back of the truck before leaving earlier by trolley-bus, were being tossed about all over the back of the truck. Ryukhin started to try and pick them up, but with a sudden burst of ill temper he hissed, "To hell with them! Why should I crawl around after them?" He pushed them away with his foot and turned away from them.

Ryukhin was in a state of depression. It was obvious that his visit to the asylum had affected him deeply. He tried to think what it was that was disturbing him. Was it the corridor with its blue lamps, which had lodged so firmly in his memory? Was it the thought that the worst misfortune in the world was to lose one's reason? Yes, it was that, of course—but that after all was a generalization, it applied to everybody. There was something else, though. What was it? The insult—that was it. Yes, those insulting words that Bezdomny had flung into his face. And the agony of it was not that they were insulting but that they were true.

The poet stopped looking about him and instead stared gloomily at the dirty, shaking floor of the truck in an agony of self-reproach.

Yes, his poetry . . . He was thirty-two! And what were his prospects? To go on writing a few poems every year. How long—until he was an old man? Yes, until he was an old man. What would these poems do for him? Make him famous? "What a bunch of crap! Stop kidding yourself. Nobody ever gets famous writing bad poetry. Why is it bad, though? He was right—he was telling the truth!" said Ryukhin pitilessly to himself. "I don't believe in a single word of what I've written!"

Embittered by an upsurge of neurotic anxiety, the poet swayed. The floor beneath had stopped shaking. Ryukhin lifted his head and saw that he was in the middle of Moscow, that day had dawned, that his truck had stopped in a traffic jam at a boulevard intersection and that very near him stood a metal man on a stone base, his head inclined slightly forward, staring blankly down the street.

Strange thoughts assailed the poet, who was beginning to feel ill. "Now there's an example of pure luck—" Ryukhin stood up in the truck and raised his fist in an inexplicable urge to attack the harmless cast-iron man—"everything he did in life, whatever happened to him, it all went his way, everything conspired to make him famous! But what did he achieve? I've never been able to discover. . . . What about that famous phrase of his that begins 'A storm of mist . . .'? What a load of crap! He was lucky, that's all, just lucky!" Ryukhin concluded venomously, feeling the truck start to move under him.

"And just because that White officer shot at him and smashed his hip, he's famous forever."

The jam was moving. Less than two minutes later the poet, now not only ill but aging, walked onto the Griboyedov veranda. It was nearly empty.

Ryukhin, laden with dishcloths, was greeted warmly by Archibald Archibaldovich and immediately relieved of the disgusting rags. If Ryukhin had not been so exhausted by the truck ride and by his experiences at the clinic, he would probably have enjoyed describing everything that had happened in the hospital and would have embellished the story with some invented details. But for the moment he was incapable. Although Ryukhin was not an observant man, now after his agony on the truck, for the first time he looked really hard at the pirate and realized that although the man was asking questions about Bezdomny and even exclaiming "Oh, poor fellow!" he was in reality totally indifferent to Bezdomny's fate and did not feel sorry for him at all. "Good for him! He's right!" thought Ryukhin with cynical, masochistic relish and, breaking off his description of the symptoms of schizophrenia, he asked, "Archibald Archibaldovich, could I possibly have a glass of vodka?"

The pirate put on a sympathetic expression and whispered, "Of course, I quite understand . . . right away," and signaled to a waiter.

A quarter of an hour later Ryukhin was sitting in absolute solitude hunched over a dish of sardines, drinking glass after glass of vodka, understanding more and more about himself and admitting that there was nothing in his life that he could put right—he could only try to forget.

The poet had wasted his night while others had spent it enjoying themselves, and now he realized that it was lost forever. He only had to lift his head up from the lamp and look at the sky to see that the night had gone beyond return. Waiters were hurriedly jerking the cloths off the tables. The cats pacing the veranda had a morning look about them. Day broke inexorably over the poet.

CHAPTER 7

THE HAUNTED APARTMENT

If next day someone had said to Stepan Likhodeyev, "Stepa! If you don't get up this minute you're going to be shot," he would have replied in a faint, languid voice, "All right, shoot me. Do what you like to me, but I'm not getting up!"

The worst of it was that he could not open his eyes, because when he did so there would be a flash of lightning and his head would shiver to fragments. A great bell was tolling in his head, brown spots with livid green edges were swimming around somewhere between his eyeballs and his closed lids. To cap it all, he felt sick and the nausea was somehow connected with the sound of a phonograph.

Stepa tried to remember what had happened, but could only recall one thing—yesterday, somewhere, God knows where, he had been holding a table napkin and trying to kiss a woman, promising her that he would come and visit her tomorrow at the stroke of noon. She had refused, saying, "No, no, I won't be at home," but Stepa had insisted, "I don't care—I'll come anyway!"

Stepa had now completely forgotten who that woman had been, what the time was, what day of what month it was, and, worst of all, he had no idea where he was. In an effort to find out, he unstuck his gummed-up left eyelid. Something glimmered in the semidarkness. At last Stepa recognized it as a mirror. He was lying crosswise on the bed in his own bedroom. Then something hit him on the head, and he closed his eyes and groaned.

Stepa Likhodeyev, manager of the Variety Theater, had waked up that morning in the apartment that he shared with Berlioz in a big six-story block of apartments on Sadovaya Street. This apartment—No. 50—had a strange reputation. Two years before, it had been owned by the widow of a jeweler called de Fougère, Anna Frantzevna, a respectable and very businesslike lady of fifty, who let three of her five rooms to lodgers. One of them was, it seems, called Belomut; the other's name has been lost.

Odd things began happening in that apartment—people started to vanish from it without a trace. One Monday afternoon a policeman called, invited the second lodger (the one whose name is no longer known) into the hall and asked him to come along to the police station for a minute or two to sign a document. The lodger told Anfisa, Anna Frantzevna's devoted servant of many years, to say that if anybody rang him up he would be back in ten minutes. He then went out accompanied by the courteous policeman in white gloves. But he not only failed to come back in ten minutes; he never came back at all. Odder still, the policeman appeared to have vanished with him.

Anfisa, a devout and frankly a rather superstitious woman, informed the distraught Anna Frantzevna that it was witchcraft, that she knew perfectly well who had enticed away the lodger and the policeman, only she dared not pronounce the name at nighttime.

Witchcraft once started, as we all know, is virtually unstoppable. The anonymous lodger disappeared on a Monday; the following Wednesday Belomut, too, vanished from the face of the earth, although admittedly in different circumstances. He was fetched as usual in the morning by the car which took him to work, but it never brought him back and never called again.

Words cannot describe the pain and distress which this caused Madame Belomut, but alas for her, she was not fated to endure even this unhappy state for long. On returning from her *dacha* that evening, whither she had hastily gone with Anfisa, Anna Frantzevna found no trace of Madame Belomut in the flat and, what was more, the doors of both rooms occupied by the Belomuts had been sealed. Two days of uncertainty and insomnia passed for Anna Frantzevna; on the third day she made another hasty visit to her *dacha*, from whence, it need hardly be said, she never returned, Anfisa, left alone, cried her eyes out and finally went to bed at two o'clock in the morning. Nobody knows what happened to her after that, but tenants of the neighboring apartment reported having heard knocking coming from No. 50 and having seen lights burning in the windows all night. By morning Anfisa, too, was gone.

Legends of all kinds about the mysterious apartment and its vanishing lodgers circulated in the building for some time. According to one of them the devout and spinsterly Anfisa used to carry twenty-five large diamonds, belonging to Anna Frantzevna, in a chamois-leather bag between her withered breasts. It was said, too, that among other things a priceless treasure consisting of those same diamonds and a hoard of czarist gold coins had been found in the coal shed behind Anna Frantzevna's dacha. Lacking proof, of course, we shall never know how true these rumors were. However, the flat only remained empty for a week before Berlioz and his wife and Stepa and his wife moved into it. Naturally as soon as they took possession of the haunted apartment the oddest things started happening to them too. Within a single month both wives had disappeared, although not without a trace. Rumor had it that Berlioz' wife had been seen in Kharkov with a ballet master, while Stepan's wife had apparently found her way to an orphanage where, the story went, the manager of the variety had used his connections to get her a room on condition that she never showed her face in Sadovaya Street again. . . .

Stepa groaned. He wanted to call his maid, Grunya, and ask her for an aspirin, but he was conscious enough to realize that it would be useless because Grunya most probably had no aspirin. He tried to call for Berlioz' help and twice moaned, "Misha . . . Misha . . ." but, as you will have guessed, there was no reply. There was complete silence in the apartment.

Wriggling his toes, Stepa deduced that he was lying in his socks. He ran a trembling hand down his hip to test whether or not he had his trousers on and found that he had not. At last, realizing that he was alone and abandoned, that there was nobody to help him, he decided to get up, whatever superhuman effort it might cost him.

Stepa pried open his eyelids and saw himself reflected in the long mirror in the shape of a man whose hair stuck out in all directions, with a puffy, stubble-grown face, with watery eyes and wearing a dirty shirt, a collar, tie, undershorts and socks.

As he looked at himself in the mirror, he also noticed standing beside it a strange man dressed in a black suit and a black beret.

Stepa sat up on the bed and did his best to focus his bloodshot eyes on the stranger. The silence was broken by the unknown visitor, who said gravely, in a low voice with a foreign accent, "Good morning, my dear Stepan Bogdanovich!"

There was a pause. Pulling himself together with fearful effort, Stepa said, "What do you want?" He did not recognize his own voice. He had spoken the word "what" in a treble, "do you" in a bass, and "want" had simply not emerged at all.

The stranger gave an amiable smile, pulled out a large gold watch with a diamond triangle on the cover, listened to it strike eleven times and said, "Eleven. I have been waiting exactly an hour for you to wake up. You gave me an appointment to see you at your apartment at ten, so here I am!"

Stepa fumbled for his trousers on the chair beside his bed and whispered, "Excuse me. . . ." He put on his trousers and asked hoarsely, "Please tell me—who are you?"

He found talking difficult, as with every word someone stuck a needle into his brain, causing him infernal agony.

"What! Have you forgotten my name too?" The stranger smiled.

"Sorry," said Stepa huskily. He could feel his hangover developing a new symptom: the floor beside his bed seemed to be on the move, and any moment now he was liable to take a dive head first down into hell.

"My dear Stepan Bogdanovich," said the visitor with a shrewd smile. "Aspirin will do you no good. Follow a wise old rule—the hair of the dog. The only thing will bring you back to life is two shots of vodka with something sharp and peppery to eat."

Ill though Stepa was, he had enough sense to realize that since he had been found in this state he had better tell all.

"Frankly . . ." he began, scarcely able to move his tongue, "I did have a bit too—"

"Say no more!" interrupted the visitor and pushed the armchair to one side.

Stepan's eyes bulged. There on a little table was a tray, laid with slices of white bread and butter, pressed caviar in a glass bowl, pickled mushrooms on a saucer, something in a little saucepan and finally vodka in one of the jeweler's ornate decanters. The decanter was so chilled that it was wet with condensation from standing in a finger bowl full of cracked ice.

The stranger cut Stepan's astonishment short by deftly pouring him out half a glass of vodka.

"What about you?" croaked Stepa.

"With pleasure!"

With a shaking hand Stepa raised the glass to his lips, and the mysterious guest swallowed his at one gulp. As he munched his caviar, Stepa was able to squeeze out the words: "Won't you have a bite to eat too?"

"Thank you, but I never eat when I'm drinking," replied the stranger, pouring out a second round. He lifted the lid of the saucepan. It contained little sausages in tomato sauce.

Slowly the awful green blobs in front of his eyes dissolved, words started to form and, most important of all, Stepa's memory began to come back. That was it—he had been at Khustov's dacha at Skhodna, and Khustov had driven Stepa out there by taxi. He even remembered hailing the taxi outside the Metropole. There had been another man with them, an actor—or was he an actor?—anyhow he had a portable phonograph. Yes, yes, they had all gone to the dacha! And the dogs, he remembered, had started howling when they played the phonograph. Only the woman Stepa had tried to kiss remained a complete blank—who the hell was she? Didn't she work for the radio? Or perhaps she didn't. . . .

Gradually the previous day came back into focus, but Stepa was much more interested in today and in particular in this odd stranger who had materialized in his bedroom complete with snacks and vodka. If only someone would explain it all!

"Well, now, I hope you've remembered my name?"

Stepa could only grin sheepishly and spread his hands.

"Well, really! I suspect you drank wine on top of vodka last night. What a way to behave!"

"Please keep this to yourself," said Stepa imploringly.

"Oh, of course, of course! But naturally I can't vouch for Khustov."

"Do you know Khustov?"

"I saw that individual for a moment or two in your office yesterday, but one cursory glance at his face was enough to convince me that he was a scheming, quarrelsome, sycophantic swine."

"He's absolutely right!" thought Stepa, amazed at such a truthful, precise and succinct description of Khustov.

The ruins of yesterday were piecing themselves together now, but the manager of the Variety still felt vaguely anxious. There was still a gaping black void in his memory. He had absolutely no recollection of having seen this stranger in his office the day before.

"Woland, professor of black magic," said the visitor gravely and, seeing that Stepa was still in difficulties, he described their meeting in detail.

He had arrived in Moscow from abroad yesterday, had immediately called on Stepa and offered himself as a guest artiste at the Variety. Stepa had telephoned the Moscow District Theatrical Commission, had agreed to the proposal (Stepa turned pale and blinked) and had signed a contract with Professor Woland for seven performances (Stepa's mouth dropped open), inviting Woland to call on him at ten o'clock the next morning to complete the arrangements. So Woland had come. When he arrived he had been met by Grunya the maid, who explained that she herself had only just arrived because she lived out, that Berlioz wasn't at home and that if the gentleman wanted to see Stepan Bogdanovich he should go into the bedroom. Stepan Bogdanovich had been sleeping so soundly that she had been unable to wake him. Seeing the condition that Stepan was in, the artiste had sent Grunya out to the nearest delicatessen for some vodka and snacks, to the drugstore for some ice and—

"You must let me settle up with you," moaned Stepa, thoroughly crushed, and began hunting for his wallet.

"Oh, what nonsense!" exclaimed the artiste and would hear no more of it.

So that explained the vodka and the food; but Stepa was miserably confused: he could remember absolutely nothing about a contract, and he would die before admitting to having seen Woland the previous day. Khustov had been there all right, but not Woland.

"Would you mind showing me the contract?" asked Stepa gently.

"Oh, but of course . . ."

Stepa looked at the sheet of paper and went numb. It was all there: his own bold signature, the backward-sloping signature of Rimsky, the treasurer, sanctioning the payment to Woland of a cash advance of ten thousand rubles against his total fee of thirty-five thousand rubles for seven performances. And what was more—Woland's receipt for ten thousand rubles!

"What the hell?" thought the miserable Stepa. His head began to spin. Was this one of his lapses of memory? Well, of course, now that the actual contract had been produced any further signs of disbelief would merely be rude. Stepa excused himself for a moment and ran to the telephone in the hall. On the way he shouted toward the kitchen, "Grunya!"

There was no reply. He glanced at the door of Berlioz' study, which opened off the hall, and stopped, as they say, dumbfounded. There, fastened to the door handle, hung an enormous wax seal.

"My God!" said a voice in Stepa's head. "If that isn't the last straw!" It would be difficult to describe Stepa's mental confusion. First this diabolical character with his black beret, the iced vodka and that incredible contract. And then, if you please, a seal on the door! Who could ever imagine Berlioz getting into any sort of trouble? No one. Yet there it was—a seal. Well!

Stepa was at once assailed by a number of uncomfortable little thoughts about an article which he had recently talked Mikhail Alexandrovich into printing in his magazine. Frankly the article had been awful—stupid, politically dubious and badly paid. Hard on the heels of his recollection of the article came a memory of a slightly equivocal conversation which had taken place, as far as he could remember, on April 24 here in the dining room when Stepa and Berlioz had been having supper together. Of course their talk had not really been shady (Stepa would not have joined in any such conversation), but it had been on a rather unnecessary subject. They could easily have avoided having it altogether. Before the appearance of this seal the conversation would undoubtedly have been dismissed as utterly trivial, but since the seal . . .

"Oh, Berlioz, Berlioz," buzzed the voice in Stepa's head. "Surely he'll never mention it!"

But there was no time for regrets. Stepa dialed the office of Rimsky, the Variety Theater's treasurer. Stepa was in a delicate position: for one thing, the foreigner might be offended at Stepa ringing up to check on him after he had been shown the contract and, for another, the treasurer was an extremely difficult man to deal with. After all he couldn't just say to him, "Look here, did I sign a contract yesterday for thirty-five thousand rubles with a professor of black magic?" It simply wouldn't do!

"Yes?" came Rimsky's harsh, unpleasant voice in the earphone.

"Hello, Grigory Danilovich," said Stepa gently. "Likhodeyev speaking. It's about this . . . er . . . this fellow . . . this artiste, in my apartment, called, er, Woland . . . I just wanted to ask you about this evening—is everything O.K.?"

"Oh, the black magician?" replied Rimsky. "The posters will be here any minute now."

"Uh-huh," said Stepa weakly. "O.K., so long . . ."

"Will you be coming over soon?" asked Rimsky.

"In half an hour," answered Stepa, and replacing the receiver he clasped his feverish head. God, how embarrassing! What an appalling thing to forget!

As it would be rude to stay in the hall for much longer, Stepa concocted a plan. He had to use every possible means of concealing his incredible forgetfulness and begin by cunningly persuading the foreigner to tell him exactly what he proposed to do in his act at the Variety.

With this Stepa turned away from the telephone, and in the hall mirror, which the lazy Grunya had not dusted for years, he clearly saw a weird-looking man, as thin as a bean pole and wearing a pince-nez. Then the apparition vanished. Stepa peered anxiously down the hallway and immediately had another shock as a huge black cat appeared in the mirror and also vanished.

Stepa's heart gave a jump and he staggered back.

"What in God's name . . .?" he thought. "Am I going out of my mind? Where are these reflections coming from?" He gave another look round the hall and shouted in alarm, "Grunya! What's this cat doing, sneaking in here? Where does it come from? And who's this other character?"

"Don't worry, Stepan Bogdanovich," came a voice, though not Grunya's—it was the visitor speaking from the bedroom. "The cat is mine. Don't be nervous. And Grunya's not here —I sent her away to her family in Voronezh. She complained that you had cheated her out of her vacation."

These words were so unexpected and so absurd that Stepa decided he had not heard them. In utter bewilderment he bounded back into the bedroom and froze on the threshold. His hair rose and a mild sweat broke out on his forehead.

The visitor was no longer alone in the bedroom. The second armchair was now occupied by the creature who had materialized in the hall. He was now to be seen quite plainly—

feathery mustache, one lens of his pince-nez glittering, the other missing. But worst of all was the third invader: a black cat of revolting proportions sprawled in a nonchalant attitude on the pouf, a glass of vodka in one paw and a fork, on which he had just speared a pickled mushroom, in the other.

Stepa felt the light in the bedroom, already weak enough, begin to fade. "This must be what it's like to go mad," he thought, clutching the door jamb.

"You seem slightly astonished, my dear Stepan Bogdano-vich," said Woland. Stepa's teeth were chattering. "But I assure you there is nothing to be surprised at. These are my assistants."

Here the cat drank its vodka and Stepa's hand dropped from the jamb.

"And my assistants need a place to stay," went on Woland, "so it seems that there is one too many of us in this flat. That one, I rather think, is you."

"Yes, that's them?" said the tall man in goatish voice, speaking of Stepa in the plural. "They've been behaving dis-gustingly lately. Getting drunk, carrying on with women, trading on their position and not doing a stroke of work— not that they could do anything even if they tried because they're completely incompetent. Pulling the wool over the boss's eyes, that's what they've been doing!"

"Drives around in a free car!" said the cat slanderously, chewing a mushroom.

Then occurred the fourth and last phenomenon, at which Stepa collapsed entirely, his weakened hand scraping down the door jamb as he slid to the floor.

Straight from the full-length mirror stepped a short but unusually broad-shouldered man with a bowler hat on his head. A fang protruding from his mouth disfigured an already hideous physiognomy that was topped with fiery red hair.

"I cannot," put in the new arrival, "understand how he ever came to be manager." His voice grew more and more nasal. "He's as much a manager as I am a bishop."

"You don't look much like a bishop, Azazello," remarked the cat, piling sausages on his plate.

"That's what I mean," snarled the man with red hair, and turning to Woland he added in a voice of respect, "Will you permit us, Messire, to kick him out of Moscow?"

"Shoo!" suddenly hissed the cat, its hair standing on end.

The bedroom began to spin around Stepa, he hit his head

on the doorpost, and as he lost consciousness he thought, "I'm dying. . . ."

But he did not die. Opening his eyes slightly, he found himself sitting on something made of stone. There was a roaring sound nearby. When he opened his eyes fully, he realized that the roaring was the sea; that the waves were breaking at his feet, that he was in fact sitting on the very end of a stone pier, a shining blue sky above him and behind him a white town climbing up the mountainside.

Not knowing quite what to do in a case like this, Stepa raised himself onto his shaking legs and walked down the pier to the shore.

On the pier stood a man, smoking and spitting into the sea. He glared at Stepa and stopped spitting.

Stepa then did an odd thing—he kneeled down in front of the unknown smoker and said, "Tell me, please, where am I?"

"Well, I'll be damned!" said the unsympathetic smoker.

"I'm not drunk," said Stepa hoarsely. "Something's happened to me, I'm ill. . . . Where am I? What town is this?"

"Yalta, of course . . ."

Stepa gave a gentle sigh and fainted, striking his head on the warm stonework of the pier.

CHAPTER 8

A DUEL BETWEEN PROFESSOR AND POET

At about half-past eleven that morning, just as Stepa lost consciousness in Yalta, Ivan Nikolayich Bezdomny regained it, waking from a deep and prolonged sleep. For a while he tried to think why he was in this strange room with its white walls, its odd little bedside table made of shiny metal and its white shutters, through which the sun appeared to be shining.

Ivan shook his head to convince himself that it was not aching and remembered that he was in a hospital. This in turn reminded him of Berlioz' death, but today Ivan no longer found this very disturbing. After his long sleep Ivan Nikolayich felt calmer and able to think more clearly. After lying for a while motionless in his spotlessly clean and comfortable spring bed, Ivan noticed a bell cord beside him. Out of a habit of fingering anything in sight, Ivan pressed it. He expected a bell to ring or a person to appear, but something quite different happened.

At the foot of Ivan's bed a frosted-glass cylinder lit up with the word "DRINK." After a short spell in that position, the cylinder began turning until it stopped at another word: "ORDERLY." Ivan found this clever machine slightly confusing. "ORDERLY" was replaced by "CALL THE DOCTOR."

"H'm . . ." said Ivan, at a loss to know what the machine expected him to do. Luck came to his rescue. Ivan pressed the button at the word "NURSE." In reply the machine gave a faint tinkle, stopped and went dark. Into the room came a kind-looking woman in a clean white coverall and said to Ivan, "Good morning!"

Ivan did not reply, as he felt the greeting out of place in the circumstances. They had, after all, dumped a perfectly healthy man in the hospital and were making it worse by pretending it was necessary! With the same kind look the woman pressed a button and raised the blind. Sunlight poured into the room through a light, wide-mesh grille that extended to the floor. Beyond the grille was a balcony, beyond that the bank of a meandering river and on the far side a cheerful pine forest.

"Bath time!" said the woman invitingly and pushed aside a folding partition to reveal a magnificently equipped bathroom.

Although Ivan had made up his mind not to talk to the woman, when he saw a broad stream of water thundering into the bath from a glittering faucet, he could not help saying sarcastically, "Look at that! Just like in the Metropole!"

"Oh, no," replied the woman proudly. "Much better. There's no equipment like this anywhere, even abroad. Professors and doctors come here especially to inspect our clinic. We have foreign tourists here every day."

At the words "foreign tourist" Ivan at once remembered the mysterious professor of the day before. He scowled and said, "Foreign tourists . . . why do you all think they're so wonderful? There are some pretty odd specimens among them, I can tell you. I met one yesterday—he was a charmer!"

He was just going to start telling her about Pontius Pilate, but changed his mind. The woman would never understand, and it was useless to expect any help from her.

Washed and clean, Ivan Nikolayich was immediately provided with everything a man needs after a bath—a freshly ironed shirt, undershorts and socks. That was only a beginning; opening the door of a wardrobe, the woman pointed inside and asked him, "What would you like to wear—a dressing gown or pajamas?"

Although he was a prisoner in his new home, Ivan found it hard to resist the woman's easy, friendly manner and he pointed to a pair of crimson flannelette pajamas.

After that Ivan Nikolayich was led along an empty, soundless corridor into a room of vast dimensions. He had decided to treat everything in this wonderfully equipped building with caustic humor, and he at once mentally christened this room "the factory kitchen."

And with good reason. It contained cupboards and glass-fronted cabinets full of gleaming nickel-plated instruments, armchairs of strangely complex design, lamps with shiny, bulbous shades, a mass of phials, Bunsen burners, electric cables and various totally mysterious pieces of apparatus.

Three people came into the room to see Ivan, two women and one man, all in white. They began by leading Ivan to a desk in the corner to interrogate him.

Ivan considered the situation. He had a choice of three courses. The first was extremely tempting—to hurl himself at these lamps and other ingenious gadgets and smash them all to pieces as a way of expressing his protest at being locked up for no reason. But today's Ivan was significantly different from the Ivan of yesterday, and he found the first course dubious; it would only make them more convinced that he was a dangerous lunatic, so he abandoned it. There was a second—to begin at once telling them the story about the professor and Pontius Pilate. However, yesterday's experience had shown him that people either refused to believe the story or completely misunderstood it, so Ivan rejected that course too, deciding to adopt the third: he would wrap himself in proud silence.

It proved impossible to keep it up, and willy-nilly he found himself answering, albeit curtly and sulkily, a whole series of questions. They carefully extracted from Ivan everything about his past life, down to an attack of scarlet fever fifteen years before. Having filled a whole page on him, they turned it over and one of the women in white started questioning him about his relatives. It was a lengthy performance—who had died, when and why, did they drink, had they suffered from venereal disease and so forth. Finally they asked him to describe what had happened on the previous day at Patriarch's Ponds, but they did not pay much attention to his recital and the story about Pontius Pilate left them cold.

The woman then handed Ivan over to the man, who took a different approach toward him, this time in silence. He took Ivan's temperature, felt his pulse and looked into his eyes while he shone a light into them. The other woman came to the man's assistance, and they struck Ivan on the back with some instruments, though not painfully, traced some signs on the skin of his chest with the handle of a little hammer, hit him on the knees with more little hammers, making Ivan's legs jerk, pricked his finger and drew blood from it, pricked his elbow joint, wrapped rubber bracelets around his arm. . . .

Ivan could only smile bitterly to himself and ponder on the absurdity of it all. He had wanted to warn them all of the danger threatening them from the mysterious professor, and had tried to catch him, yet all he had achieved was to land in this weird laboratory just to talk a lot of rubbish about his Uncle Fyodor who had died of drink in Vologda.

At last they let Ivan go. He was led back to his room, where he was given a cup of coffee, two soft-boiled eggs and a slice of white bread and butter. When he had eaten his breakfast, Ivan made up his mind to wait until someone in charge of the clinic arrived, then to make him listen and to plead for justice.

The man came soon after Ivan's breakfast. The door into Ivan's room suddenly opened and in swept a crowd of people in white coveralls. In front strode a man of about forty-five, with a clean-shaven, actorish face, kind but extremely piercing eyes and a courteous manner. The whole retinue showed him signs of attention and respect, which gave his entrance a certain solemnity. "Like Pontius Pilate!" thought Ivan.

Yes, he was undoubtedly the man in charge. He sat down on a stool. Everybody else remained standing.

"How do you do. My name is Dr. Stravinsky," he said as he sat down, looking amiably at Ivan.

"Here you are, Alexander Nikolayich," said a neatly bearded man and handed the chief Ivan's filled-in questionnaire.

"They've got it all sewn up," thought Ivan. The man in charge ran a practiced eye over the sheet of paper, muttered "M'h" and exchanged a few words with his colleagues in a strange language. "And he speaks Latin too—like Pilate," mused Ivan sadly. Suddenly a word made him shudder. It was the word "schizophrenia," which the sinister stranger had spoken at Patriarch's Ponds. Now Dr. Stravinsky was saying it. "So he knew about this, too!" thought Ivan uneasily.

The chief had adopted the line of agreeing with everybody and being pleased with whatever other people said, expressing this by the word "Splendid!"

"Splendid!" said Stravinsky, handing back the sheet of paper. He turned to Ivan.

"Are you a poet?"

"Yes, I am," replied Ivan glumly, and for the first time he suddenly felt an inexplicable revulsion to poetry. Remembering some of his own poems, they struck him as vaguely unpleasant.

Frowning, he returned Stravinsky's question by asking, "Are you a professor?"

To this Stravinsky, with engaging courtesy, inclined his head.

"Are you in charge here?" Ivan went on.

To this, too, Stravinsky nodded.

"I must talk to you," said Ivan Nikolayich in a significant tone.

"That's why I'm here," answered Stravinsky.

"Well, this is the situation," Ivan began, sensing that his hour had come. "They say I'm mad and nobody wants to listen to me!"

"Oh, no, we will listen very carefully to everything you have to say," said Stravinsky seriously and reassuringly, "and on no account shall we allow anyone to say you're mad."

"All right, then, listen: yesterday evening at Patriarch's Ponds I met a mysterious person, who may or may not have been a foreigner, who knew about Berlioz' death before it happened and who had met Pontius Pilate."

The retinue listened to Ivan, silent and unmoving.

"Pilate? Is that the Pilate who lived at the time of Jesus Christ?" inquired Stravinsky, peering at Ivan.

"Yes."

"Aha," said Stravinsky. "And this Berlioz is the one who died falling under a streetcar?"

"Yes. I was there yesterday evening when the car killed him, and this mysterious character was there too."

"Pontius Pilate's friend?" asked Stravinsky, obviously a man of exceptional intelligence.

"Exactly," said Ivan, studying Stravinsky. "He told us, before it happened, that Anna had spilt the sunflower-seed oil . . . and it was on that very spot that Berlioz slipped! How d'you like that?" Ivan concluded, expecting his story to produce a big effect.

But it produced none. Stravinsky simply asked, "And who is this Anna?"

Slightly disconcerted by the question, Ivan frowned.

"Anna doesn't matter," he said irritably. "God knows who she is. Simply some stupid girl from Sadovaya Street. What's important, don't you see, is that he knew about the sunflower-seed oil beforehand. Do you follow me?"

"Perfectly," replied Stravinsky seriously. Patting the poet's knee, he added, "Relax and go on."

"All right," said Ivan, trying to fall into Stravinsky's tone and knowing from bitter experience that only calm would help him. "So obviously this terible man (he's lying, by the way—he's no professor) has some unusual power. . . . For instance, if you chase him, you can't catch up with him . . . and there's a couple of others with him, just as peculiar in their way: a tall fellow with broken spectacles and an enormous cat who rides on the streetcar by himself. What's more," went on Ivan with great heat and conviction, "he was on the balcony with Pontius Pilate, there's no doubt of it. What about that, eh? He must be arrested immediately or he'll do untold harm."

"So you think he should be arrested? Have I understood you correctly?" asked Stravinsky.

"He's clever," thought Ivan. "I must admit there are a few bright ones among the intellectuals," and he replied, "Quite correct. It's obvious—he *must* be arrested! And meanwhile I'm being kept here by force while they flash lights at me, bathe me and ask me idiotic questions about Uncle Fyodor, who's been dead for years! I demand to be let out at once!"

"Splendid, splendid!" cried Stravinsky. "I see it all now. You're right—what's the use of keeping a healthy man in the hospital? Very well, I'll discharge you at once if you tell me you're normal. You don't have to prove it—just say it. Well, are you normal?"

There was complete silence. A fat woman, one of those who had examined Ivan that morning, glanced reverently at the professor, and once again Ivan thought, "Extremely clever!"

The professor's offer pleased him a great deal, but before replying he thought hard, frowning, until at last he announced firmly, "I am normal."

"Splendid," exclaimed Stravinsky with relief. "In that case let us reason logically. We'll begin by considering what happened to you yesterday." Here he turned and was immediately handed Ivan's questionnaire. "Yesterday, while in search of an unknown man, who had introduced himself as a friend of Pontius Pilate, you did the following." Here Stravinsky began ticking off the points on his long fingers, glancing back and forth from the paper to Ivan. "You pinned an icon to your chest. Right?"

"Right," Ivan agreed sulkily.

"You fell off a fence and scratched your face. Right? You appeared in a restaurant carrying a lighted candle, wearing only undershorts, and you hit somebody in the restaurant. You were tied up and brought here, where you rang the police and asked them to send some machine guns. You then attempted to throw yourself out of the window. Right? The question is: is that the way to set about catching or arresting somebody? If you're normal, you're bound to reply, no, it isn't. You want to leave here? Very well. But where, if you don't mind my asking, do you propose to go?"

"To the police, of course," replied Ivan, although rather less firmly and slightly disconcerted by the professor's stare.

"Straight from here?"

"M'h."

"Won't you go home first?" Stravinsky asked quickly.

"Why should I go there? While I'm going home he might get away!"

"I see. And what will you tell the police?"

"I'll tell them about Pontius Pilate," replied Ivan Nikolayich, his eyes clouding.

"Splendid!" exclaimed Stravinsky, defeated, and turning to a man with a beard, he said, "Fyodor Vasilievich, please arrange for Comrade Bezdomny to be discharged. But don't put anybody else in this room and don't change the bedclothes. Comrade Bezdomny will be back here again in two hours. Well," he said to the poet, "I won't wish you success because I see no chance whatever of your succeeding. See you soon!" He got up and his retinue started to leave.

"Why will I come back here?" asked Ivan anxiously.

"Because as soon as you appear at a police station dressed in your undershorts and say you've met a man who knew Pontius Pilate, you'll immediately be brought back here and put in this room again."

"Because of my undershorts?" asked Ivan, staring distractedly about him.

"Chiefly because of Pontius Pilate. But the undershorts will help. We shall have to take away your hospital clothes and give you back your own. And you came here wearing undershorts. Incidentally, you said nothing about going home first, despite my hint. After that you only have to start talking about Pontius Pilate, and you're done for."

At this point something odd happened to Ivan Nikolayich.

His will power seemed to crumple. He felt himself weak and in need of advice.

"Then what should I do?" he asked, timidly this time.

"Splendid!" said Stravinsky. "A most reasonable question. Now I'll tell you what has really happened to you. Yesterday someone gave you a bad fright, upsetting you with this story about Pontius Pilate and other things. So, worn out and nerve-racked, you wandered around town talking about Pontius Pilate. Quite naturally people took you for a lunatic. Your only salvation now is complete rest. And you must stay here."

"But somebody must arrest him!" cried Ivan, imploringly.

"Certainly, but why should you have to do it? Put down all your suspicions and accusations against this man on a piece of paper. Nothing could be simpler than to send your statement to the proper authorities, and if, as you suspect, the man is a criminal, it will come to light soon enough. But on one condition—don't overstrain your mind and try to think a bit less about Pontius Pilate. If you harp on that story, I don't think many people are going to believe you."

"You're right!" announced Ivan firmly. "Please give me pen and paper."

"Give him some paper and a short pencil," said Stravinsky to the fat woman, then turning to Ivan, "But I don't advise you to start writing today."

"No. no, today! I must do it today!" cried Ivan excitedly.

"All right. Only don't overtax your brain. If you don't get it quite right today, tomorrow will do.

"But he'll get away!"

"Oh, no," countered Stravinsky. "I assure you he's not going to get away. And remember—we are here to help you in every way we can, and unless we do, nothing will come of your plan. D'you hear?" Stravinsky suddenly asked, seizing Ivan Nikolayich by both hands. As he held them in his own he stared intently into Ivan's eyes, repeating, "We shall help you . . . do you hear? . . . We shall help you . . . you will be able to relax . . . it's quiet here, everything's going to be all right . . . all right . . . we shall help you. . . ."

Ivan Nikolayich suddenly yawned and his expression softened.

"Yes, I see," he said quietly.

"Splendid!" said Stravinsky, closing the conversation in his confident way and getting up. "Good-bye!" He shook Ivan by the hand, and as he went out he turned to the man with the beard and said, "Yes, and try oxygen . . . and baths."

A few moments later Stravinsky and his retinue were gone. Through the window and the grille the gay, springtime wood gleamed brightly on the far bank and the river sparkled in the noon sunshine.

CHAPTER 9

KOROVIEV'S TRICKS

Nikanor Ivanovich Bosoi, chairman of the tenants' association of No. 302A Sadovaya Street, Moscow, where the late
Berlioz had lived, was in trouble. It had all begun on the previous Wednesday night.

At midnight, as we already know, the police had arrived
with Zheldybin, had hauled Nikanor Ivanovich out of bed,
told him of Berlioz' death and followed him to apartment No.
50. There they had sealed the deceased's papers and personal
effects. Neither Grunya the maid, who lived out, nor the im-
prudent Stepan Bogdanovich was in the apartment at the time.
The police informed Nikanor Ivanovich that they would call
later to collect Berlioz' manuscripts for sorting and examina-
tion and that his quarters, consisting of three rooms (the
jeweler's study, drawing room and dining room) would revert
to the tenants' association for disposal. His effects were to be
kept under seal until the legatees' claims were proved by the
court.

The news of Berlioz' death spread through the building with
supernatural speed, and from seven o'clock on Thursday morning Bosoi started to get telephone calls. After that people
began calling in person with written pleas of their urgent need
of vacant housing space. Within the span of two hours Nikanor
Ivanovich had collected thirty-two such statements.

They contained entreaties, threats, intrigue, denunciations, promises to redecorate the apartment, remarks about over-crowding and the impossibility of sharing an apartment with hoodlums. Among them was a description, shattering in its literary power, of the theft of some meatballs from someone's jacket pocket in apartment No. 31, two threats of suicide and one confession of secret pregnancy.

Nikanor Ivanovich was again and again taken aside with a wink and assured in whispers that he would do well on the deal. . . .

This torture lasted until one o'clock, when Nikanor Ivan-ovich simply ran out of his apartment by the main entrance, only to take flight again when he found them lying in wait for him outside. Somehow contriving to throw off the people who chased him across the asphalt courtyard, Nikanor Ivan-ovich took refuge in staircase 6 and climbed to the fatal apartment.

Panting with exertion, the stout Nikanor Ivanovich rang the bell on the fifth-floor landing. No one opened. He rang again and again and began to swear quietly. Still no answer. Nikanor Ivanovich's patience gave way, and pulling a bunch of duplicate keys from his pocket he opened the door with a masterful flourish and walked in.

"Hello, there!" shouted Nikanor Ivanovich in the dim hall-way. "Are you there, Grunya?"

No reply.

Nikanor Ivanovich then took a folding ruler out of his pocket, pried the seal from the study door and strode in. At least he began by striding in, but stopped in the doorway with a start of amazement.

Behind Berlioz' desk sat a tall, thin stranger in a check jacket, jockey cap and pince-nez. . . .

"And who might you be, comrade?" asked Nikanor Ivan-ovich.

"Nikanor Ivanovich!" cried the mysterious stranger in a quavering tenor. He leaped up and greeted the chairman with an unexpectedly powerful handshake, which Nikanor Ivan-ovich found extremely painful.

"Pardon me," he said suspiciously, "but who are you? Are you somebody official?"

"Ah, Nikanor Ivanovich!" said the stranger in a man-to-man voice. "Who is official and who is unofficial these days? It all depends on your point of view. It's all so vague and changeable, Nikanor Ivanovich. Today I'm unofficial, tomorrow—presto! I'm official! Or maybe vice versa—who knows?"

None of this satisfied the chairman. By nature a suspicious man, he decided that this voluble individual was not only unofficial but had no business to be there.

"Who are you? What's your name?" said the chairman firmly, advancing on the stranger.

"My name," replied the man, quite unmoved by this hostile reception, "is . . . er . . . let's say . . . Koroviev. Wouldn't you like a bite to eat, Nikanor Ivanovich? Since we're friends?"

"Look here," said Nikanor Ivanovich disagreeably, "what the hell do you mean, eat?" (Sad though it is to admit, Nikanor Ivanovich had no manners.) "You're not allowed to enter a dead man's apartment! What are you doing here?"

"Now just sit down, Nikanor Ivanovich," said the imperturbable stranger in a wheedling voice, offering Nikanor Ivanovich a chair.

Infuriated, Nikanor Ivanovich kicked the chair away and yelled, "Who are you?"

"I am employed as interpreter to a foreign gentleman residing in this apartment," said the self-styled Koroviev by way of introduction as he clicked the heels of his dirty brown boots.

Nikanor Ivanovich's mouth fell open. A foreigner in this apartment, complete with interpreter, was a total surprise to him and he demanded an explanation.

This the interpreter willingly supplied. Monsieur Woland, an artiste from abroad, had been kindly invited by the manager of the Variety Theater, Stepan Bogdanovich Likhodeyev, to spend his stay as a guest artiste, about a week, in his apartment. Likhodeyev had written to Nikanor Ivanovich about it yesterday, requesting him to register the gentleman from abroad as a temporary resident while Likhodeyev himself was away in Yalta.

"But he hasn't written to me," said the bewildered chairman.

"Take a look in your briefcase, Nikanor Ivanovich," suggested Koroviev amiably.

Shrugging his shoulders, Nikanor Ivanovich opened his briefcase and found a letter from Likhodeyev.

"Now how could I have forgotten that?" mumbled Nikanor Ivanovich, gazing stupidly at the opened envelope.

"It happens to the best of us, Nikanor Ivanovich!" cackled Koroviev. "Absent-mindedness, overstrain and high blood pressure, my dear friend! Why, I'm dreadfully absent-minded.

Sometime over a glass or two I'll tell you a few things that have happened to me—you'll die with laughter!"

"When is Likhodeyev going to Yalta?"

"He's already gone," cried the interpreter. "He's on his way there. God knows where he is by now." And the interpreter waved his arms like windmill sails.

Nikanor Ivanovich announced that he had to see the foreign gentleman in person, but this was refused. It was quite out of the question. Monsieur Woland was busy. Training his cat.

"You can see the cat if you like," suggested Koroviev.

This Nikanor Ivanovich declined, and the interpreter then made him an unexpected but most interesting proposal: since Monsieur Woland could not bear staying in hotels and was used to spacious quarters, couldn't the tenants' association lease him the whole apartment for his week's stay, including the dead man's rooms?

"After all, what does he care? He's dead," hissed Koroviev in a whisper. "You must admit the apartment's no use to him now, is it?"

In some perplexity Nikanor Ivanovich objected that foreigners were normally supposed to stay at the Metropole and not in private apartments.

"I tell you he's so fussy, you'd never believe it," whispered Koroview. "He simply refuses! He hates hotels! I can tell you I'm fed up with these foreign tourists," complained Koroviev confidentially. "They wear me out. They come here and either they go spying and snooping or they drive me mad with their whims and fancies—this isn't right, that isn't just so! And there'd be plenty in it for your association, Nikanor Ivanovich. He's not short of money." Koroviev glanced round and then whispered in the chairman's ear, "He's a millionaire!"

The suggestion was obviously a sensible one, but there was something ridiculous about his manner, his clothes and that absurd, useless pince-nez, all of which combined to make Nikanor Ivanovich vaguely uneasy. However, he agreed to the suggestion. The tenants' association, alas, was showing an enormous deficit. In the autumn they would have to buy oil for the steam-heating plant, and there was not a kopeck in the till, but with this foreigner's money they might just manage it. Nikanor Ivanovich, however, practical and cautious as ever, insisted on clearing the matter with the Tourist Bureau.

"Of course!" cried Koroviev. "It must be done properly. There's the telephone, Nikanor Ivanovich, ring them up right away! And don't worry about money," he added in a whisper as he led the chairman to the telephone in the hall, "if anyone can pay handsomely, he can. If you could see his villa in Nice! When you go abroad next summer, you must go there especially and have a look at it—you'll be amazed!"

The matter was fixed with the Tourist Bureau with astonishing ease and speed. The Bureau appeared to know all about Monsieur Woland's intention to stay in Likhodeyev's apartment and raised no objections.

"Excellent!" cried Koroviev.

Slightly stupefied by this man's incessant cackling, the chairman announced that the tenants' association was prepared to lease apartment No. 50 to Monsieur Woland the artiste at a rent of . . . Nikanor Ivanovich stammered a little and said, "Five hundred rubles a day."

At this Koroviev surpassed himself. Winking conspiratorially toward the bedroom door, through which they could hear a series of soft thumps as the cat praticed its leaps, he said, "So for a week that would amount to three and a half thousand, wouldn't it?"

Nikanor Ivanovich fully expected the man to add, "Greedy, aren't you, Nikanor Ivanovich?" but instead he said, "That's not much. Ask him for five thousand, he'll pay."

Grinning with embarrassment, Nikanor Ivanovich did not even notice how he had suddenly come to be standing beside Berlioz' desk and how Koroviev had managed with such incredible speed and dexterity to draft a contract in duplicate. This done, he flew into the bedroom and returned with the two copies signed in the stranger's florid hand. The chairman signed in turn, and Koroviev asked him to make out a receipt for five . . .

"Write it out in words, Nikanor Ivanovich. 'Five thousand rubles.' " Then with a flourish which seemed vaguely out of place in such a serious matter— *"Ein, zwei, drei!"*—he laid five bundles of brand-new banknotes on the table.

Nikanor Ivanovich checked them, to an accompaniment of witticisms from Koroviev of the "better safe than sorry" variety. Having counted the money, the chairman took the stranger's passport to be stamped with his temporary residence permit, put contract, passport and money into his briefcase and asked shyly for a free ticket to the show.

"But of course!" exclaimed Koroviev. "How many do you want, Nikanor Ivanovich—twelve, fifteen?"

Overwhelmed, the chairman explained that he only wanted two, one for his wife Pelagea Antonovna and one for himself.

Koroviev seized a note pad and dashed off an order to the box office for two complimentary tickets in the front row. As the interpreter handed it to Nikanor Ivanovich with his left hand, with his right he gave him a thick, crackling package. Glancing at it, Nikanor Ivanovich blushed hard and started to push it away.

"It's not proper—"

"I won't hear any objection," Koroviev whispered right in his ear. "We don't do this sort of thing, but foreigners do. You'll offend him, Nikanor Ivanovich, and that might be awkward. You've earned it."

"It's strictly forbidden," whispered the chairman in a tiny voice, with a furtive glance around.

"Where are the witnesses?" hissed Koroviev into his other ear. "I ask you—where are they? Come, now . . ."

There then happened what the chairman later described as a miracle—the package jumped into his briefcase of its own accord, after which he found himself, feeling weak and battered, on the staircase. A storm of thoughts was whirling round inside his head. Among them were the villa in Nice, the trained cat, relief that there had been no witnesses and his wife's pleasure at the complimentary tickets. Yet despite these mostly comforting thoughts, in the depths of his soul the chairman still felt the pricking of a little needle. It was the needle of unease. Suddenly, halfway down the staircase, something else occurred to him—how had that interpreter found his way into the study past a sealed door? And why on earth had he, Nikanor Ivanovich, forgotten to ask him about it? For a while the chairman stared at the steps like a sheep, then decided to forget it and not to bother himself with imaginary problems. . . .

As soon as the chairman had left the flat a low voice came from the bedroom: "I don't care for that Nikanor Ivanovich. He's a sly rogue. Why not fix it so that he doesn't come here again?"

"Messire, you only have to give the order," answered Koroviev in a firm, clear voice that no longer quavered.

At once the diabolical interpreter was in the hall, had dialed a number and started to speak in a whining voice:

"Hello! I consider it my duty to report that the chairman of our tenants' association at No. 302A Sadovaya Street, Nikanor

Ivanovich Bosoi, is dealing in black-market foreign currency. He has just stuffed four hundred dollars wrapped in newspaper into the ventilation shaft of the lavatory in his apartment, No. 35. My name is Timothy Kvastov and I live in the same block, apartment No. 11. But please keep my name a secret. I'm afraid of what that man may do if he finds out."

And with that the scoundrel hung up.

What happened after that in No. 50 is a mystery, although what happened to Nikanor Ivanovich is common knowledge. Locking himself in the lavatory, he pulled the package out of his briefcase and found that it contained four hundred rubles. He wrapped it up in a sheet of old newspaper and pushed it into the ventilation shaft. Five minutes later he was sitting down at table in his little dining room. From the kitchen his wife brought in a pickled herring, sliced and thickly sprinkled with raw onion. Nikanor Ivanovich poured himself a wine-glassful of vodka, drank it, poured out another, drank that, speared three slices of herring on his fork . . . and then the doorbell rang. Pelagea Antonovna was just bringing in a steaming casserole, one glance at which was enough to tell you that in the midst of all that hot, thick borsch was one of the most delicious things in the world—a marrow bone.

Gulping down his running saliva, Nikanor Ivanovich snarled, "Who the hell is that—at this hour! They won't even allow a man to eat his supper. . . . Don't let anybody in—I'm not at home. . . . If it's about the apartment, tell them to stop worrying. There'll be a committee meeting about it in a week's time."

His wife ran into the hall, and Nikanor Ivanovich ladled the quivering marrow bone out of its steaming lake. At that moment three men came into the dining room, followed by a very pale Pelagea Antonovna. At the sight of them Nikanor Ivanovich turned white and got up.

"Where's the john?" inquired the first man urgently.

There was a crash as Nikanor Ivanovich dropped the ladle onto the oilcloth table top.

"Here, in here," babbled Pelagea Antonovna. The visitors turned and rushed back into the passage.

"What's going on?" asked Nikanor Ivanovich as he followed them. "You can't just burst into our apartment like that. Where's your identity card if you don't mind?"

The first man showed Nikanor Ivanovich his identity card

while the second clambered up onto a stool in the lavatory and thrust his arm into the ventilation shaft. Nikanor Ivanovich began to feel faint. They unwrapped the sheet of newspaper to find that the banknotes in the package were not rubles but some unknown foreign money—bluish-green in color with a picture of an old man. Nikanor Ivanovich, however, saw none of it very clearly because spots were swimming in front of his eyes.

"Dollars in the ventilation shaft . . ." said the first man thoughtfully and asked Nikanor Ivanovich politely, "Is this your little parcel?"

"No!" replied Nikanor Ivanovich in a terrified voice. "It's been planted on me!"

"Could be," agreed the first man, adding as quietly as before, "Still, you'd better give up the rest."

"There isn't any more! I swear to God I've never even seen any!" screamed the chairman in desperation. He rushed to a chest, pulled out a drawer and out of that his briefcase, shouting distractedly as he did so, "It's all in here . . . the contract . . . that interpreter must have planted them on me . . . Koroviev, the man in the pince-nez!"

He opened the briefcase, looked inside, thrust his hand in, turned blue in the face and dropped his briefcase into the borsch. There was nothing in it—no letter from Stepan, no contract, no passport, no money and no complimentary tickets. Nothing, in short, except a folding ruler.

"Comrades!" screamed the chairman frantically. "Arrest them! The forces of evil are in this house!"

Something odd happened to Pelagea Antonovna at this point. Wringing her hands she cried, "Confess, Nikanor! They'll reduce your sentence if you do!"

Eyes bloodshot, Nikanor Ivanovich raised his clenched fists over his wife's head and screamed, "Aaah! You stupid bitch!"

Then he crumpled and fell into a chair, having obviously decided to bow to the inevitable. Meanwhile, out on the landing, Timothy Kondratievich Kvastov was pressing first his ear then his eye to the keyhole of the chairman's front door, burning with curiosity.

Five minutes later the tenants saw the chairman led out into the courtyard by two men. Nikanor Ivanovich, so they said later, had been scarcely recognizable—staggering like a drunkard and muttering to himself.

Another hour after that a stranger appeared at apartment

No. 11 just when Timothy Kondratievich, gulping with pleasure, was describing to some other tenants how the chairman had been whisked away; the stranger beckoned Timothy Kondratievich out of his kitchen into the hall, said something and took him away.

CHAPTER **10**

NEWS FROM YALTA

As disaster overtook Nikanor Ivanovich in Sadovaya Street, not far from No. 302A two men were sitting in the office of Rimsky, the treasurer of the Variety Theater: Rimsky himself and the house manager, Varenukha.

From this large office on the second floor two windows gave onto Sadovaya and another, just behind the treasurer's back as he sat at his desk, onto the Variety's garden; it was used in summer and contained several bars for serving cold drinks, a shooting gallery and an open promenade. The furniture of the room, apart from the desk, consisted of a collection of old posters hanging on the wall, a small table with a carafe of water, four chairs and a stand in one corner supporting a dusty, long-forgotten model of a stage set. Naturally the office also contained a small, battered fireproof safe standing to the left of Rimsky's desk.

Rimsky had been in a bad mood all morning. Varenukha, by contrast, was extremely cheerful and lively, if somewhat nervous. Today, however, there was no outlet for his energy.

Varenukha had just taken refuge in the treasurer's office from the complimentary ticket hounds who made his life a misery, especially on the days when there was a change of program. And today was one of those days. As soon as the telephone started to ring, Varenukha picked up the receiver and lied into it, "Who? Varenukha? He's not here. He's left the theater."

"Please try and ring Likhodeyev once more," said Rimsky testily.

"But he's not at home. I've already sent Karpov; the flat's empty."

"I wish to God I knew what was going on!" hissed Rimsky, fidgeting with his adding machine.

The door opened and a theater usher dragged in a thick package of newly printed billboard posters, which announced in large red letters on a green background:

> *Tonight and All This Week*
> *in the*
> *Variety Theater*
> *A Special Act*
> **PROFESSOR WOLAND**
> *Black Magic*
> *All Mysteries Revealed*

As Varenukha stepped back from the poster, which he had propped up against the model, he admired it and ordered the usher to have all the copies posted.

"All right, get a move on," said Varenukha to the departing usher.

"I don't care for this project at all," growled Rimsky disagreeably, staring at the poster through his horn-rims. "I'm amazed that he was ever engaged."

"No, Grigory Danilovich, don't say that! It's a very smart move. All the fun is in showing how it's done—the 'mysteries revealed.' "

"I don't know, I don't know. I don't see any fun in that myself . . . just like him to dream up something of this sort. If only he'd shown us this magician. Did you see him? God knows where he's dug him up from."

It transpired that Varenukha, like Rimsky, had not seen the magician either. Yesterday Stepa had rushed ("like a madman," in Rimsky's words) into the treasurer's office clutching a draft contract, had ordered him to countersign it and pay Woland his money. The magician had vanished, and no one except Stepa himself had seen him.

Rimsky pulled out his watch, saw that it was five minutes to three and was seized with fury. Really, this was too much!

Likhodeyev had rung at about eleven o'clock, had said that he would come in in about half an hour, and now he had not only failed to appear but had disappeared from his apartment.

"It's holding up all my work," snarled Rimsky, tapping a pile of unsigned papers.

"I suppose he hasn't fallen under a streetcar, like Berlioz?" said Varenukha, holding the receiver to his ear and hearing nothing but a continual, hopeless buzz as Stepa's telephone rang unanswered.

"It would be a damned good thing if he has," said Rimsky softly between his teeth.

At that moment in came a woman in a uniform jacket, peaked cap, black skirt and sneakers. She took a square of white paper and a notebook out of a little pouch on her belt and inquired, "Which of you is Variety? Priority telegram for you. Sign here."

Varenukha scrawled some hieroglyphic in the woman's notebook and, as soon as the door had slammed behind her, opened the envelope. Having read the telegram, he blinked and handed it to Rimsky.

The telegram read as follows:

YALTA TO MOSCOW VARIETY STOP TODAY 1130 PSYCHI-
ATRIC CASE NIGHTSHIRTED TROUSERED SHOELESS STAG-
GERED POLICE STATION ALLEGING SELF LIKHODEYEV MAN-
AGER VARIETY WIRE YALTA POLICE WHERE LIKHODEYEV.

"Thanks—and I'm a Dutchman!" exclaimed Rimsky and added, "Another little surprise package!"

"The False Dmitri!" said Varenukha and spoke into the telephone: "Telegrams, please. On account, Variety Theater, Priority. Ready? 'Yalta Police stop Likhodeyev Moscow Rimsky Treasurer.'"

Disregarding the Pretender of Yalta, Varenukha tried again to locate Stepa by telephone and could not, of course, find him anywhere. While he was still holding the receiver in his hand and wondering where to ring next, the same woman came in again and handed Varenukha a new envelope. Hastily opening it, Varenukha read the text and whistled.

"What is it now?" asked Rimsky, twitching nervously.

Varenukha silently passed him the telegram, and the treasurer read the words:

BEG YOU BELIEVE TRANSPORTED YALTA WOLANDS HYP-
NOSIS WIRE POLICE CONFIRMATION MY IDENTITY LIK-
HODEYEV.

Rimsky and Varenukha put their heads together, read the
telegram again and stared at one another in silence.

"Come on, come on!" said the woman irritably. "Sign here.
Then you can sit and stare at it as long as you like. I've got
urgent telegrams to deliver!"

Without taking his eyes off the telegram, Varenukha
scribbled in her book and the woman disappeared.

"You say you spoke to him on the telephone just after
eleven? said the house manager in complete bewilderment.

"Yes, extraordinary as it may seem!" shouted Rimsky. "But
whether I did or not, he can't be in Yalta now. It's funny."

"He's drunk," said Varenukha.

"Who's drunk?" asked Rimsky, and they stared at each other
again.

There was no doubt that some lunatic or practical joker was
telegraphing from Yalta. But the strange thing was: how did
this wit in Yalta know about Woland, who had only arrived in
Moscow the evening before? How did he know of the connection between Likhodeyev and Woland?

" 'Hypnosis'," muttered Varenukha, repeating one of the
words in the telegram. "How does he know about Woland?" He
blinked and suddenly shouted firmly, "No, of course not. It
can't be! Rubbish!"

"Where the hell has this man Woland got to, damn him?"
asked Rimsky.

Varenukha at once got in touch with the Tourist Bureau and
announced, to Rimsky's utter astonishment, that Woland was
staying in Likhodeyev's apartment. Having then dialed Likhodeyev's apartment yet again, Varenukha listened for a long
time as the ringing tone buzzed thickly in the earpiece. In between the buzzes a distant baritone voice could be heard singing, and Varenukha decided that somewhere the telephone
system had got its wires crossed with the radio station.

"No reply from his apartment," said Varenukha, replacing
the receiver on its rest. "I'll try once more. . . ."

Before he could finish in came the same woman, and both
men rose to greet her as this time she took out of her pouch
not a white but a black sheet of paper.

"This is getting interesting," said Varenukha through

clenched teeth, watching the woman as she hurried out. Rimsky was the first to look at the message.

On a dark sheet of photographic paper the following lines were clearly visible:

As proof herewith specimen my handwriting and signature wire confirmation my identity. Have Woland secretly followed. Likhodeyev.

In twenty years of experience in the theater Varenukha had seen plenty, but now he felt his mind becoming paralyzed and he could find nothing to say beyond the commonplace and absurd remark: "It can't be!"

Rimsky reacted differently. He got up, opened the door and bellowed through it to the usher sitting outside on a stool, "Don't let anybody in except the telegraph girl," and locked the door.

He then pulled a sheaf of papers out of his desk drawer and began a careful comparison of the thick, backward-sloping letters in the photogram with the writing in Stepa's memoranda and his signatures, with their typically curly-tailed script. Varenukha, sprawling on the desk, breathed hotly on Rimsky's cheek.

"It's his handwriting," the treasurer finally said, and Varenukha echoed him, "It's his all right."

Looking at Rimsky's face, the house manager noticed a change in it. A thin man, the treasurer seemed to have grown even thinner and to have aged. Behind their horn-rims his eyes had lost their usual aggressiveness. Now they showed only anxiety, even alarm.

Varenukha did everything that people are supposed to do in moments of great stress. He paced up and down the office, twice spread his arms as though he were being crucified, drank a whole glass of brackish water from the carafe and exclaimed, "I don't understand it! I don't understand it! I don't understand it!"

Rimsky stared out of the window, thinking hard. The treasurer was in an extremely perplexing situation. He had to find an immediate, on-the-spot, natural solution for a number of very unusual phenomena.

Frowning, he tried to imagine Stepa in a nightshirt and without his shoes, climbing that morning at about half-past eleven into some incredibly super-rapid airplane, and then the

same Stepa, also at half-past eleven, standing in the Yalta airport in his socks. . . .

Perhaps it wasn't Stepa who had telephoned him from his
apartment? No, it had been Stepa all right! As if he didn't know
Stepa's voice. Even if it hadn't been Stepa talking to him that
morning, he had actually seen the man no earlier than the
evening before, when Stepa had rushed in from his own office
waving that idiotic contract and had so annoyed Rimsky by his
irresponsible behavior. How could he have flown out of Moscow without saying a word to the theater? And if he had flown
away yesterday evening, he couldn't have reached Yalta before
noon today. Or could he?

"How far is it to Yalta?" asked Rimsky.

Varenukha stopped pacing and cried, "I've already thought
of that! To Sevastopol by rail it's over nine hundred miles,
and it's about another fifty miles to Yalta. It's less by air, of
course."

"H'm . . . Yes . . . No question of his having gone by
train. What then? An Air Force fighter plane? Who'd let Stepa
on board a fighter in his stockinged feet? And why? Perhaps
he'd taken his shoes off by the time he got to Yalta? Same
problem—why? Anyhow, the Air Force wouldn't let him
board a fighter even with his shoes on! No, a fighter was out
of the question too. But the telegram said that he'd appeared
at the police station at half-past eleven in the morning, and
he'd been in Moscow, talking on the telephone, at . . . Just
a moment (his watch face appeared before Rimsky's eyes)
. . . He remembered where the hands had been pointing. . . .
Horrors! It had been twenty past eleven!

So what was the answer? Supposing that the moment after
his telephone call Stepa had rushed to the airport and got there
in, say, five minutes (which was impossible anyway); then if
the airplane had taken off at once, it must have covered over
six hundred miles in five minutes. Consequently it had been
flying at a speed of more than seven thousand miles per hour!
Impossible; ergo he wasn't in Yalta!

What other explanation could there be? Hypnosis? There
was no hypnosis which could hurl a man a distance of six
hundred miles. Could he be imagining that he was in Yalta?
He might, but would the Yalta police imagine it? No, no, really,
it was absurd! But they had telegraphed from Yalta, hadn't
they?

The treasurer's face was dreadful to see. By now someone

outside was twisting and rattling the door handle, and the usher could be heard shouting desperately, "No, you can't! I wouldn't let you in even if you were to kill me! They're in conference!"

Rimsky pulled himself together as well as he could, picked up the telephone receiver and said into it, "I want to put through a priority call to Yalta."

"Clever!" thought Varenukha.

But the call to Yalta never went through. Rimsky put back the receiver and said, "The line's out of order—as if on purpose."

For some reason the faulty line disturbed him a great deal and made him reflect. After some thought he picked up the receiver again with one hand and with the other wrote down what he was dictating into the telephone:

"Priority telegram. From Variety. Yes. To Yalta police. Yes. 'Today approximately 1130 Likhodeyev telephoned me Moscow stop. Thereafter failed appear theater and unreachable telephone stop. Confirm handwriting stop. Will take suggested measures observe Woland. Rimsky Treasurer.' "

"Very clever!" thought Varenukha, but an instant later he changed his mind: "No, it's absurd! He can't be in Yalta!"

Rimsky was meanwhile otherwise engaged. He carefully stacked all the telegrams in a pile and, together with a copy of his own telegram, put them into an envelope, sealed it up, wrote a few words on it and handed it to Varenukha, saying, "Take this and deliver it at once, Ivan Savyelich. Let them puzzle it out."

"Now that really is smart!" thought Varenukha as he put the envelope into his briefcase. Then just to be absolutely sure, he dialed the number of Stepa's apartment, then winked mysteriously and made a joyful face. Rimsky craned his neck to listen.

"May I speak to Monsieur Woland, please?" asked Varenukha sweetly.

"He's busy," answered the receiver in a quavering voice. "Who wants him?"

"Varenukha, house manager of the Variety Theater."

"Ivan Savyelich?" squeaked the earpiece delightedly. "How very nice to hear your voice! How are you?"

"*Merci*," replied Varenukha in some consternation. "Who's speaking?"

"This is Koroviev, his assistant and interpreter," trilled the receiver. "At your service, my dear Ivan Savyelich! Just tell me what I can do for you. What is it?"

"Please . . . is Stepan Bogdanovich Likhodeyev at home?"

"Alas, no, he isn't," cried the telephone. "He's gone out."

"Where to?"

"He went out of town on a car ride."

"Wha-at? A car ride? When is he coming back?"

"He said he just wanted a breath of fresh air and then he'd be back."

"I see . . ." said Varenukha, perplexed. *"Merci . . .* Please tell Monsieur Woland that his act this evening comes just after the second intermission."

"Very good. Of course. At once. Immediately. Certainly. I'll tell him," came the staccato reply from the earpiece.

"Good-bye," said Varenukha, in amazement.

"Please accept," said the telephone, "my warmest and most sincere good wishes for a brilliant success! It will be a great show—great!"

"There you are—I told you so!" said the house manager excitedly. "He hasn't gone to Yalta, he's just gone out of town for a drive."

"Well, if that's the case," said the treasurer, turning pale with anger, "he has behaved like an absolute bastard!"

Here the manager leaped into the air and gave such a shout that Rimsky shuddered.

"I remember! I remember now! There's a new Turkish restaurant out at Pushkino—it's just opened, and it's called the Yalta! Don't you see? He went there, got drunk and he's been sending us telegrams from there!"

"Well, he really has overdone it this time," replied Rimsky, his cheek twitching and real anger flashing in his eyes. "This little jaunt is going to cost him plenty." He suddenly stopped and added uncertainly, "But what about those telegrams from the police?"

"A lot of rubbish! More of his practical jokes," said Varenukha confidently and asked, "Shall I take this envelope all the same?"

"You must," replied Rimsky.

Again the door opened to admit the same woman. "Oh, not her!" sighed Rimsky to himself. Both men got up and walked toward her.

This time the telegram said:

THANKS CONFIRMATION IDENTITY WIRE ME FIVE HUN-
DRED RUBLES POLICE STATION FLYING MOSCOW TOMOR-
ROW LIKHODEYEV.

"He's gone mad," said Varenukha weakly.

Rimsky rattled his key chain, took some money out of the safe, counted out five hundred rubles, rang the bell, gave the money to the usher and sent her off to the post office.

"But Grigory Danilovich," said Varenukha, unable to believe his eyes, "if you ask me, you're throwing that money away."

"It'll come back," replied Rimsky quietly, "and then he'll pay dearly for this little picnic." And pointing at Varenukha's briefcase he said, "Go on, Ivan Savyelich, don't waste any time."

Varenukha picked up his briefcase and trotted off.

He went down to the ground floor, saw a very long line outside the box office and heard from the cashier that she was expecting to have to put up the "SRO" notices that evening because they were being positively overwhelmed since the special bill had been posted. Varenukha told her to be sure not to sell the thirty best seats in the boxes and orchestra, then rushed out of the box office, fought off the people begging for free tickets and slipped into his own office to pick up his cap. At that moment the telephone rang.

"Yes?" he shouted.

"Ivan Savyelich?" inquired the receiver in an odious nasal voice.

"He's not in the theater!" Varenukha was just about to shout, but the telephone cut him off.

"Don't play the fool, Ivan Savyelich, and listen. You are not to take those telegrams anywhere or show them to anybody."

"Who's that?" roared Varenukha. "Kindly stop playing these tricks! You're going to be shown up before long. What's your telephone number?"

"Varenukha," insisted the repulsive voice. "You understand Russian, don't you? Don't take those telegrams."

"So you refuse to stop this game, do you?" shouted the house manager in a rage. "Now listen to me—you're going to pay for this!" He went on shouting threats but stopped when he realized that no one was listening to him on the other end.

At that moment his office began to darken. Varenukha ran

out, slammed the door behind him and went out into the garden through the side door.

He felt excited and full of energy. After that last insolent telephone call he no longer had any doubt that some gang of hoodlums was playing some nasty practical joke and that the joke was connected with Likhodeyev's disappearance. The house manager felt inspired with the urge to unmask the villains, and, strange as it may seem, he had a premonition that he was going to enjoy it. It was a longing to be in the limelight, to be the bearer of sensational news.

Out in the garden the wind blew in his face and threw sand in his eyes as if it were trying to bar his way or warn him. A window on the second floor slammed shut with such force that it nearly broke the glass; the tops of the maples and poplars rustled alarmingly. It grew darker and colder. Varenukha wiped his eyes and noticed that a yellowish-centered thundercloud was scudding low over Moscow. From the distance came a low rumble.

Although Varenukha was in a hurry, an irresistible urge made him turn aside for a second into the open-air men's toilet to check whether the electrician had replaced a missing electric bulb.

Running past the shooting gallery, he passed through the thick clump of lilac which screened the blue-painted lavatory. The electrician seemed to have done his job: the bulb in the men's toilet had been screwed into its socket and the protective wire screen replaced, but the house manager was annoyed to notice that even in the darkness preceding the thunderstorm the penciled graffiti on the walls were still clearly visible.

"What a—" he began, then suddenly heard a purring voice behind him: "Is that you, Ivan Savyelich?"

Varenukha shuddered, turned round and saw before him a shortish, fat creature with what seemed like the face of a cat.

"Yes," replied Varenukha coldly.

"Delighted to meet you," answered the stout, catlike personage. Suddenly it swung round and gave Varenukha such a box on the ear that his cap flew off and vanished without a trace into one of the lavatory bowls.

For a moment the blow made the toilet shimmer with a flickering light. A clap of thunder came from the sky. Then there was a second flash and another figure materialized, short but athletically built, with fiery red hair, one walleye, a fang protruding from his mouth. . . . He appeared to be left-handed, as he fetched the house manager a shattering clout on his other ear. The sky rumbled again in reply, and rain started to drench the wooden roof.

"Look here, com—" whispered Varenukha, staggering. It at once occurred to him that the word "comrades" hardly fitted these thugs who went around assaulting people in public conveniences, so he groaned instead "citizens," realized that they didn't even deserve to be called that and got a third fearful punch. This time he could not see who had hit him, as blood was spurting from his nose and down his shirt.

"What have you got in your briefcase, louse?" shouted the cat figure. "Telegrams? Weren't you warned by telephone not to take them anywhere? I'm asking you—weren't you warned?"

"Yes . . . I was . . . warned," panted Varenukha.

"And you still went? Gimme the briefcase, you scum!" said the other creature in the same nasal voice that had come through the telephone and wrenched the briefcase out of Varenukha's trembling hands.

Then they both grabbed the house manager by the arms and frog-marched him out of the garden and along Sadovaya Street. The storm was in full spate, water was roaring and gurgling down the sewer holes in great bubbling waves, it poured off the roofs from the overflowing gutters and out of the drainpipes in foaming torrents. Every living person had vanished from the street, and there was no one to help Ivan Savyelich. In one second, leaping over filthy streams and lit by flashes of lightning, the thugs had dragged the half-dead Varenukha to No. 302A and fled through the doorway, where two barefoot women stood pressed against the wall, holding their shoes and stockings in their hands. Then they rushed to staircase 6, carried the nearly insane Varenukha up to the fifth floor and threw him to the floor in the familiar semidarkness of the hallway of Stepa Likhodeyev's apartment.

The two kidnappers vanished and in their place appeared a completely naked girl—a redhead with eyes that burned with a phosphorescent glitter.

Varenukha felt that this was the most terrible thing that had ever happened to him. With a groan he turned and leaned against the wall. The girl came right up to him and put her hands on his shoulders. Varenukha's hair stood on end. Even through the cold, soaking-wet material of his coat he could feel that those palms were even colder, that they were as cold as ice.

"Let me give you a kiss," said the girl tenderly, her gleaming eyes close to his. Varenukha lost consciousness before he could feel her kiss.

CHAPTER **11**

THE TWO IVANS

The wood on the far bank of the river, which an hour before had glowed in the May sunshine, had now grown dim, had blurred and dissolved.

Outside, water was pouring down in solid sheets. Now and again a rift appeared in the sky, the heavens split and the patient's room was flooded with a terrifying burst of light.

Ivan was quietly weeping as he sat on his bed and stared out at the boiling, muddied river. At every clap of thunder he cried miserably and covered his face with his hands. Sheets of paper, covered with his writing, blew about on the floor.

The poet's efforts to compose a report on the terrible professor had come to nothing. As soon as he had been given a stub of a pencil and some paper by the fat nurse, whose name was Praskovya Fyodorovna, he had rubbed his hands in a business-like way and arranged his bedside table for work. The beginning sounded rather well:

To the Police. From Ivan Nikolayich Bezdomny, Member of MASSOLIT. Statement. Yesterday evening I arrived at Patriarch's Ponds with the late M. A. Berlioz. . . .

Here the poet stumbled, chiefly because of the words "the late." It sounded wrong—how could he have "arrived" with "the late . . ."? Dead people can't walk. If he wrote like this, they really would think he was mad. So Ivan Nikolayich made some corrections, which resulted in: ". . . with M. A. Berlioz, later deceased." He did not like that either, so he wrote a third version and that was even worse than the previous two: ". . . with Berlioz, who fell under a streetcar . . ." Here he thought of the composer of the same name and felt obliged to add: ". . . not the composer."

Struggling with these two Berlioz', Ivan crossed it all out and decided to begin right off with a striking phrase that would immediately catch the reader's attention, so he first described how the cat had jumped on the streetcar and then described the episode of the severed head. The head and the professor's forecast reminded him of Pontius Pilate, so to sound more convincing Ivan decided to give the story of the Procurator in full, from the moment when he had emerged in his white, red-lined cloak into the arcade of Herod's palace.

Ivan worked hard. He crossed out some of what he had written, put in new words and even tried to draw a sketch of Pontius Pilate, then one showing the cat walking on its hind legs. But his drawings were hopeless, and the further he went, the more confused his statement grew.

By the time the storm had begun, Ivan felt that he was exhausted and would never be able to write a statement. His wind-blown sheets of paper were in a complete muddle, and he began to weep, quietly and bitterly. The kind nurse Praskovya Fyodorovna called on the poet during the storm and was worried to find him crying. She closed the blinds so that the lightning should not frighten the patient, picked up the sheets of paper and went off with them to look for the doctor.

The doctor appeared, gave Ivan an injection in his arm and assured him that he would soon stop crying, that it would pass, everything would be all right and he would forget all about it.

The doctor was right. Soon the wood across the river looked as it always did. The weather cleared until every single tree stood out against a sky which was as blue as before, and the river subsided. His injection at once made Ivan feel less depressed. The poet lay quietly down and gazed at the rainbow stretched across the sky.

He lay there until evening and did not even notice how the rainbow dissolved, how the sky faded and saddened, how the wood turned to black.

When he had drunk his hot milk, Ivan lay down again.

He was amazed to notice how his mental condition had changed. The memory of the diabolical cat had grown indistinct, he was no longer frightened by the thought of the decapitated head. Ivan started to muse on the fact that the clinic really wasn't such a bad place, that Stravinsky was very clever and famous and that he was an extremely pleasant man to deal with. The evening air, too, was sweet and fresh after the storm.

The asylum was asleep. The white frosted-glass bulbs in the silent corridors were extinguished and in their place glowed the weak blue night lights. The nurses' cautious footsteps were heard less and less frequently walking the rubber-tiled floor of the corridor.

Ivan now lay in sweet lassitude; glancing at his bedside lamp, then at the dim ceiling light and at the moon rising in the dark, he talked to himself.

"I wonder why I got so excited about Berlioz falling under that streetcar?" the poet reasoned. "After all he's dead, and we all die sometime. It's not as if I were a relation or even a really close friend. When you come to think of it, I didn't even know the man very well. What did I really know about him? Nothing, except that he was bald and horribly talkative. So, gentlemen," went on Ivan, addressing an imaginary audience, "let us consider the following problem: why, I should like to know, did I get into such a rage with that mysterious professor or magician with his empty, black eye? Why did I chase after him like a fool in those undershorts and holding a candle? Why the ridiculous scene in the restaurant?"

"Wait a moment, though!" said the old Ivan severely to the new Ivan, in a voice that was not exactly inside him and not quite by his ear. "He did know in advance that Berlioz was going to have his head cut off, didn't he? Isn't that something to get upset about?"

"What do you mean?" objected the new Ivan. "I quite agree that it's a nasty business—a child could see that. But he's a mysterious, superior being—that's what makes it so interesting. Think of it—a man who knew Pontius Pilate! Instead of creating that ridiculous scene at Patriarch's, wouldn't it have been rather more intelligent to ask him politely what happened next to Pilate and that prisoner Ha-Notsri? And I had to behave like an idiot! Of course it's a serious matter to kill the editor of a magazine. But still—the magazine won't close down just because of that, will it? Man is mortal, and, as the professor so rightly said, mortality can come so suddenly. So God rest his soul and let's get ourselves another editor, perhaps one who's even more of a chatterbox than Berlioz!"

After dozing for a while the new Ivan said spitefully to the old Ivan, "And how do I look after this affair?"

"A fool," distinctly said a bass voice that belonged to neither of the Ivans and was extremely like the professor's.

Ivan, somehow not offended by the word "fool" but even pleasantly surprised by it, smiled and sank into a half-doze. Sleep crept up on him. He had a vision of a palm tree on its elephantine leg and a cat passing by—not a terrible cat but a nice one—and Ivan was just about to fall fast asleep when suddenly the grille slid noiselessly aside. A mysterious figure appeared on the moonlit balcony and pointed a threatening finger at Ivan.

Quite unafraid, Ivan sat up in bed and saw a man on the balcony. Pressing his finger to his lips the man whispered, "Sshh!"

old vs new

BLACK MAGIC REVEALED

A little man with a crimson, pear-shaped nose, in a battered yellow bowler hat, check trousers and patent-leather boots pedaled onto the Variety stage on a bicycle. As the band played a fox trot he rode around in circles a few times, then gave a triumphant yelp, at which the bicycle reared up with its front wheel in the air. After a few rounds on the back wheel alone, the man stood on his head, unscrewed the front wheel and threw it into the wings. He then carried on with one wheel, turning the pedals with his hands.

Next a fat blonde girl, wearing a sweater and a very brief skirt strewn with sequins, came in riding a long metal pole with a saddle on the top and a single wheel at the bottom. As they met, the man gave a welcoming cry and doffed his bowler hat with his foot.

Finally a little boy of about seven, with the face of an old man, sneaked in between the two adults on a tiny two-wheeler to which was fixed an enormous motorcar horn.

After a few figures of eight the whole troupe, to an urgent roll of drums from the orchestra, rode at full tilt toward the front of the stage. The spectators in the front rows gasped and ducked, fully expecting all three to crash, cycles and all, into the orchestra pit, but they stopped at the very second that their front wheels threatened to skid into the pit onto the heads of the musicians. With a loud cry of "Allez-oop!" the three cyclists leaped from their machines and bowed, while the blonde blew kisses to the audience and the little boy played a funny tune on his horn.

The auditorium rocked with applause, the blue curtain fell and the cyclists vanished. The lighted green "Exit" signs went out and the white globes began to glow brighter and brighter in the web of girders under the dome. The second and last intermisison had begun.

The only man unaffected by the Giulli family's marvels of cycling technique was Grigory Danilovich Rimsky. He sat alone in his office, biting his thin lips, his face twitching spasmodically. First, Likhodeyev had vanished under the most bizarre circumstances, and now Varenukha had suddenly disappeared. Rimsky knew where Varenukha had been going, but the man had simply gone and never came back. He shrugged his shoulders and muttered to himself, "But why?"

Nothing would have been simpler for a sensible, practical man like Rimsky than to have telephoned the place where Varenukha had gone and to have found out what had happened to him, yet it was ten o'clock that evening before he could bring himself to do so.

At ten Rimsky finally got a grip on himself and picked up the telephone receiver. The telephone was dead. An usher reported that all the other telephones in the building were out of order. This annoying but hardly supernatural occurrence seemed to shock Rimsky, although secretly he was glad, because it absolved him from the need to telephone.

As the little red light above the treasurer's head started flashing to show that the intermission was beginning, an usher came in and announced that the foreign magician had arrived. Rimsky's expression changed, and he scowled with a mixture of anxiety and irritation. As the only member of the management left in the theater, it was his duty to go backstage and receive the guest artiste.

As the warning bells rang, inquisitive people were peeping into the star dressing room. Among them were jugglers in bright robes and turbans, a roller-skater in a knitted cardigan, a comedian with a powdered white face and a makeup man. The celebrated guest artiste amazed everyone with his unusually long, superbly cut tail coat and by wearing a black domino. Even more astounding were the black magician's two companions: a tall man in checks with an unsteady pince-nez and a fat black cat which walked into the dressing room on its hind legs and casually sat down on the divan, blinking in the light of the unshaded bulbs around the makeup mirror.

With a forced smile which only made him look acidly disagreeable, Rimsky bowed to the silent magician sitting beside the cat on the divan. There were no handshakes, but the man in checks introduced himself smoothly as "the assistant." This gave the treasurer an unpleasant shock, as there had not been a word in the contract about an assistant.

Grigory Danilovich inquired stiffly where the professor's equipment might be.

"Why, bless you, my dear sir," replied the magician's assistant, "we have all the equipment we need with us now— look! *Ein, zwei, drei!*"

Flourishing his long, knotty fingers in front of Rimsky's eyes, he made a pass beside the cat's ear and pulled out of it Rimsky's gold watch and chain, which until that moment had been resting under the treasurer's buttoned jacket in his waistcoat pocket with the chain threaded through a button-hole.

Rimsky involuntarily clutched his stomach, the spectators gasped, and the makeup man, watching from the corridor, clucked with approval.

"Your watch, sir? There you are," said the man in checks. Smiling nonchalantly, he proffered the watch to its owner on his dirty palm.

"I wouldn't sit next to *him* in a trolley," whispered the comedian cheerfully to the makeup man.

But the cat put the watch trick in the shade. Suddenly getting up from the divan, it walked on its hind legs to the dressing table, pulled the stopper out of a carafe with its forepaw, poured out a glass of water, drank it, replaced the stopper and wiped its whiskers with a makeup cloth.

Nobody even gasped. Their mouths fell open and the makeup man whispered admiringly, "Bravo!"

The last warning bell rang, and everybody, excited by the prospect of a good act, tumbled out of the dressing room.

A minute later the house lights went out, the footlights lit up the fringe of the curtain with a red glow, and in the lighted gap between the side drops the audience saw a fat, jolly, clean-shaven man in stained tails and a grubby white dickey. It was Moscow's best-known master of ceremonies, George Bengalsky.

"And now, ladies and gentlemen," said Bengalsky, smiling his boyish smile, "you are about to see . . ." Here Bengalsky broke off and started again in a completely different tone of voice: "I see that our audience has increased in numbers since the intermission. Half Moscow seems to be here tonight! D'you know, I met a friend of mine the other day and I said to him, 'Why didn't you come and see our show? Half the town was there last night.' And he said, 'I live in the other half!' " Bengalsky paused for the laugh, but none came, so he went on: "Well, as I was saying, you are about to see a very famous artiste from abroad, Monsieur Woland, with a session of black magic. Of course we know, don't we—" Bengalsky smiled confidentially—"that there's no such thing really. It's all superstition—or rather Maestro Woland is a past master of the art of conjuring, as you will see from the most interesting part of his act in which he reveals the mysteries of his technique. And now, ladies and gentlemen, since none of us can bear the suspense any longer, I give you . . . Monsieur Woland!"

Having spoken his feeble piece, Bangalsky put his hands palm to palm and raised them in a gesture of welcome toward the gap in the curtain, which then rose with a soft rustle.

The entry of the magician with his tall assistant and his cat, who trotted on stage on its hind legs, pleased the audience greatly.

"Armchair, please," said Woland quietly, and instantly an armchair appeared on stage from nowhere. The magician sat down. "Tell me, my dear Faggot," Woland inquired of the check-clad buffoon, who apparently had another name besides "Koroviev," "do you find the people of Moscow much changed?"

The magician nodded toward the audience, still silent with astonishment at seeing an armchair materialize from nowhere.

"I do, messire," replied Faggot-Koroviev in a low voice.

"You are right. The Muscovites have changed considerably —outwardly, I mean—as has the city itself. . . . Not just the clothes, but now they have all these . . . what d'you call 'em . . . streetcars, trolleys . . ."

"Buses," prompted Faggot respectfully.

The audience listened intently to this conversation, assuming it to be the prelude to some magic tricks. The wings were full of actors and stage hands and among their faces could be seen the pale, strained features of Rimsky.

Bengalsky's face, lurking in a corner of the stage, began to show consternation. With an imperceptible raise of one eyebrow he seized the opportunity of a pause in the dialogue to interject: "Our guest artiste from abroad is obviously delighted with Moscow's technological progress." This was accompanied by a smile for the orchestra and a smile for the balcony.

Woland, Faggot and the cat turned their heads toward the master of ceremonies.

"Did I say I was delighted?" the magician asked Faggot.

"You said nothing of the kind, messire," replied the latter.

"Then what *is* the man talking about?"

"He was simply telling lies!" announced the checkered clown in a loud voice for the whole theater to hear, and turning to Bengalsky he added, "D'you hear—you're a liar!"

There was a burst of laughter from the balcony as Bengalsky spluttered, his eyes popping with indignation.

"But naturally I am not so much interested in the buses and telephones and such—"

"Apparatus," prompted Faggot.

"Precisely, thank you," drawled the magician in a deep bass. "As in the much more important question: have the Muscovites changed inwardly?"

"A vital question, indeed, sir."

In the wings, glances were exchanged, shoulders shrugged; Bengalsky was turning purple, Rimsky white. Suddenly, sensing the general air of restlessness, the magician said, "That's enough talk from us, my dear Faggot—the audience is getting bored. Show us something simple to begin with."

There was a rustling in the house. Faggot and the cat walked to opposite sides of the footlights. Faggot snapped his fingers, cried, "Three, four!" and seized a pack of cards out of the air, shuffled it and threw it in an unbroken stream to the cat, who caught it and threw it back in the same way. The shiny arc of cards gave a twist, Faggot opened his mouth like a baby bird and swallowed the whole pack, card for card. With this the cat bowed and raised a storm of applause.

"Bravo! Bravo!" came the admiring cries from the wings.

Faggot pointed to the orchestra seats and announced, "That pack of cards, ladies and gentlemen, is now to be found in the seventh row, in comrade Parchevsky's wallet between a three-ruble note and a summons to appear in court for non-payment of alimony to his ex-wife."

More rustling in the auditorium, people half-rose, and finally a man who really was called Parchevsky, purple with embarrassment, removed the pack of cards from his wallet and started waving it in the air, not knowing what to do with it.

"Keep it as a souvenir!" shouted Faggot. "You may need it—didn't you say at dinner yesterday that if it weren't for your poker games life wouldn't be worth living?"

"That's an old trick!" came a shout from the balcony. "The man in the orchestra is a plant."

"Think so?" bawled Faggot, peering up at the balcony. "In that case you're a plant too, because there's a pack of cards in your pocket!"

There was a movement in the balcony and a voice cried gleefully, "He's right! There is! Here they are! . . . Wait . . . there's some money too!"

The people in the orchestra turned their heads. The embarrassed man in the balcony had found a bundle in his pocket, tied up with banker's tape and marked "One Thousand Rubles." His neighbors crowded round as he picked at the wrapping with his fingernail to find out whether it was real money or a stage prop.

"My God, it's real money!" came a joyful shout from the balcony.

"I wish you'd play cards with me if you've any more packs like that one," begged a fat man in the middle of the orchestra.

"*Avec plaisir!*" replied Faggot. "But why should you be the only one? You shall all take part! Everybody look up, please! One!" A pistol appeared in his hand. "Two!" The pistol was pointed upward. "Three!" There was a flash, a bang, and immediately a cascade of white pieces of paper began to float down from the dome above the auditorium.

Turning over and over, some were blown aside and landed in the balcony, some fell toward the orchestra pit or the stage. A few seconds later the shower of money reached the orchestra seats, and the audience began catching it.

Hundreds of hands were raised as the audience held the notes up to the light from the stage and found that the watermarks were absolutely genuine. Their smell left no doubt: it was the uniquely delicious smell of newly printed money. First amusement, then wonder, seized the entire theater. From all over the house, amid gasps and delighted laughter, came the words "Money! Money!" One man was already crawling in the aisle and fumbling under the seats. Several more were standing up on their seats to catch the drifting, twisting banknotes as they fell.

Gradually a look of perplexity came over the expressions of the police, and the artistes backstage openly pressed forward from the wings. From the dress circle a voice was heard shouting, "Let go! It's mine—I caught it first!," followed by another voice: "Stop pushing and grabbing or I'll punch your face in!" There was a muffled crash. A policeman's helmet appeared in the dress circle and a member of the audience was led away. The excitement rose and might have got out of hand if Faggot had not stopped the rain of money by suddenly blowing into the air.

Two young men, grinning purposefully, left their seats and made straight for the bar. A loud buzz filled the theater: the audience was galvanized with excitement, and in an effort to control the situation Bengalsky stirred himself and appeared on stage. With a tremendous effort of self-mastery he went through his habitual motion of washing his hands and in his most powerful voice began:

"We have just seen, ladies and gentlemen, a case of so-called mass hypnosis. A purely scientific experiment, demonstrating better than anything else that there is nothing supernatural about magic. We shall ask Maestro Woland to show us how he did that experiment. You will now see, ladies and gentlemen, how those apparent banknotes will vanish as suddenly as they appeared."

He began to clap, but he was alone. A confident smile appeared on his face, but the look in his eyes was one of entreaty.

The audience did not care for Bengalsky's speech. Faggot broke the silence.

"And that was a case of so-called fiddlesticks," he declared in a loud goatish bray. "The banknotes, ladies and gentlemen, are real."

"Bravo!" abruptly roared a bass from high up in the balcony.

"This man," Faggot pointed at Bengalsky, "is starting to bore me. He sticks his nose in everywhere without being asked and ruins the whole act. What shall we do with him?"

"Cut off his head!" said a stern voice.

"What did you say, sir?" was Faggot's instant response to

this savage proposal. "Cut off his head? That's an idea! Behemoth!" he shouted to the cat. "Do your stuff! *Ein, zwei, drei!*"

Then the most incredible thing happened. The cat's fur stood on end and it uttered a harrowing "Miaow!" It crouched, then leaped like a panther straight for Bengalsky's chest and from there to his head. Growling, the cat dug its claws into the M.C.'s glossy hair, and with a wild screech it twisted the head clean off the neck in two turns.

Two and a half thousand people screamed as one. Fountains of blood from the severed arteries in the neck spurted up and drenched the man's shirt front and tails. The headless body waved its legs stupidly and sat on the ground. Hysterical shrieks rang out through the auditorium. The cat handed the head to Faggot, who picked it up by the hair and showed it to the audience. The head moaned desperately, "Call a doctor!"

"Will you go on talking so much rubbish?" said Faggot threateningly to the weeping head.

"No, I promise I won't!" croaked the head.

"For God's sake, stop torturing him!" a woman's voice from a box suddenly rang out above the turmoil, and the magician turned toward the sound.

"Well, ladies and gentlemen, shall we forgive him?" asked Faggot, turning to the audience.

"Yes, forgive him, forgive him!" The cries came at first from a few individual voices, mostly women, then merged into a chorus with the men.

"What is your command, Messire?" Faggot asked the masked professor.

"Well, now," replied the magician reflectively. ("They're people like any others, but thoughtless . . . but they do show some compassion occasionally. They're overfond of money, but then they always were. . . . Humankind loves money, no matter if it's made of leather, paper, bronze or gold. They're thoughtless, of course, but then they sometimes feel compassion too. . . . They're ordinary people—in fact, they remind me very much of their predecessors, except that the housing shortage has soured them.") And he shouted the order: "Put back his head."

Taking careful aim, the cat popped the head back on its neck, where it sat as neatly as if head and body had never been parted. Most amazing of all, there was not even a scar on the neck. The cat wiped the tail coat and shirt front with its paw and every trace of blood vanished. Faggot lifted the seated Bengalsky to his feet, shoved a bundle of money into his coat pocket and led him off stage, saying, "Go on—off you go, it's more fun without you!"

Gazing round in a daze and staggering, the M.C. got no further than the fireman's post and collapsed. He cried miserably, "My head, my head . . ."

Among those who rushed to help him was Rimsky. The M.C. was weeping, snatching at something in the air and mumbling, "Give me back my head, my head. . . . You can have my apartment, you can have all my pictures, only give me back my head!"

An usher ran for the doctor. They tried to lay Bengalsky on a couch in his dressing room, but he resisted and became violent. An ambulance was called. When the unfortunate M.C. had been removed, Rimsky ran back to the stage, where new miracles were in progress. It was then, or perhaps a little earlier, that the magician and his faded armchair vanished from the stage. The audience did not notice this at all, as they were absorbed by Faggot's wonderful tricks.

Having seen the M.C. off the stage, Faggot announced to the audience, "Now that we have disposed of that old bore, we shall open a shop for the ladies!"

In a moment half the stage was covered with Persian carpets, some huge mirrors and a row of showcases, in which the audience was astounded to see a collection of Parisian dresses that were the last word in chic. In other showcases were hundreds of ladies' hats, some with feathers and some without, hundreds of pairs of shoes—black shoes, white shoes, yellow shoes, leather shoes, satin shoes, chamois-skin shoes, buckled shoes and shoes studded with costume jewelry. Beside the shoes there were flacons of scent, piles of handbags made of buckskin, satin and silk, and next to them piles of gilt lipstick holders.

A red-haired girl in a black evening dress who had suddenly appeared from nowhere, her beauty only marred by a curious scar on her neck, smiled from among the showcases with a proprietorial smile.

With an engaging leer Faggot announced that the firm would exchange, absolutely free of charge, any lady's old dress and shoes for model dresses and shoes from Paris, adding that the offer included handbags and the odds and ends that go in them.

The cat began bowing and scraping, its forepaw gesturing like a doorman opening a door.

In a sweet though slightly hoarse voice the girl made an announcement which sounded rather cryptic but which, judging from the faces of the women in the orchestra, was very enticing:

"Guerlain, Chanel, Mitsouko, Narcisse Noir, Chanel Number Five, evening dresses, cocktail dresses . . ."

Faggot bent double, the cat bowed and the girl opened the glass-fronted showcases.

"Step up, please!" cried Faggot. "Don't be shy!"

The audience began to fidget, but no one dared mount the stage. At last a brunette emerged from the tenth row of the orchestra and smiling nonchalantly walked up the side stairs onto the stage.

"Bravo!" cried Faggot. "Our first customer! Behemoth, a chair for the lady! Shall we start with the shoes, madam?"

The brunette sat down, and Faggot at once spread out a whole heap of shoes on the carpet in front of her. She took off her right shoe, tried on a lilac one, tested it with a walk on the carpet and inspected the heel.

"Won't they pinch?" she inquired thoughtfully.

Offended, Faggot cried, "Oh, come, now!" and the cat gave an insulted miaow.

"I'll take them, monsieur," said the brunette with dignity as she put on the other shoe of the pair. Her old shoes were tossed behind a curtain, followed by the girl herself, the redhead, and Faggot carrying several model dresses on coat hangers. The cat busied itself with helping and hung a tape measure round its neck for greater effect.

A minute later the brunette emerged from behind the curtain in a dress that sent a gasp through the entire auditorium. The bold girl, now very much prettier, paused in front of a mirror, wriggled her bare shoulders, patted her hair and twisted round to try and see herself from the rear.

"The firm begs you to accept this as a souvenir," said Faggot, handing the girl an open case containing a flacon of scent.

"Merci," replied the girl haughtily and walked down the steps to the orchestra. As she returned to her seat, people jumped up to touch her scent bottle.

The ice was broken. Women from all sides poured onto the stage. In the general hubbub of talk, laughter and cries a man's voice was heard crying, "I won't let you!" followed by a woman's saying, "Let go of my arm, you narrow-minded little tyrant!" Women were disappearing behind the curtain, leaving their old dresses there and emerging in new ones. A row of women was sitting on gilt-legged stools trying on new shoes. Faggot was on his knees, busy with a shoehorn, while the cat, weighed down by handbags and shoes, staggered from the showcases to the stools and back again, the girl with the scarred neck bustled to and fro, entering so much into the spirit of it all that she was soon chattering away in nothing but French. Strangely enough, all the women understood her at once, even those who knew not a word of French.

To everybody's astonishment, a lone man climbed onto the stage. He announced that his wife had a cold and asked to be given something to take home to her. To prove that he was really married, he offered to show his passport. This conscientious husband was greeted with a roar of laughter. Faggot declared that he believed him even without his passport and handed the man two pairs of silk stockings. The cat spontaneously added a pot of cold cream.

Late-comers still mounted the steps as a stream of happy women in ball dresses, pajama suits embroidered with dragons, severe tailor-mades and hats pranced back into the auditorium.

Then Faggot announced that because it was so late in exactly a minute's time the shop would close until tomorrow evening. This produced an incredible scuffle on stage. Without trying them on, women grabbed any shoes within reach. One woman hurtled behind the screen, threw off her clothes and seized the first thing at hand—a silk dress patterned with enormous bunches of flowers—grabbed a dressing gown and for good measure scooped up two flacons of scent. Exactly a minute later a pistol shot rang out, the mirrors disappeared, the showcases and stools melted away, carpet and curtain vanished into thin air. Last to disappear was the mountain of old dresses and shoes. The stage was bare and empty again.

At this point a new character joined the cast. A pleasant and extremely self-confident baritone was heard from Box No. 2: "It's high time, sir, that you showed the audience how you do your tricks, especially the banknote trick. We should also like to see the M.C. back on stage. The audience is concerned about him."

The baritone voice belonged to none other than the evening's guest of honor, Arkady Appolonovich Sempleyarov, chairman of the Moscow Theaters' Acoustics Commission.

Arkady Appolonovich was sharing his box with two ladies —one elderly, who was expensively and fashionably dressed, the other young and pretty and more simply dressed. The first, as was later established when the official report was compiled, was Arkady Appolonovich's wife and the other a distant relative of his, an aspiring young actress from Saratov who lodged in the Sempleyarovs' apartment.

"I beg your pardon," replied Faggot. "I'm sorry, but there's nothing to reveal. It's all quite plain."

"Excuse me, but I don't agree. An explanation is essential, otherwise your brilliant act will leave a painful impression. The audience demands an explanation."

"The audience," interrupted the insolent mountebank, "has not, to my knowledge, demanded anything of the sort. However, in view of your distinguished position, Arkady Appolonovich, I will—since you insist—reveal something of our technique. To do so, will you allow me time for another short number?"

"Of course," replied Arkady Appolonovich patronizingly. "But you must show how it's done."

"Very well, sir, very well. Now, may I ask you where you were yesterday evening, Arkady Appolonovich?"

At this impertinent question Arkady Appolonovich's expression underwent a complete and violent change.

"Yesterday evening Arkady Appolonovich was at a meeting of the Acoustics Commission," said his wife haughtily. "Surely that has nothing to do with magic?"

"Oui, madame," replied Faggot, "it has, but you naturally do not know why. As for the meeting, you are quite wrong. When he went to the meeting—which, incidentally, was never scheduled to take place yesterday—Arkady Appolonovich dismissed his chauffeur at the Acoustics Commission"— a hush came over the whole theater—"and took a bus to Yelokhovskaya Street, where he called on an actress called Militsa Andreyevna Pokobatko from the local repertory theater and spent about four hours in her flat."

"Oh!" The painful cry rang out in the complete silence.

Suddenly Arkady Appolonovich's young cousin burst into a low, malicious laugh.

"Of course!" she exclaimed. "I've suspected him for a long time. Now I see why that tenth-rate ham got the part of Luisa!" And with a sudden wave of her arm she hit Arkady Appolonovich on the head with a short, fat, mauve umbrella.

The vile Faggot, who was none other than Koroviev, shouted, "There, ladies and gentlemen, is your revelation, as requested so insistently by Arkady Appolonovich!"

"How dare you hit Arkady Appolonovich, you little bitch?" said the wife grimly, rising in the box to her full gigantic height.

The young girl was seized with another outburst of satanic laughter.

"I've as much right," she replied laughing, "to hit him as you have!" A second dull crack was heard as the umbrella bounced off Arkady Appolonovich's head.

"Police! Arrest her!" roared Madam Sempleyarov in a terrifying voice.

Here the cat bounded up to the footlights and announced in a human voice, "That concludes the evening! Maestro! Finale, please!"

The dazed conductor, scarcely aware of what he was doing, waved his baton and the orchestra struck up, or rather murdered, a disorganized excuse for a march, normally sung to obscene but very funny words. However, it was quickly drowned in the ensuing uproar. The police ran to the Sempleyarovs' box, curious spectators climbed onto the ledge to watch, there were explosions of infernal laughter and wild cries, drowned by the golden crash of cymbals from the orchestra.

Suddenly the stage was empty. The horrible Faggot and the sinister cat Behemoth melted into the air and disappeared, just as the magician in his shabby armchair had vanished earlier.

CHAPTER **13**

ENTER THE HERO

Ivan swung his legs off the bed and stared. A man was standing on the balcony, peering cautiously into the room. He was aged about thirty-eight, clean-shaven and dark, with a sharp nose, restless eyes and a lock of hair that tumbled over his forehead.

The mysterious visitor listened awhile, then, satisfied that Ivan was alone, entered the room. As he came in, Ivan noticed that the man was wearing hospital clothes—pajamas, slippers and a reddish-brown dressing gown thrown over his shoulders.

The visitor winked at Ivan, put a bunch of keys into his pocket and asked in a whisper, "May I sit down?" Receiving an affirmative reply, he settled in the armchair.

"How did you get in here?" Ivan whispered in obedience to a warning finger. "The grilles on the windows are locked, aren't they?"

"The grilles are locked," agreed the visitor. "Praskovya Fyodorovna is a dear person but, alas, terribly absent-minded. A month ago I removed this bunch of keys from her, which has given me the freedom of the balcony. It stretches along the whole floor, so that I can call on my neighbors whenever I feel like it."

"If you can get out onto the balcony, you can run away. Or is it too high to jump?" inquired Ivan with interest.

"No," answered the visitor firmly, "I can't escape from here. Not because it's too high but because I've nowhere to go." After a pause he added, "So here we are."

"Here we are," echoed Ivan, gazing into the man's restless brown eyes.

"Yes . . ." The visitor grew suddenly anxious. "You're not violent, I hope? You see, I can't bear noise, disturbance, violence or anything of that sort. I particularly hate the sound of people screaming, whether it's a scream of pain, anger or any other kind of scream. Just reassure me—you're not violent, are you?"

"Yesterday in a restaurant I clouted a fellow across the snout," the poet confessed manfully.

"What for?" asked the visitor disapprovingly.

"For no reason at all, I must admit," replied Ivan, embarrassed.

"Disgraceful," said the visitor reproachfully and added, "And I don't care for that expression of yours—clouted him across the snout. . . . People have faces, not snouts. So I suppose you mean you punched him in the face. . . . No, you must give up doing that sort of thing."

After this reprimand the visitor inquired, "What's your job?"

"I'm a poet," admitted Ivan with a slight unwillingness.

This annoyed the man.

"Just my bad luck!" he exclaimed, but immediately regretted it, apologized and asked, "What's your name?"

"Bezdomny,"

"Oh," said the man frowning.

"What, don't you like my poetry?" asked Ivan with curiosity.

"No, I don't."

"Have you read any of it?"

"I've never read any of your poetry!" said the visitor irritably.

"Then how can you say that?"

"Why shouldn't I?" retorted the visitor. "I've read plenty of other poetry. I don't suppose by some miracle that yours is any better, but I'm ready to take it on trust. Is your poetry good?"

"Stupendous!" said Ivan boldly.

"Don't write any more!" said the vititor imploringly.

"I promise not to!" said Ivan solemnly.

As they sealed the vow with a handshake, soft footsteps and voices could be heard from the corridor.

"Sshh!" whispered the man. He bounded out onto the balcony and closed the grille behind him.

Praskovya Fyodorovna looked in, asked Ivan how he felt and whether he wanted to sleep in the dark or the light. Ivan asked her to leave the light on, and Praskovya Fyodorovna departed, wishing him good night. When all was quiet again, the visitor returned.

He told Ivan in a whisper that a new patient had been put into No. 119—a fat man with a purple face who kept muttering about dollars in the ventilation shaft and swearing that the powers of darkness had taken over their house on Sadovaya Street. "He curses Pushkin for all he's worth and keeps shouting 'Encore, encore!' " said the visitor, twitching nervously. When he had grown a little calmer, he sat down and said, "However, let's forget about him," and resumed his interrupted conversation with Ivan. "How did you come to be here?"

"Because of Pontius Pilate," replied Ivan, staring glumly at the floor.

"What?" cried the visitor, forgetting his caution, then clapped his hand over his mouth. "What an extraordinary coincidence! Do tell me about it, I beg of you!"

For some reason Ivan felt that he could trust this stranger. Shyly at first, then gaining confidence, he began to describe the previous day's events at Patriarch's Ponds. His visitor treated Ivan as completely sane, showed the greatest interest in the story, and as it developed he reached a state of near ecstasy. Now and again he interrupted Ivan, exclaiming, "Yes, yes! Please go on! For heaven's sake don't leave anything out!"

Ivan left out nothing, as it made the story easier to tell, and gradually he approached the moment when Pontius Pilate, in his white cloak lined with blood red, mounted the platform.

Then the visitor folded his hands as though in prayer and whispered to himself, "Oh, I guessed it! I guessed it all!"

Listening to the terrible description of Berlioz' death, the visitor made an enigmatic comment, his eyes flashing with malice: "I'm only sorry that it wasn't Latunsky the critic or that hack Mstislav Lavrovich instead of Berlioz!" And he mouthed silently and ecstatically, "Go on!"

The visitor was highly amused by the story of how the cat had paid the conductress, and he was choking with suppressed laughter as Ivan, stimulated by the success of his storytelling, hopped about on his haunches, imitating the cat stroking his whiskers with a ten-kopeck piece.

"And so," said Ivan, saddening as he described the scene at Griboyedov, "here I am."

The visitor laid a sympathetic hand on the wretched poet's shoulder and said, "Unhappy poet! But it's your own fault, my dear fellow. You shouldn't have treated him so carelessly and rudely. Now you're paying for it. You should be thankful that you got off comparatively lightly."

"But who on earth is he?" asked Ivan, clenching his fists in excitement.

The visitor stared at Ivan and answered with a question: "You won't get violent, will you? We're all unstable people here. . . . There won't be any calls for the doctor, injections or any disturbances of that sort, will there?"

"No, no!" exclaimed Ivan. "Tell me, who is he?"

"Very well," replied the visitor, and said slowly and gravely, "At Patriarch's Ponds yesterday you met Satan."

As he had promised, Ivan did not become violent, but he was powerfully shaken.

"It can't be! He doesn't exist!"

"Come, come! Surely you of all people can't say that. You were apparently one of the first to suffer from him. Here you are, shut up in a psychiatric clinic, and you still say he doesn't exist. How strange!"

Ivan was reduced to speechlessness.

"As soon as you started to describe him," the visitor went on, "I guessed who it was that you were talking to yesterday. I must say I'm surprised at Berlioz! You, of course, are an innocent—"again the visitor apologized for his expression— "but he, from what I've heard of him, was at least fairly well read. The first remarks that this professor made to you dispelled all my doubts. He's unmistakable, my friend! You are— do forgive me again, but unless I'm wrong, you are an ignorant person, aren't you?"

"I am indeed," agreed the new Ivan.

"Well, you see, even the face you described, the different-colored eyes, the eyebrows . . . Forgive me, but have you even seen the opera *Faust?*"

Ivan mumbled an embarrassed excuse.

"There you are, it's not surprising! But, as I said before, I'm surprised at Berlioz. He's not only well read but extremely cunning. Although in his defense I must say that Woland is quite capable of throwing dust in the eyes of men who are even cleverer than Berlioz."

"What?" shouted Ivan.

"Quiet!"

With a sweeping gesture Ivan smacked his forehead with his palm and croaked, "I see it now. There was a letter 'W' on his visiting card. Well I'm damned!" He sat for a while in perplexity, staring at the moon floating past the grille and then said, "So he really might have known Pontius Pilate? He was alive then, I suppose? And they call me mad!" he added, pointing indignantly toward the door.

The visitor's mouth set in a fold of bitterness.

"We must look the facts in the face." The visitor turned his face toward the moon as it raced through a cloud. "Both you and I are mad, there's no point in denying it. He gave you a shock and it sent you mad, because you were temperamentally liable to react in that way. Nevertheless what you have described unquestionably happened in fact. But it is so unusual that even Stravinsky, a psychiatrist of genius, naturally didn't believe you. Has he examined you? Ivan nodded. "The man you were talking to *was* with Pontius Pilate, he did have breakfast with Kant and now he has paid a call on Moscow."

"But God knows what he may do here! Shouldn't we try and catch him somehow?" The old Ivan raised his head, uncertain but not yet quite extinguished.

"You've already tried and look where it's got you," said the visitor ironically. "I don't advise others to try. But he will cause more trouble, you may be sure of that. How infuriating, though, that you met him and not I. Although I'm a burnt-out man and the embers have died away to ashes, I swear that I would have given up Praskovya Fyodorovna's bunch of keys in exchange for that meeting. Those keys are all I have. I am destitute."

"Why do you want to see him so badly?"

After a long, gloomy silence the visitor said at last, "You see, it's most extraordinary, but I am in here for exactly the same reason that you are—I mean because of Pontius Pilate." The visitor glanced around uneasily and said, "The fact is that a year ago I wrote a novel about Pilate."

"Are you a writer?" asked the poet with interest.

The visitor frowned, threatened Ivan with his fist and said, "I am a master."

His expression hardened and he pulled out of his dressing

gown pocket a greasy black cap with the letter "M" embroidered on it in yellow silk. He put the cap on and showed himself to Ivan in profile and full face to prove that he was a master. "She sewed it for me with her own hands," he added mysteriously.

"What is your name?"

"I no longer have a name," replied the curious visitor with grim contempt. "I have renounced it, as I have renounced life itself. Let us forget it."

"At least tell me about your novel," asked Ivan tactfully.

"If you wish. I should say that my life has been a somewhat unusual one," began the visitor.

A historian by training, two years ago he had, it seemed, been employed in one of the Moscow museums. He was also a translator.

"From what language?" asked Ivan.

"I know five languages beside my own," replied the visitor. "English, French, German, Latin and Greek. And I read Italian a little."

"Phew!" Ivan whistled with envy.

This historian lived alone, had no relatives and knew almost no one in Moscow. One day he won a hundred thousand rubles.

"Imagine my astonishment," whispered the visitor in his black cap, "when I fished my lottery ticket out of the laundry basket and saw that it had the same number as the winning draw printed in the paper! The museum," he explained, "had given me the ticket."

Having won his hundred thousand, Ivan's mysterious guest bought some books, gave up his room on Myasnitskaya Street —"Ugh, it was a filthy hole!" he snarled—and rented two rooms in the basement of a small house with a garden near the Arbat. He gave up his job in the museum and began writing his novel about Pontius Pilate.

"Ah, that was a golden time!" whispered the narrator, his eyes shining. "A completely self-contained little apartment and a hall with a sink and running water," he emphasized proudly, "little windows just above the level of the path leading from the garden gate. Only a few steps away, by the garden fence, were a lilac, a lime tree and a maple. Ah, me! In winter I rarely saw anyone walking up the garden path or heard the crunch of snow. And there was always a blaze in my little stove! But suddenly it was spring, and through the muddied panes of my windows I saw first the bare branches, then the green of the first leaves. And then, last spring, something happened which was far more delightful than winning a hundred thousand rubles. And that, you must agree, is an enormous sum of money!"

"It is," Ivan agreed, listening intently.

"I had opened the windows and was sitting in the second room, which was quite tiny." The visitor made measuring gestures. "Like this—the couch here, another couch along the other wall, a beautiful lamp on a little table between them, a bookcase by the window and over here a little bureau. The main room was huge—a hundred and fifty square feet—books, more books and a stove. It was a marvelous little place. How deliciously the lilac used to smell! I was growing lightheaded with fatigue and Pilate was coming to an end—"

"White cloak, red lining! How I know the feeling!" exclaimed Ivan.

"Precisely! Pilate was rushing to a conclusion and I already knew what the last words of the novel would be: 'the fifth Procurator of Judea, the knight Pontius Pilate.' Naturally I used to go out for walks. A hundred thousand is a huge sum and I had a handsome suit. Or I would go out for lunch to a restaurant. There used to be a wonderful restaurant in the Arbat, I don't know whether it's still there."

Here his eyes opened wide, and as he whispered he gazed at the moon.

"She was carrying some of those repulsive yellow flowers. God knows what they're called, but they are somehow always the first to come out in spring. They stood out very sharply against her black dress. She was carrying yellow flowers! It's an ugly color. She turned off Tverskaya into a side street and turned round. You know Tverskaya, don't you? There must have been a thousand people on it, but I swear to you that she saw no one but me. She had a look of suffering, and I was struck less by her beauty than by the extraordinary loneliness in her eyes. Obeying that yellow signal, I too turned into the side street and followed her. We walked in silence down that dreary, winding little street without saying a word, she on one side, I on the other. There was not another soul in the street. I was in agony because I felt I had to speak to her and was worried that I might not be able to utter a word, she would disappear and I should never see her again. Then, if you can believe it, she said, 'Do you like my flowers?'

"I remember exactly how her voice sounded. It was pitched fairly low but with a catch in it, and, stupid as it may sound, I had the impression that it echoed across the street and reverberated from the dirty yellow wall. I quickly crossed to her side and going up to her replied, 'No.'

"She looked at me in surprise and suddenly, completely unexpectedly, I realized that I had been in love with this woman all my life. Extraordinary, isn't it? You'll say I was mad, I expect."

"I say nothing of the sort," exclaimed Ivan, adding, "Please, please go on."

The visitor continued: "Yes, she looked at me in surprise and then she said, "Don't you like flowers at all?"

"There was, I felt, hostility in her voice. I walked on alongside her, trying to walk in step with her and to my amazement, I felt completely free of shyness.

" 'No, I like flowers, only not these,' I said.

" 'Which flowers do you like?'

" 'I love roses.'

"I immediately regretted having said it, because she smiled guiltily and threw her flowers into the gutter. Slightly embarrassed, I picked them up and gave them to her, but she pushed them away with a smile and I had to carry them.

"We walked on in silence for a while until she pulled the flowers out of my hand and threw them in the roadway, then slipped her black-gloved hand into mine and we went on."

"Go on," said Ivan, "and please don't leave anything out!"

"Well," said the visitor, "you can guess what happened after that." He wiped away a sudden tear with his right sleeve and went on. "Love leaped out at us like a murderer jumping out of a dark alley. It shocked us both—the shock of a stroke of lightning, the shock of a switchblade knife. Later she said that this wasn't so, that we had of course been in love for years without knowing each other and never meeting, that she had merely been living with another man and I had been living with . . . that girl, what was her name?"

"With whom?" asked Bezdomny.

"With . . . er, that girl . . . she was called . . ." said the visitor, snapping his fingers in a vain effort to remember.

"Were you married to her?"

"Yes, of course I was, that's why it's so embarrassing to forget . . . I think it was Varya . . . or was it Manya? . . . no, Varya, that's it . . . she wore a striped dress, worked at the museum. . . . No good, can't remember. So, she used to say, she had gone out that morning carrying those yellow flowers for me to find her at last and that if it hadn't happened she would have committed suicide because her life was empty.

"Yes, the shock of love struck us both at once. I knew it within an hour when we found ourselves, quite unawares, on the embankment below the Kremlin wall. We talked as though we had only parted the day before, as though we had known each other for years. We agreed to meet the next day at the same place by the Moscow River, and we did. The May sun shone on us, and soon that woman became my mistress.

"She came to me every day at noon. I began waiting for her from early morning. The strain of waiting gave me hallucinations of seeing things on the table. After ten minutes I would sit at my little window and start to listen for the creak of that ancient garden gate. It was curious: until I met her no one ever came into our little yard. Now it seemed to me that the whole town was crowding in. The gate would creak, my heart would bound and outside the window a pair of muddy boots would appear, level with my head. A knife grinder. Who in our house could possibly need a knife grinder? What was there for him to sharpen? Whose knives?

"She only came through that gate once a day, but my heart would beat faster from at least ten false alarms every morning. Then when her time came and the hands were pointing to noon, my heart went on thumping until her shoes with their black patent-leather straps and steel buckles drew level, almost soundlessly, with my basement window.

"Sometimes for fun she would stop at the second window and tap the pane with her foot. In a second I would appear at that window, but always her shoe and her black silk dress that blocked the light had vanished and I would turn instead to the hall to let her in.

"Nobody knew about our liaison, I can swear to that, although as a rule no one can keep such affairs a complete secret. Her husband didn't know, our friends didn't know. The other tenants in that forgotten old house knew, of course, because they could see that a woman called on me every day, but they never knew her name."

"Who was she?" asked Ivan, deeply fascinated by this love story.

The visitor made a sign which meant that he would never reveal this to anyone and went on with his narrative.

The master and his unknown mistress loved one another so intensely that they became utterly inseparable. Ivan could clearly see for himself the two basement rooms, where it was always twilight from the shade of the lilac bush and the fence: the shabby red furniture, the clock on top of it which struck the half-hours, the books, books from the painted floor to the smoke-blackened ceiling, and the stove.

Ivan learned that from the very first days of their affair the man and his mistress decided that fate had brought them together on the corner of the Tverskaya and that side street and that they were made for each other to eternity.

Ivan heard his visitor describe how the lovers spent their day. Her first action on arrival was to put on an apron and light an oil stove on a wooden table in the cramped hall, with its tap and sink that the wretched patient recalled with such pride. There she cooked lunch and served it on an oval table in the living room. When the May storms blew and the water slashed noisily past the dim little windows, threatening to flood their home, the lovers stoked up the stove and baked potatoes in it. Steam poured out of the potatoes as they cut them open, the charred skins blackening their fingers. There was laughter in the basement, and after the rain the trees in the garden scattered broken branches and white blossoms.

When the storms were past and the heat of summer came, the vase was filled with the long-awaited roses that they both loved so much. The man who called himself the master worked feverishly at his novel, and the book cast its spell over the unknown woman.

"At times I actually felt jealous of it," the moonlight visitor whispered to Ivan.

Running her sharp, pointed fingernails through her hair, she ceaselessly read and reread the manuscript, sewing that same black cap as she did so. Sometimes she would squat down by the lower bookshelves or stand by the topmost ones and wipe the hundreds of dusty spines. Sensing fame, she drove him on and started to call him "the master." She waited impatiently for the promised final words about the fifth Procurator of Judea, reading out in a loud singsong random sentences that pleased her and saying that the novel was her life.

It was finished in August and handed to a typist who transcribed it in five copies. At last came the moment to leave the secret refuge and enter the outside world.

"When I emerged into the world clutching my novel, my life came to an end," whispered the master. He hung his head and for a long while wagged the black cap with its embroidered yellow "M." He went on with his story, but it grew more disjointed and Ivan could only gather that his visitor had suffered some disaster.

"It was my first sortie into the literary world, but now that it's all over and I am ruined for everyone to see, it fills me with horror to think of it!" whispered the master solemnly, raising his hand. "God, what a shock he gave me!"

"Who?" murmured Ivan, barely audible, afraid to disturb the master's inspiration.

"The editor, of course, the editor! Oh, yes, he read it. He looked at me as if I had a swollen face, avoided my eyes and even giggled with embarrassment. He had smudged and creased the typescript quite unnecessarily. He asked me questions which I thought were insane. He said nothing about the substance of the novel but asked me who I was and where I came from, had I been writing for long, why had nothing been heard of me before and finally asked what struck me as the most idiotic question of all: who had given me the idea of writing a novel on such a curious subject? Eventually I lost patience with him and asked him straight out whether he was going to print my novel or not. This embarrassed him. He began mumbling something, then announced that he personally was not competent to decide and that the other members of the editorial board would have to study the book, in particular the critics Latunsky and Ariman and the author Mstislav Lavrovich. He asked me to come back a fortnight later. I did so and was received by a girl who had developed a permanent squint from having to tell so many lies."

"That's Lapshennikova, the editor's secretary," said Ivan with a smile, knowing the world that his visitor was describing with such rancor.

"Maybe," he cut in. "Anyway, she gave me back my novel thoroughly tattered and covered with grease marks. Trying not to look at me, the girl informed me that the editors had enough material for two years ahead and therefore the question of printing my novel became, as she put it, 'redundant.' What else do I remember?" murmured the visitor, wiping his forehead. "Oh, yes, the red blobs spattered all over the title page and the eyes of my mistress. Yes, I remember those eyes."

The story grew more and more confused, full of more

and more disjointed remarks that trailed off unfinished. He said something about slanting rain and despair in their basement home, about going somewhere else. He whispered urgently that he would never, never blame her, the woman who had urged him on in the struggle.

After that, as far as Ivan could tell, something strange and sudden happened. One day he opened a newspaper and saw an article by Ariman, entitled "The Enemy Makes a Sortie," in which the critic warned all and sundry that he, that is to say our hero, had tried to drag into print an apologia for Jesus Christ.

"I remember that!" cried Ivan. "But I've forgotten what your name was."

"I repeat, let's leave my name out of it, it no longer exists," replied the visitor. "It's not important. A day or two later another article appeared in a different paper signed by Mstislav Lavrovich, in which the writer suggested striking and striking hard at all this Pilatism and religiosity which I was trying to drag (that damned word again!) into print. Stunned by that unheard-of word 'Pilatism,' I opened the third newspaper. In it were two articles, one by Latunsky, the other signed with the initials 'N.E.' Believe me, Ariman's and Lavrovich's stuff was a mere joke by comparison with Latunsky's article. Suffice it to say that it was entitled 'A Militant Old Believer.' I was so absorbed in reading the article about myself that I did not notice her standing in front of me with a wet umbrella and a sodden copy of the same newspaper. Her eyes were flashing fire, her hands cold and trembling. First she rushed to kiss me, then she said in a strangled voice, thumping the table, that she was going to murder Latunsky."

Embarrassed, Ivan gave a groan but said nothing.

"The joyless autumn days came," the visitor went on, "the appalling failure of my novel seemed to have withered part of my soul. In fact, I no longer had anything to do, and I only lived for my meetings with her. Then something began to happen to me. God knows what it was; I expect Stravinsky has unraveled it long ago. I began to suffer from depression and strange forebodings. The articles, incidentally, did not stop. At first I simply laughed at them, then came the second stage: amazement. In literally every line of those articles one could detect a sense of falsity, of unease, in spite of their confident and threatening tone. I couldn't help feeling—and the conviction grew stronger the more I read—that the people writing those articles were not saying what they had really wanted to say and that *this* was the cause of their fury. And then came the third stage: fear. Don't misunderstand me, I was not afraid of the articles; I was afraid of something else which had nothing to do with them or with my novel. I started, for instance, to be afraid of the dark. I was reaching the stage of mental derangement. I felt, especially just before going to sleep, that some very cold, supple octopus was fastening its tentacles around my heart. I had to sleep with the light on.

"My beloved had changed too. I told her nothing about the octopus, of course, but she saw that something was wrong with me. She lost weight, grew paler, stopped laughing and kept begging me to have that excerpt from the novel printed. She said I should forget everything and go south to the Black Sea, paying for the journey with what was left of the hundred thousand rubles.

"She was very insistent, so to avoid arguing with her (something told me that I never would go to the Black Sea) I promised to arrange the trip soon. However, she announced that she would buy me the ticket herself. I took out all my money, which was about ten thousand rubles, and gave it to her.

" 'Why so much?' she said in surprise.

"I said something about being afraid of burglars and asked her to keep the money until my departure. She took it, put it in her handbag, began to kiss me and said that she would rather die than leave me alone in this condition, but people were expecting her, she had to go but would come back the next day. She begged me not to be afraid.

"It was twilight, in mid-October. She went. I lay down on my couch and fell asleep without putting on the light. I was awakened by the feeling that the octopus was there. Fumbling in the dark, I just managed to switch on the lamp. My watch showed two o'clock in the morning. When I had gone to bed, I had been sickening; when I woke up, I was an ill man. I had a sudden feeling that the autumn murk was about to burst the windowpanes, flood into the room, and I would drown in it as if it were ink. I had lost control of myself. I screamed, I wanted to run somewhere, if only to my landlord upstairs. Wrestling with myself as one struggles with a lunatic, I had just enough strength to crawl to the stove and relight it. When I heard it begin to crackle and the fire door started rattling in the draft, I felt slightly better, I rushed into the hall, switched on the light, found a bottle of white wine and began gulping it down from the bottle. This calmed my fright a little, at least enough to stop me from running to my landlord. Instead, I went back to the stove. I opened the fire door. The heat began to warm my hands and face and I whispered, 'Something terrible has happened to me. . . . Come, come, please come . . . !'

"But nobody came. The fire roared in the stove, rain whipped against the windows. Then I took the heavy typescript copies of the novel and my handwritten drafts out of the desk drawer and started to burn them. It was terribly hard to do because paper that has been written over in ink doesn't burn easily. Breaking my fingernails, I tore up the manuscript books, stuffed them down between the logs and stoked the burning pages with the poker. Occasionally there was so much ash that it put the flames out, but I struggled with it until finally the whole novel, resisting fiercely to the end, was destroyed. Familiar words flickered before me, the yellow crept inexorably up the pages, yet I could still read the words through it. They only vanished when the paper turned black and I had given it a savage beating with the poker.

"There was a sound of someone scratching gently at the window. My heart leaped and, thrusting the last manuscript book into the fire, I rushed up the brick steps from the basement to the door that opened onto the yard. Panting, I reached the door and asked softly, 'Who's there?'

"And a voice, her voice, answered, 'It's me. . . .'

"I don't remember how I managed the chain and the key. As soon as she was indoors she fell into my arms, all wet, cheeks wet, hair bedraggled, shivering. I could only say, 'Is it really you?' Then my voice broke off and we ran downstairs into the flat.

"She took off her coat in the hall and we went straight into the living room. Gasping, she pulled the last bundle of paper out of the stove with her bare hands. The room at once filled with smoke. I stamped out the flames with my foot, and she collapsed on the couch and burst into convulsive, uncontrollable tears.

"When she was calm again I said, 'I suddenly felt I hated the novel and I was afraid. I'm sick. I feel terrible.'

"She sat up and said, 'God, how ill you look! Why, why? But I'm going to save you. What's the matter?'

"I could see her eyes, swollen from smoke and weeping, felt her cool hands smoothing my brow.

" 'I shall make you better,' she murmured, burying her head on my shoulder. 'You're going to write it again. Why, oh, why didn't I keep one copy myself?'

"She ground her teeth in anger and said something indistinct. Then with clamped lips she started to collect and sort the burnt sheets of paper. It was a chapter from somewhere in the middle of the book, I forget which. She carefully piled up the sheets, wrapped them up into a parcel and tied it with string. All her movements showed that she was a determined woman who was in absolute command of herself.

"She asked for a glass of wine and having drunk it said calmly, 'This is how one pays for lying, and I don't want to go on lying any more. I would have stayed with you this evening, but I didn't want to do it like that. I don't want his last memory of me to be that I ran out on him in the middle of the night. He has never done me any harm. . . . He was suddenly called out, there's a fire at his factory. But he'll be back soon. I'll tell him tomorrow morning, tell him I love someone else and then come back to you forever. If you don't want me to do that, tell me.'

" 'My poor, poor girl.' I said to her. 'I won't allow you to do it. It will be hell living with me, and I don't want you to perish here as I shall perish.'

" 'Is that the only reason?' she asked, putting her eyes close to mine.

" 'That's the only reason.'

"She grew terribly excited, hugged me, embraced my neck and said, 'Then I shall die with you. I shall be here tomorrow morning.'

"The last that I remember seeing of her was the patch of light from my hall and in that patch of light a loose curl of her hair, her beret and her determined eyes, her dark silhouette in the doorway and a parcel wrapped in white paper.

" 'I'd see you out, but I don't trust myself to come back alone, I'm afraid.'

"Don't be afraid. Just wait a few hours. I'll be back tomorrow morning.'

"Those were the last words that I heard her say."

"Sshh!" The patient suddenly interrupted himself and raised his finger. "It's a restless moonlit night." He disappeared onto the balcony. Ivan heard the sound of wheels along the corridor, there was a faint groan or cry.

When all was quiet again, the visitor came back and reported that a patient had been put into room No. 120, a man who kept asking for his head back. Both men relapsed into anxious silence for a while, but soon resumed their interrupted talk. The visitor had just opened his mouth, but the night, as he had said, was a restless one: voices were heard in the corridor, and the visitor began to whisper into Ivan's ear so softly that only the poet could hear what he was saying, with the exception of the first sentence: "A quarter of an hour after she had left me there came a knock at my window. . . ."

The man was obviously very excited by what he was whispering into Ivan's ear. Now and again a spasm would cross his face. Fear and anger sparkled in his eyes. The narrator pointed in the direction of the moon, which had long since disappeared from the balcony. Only when all the noises outside had stopped did the visitor move away from Ivan and speak louder:

"Yes, so there I stood, out in my little yard, one night in the middle of January, wearing the same overcoat but without any buttons now, and I was freezing with cold. Behind me the lilac bush was buried in snowdrifts, below and in front of me were my feebly lit windows with drawn blinds. I knelt down to the first of them and listened—a phonograph was playing in my room. I could hear it but see nothing. After a slight pause I went out of the gate and into the street. A snowstorm was howling along it. A dog which ran between my legs frightened me, and to get away from it I crossed to the other side. Cold and fear, which had become my inseparable companions, had driven me to desperation. I had nowhere to go, and the simplest thing would have been to throw myself under a trolley then and there where my side street joined the main road. In the distance I could see the approaching streetcars, looking like ice-encrusted lighted boxes, and hear the fearful scrunch of their wheels along the frostbound tracks. But the joke, my dear friend, was that every cell of my body was in the grip of fear. I was as afraid of the streetcar as I had been of the dog. I'm the most hopeless case in this building, I assure you!"

"But you could have let her know, couldn't you?" said Ivan sympathetically. "Besides, she had all your money. I suppose she kept it, did she?"

"Don't worry, of course she kept it. But you obviously don't understand me. Or rather I have lost the powers of description that I once had. I don't feel very sorry for her, as she is of no more use to me. Why should I write to her? She would be faced," said the visitor, gazing pensively at the night sky, "by a letter from the madhouse. Can one really write to anyone from an address like this? I—a mental patient—how could I make her so unhappy? I . . . I couldn't do it."

Ivan could only agree. The poet's silence was eloquent of his sympathy and compassion for his visitor, who bowed his head in pain at his memories and said, "Poor woman . . . I can only hope she has forgotten me."

"But you may recover," said Ivan timidly.

"I am incurable," said the visitor calmly. "Even though Stravinsky says that he will send me back to normal life, I don't believe him. He's a humane man and he only wants to comfort me. I won't deny, though, that I'm a great deal better now than I was. Now, where was I? Oh, yes. The frost, the moving streetcars . . . I knew that this clinic had just been opened and I crossed the whole town on foot to come here. It was madness! I would probably have frozen to death but for a lucky chance. A truck had broken down on the road, and I approached the driver. It was two miles beyond the city limits, and to my surprise he took pity on me. He was driving here and he brought me. . . . The toes of my left foot were frostbitten, but they cured them. I've been here four months now. And, do you know, I think this is not at all a bad place. I shouldn't bother to make any great plans for the future if I were you. I, for example, wanted to travel all over the world. Well, it seems that I was not fated to have my wish. I shall only see an insignificant little corner of the globe. I don't think it's necessarily the best bit, but I repeat, it's not so bad. Summer's on the way, and the balcony will be covered in ivy, so Praskovya Fyodorovna tells me. These keys have enlarged my radius of action. There'll be a moon at night. Oh, it has set! The air is fresher. Midnight is on the way. It's time for me to go."

"Tell me, what happened afterward with Yeshua and Pilate?" begged Ivan. "Please, I want to know."

"Oh, no, I couldn't," replied the visitor, wincing painfully. "I can't think about my novel without shuddering. Your friend from Patriarch's Ponds could have done it better than I can. Thanks for the talk. Good-bye."

Before Ivan had time to notice, the grille had shut with a gentle click and the visitor was gone.

SAVED BY COCKCROW

His nerves in shreds, Rimsky did not stay for the completion of the police report on the incident and took refuge in his own office. He sat down at the desk and with bloodshot eyes stared at the magic ruble notes spread out in front of him. The treasurer felt his reason slipping. A steady rumbling could be heard from outside as the public streamed out of the theater onto the street. Suddenly Rimsky's acute hearing distinctly caught the screech of a police whistle, always a sound of ill omen. When it was repeated and answered by another, more prolonged and authoritative, followed by a clearly audible bellow of laughter and a kind of ululating noise, the treasurer realized at once that something scandalous was happening in the street. However much he might like to disown it, the noise was bound to be closely connected with the terrible act put on that evening by the black magician and his assistants.

The treasurer was right. As he glanced out of the window onto Sadovaya Street, he gave a grimace and hissed, "I knew it!"

In the bright light of the street lamps he saw below him on the pavement a woman wearing nothing but a pair of violet panties, a hat and an umbrella. Round the painfully embarrassed woman, trying desperately to crouch down and run away, surged the crowd laughing in the way that had sent shivers down Rimsky's spine. Beside the woman was a man who was ripping off his coat and getting his arm hopelessly tangled in the sleeve.

Shouts and roars of laughter were also coming from the side entrance, and as he turned in that direction Grigory Danilovich saw another woman, this one in pink underwear. She was struggling across the pavement in an attempt to hide in the doorway, but the people coming out barred her way, and the wretched victim of her own rashness and vanity, duped by the sinister Faggot, could do nothing but hope to be swallowed up by the ground. A policeman ran toward the unfortunate woman, splitting the air with his whistle. He was closely followed by some cheerful, cloth-capped young men, the source of the ribald laughter and wolf whistles.

A thin, mustached horse-cab driver drove up alongside the first undressed woman and, smiling all over his whiskered face, reined in his horse with a flourish.

Rimsky punched himself on the head, spat with fury and jumped back from the window. He sat at his desk for a while listening to the noise in the street. The sound of whistles from various directions rose to a climax and then began to fade out. To Rimsky's astonishment the uproar subsided with surprising speed.

The time had come to act, to drink the bitter cup of responsibility. The telephones had been repaired during the last act, and he now had to ring up, report the incident, ask for help, blame it all on Likhodeyev and exculpate himself.

Twice Rimsky nervously picked up the receiver and twice put it down. Suddenly the deathly silence of the office was broken by the telephone itself ringing. He jumped and went cold. "My nerves are in a terrible state," he thought as he lifted the telephone. Immediately he staggered back and turned whiter than paper. A soft, sensual woman's voice whispered from the earpiece, "Don't ring up, Rimsky, or you'll regret it."

The line went dead. Feeling goose flesh spreading over his skin, the treasurer replaced the receiver and glanced around to the window behind his back. Through the sparse leaves of a sycamore tree he saw the moon flying through a translucent cloud. He seemed to be mesmerized by the branches of the tree, and the longer Rimsky stared at them, the more strongly he felt the grip of fear.

Pulling himself together, the treasurer finally turned away from the moonlit window and stood up. There was now no longer any question of telephoning, and Rimsky could only think of one thing—how to get out of the theater as quickly as possible.

He listened: the building was silent. He realized that for some time now he had been the only person left on the second floor, and a childish, uncontrollable fear overcame him at the thought. He shuddered to think that he would have to walk alone through the empty passages and down the staircase. He feverishly grabbed the magic rubles from his desk, stuffed them into his briefcase and coughed to summon up a little courage. His cough sounded hoarse and weak.

At this moment he noticed what seemed to be a damp, evil-smelling substance oozing under the door and into the office. A tremor ran down the treasurer's spine. Suddenly a clock began to strike midnight, and even this made him shudder. But his heart sank completely when he heard the sound of a latchkey being softly turned in the clock. Clutching his brief-case with damp, cold hands, Rimsky felt that if that scraping noise in the keyhole were to last much longer his nerves would snap and he would scream.

At last the door gave way and Varenukha slipped noiselessly into the office. Rimsky collapsed where he stood and sat down in an armchair. Gasping for air, he smiled what was meant to be an ingratiating smile and whispered. "God, what a fright you gave me!"

Terrifying as this sudden appearance was, it had its hopeful side—it cleared up at least one little mystery in this whole baffling affair.

"Tell me, tell me, quickly!" croaked Rimsky, clutching at his one straw of certainty in a world gone mad. "What does this all mean?"

"I'm sorry," mumbled Varenukha, closing the door. "I thought you would have left by now." Without taking his cap off he crossed to an armchair and sat down beside the desk, facing Rimsky.

There was a trace of something odd in Varenukha's reply, immediately detected by Rimsky, whose sensitivity was now on a par with the world's most delicate seismograph. For one thing, why had Varenukha come to the treasurer's office if he thought he wasn't there? He had his own office, after all. For another, no matter which entrance Varenukha had used to come into the theater he must have met one of the night watchmen, who had all been told that Grigory Danilovich was working late in his office. Rimsky, however, did not dwell long on these oddities—this was not the moment.

"Why didn't you ring me? And what the hell was all that charade about Yalta?"

"It was what I thought," replied the house manager, making a sucking noise as though troubled by an aching tooth. "They found him in a bar out at Pushkino."

"Pushkino? But that's just outside Moscow! What about those telegrams from Yalta?"

"Yalta—hell! He got the Pushkino telegrapher drunk and they started playing games, which included sending us those telegrams marked 'Yalta.' "

"Aha, aha . . . I see now," crooned Rimsky, his yellowish eyes flashing. In his mind's eye he saw Stepa being solemnly dismissed from his job. Freedom! At last Rimsky would be rid of that idiot Likhodeyev! Perhaps something even worse than being fired was in store for Stepan Bogdanovich. . . . "Tell me all the details!" cried Rimsky, banging his desk with a paperweight.

Varenukha began telling the story. As soon as he had arrived at the place where the treasurer had sent him, he was immediately shown in and listened to with great attention. No one, of course, believed for a moment that Stepa was in Yalta. Everybody at once agreed with Varenukha's suggestion that Likhodeyev was obviously at the Yalta restaurant in Pushkino.

"Where is he now?" Rimsky interrupted excitedly.

"Where do you think?" replied the house manager with a twisted smile. "In a police cell, of course, being sobered up!"

"Ah! Thank God for that!"

Varenukha went on with his story, and the more he said, the clearer Rimsky saw the long chain of Likhodeyev's misdeeds, each succeeding link in it worse than the last. What a price he was going to pay for one drunken afternoon at Pushkino! Dancing with the telegrapher. Chasing terrified women. Picking a fight with the barman at the Yalta. Throwing onions on the floor. Breaking eight bottles of white wine. Smashing a cab driver's taximeter for refusing to take him. Threatening to arrest people who tried to stop him . . .

Stepa was well known in the Moscow theater world, and everybody knew that the man was a menace, but this story was just a shade too much, even for Stepa. . . . Rimsky's sharp eyes bored into Varenukha's face across the desk, and the longer the story went on, the grimmer those eyes became. The more Varenukha embroidered his account with picturesque and revolting details, the less Rimsky believed him. When Varenukha described how Stepa was so far gone that he tried to resist the men who had been sent to bring him back to Moscow, Rimsky was quite certain that everything the house manager was telling him was a lie—a lie from beginning to end.

Varenukha had never gone to Pushkino, and Stepa had never been there either. There was no drunken telegrapher, no broken glass in the bar, and Stepa had not been hauled away in handcuffs—none of it had ever happened.

As soon as Rimsky felt sure that his colleague was lying to him, a feeling of terror crawled over his body, beginning with his feet, and for the second time he had the weird feeling that a kind of malarial damp was oozing across the floor. The house manager was sitting in a curious hunched attitude in the armchair, trying persistently to stay outside the light cast by the blue-shaded table lamp and ostensibly shading his eyes from its glare with a folded newspaper. Without taking his eyes off Varenukha for a moment, Rimsky's mind was working furiously to unravel this new mystery. Why should the man be lying to him at this late hour in the totally empty and silent building? Slowly a consciousness of danger, of an unknown but terrible danger, took hold of Rimsky. Pretending not to notice Varenukha's fidgeting and his tricks with the newspaper, the treasurer concentrated on his face, scarcely listening to what he was saying. There was something else that Rimsky found even more sinister than this slanderous and completely bogus yarn about the goings-on in Pushkino, and that something was a change in the house manager's appearance and manner.

However hard Varenukha tried to pull down the peak of his cap to shade his face and however much he waved the newspaper, Rimsky managed to discern an enormous bruise that covered most of the right side of his face, starting at his nose. What was more, this normally ruddy-cheeked man now had an unhealthy chalky pallor, and although the night was hot, he was wearing an old-fashioned striped cravat tied around his neck. If one added to this his newly acquired and repulsive habit of sucking his teeth, a distinct lowering and coarsening of his tone of voice and the furtive, shifty look in his eyes, it would be safe to say that Ivan Savyelich Varenukha was unrecognizable.

Something even more insistent was worrying Rimsky, but he could not put his finger on it however much he racked his

brain or stared at Varenukha. He was only sure of one thing—
that there was something peculiar and unnatural in the man's
posture in that familiar chair.

"Well, finally they overpowered him and shoved him into a
car," boomed Varenukha, peeping from under the newspaper
and covering his bruise with his hand.

Rimsky suddenly stretched out his arm and with an apparently unthinking gesture of his palm pressed the button of an
electric bell, drumming his fingers as he did so. His heart sank.
A loud ringing should have resounded instantly throughout the
building, but nothing happened, and the bell button merely
sank lifelessly into the desk top. The warning system was out
of order.

Rimsky's cunning move did not escape Varenukha, who
scowled and said with a clear flicker of hostility in his look,
"Why did you ring?"

"Oh, I just pressed it by mistake, without thinking,"
mumbled Rimsky, pulling back his hand, and asked in a shaky
voice, "What's that on your face?"

"The car braked suddenly and I hit myself on the door
handle," replied Varenukha, averting his eyes.

"He's lying!" said Rimsky to himself. Suddenly his eyes
gaped with utter horror, and he pressed himself against the
back of his chair.

On the floor behind Varenukha's chair lay two intersecting
shadows, one thicker and blacker than the other. The shadows
cast by the back of the chair and its tapering legs were clearly
visible, but above the lighter shadow of the chair back there
was no shadow of Varenukha's head, just as there was no
shadow of his feet to be seen under the chair legs.

"He throws no shadow!" cried Rimsky in a silent shriek of
despair. He shuddered helplessly.

Following Rimsky's horrified stare, Varenukha glanced furtively behind the chair and realized that he had been found
out. He got up (Rimsky did the same) and took a pace away
from the desk, clutching his briefcase.

"You've guessed, damn you! You always were clever," said
Varenukha, smiling evilly right into Rimsky's face. Then he
suddenly leaped for the door and quickly pushed down the
safety catch on the lock. The treasurer looked round in desperation, retreated toward the window that gave onto the
garden, and in that moon-flooded window he saw the face of
a naked girl pressed to the glass, her bare arm reaching through

the transom-like opening at the top in an attempt to unlatch the lower casement.

It seemed to Rimsky that the light of the desk lamp was going out and that the desk itself was tilting. A wave of icy cold washed over him, but luckily he fought it off and did not fall. He felt that he had barely enough strength to whisper, "Help . . ."

Varenukha, guarding the door, was jumping up and down beside it. He hissed and sucked, signaling to the girl in the window and pointing his crooked fingers at Rimsky.

The girl, increasing her efforts, pushed her auburn head through the little upper opening, stretched out her arm as far as she could and began to pluck at the lower catch with her fingernails and shake the frame. Her arm, colored deathly green, started to stretch as if it were made of rubber. Finally her green cadaverous fingers caught the knob of the window catch, turned it and the casement opened. Rimsky gave a weak cry and pressed himself to the wall, holding his briefcase in front of him like a shield. His last hour, he knew, had come.

The window swung wide open, but instead of fresh night air and the scent of lime blossom the room was flooded with the stench of the grave. The walking corpse stepped onto the window sill. Rimsky clearly saw patches of decay on her breast.

At that moment the sudden, joyful sound of a cock crowing rang out in the garden from the low building behind the shooting gallery where the cage birds used on the Variety stage were kept. With his full-throated cry the tame cock was announcing the approach of dawn over Moscow from the east.

Sudden fury distorted the girl's face as she swore hoarsely, and by the door Varenukha whimpered and collapsed to the floor.

The cock crowed again, the girl ground her teeth, and her auburn hair stood on end. At the third crow she turned and flew out. Behind her, flying horizontally through the air like an oversized Cupid, Varenukha floated slowly across the desk and out of the window.

His head as white as snow, without a black hair left on it, the old man who a short while before had been Rimsky ran to the door, freed the latch and rushed down the dark corridor. At the top of the stairs, groaning with terror, he fumbled for the switch and lit the lights on the staircase. The shattered, trembling old man stumbled down the stairs, imagining that Varenukha was gently pushing him from above.

At the bottom Rimsky saw the night watchman, who had fallen asleep on a chair in the foyer beside the box office. Rimsky tiptoed past him and slipped out the main door. Once in the street he felt slightly better. He came to his senses enough to realize, as he clutched his head, that he had left his hat in his office.

Nothing would have induced him to go back for it, and he ran panting across the wide street to the movie theater on the opposite corner, where a solitary cab stood on the rank. He reached it before anyone else could snatch it from him.

"To the Leningrad Station—hurry and I'll make it worth your while," said the old man, breathing heavily and clutching his heart.

"I'm only going to the garage," replied the driver, turning away with a surly face.

Rimsky unfastened his briefcase, pulled out fifty rubles and thrust them at the driver through the open window.

A few moments later the taxi, shaking like a leaf in a storm, was flying along the ring boulevard. Bouncing up and down in his seat, Rimsky caught occasional glimpses of the driver's delighted expression and his own wild look in the mirror.

Jumping from the car at the station, Rimsky shouted to the first man he saw, who was wearing a white apron and a numbered metal disc, "First class single—here's thirty rubles." As he fumbled for the money in his briefcase, he added, "If there aren't any seats left in the first, I'll take second . . . if there aren't any in the second, get me third class!"

Glancing round at the illuminated clock, the man with the apron snatched the money from Rimsky's hand.

Five minutes later the express pulled out of the glass-roofed station and steamed into the dark. With it vanished Rimsky.

THE DREAM OF
NIKANOR IVANOVICH

It is not hard to guess that the fat man with the purple face who was put into room No. 119 at the clinic was Nikanor Ivanovich Bosoi.

He had not, however, been put into Professor Stravinsky's care at once, but had first spent some time in another place, of which he could remember little except a desk, a cupboard and a sofa.

There some men had questioned Nikanor Ivanovich, but since his eyes were clouded by a flux of blood and extreme mental anguish, the interview was muddled and inconclusive.

"Are you Nikanor Ivanovich Bosoi," they began, "chairman of the house committee of No. 302A Sadovaya Street?"

Nikanor Ivanovich gave a wild peal of laughter and replied, "Of course I'm Nikanor! But why call me chairman?"

"What do you mean?" they asked, frowning.

"Well," he replied, "if I'm a chairman, I would have seen at once that he was an evil spirit, wouldn't I? I should have realized, what with his shaky pince-nez, his tattered clothes, how could he have been an interpreter?"

"Who are you talking about?"

"Koroviev!" cried Nikanor Ivanovich. "The man who's moved into No. 50. Write it down—Koroviev! You must find him and arrest him at once. Staircase 6—write it down—that's where you'll find him."

"Where did you get the foreign currency from?" they asked insinuatingly.

"As Almighty God's my witness," said Nikanor Ivanovich, "I never touched any and I never even suspected that it was foreign money. God will punish me for my sin," Nikanor Ivanovich went on feelingly, unbuttoning his shirt, buttoning it up again and crossing himself. "I took the money—I admit that—but it was Soviet money. I even signed a receipt for it. Our secretary, Prolezhnev, is just as bad—frankly we're all thieves on our house committee—but I never took any foreign money."

On being told to stop playing the fool and to tell them how the dollars found their way into his ventilation shaft, Nikanor Ivanovich fell on his knees and rocked backward and forward with his mouth wide open as though he were trying to swallow the wooden parquet blocks.

"I'll do anything you like," he groaned, "that'll convince you I didn't take the stuff. That Koroviev's nothing less than a devil!"

Everyone's patience has its limit; voices were raised behind the desk, and Nikanor Ivanovich was told that it was time he stopped talking gibberish.

Suddenly the room was filled with a savage roar from Nikanor Ivanovich as he jumped up from his knees: "There he is! There—behind the cupboard! There—look at him grinning! And his pince-nez . . . Stop him! Arrest him! Surround the building!"

The blood drained from Nikanor Ivanovich's face. Trembling, he made the sign of the cross in the air, bolted toward the door, then back again, intoned a prayer and then relapsed into complete delirium.

It was plain that Nikanor Ivanovich was incapable of talking rationally. He was removed and put in a room by himself, where he calmed down slightly and merely prayed and sobbed.

Men were sent to the house on Sadovaya Street to inspect apartment No. 50, but they found no Koroviev and no one in the building who had either seen or heard of him. The apartment belonging to Berlioz and Likhodeyev was empty, and the wax seals, quite intact, hung on all the cupboards and drawers in the study. The men left the building, taking with them the bewildered and crushed Prolezhnev, secretary of the house committee.

That evening Nikanor Ivanovich was delivered to Stravinsky's clinic. There he behaved so violently that he had to be given one of Stravinsky's special injections, and it was midnight before Nikanor Ivanovich fell asleep in room No. 119, uttering an occasional deep, tormented groan.

But the longer he slept, the calmer he grew. He stopped tossing and moaning, his breathing grew light and even, until finally the doctors left him alone.

Nikanor Ivanovich then had a dream, which was undoubtedly influenced by his recent experiences. It began with some men who carried golden trumpets leading him, with great solemnity, to a pair of huge painted doors, where his companions blew a fanfare in Nikanor Ivanovich's honor. Then a bass voice boomed at him from the sky, "Welcome, Nikanor Ivanovich! Hand over your foreign currency!"

Amazed beyond words, Nikanor Ivanovich saw in front of him a black loudspeaker. Soon he found himself in an auditorium lit by a crystal chandelier beneath a gilded ceiling and by sconces on the walls. Everything resembled a small but luxurious theater. There was a stage, with a velvet curtain whose dark cerise background was strewn with enlargements of gold ten-rouble pieces; there was a prompter's box and even an audience.

Nikanor Ivanovich was surprised to notice that the audience was an all-male one and that its members all wore beards. An odd feature of the auditorium was that it had no seats and the entire assembly was sitting on the beautifully polished and extremely slippery floor.

Embarrassed at finding himself in this large and unexpected company, after some hesitation Nikanor Ivanovich followed the general example and sat down Turkish-fashion on the parquet, wedging himself between a stout red-beard and a pale and extremely hirsute citizen. None of the audience paid any attention to the newcomer.

There came the gentle sound of a bell, the house lights went out, and the curtains parted to reveal a lighted stage set with an armchair, a small table on which was a little golden bell, and a heavy black velvet backdrop.

Onto the stage came an actor, dinner-jacketed, clean-shaven, his hair parted in the middle above a young, charming face. The audience grew lively and everybody turned to look at the stage. The actor advanced to the footlights and rubbed his hands.

"Are you all sitting down?" he inquired in a soft baritone and smiled at the audience.

"We are, we are," chorused the tenor and bass voices.

"H'm . . ." said the actor thoughtfully. "I realize, of course, how bored you must be. Everybody else is out of doors now, enjoying the warm spring sunshine, while you have to squat on the floor in this stuffy auditorium. Is the program really worthwhile? Ah well, *chacun à son goût,*" he said philosophically.

At this he changed the tone of his voice and announced gaily: "And the next number on our program is—Nikanor Ivanovich Bosoi, tenants' committee chairman and manager of a diabetic restaurant. This way please, Nikanor Ivanovich!"

At the sound of the friendly applause which greeted his name, Nikanor Ivanovich's eyes bulged with astonishment and the master of ceremonies, shading his eyes against the glare of the footlights, located him among the audience and beckoned him to the stage. Without knowing how he got here, Nikanor Ivanovich found himself on stage. His eyes were dazzled from above and below by the glare of colored lights which blotted out the audience from his sight.

"Now, Nikanor Ivanovich, set us an example," said the young actor gently and confidingly, "and hand over your foreign currency."

Silence. Nikanor Ivanovich took a deep breath and said in a low voice, "I swear to God, I—"

Before he could finish, the whole audience had burst into shouts of disapproval. Nikanor Ivanovich relapsed into uncomfortable silence."

"Am I right," asked the MC, "in thinking that you were about to swear by God that you had no foreign currency?" He gave Nikanor Ivanovich a sympathetic look.

"That's right. I haven't any."

"I see," said the actor. "But . . . if you'll forgive the indelicacy . . . where did those four hundred dollars come from that were found in the lavatory of your flat, of which you and your wife are the sole occupants?"

"They were magic ones!" said a sarcastic voice somewhere in the dark auditorium.

"That's right, they were magic ones," said Nikanor Ivanovich timidly, addressing no one in particular but adding, "An evil spirit, that interpreter in a check suit, planted them on me."

Again the audience roared in protest. When calm was restored, the actor said, "This is better than La Fontaine's fables! Planted four hundred dollars! Listen, you're all in the currency racket—I ask you now, as experts: is that possible?"

"We're not currency racketeers," cried a number of offended voices from the audience, "but it's impossible!"

"I entirely agree," said the actor firmly, "and now I'd like to ask you: what sort of things do people plant on other people?"

"Babies!" cried someone at the back.

"Quite right," agreed the MC. "Babies, anonymous letters, manifestoes, time bombs and God knows what else, but no one would ever plant four hundred dollars on a person because there just isn't anyone idiotic enough to try." Turning to Nikanor Ivanovich, the artist added sadly and reproachfully, "You've disappointed me, Nikanor Ivanovich. I was relying on you. Well, that number was a flop, I'm afraid."

The audience began to boo Nikanor Ivanovich.

"He's in the currency black market all right," came a shout from the crowd, "and innocent people like us have to suffer because of the likes of him."

"Don't shout at him," said the MC gently. "He'll repent." Turning his blue eyes, brimming with tears, toward Nikanor Ivanovich, he said, "Go back to your place, Nikanor Ivanovich."

After this the actor rang the bell and loudly announced, "Intermission!"

Shattered by his involuntary debut in the theater, Nikanor Ivanovich found himself back at his place on the floor. Then he began dreaming that the auditorium was plunged into total darkness and fiery red words leaped out from the walls: "Hand over all foreign currency!"

After a while the curtains opened again and the MC announced: "Sergei Gerardovich Dunchill on stage, please!"

Dunchill was a good-looking though very stout man of about fifty.

"Sergei Gerardovich," the MC addressed him, "you have been sitting here for six weeks now, firmly refusing to give up your remaining foreign currency, at a time when your country has desperate need of it. You are extremely obstinate. You're an intelligent man, you understand all this perfectly well, yet you refuse to come forward."

"I'm sorry, but how can I, when I have no more currency?" was Dunchill's calm reply.

"Not even any diamonds, perhaps?" asked the actor.

"No diamonds either."

The actor hung his head, reflected for a moment, then clapped his hands. From the wings emerged a fashionably dressed middle-aged woman. The woman looked worried as Dunchill stared at her without the flicker of an eyelid.

"Who is this lady?" the MC inquired of Dunchill.

"She is my wife," replied Dunchill with dignity, looking at the woman with an expression of faint repugnance.

"We regret the inconvenience to you, Madame Dunchill," said the MC, "but we have invited you here to ask you whether your husband has surrendered all his foreign currency."

"He handed it all in when he was told to," replied Madame Dunchill anxiously.

"I see," said the actor, "well, if you say so, it must be true. If he really has handed it all in, we must regretfully deprive ourselves of the pleasure of Sergei Gerardovich's company. You may leave the theater if you wish, Sergei Gerardovich," announced the MC with a regal gesture.

Calmly and with dignity Dunchill turned and walked toward the wings.

"Just a minute!" The MC stopped him. "Before you go just let me show you one more number from our program." Again he clapped his hands.

The dark backdrop parted and a beautiful young woman in a ball gown stepped on stage. She was holding a golden salver, on which lay a thick parcel tied with colored ribbon, and round her neck she wore a diamond necklace that flashed blue, yellow and red fire.

Dunchill took a step back and his face turned pale. Complete silence gripped the audience.

"Eighteen thousand dollars and a necklace worth forty thousand gold roubles," the MC solemnly announced, "belonging to Sergei Gerardovich and kept for him in Kharkov in the apartment of his mistress, Ida Herkulanovna Vors, whom you have the pleasure of seeing before you now and who has kindly consented to help in displaying these treasures which, priceless as they are, are useless in private hands. Thank you very much, Ida Herkulanovna."

The beauty flashed her teeth and fluttered her long eyelashes. "And as for you," the actor said to Dunchill, "we now know that beneath that dignified mask lurks a vicious spider, a liar and a disgrace to our society. For six weeks you have worn us all out with your stupid obstinacy. Go home now and may the hell which your wife is preparing for you be your punishment."

Dunchill staggered and was about to collapse when a sympathetic pair of arms supported him. The curtain then fell and hid the occupants of the stage from sight.

Furious applause shook the auditorium until Nikanor Ivanovich thought the bulbs were going to jump out of the chandelier. When the curtain rose again there was no one on stage except the actor. To another salvo of applause he bowed and said, "We have just shown you a typically stubborn case. Only yesterday I was saying how senseless it was to try and conceal a secret hoard of foreign currency. No one who has one can make use of it. Take Dunchill, for example. He is well paid and never short of anything. He has a splendid apartment, a wife and a beautiful mistress. Yet instead of acting like a law-abiding citizen and handing in his currency and jewelry, all that this incorrigible rogue has achieved is public exposure and a family scandal. So who wants to hand in his currency? Nobody? In that case, the next number on our program will be the famous actor Savva Potapovich Kurolesov in excerpts from 'The Covetous Knight' by the poet Pushkin."

Kurolesov entered, a tall, fleshy, clean-shaven man in tails and white tie. Without a word of introduction he scowled, frowned and, squinting at the golden bell, began to recite in an unnatural voice: "Hastening to meet his courtesan, the young gallant . . ."

Kurolesov's recital described a tale of evil. He confessed how an unhappy widow had knelt weeping before him in the rain, but the actor's hard heart had remained untouched.

Until this dream, Nikanor Ivanovich had known nothing of the works of Pushkin, although he knew his name well enough and almost every day he used to make remarks like "Who's going to pay the rent—Pushkin?" or "I suppose Pushkin stole the light bulb on the staircase" or "Who's going to buy the fuel oil for the boilers—Pushkin, I suppose?" Now as he listened to one of Pushkin's dramatic poems for the first time Nikanor Ivanovich felt miserable, imagining the woman on her knees in the rain with her orphaned children, and he could not help thinking what a beast this fellow Kurolesov must be.

The actor himself, his voice constantly rising, poured out his repentance and finally he completely muddled Nikanor Ivanovich by talking to someone who wasn't on the stage at all, then answered for the invisible man, all the time calling himself first "king," then "baron," then "father," then "son," until the confusion was total. Nikanor Ivanovich only managed to understand that the actor died a horrible death shouting "My keys! My keys!" at which he fell croaking to the ground, having first taken care to pull off his white tie.

Having died, Kurolesov got up, brushed the dust from his trousers, bowed, smiled an insincere smile and walked off to faint applause.

The MC then said, "In Savva Potapovich's masterly interpretation we have just heard the story of 'The Covetous Knight.' That knight saw himself as a Casanova; but, as you saw, nothing came of his efforts, no nymphs threw themselves at him, the muses refused him their tribute, he built no palaces and, instead, he ended miserably after his hoard of money and jewels was plundered. I warn you that something of the kind will happen to you, if not worse, unless you hand over your foreign currency!"

It may have been Pushkin's verse or it may have been the MC's prosaic remarks which had the desired effect; in any event a timid voice was heard from the audience: "I'll hand over my currency."

"Please come up on stage," was the MC's welcoming response as he peered into the dark auditorium.

A short blond man, three weeks unshaven, appeared on stage.

"What is your name, please?" inquired the MC.

"Nikolai Kanavkin" was the shy answer.

"Ah! Delighted, Citizen Kanavkin. Well?"

"I'll hand it over."

"How much?"

"A thousand dollars and twenty gold ten-rouble pieces."

"Bravo! Is that all you have?" The MC stared straight into Kanavkin's eyes, and it seemed to Nikanor Ivanovich that those eyes emitted rays which saw through Kanavkin like X-rays. The audience held its breath.

"I believe you!" cried the actor at last and extinguished his gaze. "I believe you! Those eyes are not lying! How many times have I said that your fundamental error is to under-estimate the significance of the human eye. The tongue may hide the truth, but the eyes—never! If somebody springs a question you may not even flinch; in a second you are in control of yourself and you know what to say in order to conceal the truth. You can be very convincing and not a muscle will flicker in your expression, but alas! The truth will start forth in a flash from the depths of your soul to your eyes and the game's up! You're caught!"

Having made this highly persuasive speech, the actor politely asked Kanavkin, "Where is the money hidden?"

"At my aunt's in Prechistenka."

"Ah! That will be . . . wait . . . yes, that's Claudia Ilyin-ishna Porokhovnikova, isn't it?"

"Yes."

"Yes, yes, of course. A little bungalow, isn't it? Opposite a high fence? Of course, I know it. And where have you put it?"

"In a box in the cellar."

The actor clapped his hands. "Oh, no! Really!" he cried angrily. "It's so damp there—it'll get moldy! People like that aren't to be *trusted* with money! What childlike innocence. What will they do next?"

Kanavkin, realizing that he was doubly at fault, hung his curly head.

"Money," the actor went on, "should be kept in the State Bank, in dry and specially guarded strong rooms, but never in your aunt's cellar, where apart from anything else the rats may get at it. Really, Kanavkin, you should be ashamed—you, a grown man!"

Kanavkin did not know which way to look and could only twist the hem of his jacket with his finger.

"All right," the artist relented slightly, "since you have owned up we'll be lenient." Suddenly he added unexpectedly, "By the way—we might as well kill two birds with one stone and not waste a car journey—I expect your aunt has some of her own hidden away, hasn't she?"

Not expecting the conversation to take this turn, Kanavkin gave a start and silence settled again on the audience.

"Really, now, Kanavkin," said the MC in a tone of kindly reproach, "I was just going to say what a good boy you were! And now you have to go and upset it all! That wasn't very clever, Kanavkin! Remember what I said just now about your eyes? Well, I can see from your eyes that your aunt has something hidden. Come on—don't tantalize us!"

"Yes, she has!" shouted Kanavkin boldly.

"Bravo!" cried the MC.

"Bravo!" roared the audience.

When the noise had died down the MC congratulated Kanavkin, shook him by the hand, offered him a car to take him home and ordered somebody in the wings to go and visit the aunt in the same car and invite her to appear in the ladies' section of the program.

"Oh, yes, I nearly forgot to ask you—did your aunt tell you where she has hidden hers?" inquired the MC, offering Kanavkin a cigarette and a lighted match. His cigarette lit, the wretched man gave an apologetic sort of grin.

"Of course, I believe you. You don't know," said the actor with a sigh. "I suppose the old skinflint wouldn't tell her nephew. Ah, well, we shall just have to try and appeal to her better nature. Perhaps we can still touch a chord in her miserly old heart. Good-bye, Kanavkin—and good luck!"

Kanavkin departed relieved and happy. The actor then asked whether anyone else wished to surrender his foreign currency, but there was no response.

"Funny, I must say!" said the MC with a shrug of his shoulders, and the curtain fell.

The lights went out, there was darkness for a while, broken only by the sound of a quavering tenor voice singing: "Heaps of gold—and mine, all mine . . ."

After a burst of applause, Nikanor Ivanovich's red-bearded neighbor suddenly announced: "There's bound to be a confession or two in the ladies' program." Then with a sigh he added: "Oh, if only they don't get my geese! I have a flock of geese at Lianozov, you see. They're savage birds, but I'm afraid they'll die if I'm not there. They need a lot of looking after. Oh, if only they don't take my geese! They don't impress *me* by quoting Pushkin." And he sighed again.

The theater was suddenly flooded with light, and Nikanor Ivanovich began dreaming that a gang of cooks started pouring through all the doors into the auditorium.They wore white chef's hats and carried ladles, and they dragged into the theater a vat full of soup and a tray of sliced black bread. The audience livened up as the cheerful cooks pushed their way down the aisles pouring the soup into bowls and handing out bread.

"Eat up, lads," shouted the cooks, "and hand over your currency! Why waste your time sitting here? Own up and you can all go home!"

"What are you doing here, old man?" said a fat, red-necked

cook to Nikanor Ivanovich as he handed him a bowl of soup with a lone cabbage leaf floating in it.

"I haven't got any! I haven't, I swear it," shouted Nikanor Ivanovich in a terrified voice.

"Haven't you?" growled the cook in a fierce bass. "Haven't you?" he inquired in a feminine soprano. "No, I'm sure you haven't," he muttered gently as he turned into the nurse Praskovya Fyodorovna.

She gently shook Nikanor Ivanovich by the shoulder as he groaned in his sleep. Cooks, theater, curtain and stage dissolved. Through the tears in his eyes Nikanor Ivanovich stared around at his hospital room and at two men in white coveralls. They turned out not to be cooks but doctors, standing beside Praskovya Fyodorovna, who instead of a soup bowl was holding a gauze-covered white-enameled dish containing a hypodermic syringe.

"What are you doing?" said Nikanor Ivanovich bitterly as they gave him an injection. "I haven't any, I tell you! Why doesn't Pushkin hand over his foreign currency? I haven't got any!"

"No, of course you haven't," said kind Praskovya Fyodorovna, "and no one is going to take you to court, so you can forget it and relax."

After his injection Nikanor Ivanovich calmed down and fell into a dreamless sleep. His unrest, however, had communicated itself to No. 120, where the patient woke up and began looking for his head; No. 118, where the nameless master wrung his hands as he gazed at the moon, remembering that last bitter autumn night, the patch of light under the door in his basement and the girl's hair blown loose.

The anxiety from No. 118 traveled along the balcony to Ivan, who woke up and burst into tears.

The doctor soon calmed all his distraught patients and they went back to sleep. Last of all was Ivan, who only dozed off as dawn began to break over the river. As the sedative spread through his body, tranquillity covered him like a slow wave. His body relaxed and his head was filled with the warm breeze of slumber. As he fell asleep the last thing that he heard was the dawn chorus of birds in the wood. But they were soon silent again, and he began dreaming that the sun had already set over Mount Golgotha and that the hill was ringed by a double cordon. . . .

CHAPTER 16

The Execution

The sun had already set over Mount Golgotha, and the hill was ringed by a double cordon.

The cavalry ala that had held up the Procurator that morning had left the city at a trot by the Hebron Gate, its route cleared ahead of it. Infantrymen of the Cappadocian cohort pressed back a crowd of people, mules and camels, and the ala, throwing up pillars of white dust, trotted toward the crossroads where two ways met—one running southward to Bethphagy, the other northwestward to Jaffa. The ala took the northwestward route. More of the Cappadocians had been posted along the edge of the road in time to clear the route of all the caravans moving into Jerusalem for the Passover. Crowds of pilgrims stood behind the line of troops, leaving the temporary shelter of their tents pitched on the grass. After about a half-mile the ala overtook the second cohort of the Lightning Legion and having gone another half-mile arrived first at the foot of Mount Golgotha. There the commander hastily divided the ala into troops and cordoned off the base of the low hill, leaving only a small gap where a path led from the Jaffa road to the hilltop.

After a while the second cohort arrived, climbed up and formed another cordon around the hill.

Last on the scene was the century under the command of

Mark Muribellum. It marched in two single files, one along each edge of the road, and between them, escorted by a secret service detachment, drove the cart carrying the three prisoners. Each wore a white board hung around his neck on which were written the words "Robber and Rebel" in Aramaic and Greek. Behind the prisoners' cart came others, loaded with freshly sawed posts and crosspieces, ropes, spades, buckets and axes. They also carried six executioners. Last in the convoy rode Mark the centurion, the captain of the temple guard and the same hooded man with whom Pilate had briefly conferred in a darkened room of the palace.

Although the procession was completely enclosed by troops, it was followed by about two thousand curious sight-seers determined to watch this interesting spectacle despite the infernal heat. These spectators from the city were now being joined by crowds of pilgrims, who were allowed to follow the tail of the procession unhindered, as it made its way toward Mount Golgotha to the bark of the heralds' voices as they repeated Pilate's announcement.

The ala allowed them through as far as the second cordon, beyond which the century admitted only those concerned with the execution and then, with a brisk maneuver, spread the crowd around the hill between the mounted cordon below and the upper ring formed by the infantry, permitting the spectators to watch the execution through a thin line of soldiery.

More than three hours had gone by since the procession had reached the hill and, although the sun over Mount Golgotha had already begun its descent, the heat was still unbearable. The troops in both cordons were suffering from it; stupefied with boredom, they cursed the three robbers and sincerely wished them a quick death.

At the gap in the lower cordon the diminutive commander of the ala, his forehead damp and his white tunic soaked with the sweat of his back, occasionally walked over to the leather bucket in the No. 1 troop's lines, scooped up the water in handfuls, drank and moistened his turban. With this slight relief from the heat he would return and recommence pacing up and down the dusty path leading to the top. His long sword bumped against his laced leather boot. As commander he had to set an example of endurance to his men, but he considerately allowed them to stick their lances into the ground and drape their white cloaks over the tips of the shafts. The Syrians then sheltered themselves from the pitiless sun under these makeshift tents. The buckets emptied quickly, and a detail of troops was kept busy fetching water from a ravine at the foot of the hill, where a muddy stream flowed in the shade of a clump of gaunt mulberry trees. There, making the most of the inadequate shade, the bored grooms lounged beside the horse lines.

The troops were exhausted, and their resentment of the victims was understandable. Fortunately, however, Pilate's fear proved unjustified. When the fourth hour of the execution had passed, contrary to all expectation not a man remained between the two cordons. The sun had scorched the crowd and driven it back to Jerusalem. Beyond the ring formed by the two Roman centuries there were only a couple of stray dogs. The heat had exhausted them too, and they lay panting with their tongues out, too weary even to chase the green-backed lizards, the only creatures unafraid of the sun, which darted among the broken stones and the spiny, ground-creeping cactus plants.

No one had tried to attack the prisoners, either in Jerusalem, which was packed with troops, or on the cordoned hill. The crowd had drifted back into town, bored by this dull execution and eager to join in the preparations for the feast which were already under way in the city.

The Roman infantry forming the second tier was suffering even more acutely than the cavalrymen. Centurion Muribellum's only concession to his men was to allow them to take off their helmets and put on white headbands soaked in water, but he kept them standing, lance in hand. The centurion himself, also wearing a headband, though a dry one, walked up and down the short distance from the group of executioners without even removing his heavy silver badges of rank, his sword or his dagger. The sun beat straight down on the centurion without causing him the least distress, and such was the glitter from his silver lions' muzzles that a glance at them was almost blinding.

Muribellum's disfigured face showed neither exhaustion nor displeasure and the giant centurion seemed strong enough to keep pacing all day, all night and all the next day. For as long as might be necessary he would go on walking with his hands on his heavy bronze-studded belt, he would fasten his stern gaze either on the crucified victims or on the line of troops or just kick at the rubble on the ground with the toe of his rough hide boot, indifferent to whether it was a whitened human bone or a small flint.

The hooded man had placed himself a short way from the gibbets on a three-legged stool and sat in calm immobility, occasionally out of boredom poking the sand with a stick.

It was not quite true that no one was left of the crowd between the cordons. There was one man, but he was partly hidden. He was not near the path, which was the best place from which to witness the execution, but on the northern side, where the hill was not smooth and passable but rough and jagged with gulleys and fissures, at a spot where a sickly fig tree had struggled to keep alive on that arid soil by rooting itself in a crevice.

Although the fig tree gave no shade, this sole remaining spectator had been sitting beneath it on a stone since the very start of the execution four hours before. He had chosen the worst place from which to watch the crucifixion, although he had an unimpeded view of the gibbets and could even see the two glittering badges on the centurion's chest. His vantage point appeared adequate, however, for a man who seemed anxious to remain out of sight.

Yet four hours ago this man had behaved quite differently and had made himself all too conspicuous, which was probably the reason why he had since changed his tactics and withdrawn to solitude. When the procession had reached the top of the hill, he had been the first of the crowd to appear and he had shown all the signs of a man arriving late. He had run panting up the hill, pushing people aside, and when halted by the cordon he had made a naïve attempt, by pretending not to understand their angry shouts, to break through the line of soldiers and reach the place of execution where the prisoners were already being led off the cart. For this he had earned a savage blow on the chest with the blunt end of a lance and had staggered back with a cry, not of pain but of despair. He had stared at the legionary who had hit him with the bleary, indifferent look of a man past feeling physical pain.

Gasping and clutching his chest, he had run around to the northern side of the hill, trying to find a gap in the cordon where he might slip through. But it was too late, the chain had been closed. And the man, his face contorted with grief, had had to give up trying to break through to the carts, from which men were now unloading the gibbet posts. Any such attempt would have led to his arrest, and as his plans for that day did not include being arrested, he had hidden himself in the crevice where he could watch unmolested.

Now as he sat on his stone, his eyes swollen from heat, dust and lack of sleep, the black-bearded man felt miserable. First he would sigh, opening his travel-worn tallith, once blue but now turned dirty gray, and bare his sweating, bruised chest; then he would raise his eyes to the sky in inexpressible anguish, following the three vultures who had long been circling the hilltop in expectation of a feast, then gaze hopelessly at the yellow soil where he stared at the half-crushed skull of a dog and the lizards that scurried around it.

The man was in such distress that now and again he would talk to himself.

"Oh, I am a fool," he mumbled, rocking back and forth in agony of soul and scratching his swarthy chest. "I'm a fool, as stupid as a woman—and I'm a coward! I'm a lump of carrion, not a man!"

He hung his head in silence, then, revived by a drink of tepid water from his wooden flask, he gripped the knife hidden under his tallith or fingered the piece of parchment lying on a stone in front of him along with a stylus and a bladder of ink.

On the parchment were some scribbled notes:

"Minutes pass while I, Matthew the Levite, sit here on Mount Golgotha and still he is not dead!"

Later:

"The sun is setting and death not yet come."

Hopelessly, Matthew now wrote with his sharp stylus:

"God! Why are you angry with him? Send him death."

Having written this, he gave a tearless sob and again scratched his chest.

The cause of the Levite's despair was his own and Yeshua's terrible failure. He was also tortured by the fatal mistake which he, Matthew, had committed. Two days before, Yeshua and Matthew had been in Bethphagy near Jerusalem, where they had been staying with a market gardener who had taken great pleasure in Yeshua's preaching. All that morning the two men had helped their host at work in his garden, intending to walk on to Jerusalem in the cool of the evening. But for some reason Yeshua had been in a hurry, saying that he had something urgent to do in the city, and had set off alone at noon. That was Matthew the Levite's first mistake. Why, why had he let him go alone?

That evening Matthew had been unable to go to Jerusalem, as he had suffered a sudden and unexpected attack of sickness.

He shivered, his body felt as if it were on fire and he begged constantly for water.

To go anywhere was out of the question. He had collapsed onto a rug in the gardener's courtyard and had lain there until dawn on Friday, when the sickness left Matthew as suddenly as it had struck him. Although still weak, he had felt oppressed by a foreboding of disaster and bidding his host farewell had set out for Jerusalem. There he had learned that his foreboding had not deceived him and that the disaster had occurred. The Levite had been in the crowd that had heard the Procurator pronounce sentence.

When the prisoners were taken away to Mount Golgotha, Matthew the Levite ran alongside the escort amid the crowd of sight-seers, trying to give Yeshua an inconspicuous signal that at least he, the Levite, was here with him, that he had not abandoned him on his last journey and that he was praying for Yeshua to be granted a quick death. But Yeshua, staring far ahead to where they were taking him, could not see Matthew.

Then, when the procession had covered half a mile or so of the way, Matthew, who was being pushed along by the crowd level with the prisoners' cart, was struck by a brilliant and simple idea. In his fervor he cursed himself for not having thought of it before. The soldiers were not marching in close order, but with a gap between each man. With great dexterity and very careful timing it would be possible to bend down and jump between two legionaries, reach the cart and jump up on it. Then Yeshua would be saved from an agonizing death. A moment would be enough to stab Yeshua in the back with a knife, having shouted to him, "Yeshua! I shall save you and depart with you! I, Matthew, your faithful and only disciple!"

And if God were to bless him with one more moment of freedom, he could stab himself as well and avoid a death on the gallows. Not that Matthew, the erstwhile tax collector, cared much how he died; he wanted only one thing—that Yeshua, who had never done anyone the least harm in his life, should be spared the torture of crucifixion.

The plan was a very good one, but it had a great flaw—the Levite had no knife and no money with which to buy one.

Furious with himself, Matthew pushed his way out of the crowd and ran back to the city. His head burned with the single thought of how he might at once, by whatever means, find a knife somewhere in town and then catch up with the procession again.

He ran as far as the city gate, slipping through the crowd of pilgrims' caravans pouring into town, and saw on his left the open door of a baker's shop. Breathless from running on the hot road, the Levite pulled himself together, entered the shop very sedately, greeted the baker's wife standing behind the counter, asked her for a loaf from the top shelf which he affected to prefer to all the rest, and as she turned round, he silently and quickly snatched off the counter the very thing he had been looking for—a long, razor-sharp bread knife—and fled from the shop.

A few minutes later he was back on the Jaffa road, but the procession was out of sight. He ran. Once or twice he had to drop and lie motionless to regain his breath, to the astonishment of the passers-by making for Jerusalem on muleback or on foot. As he lay he could hear the beat of his heart in his chest, in his head and his ears. Rested, he stood up and began running again, although his pace grew slower and slower. When he finally caught sight again of the long, dusty procession, it had already reached the foot of the hill.

"Oh, God!" groaned the Levite. He knew he was too late.

With the passing of the fourth hour of the execution Matthew's torments reached their climax and drove him to a frenzy. Rising from his stone, he hurled the stolen knife to the ground, crushed his flask with his foot, thus depriving himself of water, snatched the kaffiyeh from his head, tore his flowing hair and cursed himself. As he cursed in streams of gibberish, bellowed and spat, Matthew slandered his father and mother for begetting such a fool.

Since cursing and swearing had no apparent effect and changed nothing in that sun-scorched inferno, he clenched his dry fists and raised them heavenward to the sun as it slowly descended, lengthening the shadows before setting into the Mediterranean. The Levite begged God to perform a miracle and allow Yeshua to die.

When he opened his eyes again, nothing on the hill had changed, except that the light no longer flashed from the badges on the centurion's chest. The sun was shining on the victims' backs, as their faces were turned east toward Jerusalem. Then the Levite cried out, "I curse you, God!"

In a hoarse voice he shouted that God was unjust and that he would believe in him no more.

"You are deaf!" roared Matthew. "If you were not deaf, you would have heard me and killed him that instant!"

His eyes tight shut, the Levite waited for the fire to strike him from heaven. Nothing happened. Without opening his eyes, he vented his spite in a torrent of insults to heaven. He shouted that his faith was ruined, that there were other gods and better. No other god would have allowed a man like Yeshua to be scorched to death on a pole.

"No—I was wrong!" screamed the Levite, now quite hoarse. "You are a God of evil! Or have your eyes been blinded by the smoke of sacrifices from the temple and have your ears grown deaf to everything but the trumpet calls of the priests? You are not an almighty God—you are an evil God! I curse you, God of robbers, their patron and protector!"

At that moment there was a puff of air in his face and something rustled under his feet. Then came another puff, and as he opened his eyes the Levite saw that everything, either as a result of his imprecations or from some other cause, had changed. The sun had been swallowed by a thundercloud looming up, threatening and inexorable, from the west. Its edges were white and ragged, its rumbling black paunch tinged with sulphur. White pillars of dust, raised by the sudden wind, flew along the Jaffa road. The Levite was silent, wondering if the storm which was about to break over Jerusalem might alter the fate of the wretched Yeshua. Watching the tongues of lightning that flickered round the edges of the cloud, he began to pray for one to strike Yeshua's gibbet. Glancing penitently up at the remaining patches of blue sky in which the vultures were winging away to avoid the storm, Matthew knew that he had cursed too soon: God would not listen to him now.

Turning round to look toward the foot of the hill, the Levite stared at the calvary lines and saw that they were on the move. From his height he had a good view of the soldiers' hasty preparations as they pulled their lances out of the ground and threw their cloaks over their shoulders. The grooms were running toward the path, leading strings of troop horses. The regiment was moving out. Shielding his face with his hand and spitting out the sand that blew into his mouth, the Levite tried to think why the calvary should be preparing to go. He shifted his glance higher up the hill and made out a figure in a purple military chlamys climbing up toward the place of execution. Matthew's heart leaped; he sensed a quick end.

The man climbing Mount Golgotha in the victims' fifth hour

of suffering was the Tribune of the Cohort, who had galloped from Jerusalem accompanied by an orderly. At a signal from Muribellum the cordon of soldiers opened and the centurion saluted the Tribune, who took Muribellum aside and whispered something to him. The centurion saluted again and walked over to the executioners, seated on stones under the gibbets. The Tribune meanwhile turned toward the man on the three-legged stool. The seated man rose politely as the Tribune approached him. The officer said something to him in a low voice and both walked over to the gallows, where they were joined by the captain of the temple guard.

Muribellum, with a fastidious grimace at the filthy rags lying on the ground near the crosses—the prisoners' clothes, which even the executioners had spurned—called to two of them and gave an order: "Follow me!"

A hoarse, incoherent song could just be heard coming from the nearest gibbet. Hestas had been driven out of his mind two hours ago by the flies and the heat and was now softly croaking something about a vineyard. His turbaned head still nodded occasionally, sending up a lazy cloud of flies from his face.

Dismas on the second cross was suffering more than the other two because he was still conscious and shaking his head regularly from side to side.

Yeshua was luckier. He had begun to faint during the first hour, and had then lapsed into unconsciousness, his head drooping in its ragged turban. As a result the mosquitoes and horseflies had settled on him so thickly that his face was entirely hidden by a black, heaving mass. All over his groin, his stomach and under his armpits sat bloated horseflies, sucking at the yellowing naked body.

At a gesture from the man in the hood one of the executioners picked up a lance and the other carried a bucket and sponge to the gibbet. The first executioner raised the lance and used it to hit Yeshua first on one extended arm and then on the other. The emaciated body gave a twitch. The executioner then poked Yeshua in the stomach with the handle of the lance. At this Yeshua raised his head, the flies rose with a buzz and the victim's face was revealed, swollen with bites, puff-eyed, unrecognizable.

Forcing open his eyelids, Ha-Notsri looked down. His usually clear eyes were now dim and glazed.

"Ha-Notsri!" said the executioner.

Ha-Notsri moved his swollen lips and answered in a hoarse gasp, "What do you want? Why have you come?"

"Drink!" said the executioner, and a water-soaked sponge was raised to Yeshua's lips on the point of a lance. Joy lit up his eyes, he put his mouth to the sponge and greedily sucked its moisture. From the next gibbet came the voice of Dismas: "It's unjust! He's as much a crook as me!"

Dismas strained ineffectually, his arms being lashed to the crossbar in three places. He arched his stomach, clawed the end of the crossbeam with his nails and tried to turn his eyes, full of envy and hatred, toward Yeshua's cross.

"Silence on the second gibbet!"

Dismas was silent. Yeshua turned aside from the sponge. He tried to make his voice sound kind and persuasive, but failed and could only croak huskily, "Give him a drink too."

It was growing darker. The cloud now filled half the sky as it surged toward Jerusalem; smaller white clouds fled before the black monster charged with fire and water. There was a flash and a thunderclap directly over the hill. The executioner took the sponge from the lance.

"Hail to the merciful hegemon!" he whispered solemnly and gently pierced Yeshua through the heart. Yeshua shuddered and whispered, "Hegemon . . ."

Blood ran down his stomach, his lower jaw twitched convulsively and his head dropped.

At the second thunderclap the executioner gave the sponge to Dismas and with the same words—"Hail, hegemon"—he killed him.

Hestas, his reason gone, cried out in fear as the executioner approached him, but when the sponge touched his lips he gave a roar and sank his teeth into it. A few seconds later his body was hanging as limply as the ropes would allow.

The man in the hood followed the executioner and the centurion; behind him in turn came the captain of the temple guard. Stopping at the first gibbet, the hooded man carefully inspected Yeshua's bloodstained body, touched the post with his white hand and said to his companions, "Dead."

He did the same at the other two gallows.

After this the Tribune gestured to the centurion and turned to walk down the hill with the captain of the temple guard and the hooded man.

It was now twilight and lightning was furrowing the black sky. Suddenly there was a brilliant flash and the centurion's shout of "Cordon, fall out!" was drowned in thunder. The delighted soldiers started running downhill, buckling on their helmets as they went.

A mist had covered Jerusalem.

The downpour struck suddenly and caught the centurion halfway down the hill. The rain fell with such force that turbulent streams began catching up with them as they ran. The troops slithered and fell on the muddy soil as they hurried to reach the main road. Moving fast, now scarcely visible in a veil of water, the rain-soaked cavalry was already on its way back to Jerusalem. After a few minutes only one man was left on the hill in the smoking caldron of wind, water and fire.

Brandishing his stolen knife, for which he now had a use after all, leaping over the slippery rocks, grasping whatever came to hand, at times crawling on his knees, he stumbled toward the gallows in alternate spells of complete darkness and flashes of light.

When he reached the gallows, he was already ankle-deep in water and threw off his soaking tallith. Wearing only his shirt, Matthew fell at Yeshua's feet. He cut the ropes round his knees, climbed onto the lower crossbar, embraced Yeshua and freed his arms from their bonds. Yeshua's wet, naked body collapsed onto Matthew and dragged him to the ground. The Levite was just about to hoist him onto his shoulders when another thought stopped him. He left the body on the watery ground, its head thrown back and arms outstretched, and ran, slithering, to the other gibbet posts. He cut their ropes and the two bodies fell to the ground.

A few minutes later only those two water-lashed bodies and three empty gibbets remained on Mount Golgotha. Matthew the Levite and Yeshua were gone.

CHAPTER 17

A DAY OF ANXIETY

On Friday morning, the day after the disastrous show, the permanent staff of the Variety Theater—Vassily Stepanovich Lastochkin the accountant, two bookkeepers, three typists, the two cashiers, the ushers, the backstage crew and the cleaners— were not at work but were instead sitting on the window ledges looking out onto Sadovaya Street and watching what was happening outside the theater. There beneath the theater walls wound a double line of several thousand people whose tail end had already reached Kudrinskaya Square. At the head of the line stood a couple of dozen of the leading lights of the Moscow theatrical world.

The ticket line was in a state of high excitement, attracting the attention of the passers-by and busily swapping hair-raising stories about the previous evening's incredible performance of black magic. Vassily Stepanovich the accountant, who had not been at yesterday's show, was growing more and more uneasy. The backstage people were saying unbelievable things, such as how after the show a number of ladies had been seen on the street in a highly improper state. The shy and unassuming Vassily Stepanovich could only blink as he listened to the description of all these sensations and felt utterly unable to decide what to do; meanwhile something *had* to be done, and it was he who had to do it, as he was now the senior remaining member of the Variety's management.

By ten o'clock the ticket line had swollen to such a size that the police heard about it and rapidly sent some detachments of horse and foot officers to reduce it to order. Unfortunately the mere existence of a mile-long ticket line was enough to cause a minor riot in spite of everything the police could do.

Inside the Variety things were as confused as they were outside. The telephone had been ringing since early morning—ringing in Likhodeyev's office, in Rimsky's office, in the accounts department, in the box office and in Varenukha's office. At first Vassily Stepanovich had attempted to answer, the cashier had tried to cope, the stage manager had mumbled something into the telephone when it rang, but soon they stopped answering altogether because there was simply no answer to give the people asking where Likhodeyev, Rimsky and Varenukha were. They had been able to put them off the scent for a while by saying that Likhodeyev was in his apartment, but this only produced more angry calls later, declaring that they had rung Likhodeyev's apartment and been told that he was at the Variety.

One agitated lady rang up and demanded to speak to Rimsky and was advised to ring his wife at home, at which the earpiece, sobbing, replied that she was Rimsky's wife and he was nowhere to be found. Odd stories began to circulate. One of the cleaning women was telling everyone that when she had gone to clean the treasurer's office she had found the door ajar, the lights burning, the window onto the garden smashed, a chair overturned on the floor and no one in the room.

At eleven o'clock Madam Rimsky descended on the Variety, weeping and wringing her hands. Vassily Stepanovich was by now utterly bewildered and unable to offer her any advice. Then at half-past eleven the police appeared. Their first and very reasonable question was: "What's happening here? What is all this?"

The staff retreated, pushing forward the pale and agitated Vassily Stepanovich. Describing the situation as it really was, he had to admit that the entire management of the Variety, including the general manager, the treasurer and the house manager, had vanished without trace, that last night's M.C. had been removed to a lunatic asylum and that, in short, yesterday's show had been a catastrophe.

Having done their best to calm her, the police sent the

sobbing Madam Rimsky home, then turned with interest to the cleaning woman's story about the state of the treasurer's office. The staff were told to go and get on with their jobs, and after a short while the detective squad turned up, leading a sharp-eared muscular dog, the color of cigarette ash and with extremely intelligent eyes. At once a rumor spread among the Variety Theater staff that the dog was none other than the famous Ace of Diamonds. It was. Its behavior amazed everybody. No sooner had the animal walked into the treasurer's office than it growled, bared its monstrous yellowish teeth, then crouched on its stomach and crept toward the broken window with a look of mingled terror and hostility. Mastering its fear, the dog suddenly leaped onto the window ledge, raised its great muzzle and gave an eerie, savage howl. It refused to leave the window, growled, trembled and crouched as though wanting to jump out of the window.

The dog was led out of the office to the lobby, from whence it went out through the main doors into the street and across the road to the taxi rank. There it lost the scent. After that Ace of Diamonds was taken away.

The detectives settled into Varenukha's office, where one after the other they called in all the members of the Variety staff who had witnessed the events of the previous evening. At every step the detectives were beset with unforeseen difficulties. The thread kept breaking in their hands.

Had there been any posters advertising the performance? Yes, there had. But since last night new ones had been pasted over them and now there was not a single one to be found anywhere. Where did this magician come from? Nobody knew. Had a contract been signed?

"I suppose so," replied Vassily Stepanovich miserably.

"And if so it will have gone through the books, won't it?"

"Certainly," replied Vassily Stepanovich in growing agitation.

"Then where is it?"

"It's not here," replied the accountant, turning paler and spreading his hands. It was true: there was no trace of a contract in the accounts department files, the treasurer's office, Likhodeyev's office or Varenukha's office.

What was the magician's surname? Vassily Stepanovich did not know, he had not been at yesterday's show. The backstage people did not know, the box-office cashier frowned and frowned, thought and thought, and finally said, "Wo . . . I think it was Woland."

Perhaps it wasn't Woland? Perhaps it wasn't. Perhaps it was Foland.

The Aliens Bureau, it appeared, had never heard of anyone called Woland or Foland or any other black magician. Karpov, an usher, said that as far as he knew the magician was staying at Likhodeyev's apartment. Naturally they immediately went to the apartment, but there was no sign of a magician living there. Likhodeyev himself was also missing. The maid Grunya was not there, and nobody knew where she was. Both the house committee chairman, Nikanor Ivanovich, and the secretary, Prolezhnev, had also vanished.

The investigation so far appeared to amount to a total absurdity: the entire management had vanished, there had been a scandalous show the previous evening—but who had arranged it? Nobody knew.

Meanwhile it was nearly noon, time for the box office to open. This, of course, was out of the question. A large piece of cardboard was hung on the Variety's doors with the announcement:

TODAY'S
PERFORMANCE
CANCELED

This caused a stir in the ticket line, begining at its head, but the excitement subsided and the line began to disperse. After an hour there was scarcely a trace of it on Sadovaya Street. The detectives left to pursue their inquiries elsewhere, the staff, except for the watchman, were dismissed, and the doors of the Variety were closed.

Vassily Stepanovich the accountant had two urgent tasks to perform: first, to go to the Commission for Theatrical Spectacles and Light Entertainment with a report on the previous day's events and then to deposit yesterday's takings of 21,711 rubles at the Commission's finance department.

The meticulous and efficient Vassily Stepanovich wrapped the money in newspaper, tied it up with string, put it into his briefcase and, following his standing instructions, avoided taking a bus or trolley but went instead to the nearby taxi rank.

As soon as the three cab drivers on the rank saw a fare approaching with a bulging briefcase under his arm, all three of them instantly drove off empty, scowling back as they went. Amazed, the accountant stood for a while wondering what this odd behavior could mean. After about three minutes an empty cab drove up to the rank, the driver grimacing with hostility when he saw his fare.

"Are you free?" asked Vassily Stepanovich with an anxious cough.

"Show me your money," snarled the driver.

Even more amazed, the accountant clutched his precious briefcase under one arm, pulled a ten-ruble note out of his wallet and showed it to the driver.

"I'm not taking you," he said curtly.

"Excuse me, but—" The accountant began, but the driver interrupted him: "Got a three-ruble note?"

The bewildered accountant took out two three-ruble notes from his wallet and showed them to the driver.

"O.K., get in," he shouted, slamming down the flag of his meter so hard that he almost broke it. "Let's go."

"Are you short of change?" inquired the accountant timidly.

"Plenty of change!" roared the driver and his eyes, reddened with fury, glared at Vassily Stepanovich from the mirror. "Third time it's happened to me today. Just the same with the others. Some son of a bitch gives me a tenner and I give him four-fifty change. Out he gets, the bastard! Five minutes later I look—instead of a tenner there's a label off a soda-water bottle!" Here the driver said several unprintable words. "Picked up another fare on Zaborskaya. Gives me a tenner—I give him three rubles change. Gets out. I look in my bag and out flies a bee! Stings me on the finger! I'll . . ." The driver spat out more unprintable words. "And there was no tenner. There was a show on at that [unprintable] Variety yesterday evening and some [unprintable] conjurer did a turn with a lot of [unprintable] ten-ruble notes."

The accountant was dumbstruck. He hunched himself up and tried to look as if he were hearing the word "Variety" for the first time in his life as he thought to himself, "Well I'm damned!"

Arrived at his destination and paying in proper money, the accountant went into the building and hurried along the corridor to the chief cashier's office, but even before he reached it he realized that he had come at a bad moment. A rumpus was going on in the offices of the Theatrical Commission. A cleaner ran past him with her head scarf awry and bulging eyes.

"He's not there! He's not there, dear," she screamed, turning to another man hurrying along the passage. "His jacket and trousers are there, but there's nobody in 'em!"

She disappeared through a door, from which there at once came the sound of smashing crockery. Vassily Stepanovich then saw the familiar figure of the chief cashier come running out of the secretaries' office and vanish, but the man was in such a state that Vassily Stepanovich failed to recognize him.

Slightly shaken, the accountant reached the door of the secretaries' office, which was the anteroom to the chairman's office, and received his greatest shock of all.

Through the far door came a terrible voice, unmistakably belonging to Prokhor Petrovich, the chairman of the Commission. "I suppose he's telling somebody off," thought the puzzled accountant. Looking round, he saw something else: there, in a leather armchair, her head resting on the back, sobbing uncontrollably and clutching a wet handkerchief, her legs stretched out to the middle of the floor, lay Prokhor Petrovich's secretary, the beautiful Anna Richardovna. Her chin was smeared with lipstick, and streaks of dissolved mascara were running down her peach-skin cheeks.

Seeing him come in, Anna Richardovna jumped up, ran to Vassily Stepanovich, clutched his lapels and began to shake him, howling, "Thank God! At least there's one of you brave enough! They've all run away, they've all let us down! Come and see him, I don't know what to do!" Still sobbing, she dragged him into the chairman's office.

Once inside Vassily Stepanovich dropped his briefcase in horror.

Behind the huge desk with its massive inkwell sat an empty suit. A dry pen was hurrying, unheld, across a sheet of paper. The suit had a shirt and tie, a fountain pen was clipped to its breast pocket, but above the collar there was no neck and no head and there were no wrists protruding from the cuffs. The suit was hard at work and oblivious of the uproar surrounding it. Hearing someone come in, the suit leaned back in its chair, and from somewhere just above the collar came the familiar voice of Prokhor Petrovich: "What is it? There's a notice on the door saying that I'm not seeing visitors."

The beautiful secretary moaned and cried, wringing her

hands, "Don't you see? He's not there! Bring him back, oh, bring him back!"

Someone peeped around the door, groaned and flew out again. Vassily Stepanovich felt his legs shaking, and he sat down on the edge of a chair—not forgetting, though, to hold onto his briefcase.

Anna Richardovna pranced around Vassily Stepanovich, pulling at his coat and shrieking, "I've always, always stopped him whenever he began swearing! Now he's sworn once too often!" The girl ran to the desk and exclaimed in a tender, musical voice, slightly nasal from so much weeping, "Prosha dear, where are you?"

"Who are you addressing as 'Prosha'?" inquired the suit haughtily, drawing further back into the chair.

"He doesn't recognize me! He doesn't recognize me! Don't you see?" sobbed the girl.

"Kindly stop crying in my office!" said the striped suit irritably, stretching out its sleeve for a fresh pile of paper.

"No, I can't look, I can't look!" cried Anna Richardovna and ran back into her office, followed, like a bullet, by the accountant.

"Just imagine—I was sitting here," began Anna Richardovna, trembling with horror and clutching Vassily Stepanovich's sleeve, "when in came a cat. A great black animal as big as Behemoth. Naturally I shooed it out and it went, but then a fat man came in who also had a face like a cat and said, 'Do you always say "shoo" to visitors?' and went right straight in to Prokhor Petrovich. So I shouted, 'What d'you mean by going in there—have you gone crazy?' But the brazen brute marched straight in to Prokhor Petrovich and sat down in the chair facing him. Well, Prokhor is the nicest man alive, but he's high-strung. He lost his temper. He works like a Trojan, but he's apt to be nervous, and he just flared up. 'Why have you come in here without being announced?' he said. And then, if you please, that impudent creature stretched out in his chair and said with a smile, 'I've come to have a chat with you on a little matter of business.' Prokhor Petrovich snapped at him again. 'I'm busy,' to which the beast said, 'You're not busy at all.' How d'you like that? Well, of course, Prokhor Petrovich lost all patience then and shouted, 'What is all this? I'm damned if I don't have you thrown out of here!' The beast just smiled and said, 'You'll be damned, I think you said? Very well!' And—bang! Before I could even scream, I looked and cat-face had

gone and there was this . . . suit . . . sitting . . . Ooooh!"
Stretching her mouth into a shapeless cavity, Anna Richardovna let out a howl.

Choking back her sobs, she took a deep breath but could only gulp nonsensically: "And it goes on writing and writing and writing; I must be going out of my mind! It talks on the telephone— the suit! They've all run away like rabbits!"

Vassily Stepanovich could only stand there, trembling. Fate rescued him. Into the secretaries' office with a firm, regular tread marched two policemen. Catching sight of them, the lovely girl began sobbing even harder and pointed toward the office door.

"Now, now, miss, let's not cry," said the first man calmly. Vassily Stepanovich, deciding that he was superfluous, skipped away and a minute later was out in the fresh air. His head felt hollow, something inside it was booming like a trumpet, and the noise reminded him of the story told by one of the stage crew about a cat which had taken part in yesterday's show. "Aha! Perhaps it's our little pussy up to his tricks again?"

Having failed to hand in the money at the Commission's main office, the conscientious Vassily Stepanovich decided to go to the branch office, which was in Vagankovsky Street, and to calm himself a little he made his way there on foot.

The branch office of the Theatrical Commission was quartered in a peeling old house at the far end of a courtyard, which was famous for the porphyry columns in its hallway. That day, however, the visitors to the house were not paying much attention to the porphyry columns.

Several visitors were standing numbly in the hall and staring at a weeping girl seated behind a deskful of theatrical brochures which it was her job to sell. The girl seemed to have lost interest in her literature and only waved sympathetic inquirers away, while from above, below and all parts of the building came the pealing of at least twenty desperate telephones.

Weeping, the girl suddenly gave a start and screamed hysterically, "There it is again!" and began singing in a wobbly soprano, *"Yo-o, heave-ho! Yo-o heave-ho!"*

A messenger, who had appeared on the staircase, shook his fist at somebody and joined the girl, singing in a rough, tuneless baritone, *"One more heave, lads, one more heave . . ."*

Distant voices chimed in, the choir began to swell until finally the song was booming out all over the building. In nearby room No. 6, the auditor's department, a powerful hoarse bass voice boomed out an octave below the rest. The chorus was accompanied by a crescendo peal of telephone bells.

"All day lo-ong we must trudge the shore," roared the messenger on the staircase.

Tears poured down the girl's face as she tried to clench her teeth, but her mouth opened of its own accord and she sang an octave above the messenger: *"Work all da-ay and then work more. . . ."*

What surprised the dumfounded visitors was the fact that the singers, spread throughout the building, were keeping excellent time, as though the whole choir were standing together and watching an invisible conductor.

Passers-by in Vagankovsky Street stopped outside the courtyard gates, amazed to hear such sounds of harmony coming from the Commission.

As soon as the first verse was over, the singing stopped at once, as though in obedience to a conductor's baton. The messenger swore under his breath and ran off.

The front door opened and in walked a man wearing a light coat over a white coverall, followed by a policeman.

"Do something, Doctor, please!" screamed the hysterical girl.

The secretary of the branch office ran out onto the staircase and, obviously burning with embarrassment and shame, said between hiccups, "Look, Doctor, we have a case of some kind of mass hypnosis, so you must . . ." He could not finish his sentence, stuttered and began singing "Shilka and Nerchinsk."

"Fool!" the girl managed to shout, but never managed to say who she meant and instead found herself forced into a trill and joined in the song about Shilka and Nerchinsk.

"Pull yourselves together! Stop singing!" said the doctor to the secretary.

It was obvious that the secretary would have given anything to stop singing but could not.

When the verse was finished, the girl at the desk received a dose of valerian from the doctor, who hurried off to give the secretary and the others the same treatment.

"Excuse me, miss," Vassily Stepanovich suddenly asked the girl, "has a black cat been in here?"

"What cat?" cried the girl angrily. "There's a donkey in this office—a donkey!" And she went on: "If you want to hear about it, I'll tell you exactly what's happened."

Apparently the director of the branch office had a mania for organizing clubs.

"He does it all without permission from the main office!" said the girl indignantly.

In the course of a year the branch director had succeeded in organizing a Lermontov Club, a Chess and Checkers Club, a Ping-pong Club and a Riding Club. In summer he threatened to organize a rowing club and a mountaineering club. And then this morning in came the director at lunchtime . . .

". . . arm in arm with some villain," said the girl, "that he'd picked up God knows where, wearing check trousers, with a wobbling pince-nez . . . and an absolutely impossible face!"

There and then, according to the girl, he had introduced him to all the lunchers in the cafeteria as a famous specialist in organizing choral societies.

The faces of the budding mountaineers darkened, but the director told them to cheer up and the specialist made jokes and assured them on his oath that singing would take up very little time and was a wonderfully useful accomplishment.

Well, of course, the girl went on, the first two to jump up were Fanov and Kosarchuk, both well-known toadies, and announced that they wanted to join. The rest of the staff realized that there was no way out of it, so they all joined the choral society too. It was decided to practice during the lunch break, because all the rest of their spare time was already taken up with Lermontov and checkers. To set an example, the director announced that he sang tenor. What happened then was like a bad dream. The check-clad chorus master bellowed: "Do, mi, sol, do!" He dragged some of the shy members out from behind a cupboard where they had been trying to avoid having to sing, told Kosarchuk that he had perfect pitch, whined, whimpered, begged them to show him some respect as an old choirmaster, struck a tuning fork with his finger and announced that they would begin with "The Song of the Volga Boatmen."

They began to sing. And they sang very well—the man in the check suit really did know his job. They sang to the end of the first verse. Then the choirmaster excused himself, saying, "I'll be back in a moment," and vanished. Everybody expected him back in a minute or two, but ten minutes went by and there was still no sign of him. The staff were delighted—he had run away!

Then suddenly, as if on order, they all began singing the second verse, led by Kosarchuk, who may not have had perfect pitch but who had quite a pleasant high tenor. They finished the verse. Still no conductor. They started to go back to their tables, but they had no time to eat before, quite against their will, they all started singing again. And they could not stop. There would be three minutes' silence and they would burst into song again. Silence—then more singing! Soon people began to realize that something terrible was happening. The director locked himself in his office out of shame.

With this the girl's story broke off—even valerian was no use.

A quarter of an hour later three trucks drove up to the gateway on Vagankovsky Street and the entire branch staff, headed by the director, was herded into them. Just as the first truck drove through the gate and out into the street, the staff, standing in the back and clasping each other around the shoulders, all opened their mouths and deafened the whole street with a song. The second truckload joined in and then the third. On they drove, singing. Passers-by hurrying about their own business gave the trucks no more than a glance and took no notice, thinking that it was some works party going on an excursion out of town. They were certainly heading out of town, but not for an outing: they were bound for Professor Stravinsky's clinic.

Half an hour later the distracted Vassily Stepanovich reached the accounts department, hoping at last to be able to get rid of his large sum of money. Having learned from experience, he first threw a cautious glance into the long hall, where the cashiers sat behind frosted-glass windows with gilt markings. He saw no sign of disturbance or upheaval. All was as quiet as it should be in such a respectable establishment.

Vassily Stepanovich stuck his head through the window marked "In Payments," said good day to the clerk and politely asked for an in-payment slip.

"What do you want?" asked the clerk behind the window.

The accountant looked amazed. "I want to make a payment, of course. I'm from the Variety."

"One minute," replied the clerk and instantly shut his little window.

"Funny!" thought Vassily Stepanovich. This was the first time in his life that he had been treated like this. We all know how hard it is to acquire money—the process is strewn with

obstacles; but in his thirty years' experience Vassily Stepanovich had never yet found anyone who had made the least
objection to taking money when it was offered him.

At last the window was pushed open again and the accountant leaned forward once more.

"How much have you got?" asked the clerk.

"Twenty-one thousand, seven hundred and eleven rubles."

"Oho!" replied the clerk ironically and handed Vassily Stepanovich a green form. Thoroughly familiar with it, he filled it
out in a moment and began untying the string on his package.
As he unpacked it, a red film came over his eyes and he
groaned in agony. In front of him lay heaps of foreign money
—Canadian dollars, English pounds, Dutch gulden, Latvian
lats, Estonian crowns . . .

"Here's another of these jokers from the Variety!" said a
grim voice behind the accountant. And Vassily Stepanovich
was immediately placed under arrest.

CHAPTER **18**

UNWELCOME VISITORS

Just as Vassily Stepanovich was taking a taxi ride to meet the suit that wrote by itself, among the passengers on the Kiev express a respectably dressed man carrying a little fiber suitcase emerged from a first-class sleeper onto the Moscow platform. This passenger was none other than the uncle of the late Misha Berlioz, Maximilian Andreyevich Poplavsky, an economist who worked in the Planning Commission and lived in Kiev. The cause of his arrival in Moscow was a telegram that he had received late in the evening two days earlier:

HAVE BEEN RUN OVER BY STREETCAR AT PATRIARCHS FU-
NERAL THREE O'CLOCK FRIDAY PLEASE COME   BERLIOZ

Maximilian Andreyevich was regarded, and rightly so, as one of the most intelligent men in Kiev, but a telegram like this would be liable to put even the brightest of us in a dilemma. If a man telegraphs that he has been run over, obviously he has not been killed. But then why the funeral? Or is he so desperately ill that he can foresee his own death? It is possible, but extremely odd to be quite so precise—even if he can predict his death, how does he know that he's going to be buried at three o'clock on Friday? What an astonishing telegram!

Intelligent people, however, become intelligent by solving complicated problems. It was very simple. There had been a mistake and the wire had arrived in a garbled form. Obviously the word "have" belonged to some other telegram and had been transmitted in error instead of the word "Berlioz," which had been put at the end of the telegram by mistake. Thus corrected, the meaning was quite clear, though, of course, tragic.

When his wife had recovered from her first grief, Maximilian Andreyevich at once prepared to go to Moscow.

Here I should reveal a secret about Maximilian Andreyevich. He genuinely mourned the death of his wife's cousin, cut off in the prime of life, but at the same time, being a practical man, he fully realized that there was no special need for his presence at the funeral. Yet Maximilian Andreyevich was in a great hurry to go to Moscow. What for? For one thing—the apartment. An apartment in Moscow was a serious matter. He did not know why, but Maximilian Andreyevich did not like Kiev, and the thought of moving to Moscow had lately begun to nag at him with such insistence that it was affecting his sleep.

He took no delight in the spring floods of the Dnieper when, as it drowned the islands on the lower shore, the water spread until it merged with the horizon. He found no pleasure in the staggeringly beautiful view from the foot of the monument to Prince Vladimir. The patches of sunlight that play in spring over the brick pathways leading to the top of St. Vladimir's hill meant nothing to him. He wanted none of it. He wanted only to go to Moscow.

Advertisements in the newspapers offering to exchange an apartment on University Street in Kiev for a smaller apartment in Moscow produced no results. Nobody could be found who wanted to move, except a few whose offers turned out to be fraudulent.

The telegram came as a shock to Maximilian Andreyevich. It was a chance that would be sinful to miss. Practical people know that opportunities of that sort never come twice.

In short, he had to make sure, at no matter what cost, that he inherited his nephew's apartment in Sadovaya Street. It was going to be complicated, very complicated, but come what might, these complications had to be overcome. An experienced man, Maximilian Andreyevich knew that the first and essential step was to arrange a temporary residence permit to stay, for however short a time, in his late nephew's apartment.

So on Friday morning Maximilian Andreyevich walked into the office of the tenants' association of No. 302A Sadovaya Street, Moscow. In a mean little room, its wall enlivened by a poster showing in several graphic diagrams how to revive a drowned man, behind a wooden desk there sat a lonely, unshaven middle-aged man with a worried look.

"May I see the chairman, please?" inquired the economist politely, taking off his hat and placing his attaché case on a chair by the door. This apparently simple question upset the man behind the desk so much that a complete change came over his expression. Squinting with anxiety, he muttered something incoherent about the chairman not being there.

"Is he in his apartment?" asked Poplavsky. "I have some very urgent business with him."

The man gave another indistinct mumble, which meant that he wasn't in his apartment either.

"When will he be back?"

To this the seated man gave no reply except to stare glumly out of the window.

"Aha!" said the intelligent Poplavsky to himself and inquired after the secretary. At this the strange man behind the desk actually went purple in the face with strain and again muttered vaguely that the secretary wasn't there either . . . nobody knew when he'd be back again . . . the secretary was ill. . . .

"Oho!" said Poplavsky to himself. "Is there anybody here from the association's management committee?"

"Me," said the man in a weak voice.

"Look," said Poplavsky ingratiatingly, "I am the sole heir of my nephew Berlioz, who, as you know, died the other day at Patriarch's Ponds, and according to law I have to claim my inheritance. All his things are in our apartment—No. 50—"

"I don't know anything about it, comrade," the man interrupted gloomily.

"Excuse me," said Poplavsky in his most charming voice, "you are a member of the management committee and you must—"

Just then a stranger came into the room. The man behind the desk went pale.

"Are you Pyatnazhko of the management committee?" said the stranger.

"Yes, I am," said the seated man in a tiny voice.

The stranger whispered something to him, and the man behind the desk, now completely bewildered, got up and left Poplavsky entirely alone in the empty committee room.

"What a nuisance! I should have seen the whole committee at once," thought Poplavsky with annoyance as he crossed the courtyard and hurried up to apartment No. 50.

He rang the bell, the door was opened, and Maximilian Andreyevich walked into the semidarkness of the hall. He was slightly surprised not to be able to see who had opened the door to him; there was no one in the hall except an enormous black cat sitting on a chair. Maximilian Andreyevich coughed and tapped his foot, at which the study door opened and Koroviev came into the hall. Maximilian Andreyevich gave him a polite but dignified bow and said, "My name is Poplavsky. I am the uncle—"

But before he could finish Koroviev pulled a dirty handkerchief out of his pocket, blew his nose and burst into tears.

"Of course, of course!" said Koroviev, removing the handkerchief from his face. "I only had to see you to know who you were!" He shook with tears and began sobbing, "Oh, what a tragedy! How could such a thing happen?"

"Was he run over by a streetcar?" asked Poplavsky in a whisper.

"Completely!" cried Koroviev, tears streaming past his pince-nez. "Completely! I saw it happen. Can you believe it? Bang—his head was off; scrunch—away went his right leg; scrunch—off came his left leg! What these trolleys can do." In his grief, Koroviev leaned his nose against the wall beside the mirror and shook with sobs.

Berlioz' uncle was genuinely moved by the stranger's behavior. "There—and they say people have no feelings nowadays!" he thought, feeling his own eyes beginning to prickle. At the same time, however, an uneasy thought snaked across his mind that perhaps this man had already registered himself in the apartment; such things had been known to happen.

"Excuse me, but were you a friend of Misha's?" he inquired, wiping his dry left eye with his sleeve and studying the grief-stricken Koroviev with his right eye. But Koroviev was sobbing so hard that his words were inaudible except for "Scrunch and off it came!"

His weeping fit over, Koroviev finally unstuck himself from the wall and said, "No, I can't bear it! I shall go and take three hundred drops of valerian in ether." Turning his tear-stained face to Poplavsky, he added, "Ah, these trolleys!"

"I beg your pardon, but did you send me a telegram?" asked Maximilian Andreyevich, racking his brains to think who this extraordinary weeping creature might be.

"He sent it," replied Koroviev, pointing to the cat.

Poplavsky, his eyes bulging, assumed that he had misheard.

"No, I can't face it any longer," went on Koroviev, sniffing. "When I think of that wheel going over his leg—each wheel weighs 360 pounds—scrunch! . . . I must go and lie down, sleep is the only cure." And he vanished from the hall.

The cat jumped down from the chair, stood up on its hind legs, put its forelegs akimbo, opened its mouth and said, "I sent the telegram. So what?"

Maximilian Andreyevich's head began to spin, his arms and legs gave way so that he dropped his case and sat down in a chair facing the cat.

"Don't you understand Russian?" said the cat severely. "What do you want to know?"

Poplavsky was speechless.

"Passport!" barked the cat and stretched out a fat paw.

Completely dumfounded and blind to everything except the twin sparks in the cat's eyes, Poplavsky pulled his passport out of his pocket like a dagger. The cat picked up a pair of spectacles with thick black rims from the table under the mirror, put them on its snout—which made it look even more imposing—and took the passport from Poplavsky's shaking hand.

"I wonder—have I fainted or what?" thought Poplavsky. From the distance came the sound of Koroviev's blubbering, the hall was filled with the smell of ether, valerian and some other nauseating abomination.

"Which department issued this passport?" asked the cat. There was no answer.

"Department four hundred and twenty," said the cat to itself, drawing its paw across the passport, which it was holding upside down. "Well, of course! I know that department, they issue passports to anybody who comes along. I wouldn't have given one to someone like you. Not on any account. One look at your face and I'd have refused!" The cat had worked itself up into such a temper that it threw the passport to the floor. "You may not attend the funeral,"

went on the cat in an official voice. "Kindly go home at once."
And it shouted toward the door: "Azazello!"

At this a small, red-haired man limped into the hall. He
had one yellow fang, a walleye and was wearing a black
sweater with a knife stuck into a leather belt. Feeling himself
suffocating, Poplavsky stood up and staggered back, clutching
his heart.

"See him out, Azazello!" ordered the cat and left the room.

"Poplavsky," said the fanged horror in a nasal whine, "I
hope you understand?"

Poplavsky nodded.

"Go back to Kiev at once," Azazello went on, "stay at
home as quiet as a mouse and forget that you ever thought
of getting an apartment in Moscow. Got it?"

The little man only came up to Poplavsky's shoulder, but
he reduced him to mortal terror with his fang, his knife and
his walleyed squint, and he had an air of cool, calculating
energy.

First he picked up the passport and handed it to Maximilian
Andreyevich, who took it with a limp hand. Then Azazello
took the suitcase in his left hand, flung open the front door
with his right and taking Berlioz' uncle by the arm led him
out onto the landing. Poplavsky leaned against the wall. Without a key Azazello opened the little suitcase, took out of it
an enormous roast chicken minus one leg wrapped in grease-
proof paper and put it on the floor. Then he pulled out two
sets of clean underwear, a razor strop, a book and a leather
case and kicked them all downstairs except the chicken. The
empty suitcase followed. It could be heard banging on the
stairs and, to judge by the sound, the lid broke off as it went.

Then the carrot-haired ruffian picked up the chicken by its
leg and hit Poplavsky a terrible blow across the neck with it,
a blow so violent that the carcass flew apart leaving Azazello
with the leg in his hand. "Everything was in a mess in the
Oblonskys' house," as Leo Tolstoy so truly put it, a remark
which applied exactly to the present situation. Everything was
in a mess for Poplavsky. A long sliver of light flashed in front
of him, then he had a vision of a funeral procession on a May
afternoon, and Poplavsky fell downstairs.

When he hit the landing, he knocked a pane out of the
window with his foot and sat down on the step. A legless
chicken rolled past him, disintegrating as it went. On the
upper landing Azazello devoured the chicken leg in a flash,

stuffed the bone into his pocket, turned back into the apartment and slammed the door behind him.

From below there came the sound of a man's cautious steps coming upstairs. Poplavsky ran down another flight and sat down on a little wooden bench on the landing to catch his breath.

A tiny little old man with a painfully sad face, wearing an old-fashioned tussore-silk suit and a straw hat with a green ribbon, came up the stairs and stopped beside Poplavsky.

"Would you mind telling me, sir," inquired the man in tussore sadly, "where No. 50 might be?"

"Upstairs," gasped Poplavsky.

"Thank you very much, sir," said the little man as gloomily as before and plodded upward, while Poplavsky stood up and walked on downstairs.

You may ask whether Maximilian Andreyevich hurried to the police to complain about the ruffians who had handled him with such violence in broad daylight. He most certainly did not. How could he walk into a police station and say that a cat had been reading his passport and that a man in a sweater armed with a knife . . . ? No, Maximilian Andreyevich was altogether too intelligent for that.

He had by now reached the ground floor and noticed just beside the main door another little door, with a broken glass pane, leading to a storage closet. Poplavsky put his passport into his pocket and hunted round for the scattered contents of his suitcase. There was no trace of them. He was amazed to notice how little this worried him. Another and rather intriguing idea now occupied him—to stay and see what happened when the little old man went into the sinister apartment. Since he had asked the way to No. 50, he must be going there for the first time and was heading straight for the clutches of the gang that had moved into the apartment. Something told Poplavsky that the little man was going to come out of that apartment again in double-quick time. Naturally he had given up any idea of going to his nephew's funeral, and there was plenty of time before the train left for Kiev. The economist glanced round and slipped into the closet.

Just then came the sound of a door closing upstairs. "He's gone in," thought Poplavsky anxiously. It was damp and cold in the closet and it smelled of mice and boots. Maximilian Andreyevich sat down on a log of wood and decided to wait.

He was in a good position to watch the staircase as well as the doorway leading into the courtyard.

However, he had to wait longer than he had expected. The staircase remained empty. At last the door on the fifth floor was heard shutting. Poplavsky froze. Yes, those were his footsteps. "He's coming down." A door opened one floor lower. The footsteps stopped. A woman's voice. A sad man's voice —yes, that was him—saying something like "Stop it, for heaven's sake." Poplavsky stuck his ear through the broken pane and caught the sound of a woman's laughter. Quick, bold steps coming downstairs, and a woman flashed past. She was carrying a green oilcloth bag and hurried out into the courtyard. Then came the little man's footsteps again. "That's odd! He's going back into the apartment again! Surely he's not one of the gang? Yes, he's going back. They've opened the door upstairs again. Well, let's wait a little longer and see. . . ."

This time there was not long to wait. The sound of the door. Footsteps. The footsteps stopped. A despairing cry. A cat miaowing. A patter of quick footsteps coming down, down, down!

Poplavsky waited. Crossing himself and muttering, the sad little man rushed past, hatless, an insane look on his face, his bald head covered with scratches, his trousers soaking wet. He began struggling with the door handle, so terrified that he failed to notice whether it opened inward or outward, finally mastered it and flew out into the sunlit courtyard.

The experiment over and without a further thought for his dead nephew or his apartment, trembling to think of the danger he had been through and muttering "I see it all, I see it all!" Maximilian Andreyevich ran outside. A few minutes later a trolley-bus was carrying the economist toward the Kiev station.

While the economist had been lurking in the downstairs closet, the little old man had been through a distressing experience. He was a bartender at the Variety Theater, and his name was Andrei Fokich Sokov. During the police investigation at the theater, Andrei Fokich had kept apart from it all, and his only noticeable reaction was that he grew even sadder-looking than usual. He also found out from Karpov, the usher, where the magician was staying.

So, leaving the economist on the landing, the bartender climbed up to the fifth floor and rang the bell at No. 50.

The door was opened immediately, but the bartender shuddered and staggered back without going in. The door had been opened by a girl, completely naked except for an indecent little lace apron, a white cap and a pair of little gold slippers. She had a perfect figure, and the only flaw in her looks was a livid scar on her neck.

"Well, come on in, since you rang," said the girl, giving the bartender an enticing look.

Andrei Fokich groaned, blinked and stepped into the entrance hall, removing his hat. At that moment the telephone rang. The shameless maid put one foot on a chair, lifted the receiver and said into it, "Hello!"

The bartender did not know where to look and shifted from foot to foot, thinking, "These foreigners and their maids! Really, it's disgusting!" To save himself from being disgusted he stared the other way.

The large, dim hallway was full of strange objects and pieces of clothing. A black cloak lined with fiery red was thrown over the back of a chair, while a long sword with a shiny gold hilt lay on the console under the mirror. Three swords with silver hilts stood in one corner as naturally as if they had been umbrellas or walking sticks, and berets adorned with eagles' plumes hung on the antlers of a stag's head.

"Yes," said the girl into the telephone. "I beg your pardon? Baron Maigel? Very good, sir. Yes. The professor is in today. Yes, he'll be delighted to see you. Yes, it's formal. Tails or dinner jacket. When? At midnight." The conversation over, she put back the receiver and turned to the bartender.

"What do you want?"

"I have to see the magician."

"What, the professor himself?"

"Yes," replied the barman miserably.

"I'll see," said the maid, hesitating, then she opened the door into Berlioz' study and announced, "Sir, there's a little man here. He says he has to see Messire in person."

"Show him in," said Koroviev's cracked voice from the study.

"Go in, please," said the girl as naturally as if she had been normally dressed, then opened the door and left the hall.

As he walked in, the bartender was so amazed at the furnishings in the room that he forgot why he had come. Through the stained-glass windows (a fantasy of the jeweler's window) poured a strange ecclesiastical light. Although the day was hot, there was a log fire in the vast old-fashioned fireplace, yet it gave no heat and instead the visitor felt a wave of damp and cold as though he had walked into a tomb. In front of the fireplace sat a great black tomcat on a tiger skin rug blinking pleasurably at the fire. There was a table, the sight of which made the God-fearing bartender shudder: it was covered with an altar cloth, and on top of it was an army of bottles— bulbous, covered with mold and dust. Among the bottles glittered a plate, obviously of solid gold. By the fireplace a little red-haired man with a knife in his belt was roasting a piece of meat on the end of a long steel blade. The fat dripped into the flames and the smoke curled up the chimney. There was a smell of roasting meat, another powerful scent and the odor of incense, which made the bartender wonder, as he had read of Berlioz' death and knew that this had been his apartment, whether they were performing some kind of requiem for the dead man, but as soon as it came to him he abandoned the idea as clearly ridiculous.

Suddenly the confused bartender heard a deep bass voice: "Well, sir, and what can I do for you?"

Andrei Fokich turned round and saw the man he was looking for.

The black magician was lolling on a vast, low, cushion-strewn divan. As far as the bartender could see, the professor was wearing nothing but black underwear and black slippers with pointed toes.

"I am," said the little man bitterly, "the head bartender at the Variety Theater."

The professor stretched out a hand glittering with precious stones as though to stop the bartender's mouth and interrupted heatedly: "No, no, no! Not another word! Never, on any account! I shall never eat or drink a single mouthful at that buffet of yours! I went past your counter the other day, my dear sir, and I shall never forget the sight of that smoked sturgeon and that cheese! My dear fellow, cheese isn't supposed to be green, you know—someone must have given you the wrong idea. It's meant to be white. And the tea! It's more like rinse water. With my own eyes I saw a slut of a girl pouring gray water into your enormous samovar while you went on serving tea from it. No, my dear fellow, that's not the way to do it!"

"I'm sorry," said Andrei Fokich, appalled by this sudden

attack, "but I came about something else, I don't want to talk about the smoked sturgeon—"

"But I insist on talking about it—it was stale!"

"The sturgeon they sent was second-grade-fresh," said the bartender.

"Really, what nonsense!"

"Why nonsense?"

" 'Second-grade-fresh'—that's what I call nonsense! There's only one degree of freshness—the first—and it's the last. If your sturgeon is 'second-grade-fresh,' that means it's stale."

"I'm sorry," began the bartender, at a loss how to parry this insistent criticism.

"No, it's unforgivable," said the professor.

"I didn't come to see you about that," said the bartender again, now utterly confused.

"Didn't you?" said the magician, astonished. "What did you come for then? As far as I remember, I've never known anybody connected with your profession, except for a vivandière, but that was long before your time. However, I'm delighted to make your acquaintance. Azazello! A stool for the head barman!"

The man who was roasting meat turned around, terrifying the bartender with his walleye, and neatly offered him one of the dark oaken stools. There were no other seats in the room.

The bartender said, "Thank you very much," and sat down on the stool. One of its back legs immediately broke with a crash and the bartender, with a groan, fell painfully backward onto the floor. As he fell he kicked the leg of another stool and upset a full glass of red wine all over his trousers.

The professor exclaimed, "Oh! Clumsy!"

Azazello helped the bartender to get up and gave him another stool. In a miserable voice the bartender declined his host's offer to take off his trousers and dry them in front of the fire. Feeling unbearably awkward in his wet trousers and underwear, he took a cautious seat on the other stool.

"I love a low seat," began the professor. "One's not so likely to fall. Ah, yes, we were talking about sturgeon. First and last, my dear fellow, it must be fresh, fresh, fresh! That should be the motto of every man in your trade. Oh, yes, would you like to taste . . ."

In the red glow of the fire a sword glittered in front of the bartender, and Azazello laid a sizzling piece of meat on a gold plate, sprinkled it with lemon juice and handed the bartender a golden two-pronged fork.

"Thank you, but I—"

"No, do taste it!"

Out of politeness the bartender put a little piece into his mouth and found that he was chewing something really fresh and unusually delicious. As he ate the succulent meat, however, he almost fell off his stool again. A huge dark bird flew in from the next room and softly brushed the top of the bartender's bald head with its wing. As it perched on the mantelpiece beside a clock, he saw that the bird was an owl. "Oh, my God!" thought Andrei Fokich, nervous as all bartenders are, "what a place!"

"Glass of wine? White or red? What sort of wine do you like at this time of day?"

"Thanks but . . . I don't drink."

"You poor fellow! What about a game of dice then? Or do you prefer some other game? Dominoes? Cards?"

"I don't play," replied the bartender, feeling weak and thoroughly muddled.

"How dreadful for you," said the host. "I always think, present company excepted of course, that there's something unpleasant lurking in people who avoid drinking, gambling, table talk, and pretty women. People like that are either sick or secretly hate their fellow men. Of course there may be exceptions. I have had some outright scoundrels sitting at my table before now! Now tell me what I can do for you."

"Yesterday you did some tricks—"

"I did? Tricks?" exclaimed the magician indignantly. "I beg your pardon! What a rude suggestion!"

"I'm sorry," said the bartender in consternation. "I mean . . . black magic . . . at the theater."

"Oh, that! Yes, of course. I'll tell you a secret, my dear fellow. I'm not really a magician at all. I simply wanted to see some Muscovites en masse and the easiest way to do so was in a theater. So my staff—" he nodded toward the cat—"arranged this little act and I just sat on stage and watched the audience. Now, if that doesn't shock you too much, tell me what brings you here in connection with my performance?"

"During your act you made banknotes float down from the ceiling." The bartender lowered his voice and looked around in embarrassment. "Well, all the audience picked them up, and a young man came to my bar and handed me a ten-ruble note, so I gave him eight rubles fifty change. . . . Then another one came—"

"Another young man?"

"No, he was older. Then there was a third and a fourth. . . . I gave them all change. And today when I came to check the till there was nothing in it but a lot of strips of paper. The bar was a hundred and nine rubles short."

"Oh, dear, dear, dear!" exclaimed the professor. "Don't tell me people thought those notes were real? I can't believe they did it on purpose."

The bartender merely stared miserably around him and said nothing.

"They weren't swindlers, were they?" the magician asked in a worried voice. "Surely there aren't any swindlers here in Moscow?"

The bartender replied with such a bitter smile that there could be no doubt about it: there were plenty of swindlers in Moscow.

"That's mean!" said Woland indignantly. "You're a poor man—you are a poor man, aren't you?"

Andrei Fokich hunched his head into his shoulders to show that he was a poor man.

"How much have you managed to save?"

Although the question was put in a sympathetic voice, it was tactless. The bartender squirmed.

"Two hundred and forty-nine thousand rubles in five different savings banks," said a quavering voice from the next room, "and under the floor at home he's got two hundred gold ten-ruble pieces."

Andrei Fokich seemed to sink into his stool.

"Well, of course, that's no great sum of money," said Woland patronizingly. "All the same, you don't need it. When are you going to die?"

Now it was the bartender's turn to be indignant.

"Nobody knows and it's nobody's business," he replied.

"Yes, nobody knows," said the same horrible voice from the next room. "But by Newton's binomial theorem I predict that he will die in nine months' time in February of next year of cancer of the liver, in Ward No. 4 of the First Moscow City Hospital."

The bartender's face turned yellow.

"Nine months . . . " Woland calculated thoughtfully. "Two hundred and forty-nine thousand . . . that works out to twenty-seven thousand a month in round figures—not much, but enough for a man of modest habits . . . then there are the gold coins—"

"The coins will not be cashed," said the same voice, turning Andrei Fokich's heart to ice. "When he dies, the house will be demolished and the coins will be impounded by the State Bank."

"If I were you, I shouldn't bother to go to the hospital," went on the professor. "What's the use of dying in a ward surrounded by a lot of groaning and croaking incurables? Wouldn't it be much better to throw a party with that twenty-seven thousand and take poison and depart for the other world to the sound of violins, surrounded by lovely drunken girls and happy friends?"

The bartender sat motionless. He had aged. Black rings encircled his eyes, his cheeks were sunken, his lower jaw sagged.

"But we're daydreaming," exclaimed the host. "To business! Show me those strips of paper."

Fumbling, Andrei Fokich took a package out of his pocket, untied it and sat petrified—the sheet of newspaper was full of ten-ruble notes.

"My dear chap, you really are sick," said Woland, shrugging his shoulders.

Grinning stupidly, the bartender got up from his stool.

"B-b-but . . . " he stammered, hiccupping, "if they vanish again . . . what then?"

"H'm," said the professor thoughtfully. "In that case come back and see us. Delighted to have met you."

At this Koroviev leaped out of the study, clasped the bartender's hand and shook it violently as he begged Andrei Fokich to give his kindest regards to everybody at the theater. Bewildered, Andrei Fokich stumbled out into the hall.

"Hella, see him out!" shouted Koroviev.

The same naked girl appeared in the hall. The bartender staggered out, just able to squeak "Good-bye," and left the apartment as though he were drunk. Having gone a little way down, he stopped, sat down on a step, took out the package and checked—the money was still there.

Just then a woman with a green bag came out of one of the apartments on that landing. Seeing a man sitting on the step and staring dumbly at a packet of banknotes, she smiled and said wistfully, "What a dump this is . . . drunks on the staircase at this hour of the morning . . . and they've smashed a window on the staircase again!"

After a closer look at Andrei Fokich she added, "Mind the rats don't get all that money of yours. . . . Wouldn't you like to share some of it with me?"

"Leave me alone, for Christ's sake!" said the bartender and promptly hid the money.

The woman laughed. "Oh, go to hell, you old miser! I was only joking." And she went on downstairs.

Andrei Fokich slowly got up, raised his hand to straighten his hat and discovered that it was not on his head. He desperately wanted not to go back, but he missed his hat. After some hesitation he made up his mind, went back and rang the bell.

"What do you want now?" asked Hella.

"I forgot my hat," whispered the bartender, tapping his bald head. Hella turned round, and the little man shut his eyes in horror. When he opened them, Hella was offering him his hat and a sword with a black hilt.

"That's not mine," whispered the bartender, pushing away the sword and quickly putting on his hat.

"Surely you didn't come without a sword?" asked Hella in surprise.

Andrei Fokich muttered something and hurried off downstairs. His head felt uncomfortable and somehow too hot. He took off his hat and gave a squeak of horror—he was holding a velvet beret with a bedraggled cock's feather. The bartender crossed himself. At that moment the beret gave a miaow and changed into a black kitten. It jumped onto Andrei Fokich's head and dug its claws into his bald patch. Letting out a shriek of despair, the wretched man hurled himself downstairs as the kitten jumped off his head and flashed back to No. 50.

Bursting out into the courtyard, the bartender trotted out of the gate and left the diabolical No. 302A forever.

It was not, however, the end of his adventures. Once in the street he stared wildly around as if looking for something. A minute later he was in a druggist's shop on the far side of the road. No sooner had he said, "Tell me, please . . ." than the woman behind the counter screamed, "Look! Your head! It's cut to pieces!"

Within five minutes Andrei's head was bandaged and he had discovered that the two best specialists in diseases of the liver were Dr. Bernadsky and Dr. Kuzmin. Inquiring which was nearer, he was overjoyed to learn that Kuzmin lived literally around the corner in a little white house, and two minutes later he was there.

It was an old-fashioned but very comfortable little house. Afterward the bartender remembered first meeting a little old woman who wanted to take his hat, but since he had no hat the old woman hobbled off, chewing her toothless gums. In her place appeared a middle-aged woman, who immediately announced that new patients could only be registered on the nineteenth of the month and not before. Instinct told Andrei Fokich what to do. Casting a swooning glance toward the three people in the waiting room, he whispered, "I'm dying. . . ."

The woman glanced uncertainly at his bandaged head, hesitated, then said, "Very well," and led the bartender down the hall.

At that moment a door opened to reveal a bright gold pince-nez. The woman in the white coverall said, "Citizens, this patient has priority."

Andrei Fokich had not time to look around before he found himself in Dr. Kuzmin's consulting room. It was a long, well-proportioned room with nothing frightening, solemn or medical about it.

"What is your trouble?" inquired Dr. Kuzmin in a pleasant voice, glancing with some concern at the bandaged head.

"I have just learned from a reliable source," answered the bartender, staring wildly at a framed group photograph, "that I am going to die next February from cancer of the liver. You must do something to stop it."

Dr. Kuzmin sat down and leaned against the tall leather back of his Gothic chair.

"I'm sorry I don't understand you. You mean . . . you saw a doctor? Why is your head bandaged?"

"Him? He's no doctor," replied the bartender, and suddenly his teeth began to chatter. "Don't bother about my head, that's got nothing to do with it. . . . I haven't come about my head. . . . I've got cancer of the liver—you must do something about it!"

"But who told you?"

"You must believe him!" Andrei Fokich begged fervently. "He knows!"

"I simply don't understand," said the doctor, shrugging his shoulders and pushing his chair back from the desk. "How can he know when you're going to die? Especially as he's not a doctor."

"In Ward No. 4," was all the bartender could say.

The doctor stared at his patient, at his head, at his damp trousers, and thought, "This is the last straw—some madman." He asked, "Do you drink?"

"Never touch it," answered the bartender.

In a minute he was undressed and lying on a chilly striped couch with the doctor kneading his stomach. This cheered the bartender considerably. The doctor declared categorically that at the present moment at least there were no signs of cancer, but since . . . since he was worried about it and some charlatan had given him a fright, he had better have some tests done.

The doctor scribbled on some sheets of paper, explaining where Andrei Fokich was to go and what he should take with him. He also gave him a note to a colleague, Dr. Burye, the neuropathologist, saying that his nerves, at any rate, were in a shocking condition.

"How much should I pay you, Doctor?" asked the bartender in a trembling voice, pulling out a fat wallet.

"As much as you like," replied the doctor dryly.

Andrei Fokich pulled out thirty rubles and put them on the table, then furtively, as though his hands were cat's paws, put a cylindrical, clinking, newspaper-wrapped package on top of the ten-ruble notes.

"What's that?" asked Kuzmin, twirling one end of his mustache.

"Don't be squeamish, Doctor," whispered the bartender. "You can have anything you want if you'll stop my cancer."

"Take your gold," said the doctor, feeling proud of himself as he said it. "You'd be putting it to better use if you spent it on having your nerves treated. Produce a specimen of urine for analysis tomorrow, don't drink too much tea and don't eat any salt in your food."

"Can't I even put salt in my soup?" asked the bartender.

"Don't put salt in anything," said Kuzmin firmly.

"Oh, dear," exclaimed the bartender gloomily, as he gazed imploringly at the doctor, picked up his parcel of gold coins and shuffled backward to the door.

The doctor did not have many patients that evening, and as twilight began to set in, the last one was gone. As he was taking off his white coverall, the doctor glanced at the place on the desk where Andrei Fokich had left the three ten-ruble notes and saw that there were no longer any banknotes there, but three old champagne bottle labels instead.

"Well, I'll be damned!" muttered Kuzmin, trailing his coverall across the floor and fingering the pieces of paper. "Apparently he's not only a schizophrenic but a crook as well. But what can he have wanted out of me? Surely not an order for a urine test? Ah! Perhaps he stole my overcoat!" The doctor dashed into the hall, dragging his coverall by one sleeve. "Xenia Nikitishna!" he screamed in the hall. "Will you look and see if my overcoat's in the cupboard?"

It was. But when the doctor returned to his desk, having finally taken off his coverall, he stopped as though rooted to the floor, staring at the desk. Where the labels had been there now sat a black kitten with a pathetically unhappy little face, miaowing over a saucer of milk.

"What is going on here? This is . . ." And Kuzmin felt a chill run up his spine.

Hearing the doctor's plaintive cry, Xenia Nikitishna came running in and immediately calmed him by saying that the kitten had obviously been abandoned there by one of the patients, a thing they were sometimes prone to do.

"I expect they're poor," explained Xenia Nikitishna, "whereas we . . ."

They tried to guess who might have left the animal there. Suspicion fell on an old woman with a gastric ulcer.

"Yes, it must be her," said Xenia Nikitishna. "She'll have thought to herself, 'I'm going to die anyway, but it's hard on the poor little kitty.' "

"Just a moment!" cried Kuzmin. "What about the milk? Did she bring the milk? And the saucer too?"

She must have had a saucer and a bottle of milk in her bag and poured it out here," explained Xenia Nikitishna.

"At any rate remove the kitten and the saucer, please," said Kuzmin and accompanied Xenia Nikitishna to the door.

As he hung up his coverall the doctor heard laughter from the courtyard. He looked around and hurried over to the window. A woman, wearing nothing but a shirt, was running across the courtyard toward the house opposite. The doctor knew her—she was called Marya Alexandrovna. A boy was laughing at her.

"Really, what behavior," said Kuzmin contemptuously.

Just then the sound of a phonograph playing a fox trot came

from his daughter's room, and at the same moment the doctor heard the chirp of a sparrow behind his back. He turned round and saw a large sparrow hopping about on his desk.

"Whoa . . . steady now!" thought the doctor. "It must have flown in when I walked over to the window. I'm quite all right!" said the doctor to himself sharply, feeling that he was all wrong, thanks to this intruding sparrow. As he looked at it closer, the professor at once realized that it was no ordinary sparrow. The revolting bird was resting its weight on its left leg, making faces and waving its other leg in syncopation—in short, it was dancing a fox trot in time to the phonograph, cavorting like a drunk around a lamp post and staring insolently at the doctor.

Kuzmin's hand was on the telephone, and he was just about to ring up his old college friend Burye and ask him what it meant to start seeing sparrows at sixty, especially if they made your head spin at the same time.

Meanwhile the sparrow had perched on his presentation inkstand, fouled it, then flew up, hung in the air and dived with shattering force at a photograph showing the whole class of '94 on graduation day, smashing the glass to smithereens. The bird then wheeled smartly and flew out of the window.

The doctor changed his mind and instead of ringing up Burye dialed the number of the Leech Bureau and asked them to send a leech to his house at once. Replacing the receiver, the doctor turned back to his desk and let out a wail. On the far side of the desk sat a woman in nurse's uniform with a bag marked "Leeches." The sight of her mouth made the doctor groan again—it was a wide, crooked man's mouth with a fang sticking out of it. The nurse's eyes seemed completely dead.

"I'll take the money," said the nurse, "it's no good to you now." She grasped the labels with a birdlike claw and began to melt into the air.

Two hours passed. Dr. Kuzmin was sitting up in bed with leeches dangling from his temples, his ears and his neck. At his feet on the quilt sat the gray-haired Dr. Burye, gazing sympathetically at Kuzmin and comforting him by assuring him that it was all nonsense. Outside it was night.

We do not know what other marvels happened in Moscow that night and we shall not, of course, try to find out—especially as the time is approaching to move into the second half of this true story. Follow me, reader!

BOOK TWO

MARGARITA

Follow me, reader! Who told you that there is no such thing as real, true, eternal love? Cut out his lying tongue!

Follow me, reader, and only me, and I will show you that love!

The master was wrong when he told Ivan with such bitterness, in the hospital that hour before midnight, that she had forgotten him. It was impossible. Of course she had not forgotten him.

First let us reveal the secret that the master refused to tell Ivan. His beloved mistress was called Margarita Nikolayevna. Everything the master said about her to the wretched poet was the strict truth. She was beautiful and clever. It is also true that many women would have given anything to change places with Margarita Nikolayevna. Thirty years old and childless, Margarita was married to a brilliant scientist, whose work was of national importance. Her husband was young, handsome, kind, honest, and he adored his wife. Margarita Nikolayevna and her husband lived alone in the whole of the top floor of a delightful house in a garden on one of the side streets near the Arbat. It was a charming place. You can see for yourself whenever you feel like having a look. Just ask me and I'll tell you the address and how to get there; the house is standing to this day.

Margarita Nikolayevna was never short of money. She could buy whatever she liked. Her husband had plenty of interesting friends. Margarita never had to cook. Margarita knew nothing of the horrors of living in a shared apartment. In short . . . was she happy? Not for a moment. Since the age of nineteen, when she had married and moved into her house, she had never been happy. Good God! What more did the woman need? Why did her eyes always glow with a strange fire? What else did she want, that witch with a very slight squint in one eye, who always decked herself with mimosa every spring? I don't know. Obviously she was right when she said she needed him, the master, instead of a Gothic house, instead of a private garden, instead of money. She was right—she loved him.

Even I, the truthful narrator, yet a mere onlooker, feel a pang when I think what Margarita went through when she came back to the master's basement the next day (fortunately she had not been able to talk to her husband, who failed to come home at the time arranged) and found that the master was not there. She did everything she could to discover where he might be, but in vain. Then she returned home and took up her old life.

But when the dirty snow disappeared from the roads and pavements, as soon as the raw, live wind of spring blew in through the upper casement, Margarita Nikolayevna felt even more wretched than she had in the winter. She often wept in secret, long and bitterly. She had no idea whether her lover was dead or alive. The longer the hopeless days marched on, the oftener, especially at twilight, she began to suspect that her man was dead. She must either forget him or die herself. Her present existence was intolerable. She had to forget him at all costs. But unfortunately he was not a man one could forget.

"Yes, I made exactly the same mistake," said Margarita, sitting by the stove and watching the fire, lit in memory of the fire that used to burn while he was writing Pontius Pilate. "Why did I leave him that night? Why? I must have been mad. I came back the next day just as I had promised, but it was too late. Yes, I came too late like poor Matthew the Levite!"

All this, of course, was nonsense, because what would have been changed if she had stayed with the master that night? Would she have saved him? The idea's absurd . . . but she was a woman and she was desperate.

On the same day that witnessed the ridiculous scandal caused by the black magician's appearance in Moscow, that Friday when Berlioz' uncle was sent packing back to Kiev, when the accountant was arrested and a host of other weird and improbable events took place, Margarita woke up around midday in her bedroom, that looked out of an attic window of their top-floor apartment.

Waking, Margarita did not burst into tears, as she frequently did, because she had waked up with a presentment that today, at last, something was going to happen. She kept the feeling warm and encouraged it, afraid that it might leave her.

"I believe it!" whispered Margarita solemnly. "I believe something is going to happen, must happen, because what have I done to be made to suffer all my life? I admit I've lied and been unfaithful and lived a secret life, but even that doesn't deserve such a cruel punishment. . . . Something will happen, because a situation like this can't drag on forever. Besides, my dream was prophetic, that I'll swear."

With a sense of unease Margarita Nikolayevna dressed and brushed her short curly hair in front of her triple dressing-table mirror.

The dream that Margarita had dreamed that night had been most unusual. Throughout her agony of the past winter she had never dreamed of the master. At night he left her, and it was only during the day that the memory of him tormented her. And now she had dreamed of him.

(Margarita had dreamed of a place, mournful, desolate under a dull sky of early spring. The sky was laden, with tufts of low, scudding gray cloud and filled with a numberless flock of rooks. There was a little humpbacked bridge over a muddy, swollen stream; joyless, beggarly, half-naked trees. A lone aspen and in the distance, beyond a vegetable garden, stood a log cabin that looked like a kind of outhouse. The surroundings looked so lifeless and miserable that one might easily have been tempted to hang oneself on that aspen by the little bridge. Not a breath of wind, not a cloud, not a living soul. In short—hell. Suddenly the door of this hut was flung open, and he appeared in it, at a fair distance but clearly visible. He was dressed in some vague, slightly tattered garment, his hair in untidy tufts, unshaven. His eyes looked anxious and sick. He waved and called. Panting in the lifeless air, Margarita started running toward him over the uneven, tussocky ground. At that moment she woke up.)

"That dream can only mean one of two things," Margarita Nikolayevna reasoned with herself. "If he is dead and beckoned me, that means that he came for me and I shall die soon. If so, I'm glad; that means that my agony will soon be over. Or if he's alive, the dream can only mean that he is reminding me of himself. He wants to tell me that we shall meet again . . . yes, we shall meet again—soon."

Still in a state of excitement, Margarita dressed, telling herself that everything was working out very well, that one should know how to seize such moments and make use of them. Her husband had gone away on business for three whole days. She would be left to herself for three days, and no one was going to stop her thinking or dreaming or whatever she wished. All five rooms on the top floor of the house, an apartment so big that tens of thousands of people in Moscow would have envied her, was entirely at her disposal.

Yet free as she was for three days in such luxurious quarters, Margarita chose the oddest part of it in which to spend her time. After a cup of tea she went into the dark, windowless attic where they kept trunks, lumber and two large chests of drawers full of old junk. Squatting down, she opened the bottom drawer of the first chest, and from beneath a pile of odds and ends of material she drew out the one thing that she valued most in the world. It was an old album bound in brown leather, which contained a photograph of the master, a savings bank book with a deposit of ten thousand rubles in his name, a few dried rose petals pressed between some pieces of cigarette paper and several sheets of typescript with singed edges.

Returning to her bedroom with this treasure, Margarita Nikolayevna propped up the photograph against her dressing-table mirror and sat for about an hour, the burnt typescript on her knees, turning the pages and rereading what the fire had not destroyed:

The mist that came from the Mediterranean Sea blotted out the city that Pilate so detested. The suspension bridges connecting the temple with the grim fortress of Antonia vanished, the murk descended from the sky and drowned the winged gods above the hippodrome, the crenelated Hasmonaean palace, the bazaars, the caravanserais, the alleyways, the pools. . . . Jerusalem, the great city, vanished as though it had never been. . . .

Margarita wanted to read on, but there was nothing more except the charred, uneven edge.

Wiping away her tears, Margarita Nikolayevna put down the script, leaned her elbows on the dressing table and sat for a long time in front of her reflection in the mirror staring at the photograph. After a while she stopped crying. Margarita carefully folded away her hoard, a few minutes later it was buried again under the scraps of silk and the lock shut with a click in the dark room.

Margarita put on her overcoat in the hall to go out for a walk. Her pretty maid Natasha inquired what she was to do tomorrow and, being told that she could do what she liked, she started talking to her mistress to pass the time and said something vague about a magician who had done such fantastic tricks at the theater yesterday that everybody had gasped, that he had handed out two bottles of French perfume and two pairs of stockings to everybody for nothing, and then, when the show was over and the audience was coming out—bang!—they were all naked! Margarita Nikolayevna collapsed onto the hall chair and burst out laughing.

"Natasha, really! Aren't you ashamed of yourself?" said Margarita. "You're a sensible, educated girl, and yet you repeat every bit of rubbishy gossip that you pick up in waiting lines!"

Natasha blushed and objected hotly, saying that she never listened to waiting-line gossip and that she had actually seen a woman that morning come into a delicatessen on the Arbat wearing some new shoes and while she was standing at the cash desk to pay, her shoes had vanished and she was left standing in her stockinged feet. She looked horrified, because she had a hole in the heel of one stocking! The shoes were the magic ones that she had got at the show.

"And she walked out barefoot?"

"Yes, she did!" cried Natasha, turning even pinker because no one would believe her. "And yesterday evening, Margarita Nikolayevna, the police arrested a hundred people. Some of the women who'd been at the show were running along Tverskaya Street in nothing but a pair of panties."

"That sounds to me like one of your friend Darya's stories," said Margarita Nikolayevna. "I've always thought she was a frightful liar."

This hilarious conversation ended with a pleasant surprise for Natasha. Margarita Nikolayevna went into her bedroom and came out with a pair of stockings and a bottle of eau de cologne. Telling Natasha that she wanted to do a magic trick too, Margarita gave her the stockings and the scent; she told her that she could have them on one condition—that she promised not to run along Tverskaya Street in nothing but stockings and not to listen to Darya's gossip. With a kiss mistress and maid parted.

Leaning back in her comfortable upholstered seat in the trolley-bus, Margarita Nikolayevna rolled along the Arbat, thinking of her own affairs and half-listening to what two men on the seat in front were whispering. Glancing around occasionally for fear of being overheard, they seemed to be talking complete nonsense. One, a plump, hearty man with sharp piglike eyes, who was sitting by the window, was quietly telling his smaller neighbor how they had been forced to cover the open coffin with a black cloth. . . .

"Incredible!" whispered the short one in amazement. "It's unheard of! So what did Zheldybin do?"

Above the steady hum of the trolley-bus came the reply from the window seat: "Police . . . scandal . . . absolute mystery!"

Somehow Margarita Nikolayevna managed to construct a fairly coherent story from these snatches of talk. The men were whispering that someone had stolen the head of a corpse (they did not mention the dead man's name) from a coffin that morning. This, apparently, was the cause of Zheldybin's anxiety, and the two men whispering in the trolley-bus also appeared to have some connection with the victim of this ghoulish theft.

"Shall we have time to buy flowers?" inquired the smaller man anxiously. "You said the cremation was at two o'clock, didn't you?"

In the end Margarita Nikolayevna grew bored with their mysterious whispering about the stolen head, and she was glad when it was time for her to get out.

A few minutes later she was sitting under the Kremlin wall on one of the benches in the Alexander Gardens facing the Manège. Margarita squinted in the bright sunlight, recalling her dream, and she remembered that exactly a year ago to the hour she had sat on this same bench beside him. Just as it had then, her black handbag lay on the bench at her side. Although the master was not there this time, Margarita Nikolayevna carried on a mental conversation with him: "If you've been sent into exile, why haven't you at least written to tell me? Don't you love me any more? No, somehow I don't believe that. In that case you have died in exile. . . . If you have, please release me, let me go free to lead my life like other people!" Margarita answered for him: "You're free. . . . I'm not keeping you by force." Then she replied: "What sort of an answer is that? I won't be free until I stop thinking of you."

People were walking past. One man threw a sideways glance at this well-dressed woman. Attracted by the sight of a pretty girl alone, he coughed and sat down on the other half of Margarita Nikolayevna's bench. Plucking up his courage he said, "What lovely weather it is today. . . ."

Margarita turned and gave him such a grim look that he got up and went away.

"That's what I mean," said Margarita silently to her lover. "Why did I chase that man away? I'm bored, there was nothing wrong with that Casanova, except perhaps for his highly unoriginal remark. . . . Why do I sit here alone like an owl? Why am I cut off from life?"

She had worked herself into a state of complete depression, when suddenly the same wave of urgent expectancy that she had felt that morning came over her. "Yes, something's going to happen!" The wave struck her again, and she then realized that it was a wave of sound. Above the noise of the traffic there rose clearly the sound of approaching drumbeats and the braying of off-key trumpets.

First to pass the park railing was a mounted policeman, followed by three more on foot. Next came the band on a truck, then a slow-moving open hearse carrying a coffin banked with wreaths and a guard of honor of four people—three men and a woman. Even from a distance Margarita could see that the members of the honor guard looked curiously distraught. This was particularly noticeable in the woman, who was walking at the left-hand rear corner of the hearse. Her fat cheeks seemed to be more than normally puffed out by some secret joke and her protuberant little eyes shone with a curiously ambiguous sparkle. It was as if the woman were liable at any moment to wink at the corpse and say, "Did you ever see such a thing? Stealing a dead man's head . . . !" The three hundred-odd mourners, who were slowly following the cortege on foot, looked equally mystified.

Margarita watched the cortege go by, listening to the mournful beat of the kettle drum as its monotonous "boom, boom, boom" slowly faded away, and she thought: "What a strange funeral . . . and how sad that drum sounds! I'd sell my soul to the devil to know whether he's alive or not. . . . I wonder who that odd-looking crowd is going to bury?"

"Mikhail Alexandrovich Berlioz," said a slightly nasal man's voice beside her, "the late chairman of MASSOLIT."

Margarita Nikolayevna turned in astonishment and saw a man on her bench who must have sat down noiselessly while she was watching the funeral procession. Presumably she had absentmindedly spoken her last question aloud. Meanwhile the procession had stopped, apparently held up by traffic lights.

"Yes," the stranger went on, "it's an odd sort of funeral. They're carrying the man off to the cemetery in the usual way, but all they can think about is—what's happened to his head?"

"Whose head?" asked Margarita, glancing at her unexpected neighbor. He was short, with fiery red hair and one protruding fang, and wore a starched shirt, a good striped suit, patent-leather shoes and a bowler hat. His tie was bright. One strange feature was his breast pocket: instead of the usual handkerchief or fountain pen, it contained a gnawed chicken bone.

"This morning," explained the red-haired man, "the head was pulled off the dead man's body during the lying-in-state at Griboyedov."

"How ever could that have happened?" asked Margarita, suddenly remembering the two whispering men in the trolley-bus.

"The devil knows how," said the man vaguely. "I suspect Behemoth might be able to tell you. It must have been a neat job, but why bother to steal a head? After all who on earth would want it?"

Preoccupied though she was, Margarita Nikolayevna could not help being intrigued by this stranger's extraordinary conversation.

"Just a minute!" she suddenly exclaimed. "Who is Berlioz? Is he the one in the newspapers today who . . ."

"Yes, yes."

"So those are writers in the guard of honor around the coffin?" inquired Margarita.

"Yes, of course."

"Do you know them by sight?"

"Every one," the man replied.

"Tell me," said Margarita, her voice dropping, "is one of them a critic by the name of Latunsky?"

"How could he fail to be there?" answered the man with red hair. "That's him, on the far side, fourth in line."

"The one with fair hair?" asked Margarita, frowning.

"Ash-blond. Look, he's staring up at the sky."

"Looking rather like a Catholic priest?"

"That's him!"

Margarita asked no more questions but stared hard at Latunsky.

"You, I see," said the stranger with a smile, "hate that man Latunsky."

"Yes, and someone else too," said Margarita between clenched teeth, "but I'd rather not talk about it."

Meanwhile the procession had moved on again, the mourners being followed by a number of mostly empty cars.

"Then we won't discuss it, Margarita Nikolayevna!"

Astounded, Margarita said, "Do you know me?"

Instead of replying, the man took off his bowler hat and held it in his outstretched hand.

"A face like a crook," thought Margarita, as she stared at him. "But I don't know you," she said frigidly.

"Why should you? However, I have been sent on a little matter that concerns you."

Margarita paled and edged away. "Why didn't you say so at once," she said, "instead of making up that fairy tale about a stolen head? Have you come to arrest me?"

"Nothing of the sort!" exclaimed the man with red hair. "Why does one only have to speak to a person for them to imagine they're going to be arrested? I simply have a little matter to discuss with you."

"I don't understand—what matter?"

The stranger glanced round and said mysteriously, "I have been sent to give you an invitation for this evening."

"What are you talking about? An invitation to what?"

"You are invited by a very distinguished foreign gentleman," said the red-haired man portentously, with a frown.

Margarita blazed with anger. "I see that pimps work in the streets now!" she said as she got up to go.

"Is that all the thanks I get?" exclaimed the man, offended. And he growled at Margarita's retreating back, "Stupid bitch!"

"Swine!" she flung back at him over her shoulder. Immediately she heard the stranger's voice behind her:

" 'The mist that came from the Mediterranean Sea blotted out the city that Pilate so detested. The suspension bridges connecting the temple with the grim fortress of Antonia vanished, the murk descended from the sky and drowned the winged gods above the hippodrome, the crenelated Hasmonaean palace, the bazaars, the caravanserais, the alleyways, the pools. . . . Jerusalem, the great city, vanished as though it had never been. . . .' So much for your charred manuscript and your dried rose petals! Yet you sit here alone on a bench and beg him to let you go, to allow you to be free and to forget him!"

White in the face, Margarita turned back to the bench. The man sat frowning up at her.

"I don't understand it," said Margarita Nikolayevna in a hushed voice. "You might have found out about the manuscript—you might have broken in, stolen it, looked at it—I suppose you bribed Natasha—but how could you know what I was thinking?" She wrinkled her brow painfully and added, "Tell me, who are you? What organization do you belong to?"

"Oh, lord, not that," muttered the stranger in exasperation. In a louder voice he said, "I'm sorry. As I said, I have not come to arrest you and I don't belong to any 'organization.' Please sit down."

Margarita obediently did as she was told, but once seated could not help asking again, "Who are you?"

"Well, if you must know, my name is Azazello, although it won't mean anything to you."

"And won't you tell me how you knew about the manuscript and how you read my thoughts?"

"I will not," said Azazello curtly.

"Do you know anything about him?" whispered Margarita imploringly.

"Well, let's say I do."

"Tell me, I beg of you, just one thing—is he alive? Don't torture me!"

"Yes, he's alive all right," said Azazello reluctantly.

"Oh, God!"

"No scenes, please," said Azazello with a frown.

"I'm sorry, I'm sorry," said Margarita humbly. "I'm sorry I lost my temper with you. But you must admit that if someone comes up to a woman in the street and invites her . . . I have no prejudices, understand." Margarita laughed mirthlessly. "But I never go with foreigners and I have never wanted to . . . besides that, my husband . . . my tragedy is that I live with a man I don't love, but I can't bring myself to ruin his life . . . he has never shown me anything but kindness."

Azazello listened to this incoherent confession and said severely, "Please be quiet for a moment."

Margarita obediently stopped talking.

"My invitation to this foreigner is quite harmless. And not a soul will know about it. That I swear."

"And what does he want me for?" asked Margarita insinuatingly.

"You will discover that later."

"I see now. . . . I am to go to bed with him," said Margarita thoughtfully.

To this Azazello snorted and replied, "Any woman in the world, I can assure you, would give anything to do so"— his face twisted with a laugh—"but I must disappoint you. He doesn't want you for that."

"Who is this foreigner?" exclaimed Margarita in perplexity, so loudly that several passers-by turned to look at her. "And why should I want to go and see him?"

Azazello leaned toward her and whispered meaningfully, "For the best possible reason: you can use the opportunity . . ."

"What?" cried Margarita, her eyes growing round. "If I've understood you correctly, you're hinting that I may hear some news of him there?"

Azazello nodded silently.

"I'll go!" Margarita burst out and seized Azazello by the arm. "I'll go wherever you like!"

With a sigh of relief Azazello leaned against the back of the bench, covering up the name "Manya" carved deep into its wood and said ironically, "Difficult people, these women!" He stuck his hands into his pocket and stretched his feet out far in front of him. "Why did he have to send me on this job? Behemoth should have done it, he's got such charm."

With a bitter smile Margarita said, "Stop mystifying me and talking in riddles. I'm happy and you're taking advantage of it. . . . I may be about to let myself in for some dubious adventure, but I swear it's only because you have enticed me by talking about him! All this mystery is making my head spin."

"Please don't make a drama out of it," replied Azazello with a grimace, "Think of what it's like being in my position. Punch a man on the nose, kick an old man downstairs, shoot somebody or any old thing like that, that's my job. But argue with women in love—no thank you! Look, I've been at it with you for half an hour now. Are you going or not?"

"I'll go," replied Margarita Nikolayevna simply.

"In that case allow me to present you with this," said Azazello, taking a little round gold box out of his pocket and saying as he handed it to Margarita, "Hide it, or people will see it. It will do you good, Margarita Nikolayevna; unhappiness has aged you a lot in the last six months." Margarita bridled but said nothing, and Azazello went on: "This evening, at exactly half-past eight, you will kindly strip naked and rub this ointment all over your face and your body. After that you can do what you like, but don't go far from the telephone. At nine I shall ring you up and tell you what you have to do. You won't have to worry about anything, you'll be taken to where you're going and nothing will be done to upset you. Understood?"

Margarita said nothing for a moment, then replied, "I understand. This thing is solid gold, I can tell by its weight. I quite see that I am being seduced into something shady which I shall bitterly regret."

"What's that?" Azazello almost hissed. "You're not having second thoughts, are you?"

"No, no, wait!"

"Give me back the cream!"

Margarita gripped the box tighter and went on, "No, please wait. . . . I know what I'm letting myself in for. I'm ready to go anywhere and do anything for his sake, only because I have no more hope left. But if you are planning to ruin me or destroy me, you will regret it. Because if I die for his sake I shall have died out of love."

"Give it back!" shouted Azazello in fury. "Give it back and to hell with the whole business. They can send Behemoth!"

"Oh, no!" cried Margarita to the astonishment of the passersby. "I agree to everything, I'll go through the whole routine of smearing on the ointment, I'll go to the ends of the earth! I won't give it back!"

"Bah!" Azazello suddenly roared and, staring at the park railings, pointed at something with his finger.

Margarita turned in the direction he was pointing, but saw nothing special. Then she turned to Azazello for some explanation of his absurd cry of "Bah!" but there was no one to explain: Margarita Nikolayevna's mysterious companion had vanished.

Margarita felt in her handbag and made sure that the gold box was still where she had put it. Then without stopping to reflect she hurried away from the Alexander Gardens.

CHAPTER 20

AZAZELLO'S CREAM

Through the branches of the maple tree a full moon hung in the clear evening sky. The limes and acacias traced a complex pattern of shadows on the grass. A triple casement window in the attic, open but with the blind drawn, shone with a glare of electric light. Every bulb was burning in Margarita Nikolayevna's bedroom and lighting up the chaotically untidy chamber.

On the bedspread lay blouses, stockings and underwear, more crumpled underwear was piled on the floor beside a pack of cigarettes that had been squashed in excitement. A pair of slippers was on the bedside table alongside a cold, unfinished cup of coffee and an ashtray with a smoldering cigarette butt. A black silk dress hung across the chair back. The room smelled of perfume, and from somewhere there came the reek of a hot iron.

Margarita Nikolayevna was sitting in front of a full-length mirror in nothing but black velvet slippers and a bath wrap thrown over her naked body. Her gold wristwatch lay in front of her alongside the little box given her by Azazello, and Margarita was staring at the watch face.

At times she felt that the watch had broken and the hands were not moving. They were moving, but so slowly that they seemed to have stuck. At last the minute hand pointed to twenty-nine minutes past eight. Margarita's heart was thumping so violently that at first she could hardly pick up the box. With an effort she opened it and saw that it contained a greasy yellowish cream. It seemed to smell of swamp mud. With the tip of her finger Margarita put a little blob of the cream on her palm, which produced an even stronger smell of marsh and forest, and then she began to massage the cream into her forehead and cheeks.

The ointment rubbed in easily and produced an immediate tingling effect. After several rubs Margarita looked into the mirror and dropped the box right onto the watch crystal, which shattered into a web of fine cracks. Margarita shut her eyes, then looked again and burst into hoots of laughter.

Her eyebrows, that she had so carefully plucked into a fine line, had thickened into two even arcs above her eyes, which had taken on a deeper green color. The fine vertical furrow between her eyebrows, which had first appeared in October when the master disappeared, had vanished without a trace. Gone, too, were the yellowish shadows at her temples and two barely detectable sets of crow's feet at the corners of her eyes. The skin of her cheeks was evenly suffused with pink, her brow had become white and smooth, and the frizzy, artificial wave in her hair had straightened out.

A dark, naturally curly-haired woman of twenty, teeth bared and laughing uncontrollably, was looking out of the mirror at the thirty-year-old Margarita.

Laughing, Margarita jumped out of her bath wrap with one leap, scooped up two large handfuls of the slightly fatty cream and began rubbing it vigorously all over her body. She immediately glowed and turned a healthy pink. In a moment the headache which had pained her all day since the encounter in the Alexander Gardens was gone. The muscles of her arms and legs grew firmer, and she even lost weight.

She gave a little jump and remained suspended in the air just above the carpet, then slowly and gently dropped back to the floor.

"Hurray for the cream!" cried Margarita, throwing herself into an armchair.

The anointing had not only changed her appearance. Joy surged through every part of her body, she felt as though bubbles were shooting along every limb. Margarita felt free, free of everything, realizing with absolute clarity that what was happening was the fulfillment of her presentiment of that morning, that she was going to leave her house and her past life forever. But one thought from her past life hammered persistently in her mind, and she knew that she had one last duty to perform before she took off into the unknown, into the air. Naked as she was, she ran out of the bedroom, flying through the air, and into her husband's study, where she turned on the light and flew to his desk. She tore a sheet off his note pad, and in one sweep, erasing nothing and changing nothing, she quickly and firmly penciled this message.

> Forgive me and forget me as quickly as you can. I am leaving you forever. Don't look for me, it will be useless. Misery and unhappiness have turned me into a witch. It is time for me to go. Farewell. Margarita.

With a sense of absolute relief Margarita flew back into the bedroom. Just then Natasha came in, loaded with clothes and shoes. At once the whole pile, dresses on coat hangers, lace blouses, blue silk shoes on shoe trees, belts, all fell to the floor, and Natasha clasped her hands.

"Pretty, aren't I?" cried Margarita Nikolayevna in a loud, slightly husky voice.

"What's happened?" whispered Natasha, staggering back. "What have you done, Margarita Nikolayevna?"

"It's the cream! The cream!" replied Margarita, pointing to the gleaming gold box and whirling in front of the mirror.

Forgetting the heap of crumpled clothes on the floor, Natasha ran to the dressing table and stared, eyes hot with longing, at the remains of the ointment. Her lips whispered a few words in silence. She turned to Margarita and said with something like awe, "Oh, your skin—look at your skin, Margarita Nikolayevna, it's shining!" Then she suddenly remembered herself, picked up the dress she had dropped and started to smooth it out.

"Leave it, Natasha! Drop it!" Margarita shouted at her. "To hell with it! Throw it all away! No—wait—you can have it. As a present from me. You can have everything in the room!"

Dumfounded, Natasha gazed at Margarita for a moment, then clasped her round the neck, kissing her and shouting, "You're like satin! Shiny satin! And look at your eyebrows!"

"Take all these rags, take all my scent and put it all in your bottom drawer, you can keep it," shouted Margarita, "but don't take the jewelry or they'll say you stole it."

Natasha rummaged in the heap for whatever she could find —stockings, shoes, dresses, underwear—and ran out of the bedroom.

At that moment from an open window on the other side of the street came the loud strains of a waltz, then the spluttering of a car engine as it drew up to the gate.

"Azazello will ring soon!" cried Margarita, listening to the sound of the waltz. "He's going to ring! And this foreigner is harmless, I realize now that he can never harm me!"

The car's engine roared as it sped away. The gate slammed and footsteps could be heard on the flagstone path.

"It's Nikolai Ivanovich, I recognize his tread," thought Margarita. "I must do something amusing as a way of saying good-bye to him!"

Margarita flung open the shutters and sat sideways on the window sill, clasping her knees with her hands. The moonlight caressed her right side. Margarita raised her head toward the moon and assumed a reflective and poetic expression. Two more footsteps were heard and then they suddenly stopped. With another admiring glance at the moon and a sigh for fun, Margarita turned to look down into the garden, where she saw her neighbor of the floor below, Nikolai Ivanovich. He was clearly visible in the moonlight, seated on a bench on which he had obviously just sat down with a bump. His pince-nez was lopsided, and he was clutching his briefcase in his arms.

"Hello, Nikolai Ivanovich!" said Margarita Nikolayevna in a sad voice. "Good evening! Have you just come from the office?"

Nikolai Ivanovich said nothing.

"And here am I," Margarita went on, leaning farther out into the garden, "sitting all alone, as you can see, bored, looking at the moon and listening to a waltz."

Margarita Nikolayevna ran her left hand along her temple, arranging a lock of hair, then said crossly, "It's very impolite of you, Nikolai Ivanovich! I am a woman, after all! It's rude not to answer when someone speaks to you."

Nikolai Ivanovich, visible in the bright moonlight down to the last button on his gray waistcoat and the last hair on his little pointed beard, suddenly gave an idiotic grin and got up from his bench. Obviously half-crazed with embarrassment, instead of taking off his hat he waved his briefcase and flexed his knees as though just about to break into a Russian dance.

"Oh, how you bore me, Nikolai Ivanovich!" Margarita went on. "You all bore me inexpressibly, and I can't tell you how happy I am to be leaving you! You can all go to hell!"

Just then the telephone rang in Margarita's bedroom. She slipped off the window sill and, forgetting Nikolai Ivanovich completely, she snatched up the receiver.

"Azazello speaking," said a voice.

"Dear, dear Azazello," cried Margarita.

"It's time for you to fly away," said Azazello, and she could tell from his tone that he was pleased by Margarita's sincere outburst of affection. "As you fly over the gate, shout, 'I'm invisible'—then fly about over the town a bit to get used to it and then turn south, away from Moscow straight along the river. They're waiting for you!"

Margarita hung up, and at once something wooden in the next room started bumping about and tapping on the door. Margarita flung it open, and a broom, bristles up, danced into the bedroom. Its handle beat a tattoo on the floor, tipped itself up horizontally and pointed toward the window. Margarita whimpered with joy and jumped astride the broomstick. Only then did she remember that in the excitement she had forgotten to get dressed. She galloped over to the bed and picked up the first thing at hand, which was a blue slip. Waving it like a banner, she flew out of the window. The waltz rose to a crescendo.

Margarita dived down from the window and saw Nikolai Ivanovich sitting on the bench. He seemed to be frozen to it, listening stunned to the shouts and bangs that had been coming from the top-floor bedroom.

"Good-bye, Nikolai Ivanovich!" cried Margarita, swooping about in front of him.

The wretched man groaned, fidgeted and dropped his briefcase.

"Farewell forever, Nikolai Ivanovich! I'm flying away!" shouted Margarita, drowning the music of the waltz. Realizing that her slip was useless, she gave a malicious laugh and threw it over Nikolai Ivanovich's head. Blinded, Nikolai Ivanovich fell off the bench onto the flagstone path with a thud.

Margarita turned round for a last look at the house where she had spent so many years of unhappiness and saw the astonished face of Natasha in the lighted window.

"Good-bye, Natasha!" Margarita shouted, waving her

broom. "I'm invisible! Invisible!" she shouted at the top of her voice as she flew off, the maple branches whipping her face, over the gate and out into the street. Behind her flew the strains of the waltz, rising to a mad climax.

CHAPTER **21**

THE FLIGHT

Invisible and free! Reaching the end of her street, Margarita turned sharp right and flew on down a long, crooked street with its plane trees and its patched roadway, its oil shop with a warped door where they sold kerosene by the jugful and the bottled juice of parasites. Here Margarita discovered that although she was invisible, free as air and thoroughly enjoying herself, she still had to take care. Stopping herself by a miracle, she just avoided a lethal collision with an old, crooked lamp post. As she swerved away from it, Maragarita gripped her broomstick harder and flew on more slowly, watching out for the passing signboards and electric cables.

The next street led straight to the Arbat. By now she had thoroughly mastered the business of steering her broom, having found that it answered to the slightest touch of her hands or legs and that when flying around the town she had to be very careful to avoid collisions. It was now quite obvious that the people in the street could not see her. Nobody turned their head, nobody shouted "Look, look!" nobody stepped aside, nobody screamed, fell into a faint or burst into laughter.

Margarita flew silently and very slowly at about second-story height. Slow as her progress was, however, she made slightly too wide a sweep as she flew into the blindingly lit Arbat and struck her shoulder against an illuminated glass traffic sign.

This annoyed her. She stopped the obedient broomstick; flew back, aimed for the sign and with a sudden flick of the end of her broom, smashed it to fragments. The pieces crashed to the ground, passers-by jumped aside, a whistle blew and Margarita burst into laughter at her little act of wanton destruction.

"I shall have to be even more careful on the Arbat," she thought to herself. "There are so many obstructions, it's like a maze." She began weaving among the cables. Beneath her flowed the roofs of streetcars, buses and cars, and rivers of hats surged along the pavements. Little streams diverged from these rivers and trickled into the lighted caves of all-night stores.

"What a maze!" thought Margarita. "There's no room to maneuver here!"

She crossed the Arbat, climbed to fourth-floor height, past the brilliant neon tubes of a corner theater and turned into a narrow side street flanked with tall houses. All their windows were open and radio music poured out from all sides. Out of curiosity Margarita glanced into one of them. She saw a kitchen. Two alcohol burners were roaring away on a marble ledge, attended by two women standing with spoons in their hands and swearing at each other.

"You should put the light out when you come out of the lavatory, I've told you before, Pelagea Petrovna," said the woman with a saucepan of some steaming decoction, "otherwise we'll have you chucked out of here."

"You should talk!" replied the other.

"You're each as bad as the other," said Margarita clearly, leaning over the window sill into the kitchen.

The two quarreling women stopped at the sound of her voice and stood petrified, clutching their dirty spoons. Margarita carefully stretched out her arm between them and turned off both burners. The women gasped. But Margarita was already bored with this prank and had flown out again into the street.

Her attention was caught by a massive and obviously newly built eight-story block of apartments at the far end of the street. Margarita flew toward it, and as she landed she saw that the building was faced with black marble, that its doors were wide, that a porter in gold-laced peaked cap and buttons stood in the hall. Over the doorway was a gold inscription reading "Dramlit House."

Margarita frowned at the inscription, wondering what the

word "Dramlit" meant. Tucking her broomstick under her arm, Margarita pushed open the front door, to the amazement of the porter, walked in and saw a huge black bulletin board that listed the names and apartment numbers of all the residents. The inscription over the board, reading "Drama and Literature House," made Margarita have a suppressed yelp of predatory anticipation. Rising a little in the air, she began eagerly to read the names: Khustov, Dvubratsky, Quant, Beskudnikov, Latunsky . . .

"Latunsky!" yelped Margarita. "Latunsky! He's the man who ruined the master!"

The porter jumped up in astonishment and stared at the name board, wondering why it had suddenly given a shriek.

Margarita was already flying upstairs, excitedly repeating, "Latunsky, eighty-four . . . Latunsky, eighty-four . . . Here we are, left—eighty-two, right—eighty-three, another floor up, left—eighty-four! Here it is and there's his name—'O. Latunsky.' "

Margarita jumped off her broomstick, and the cold stone floor of the landing felt pleasantly cool to her hot bare feet. She rang once, twice. No answer. Margarita pressed the button harder and heard the bell ringing deep inside Latunsky's flat. Latunsky should have been grateful to his dying day that the chairman of MASSOLIT had fallen under a streetcar and that the memorial gathering was being held that very evening. Latunsky must have been born under a lucky star, because the coincidence saved him from an encounter with Margarita, newly turned witch that Friday.

No one came to open the door. At full speed Margarita flew down, counting the floors as she went, reached the bottom, flew out into the street and looked up. She counted the floors and tried to guess which of the windows belonged to Latunsky's apartment. Without a doubt they were the five unlighted windows on the eighth floor at the corner of the building. Feeling sure that she was right, Margarita flew up and a few seconds later found her way through an open window into a dark room lit only by a silver patch of moonlight. Margarita walked across and fumbled for the switch. Soon all the lights in the apartment were burning. Parking her broom in a corner and making sure that nobody was at home, Margarita opened the front door and looked at the name plate. This was it.

People say that Latunsky still turns pale when he remembers that evening and that he always pronounces Berlioz' name with gratitude. If he had been at home, God knows what violence might have been done that night.

Margarita went into the kitchen and came out with a massive hammer.

Naked and invisible, unable to restrain herself, her hands shook with impatience. Margarita took careful aim and hit the keys of the grand piano, sending a crashing discord echoing through the apartment. The innocent piano, a Bäcker baby grand, howled in protest. The keys broke and their ivory tops splintered in all directions. The instrument moaned, screeched and sobbed. With the sound of a revolver shot, the polished sounding board split under a hammer blow. Breathing hard, Margarita smashed and battered the strings until she collapsed into an armchair to rest.

An ominous sound of water came from the kitchen and the bathroom. "It must be overflowing by now," thought Margarita and added aloud, "But there's no time to sit and gloat."

A flood was already pouring from the kitchen into the passage. Wading barefoot, Margarita carried water by the gallon into the critic's study and emptied them into the drawers of his desk. Then having smashed the glass-fronted bookcase with a few hammer blows, she ran into the bedroom. There she shattered the mirror in the wardrobe door, pulled out all Latunsky's suits and flung them into the bathtub. She found a large bottle of ink in the study and poured its contents all over the huge, luxurious double bed.

Although this destruction was giving her the deepest pleasure, she somehow felt that its total effect was inadequate and too easily repaired. She grew wilder and more indiscriminate. In the room with the piano, she smashed the flower vases and the pots holding rubber plants. With savage delight she rushed into the bedroom with a cook's knife, slashed all the sheets and broke the glass in the photograph frames. Far from feeling tired, she wielded her weapon with such ferocity that the sweat poured in streams down her naked body.

Meanwhile in No. 82, immediately beneath Latunsky's apartment, Quant's maid was drinking a cup of tea in the kitchen and wondering vaguely why there was so much noise and running about upstairs. Looking up at the ceiling, she suddenly saw it change color from white to a deathly gray-blue. The patch spread visibly and it began to spout drops of water. The maid sat there for a few minutes, bewildered at this phenomenon, until a regular shower began raining down from the ceiling and pattering on the floor. She jumped up and put a bowl under the stream, but it was useless as the shower was spreading and was already pouring over the gas stove and the dresser. With a shriek Quant's maid ran out of the flat onto the staircase and started ringing Latunsky's front-door bell.

"Ah, somebody's ringing . . . time to go," said Margarita. She mounted the broom, listening to a woman's voice shouting through the keyhole.

"Open up, open up! Open the door, Dusya! Your water's overflowing! We're being flooded!"

Margarita flew up a few feet and took a swing at the chandelier. Two bulbs broke and glass fragments flew everywhere. The shouts at the keyhole had stopped and there was a tramp of boots on the staircase. Margarita floated out of the window, where she turned and hit the glass a gentle blow with her hammer. It shattered and cascaded in a shower down the marble façade onto the street below. Margarita flew on to the next window. Far below people were running about on the pavement, and one of the cars standing outside the entrance started up and drove away.

Having dealt with all Latunsky's windows, Margarita floated on toward the next flat. The blows became more frequent, the street resounded with bangs and tinkles. The porter ran out of the front door, looked up, hesitated for a moment in amazement, popped a whistle into his mouth and blew like a maniac. The noise inspired Margarita to even more violent action on the eighth-floor windows and then to drop down a story and to start work on the seventh.

Bored by his idle job of hanging around the entrance hall, the porter put all his pent-up energy into blowing his whistle, playing a woodwind obbligato in time to Margarita's enthusiastic percussion. In the intervals as she moved from window to window, he drew breath and then blew an ear-splitting blast from distended cheeks at each stroke of Margarita's hammer. Their combined efforts produced the most impressive results. Panic broke out in Dramlit House. The remaining unbroken windowpanes were flung open, heads were popped out and instantly withdrawn, while open windows were hastily shut. At the lighted windows of the building opposite appeared figures, straining forward to try and see why for no reason all the windows of Dramlit House were spontaneously exploding.

All along the street people began running toward Dramlit

House, and inside it others were dashing senselessly up and down the staircase. The Quants' maid shouted to them that they were being flooded out, and she was soon joined by the Khustovs' maid from No. 80, which lay underneath the Quants. Water was pouring through the Khustovs' ceiling into the bathroom and kitchen. Finally an enormous chunk of plaster crashed down from Quant's kitchen ceiling, smashing all the dirty dishes on the drain board and letting loose a deluge as though someone upstairs were pouring out buckets of dirty rubbish and lumps of sodden plaster. Meanwhile a chorus of shouts came from the staircase.

Flying past the last window but one on the fourth floor, Margarita glanced into it and saw a panic-stricken man putting on a gas mask. Terrified at the sound of Margarita's hammer tapping on the window, he vanished from the room.

Suddenly the uproar stopped. Floating down to the third floor, Margarita looked into the far window, which was shaded by a flimsy blind. The room was lit by a little night light. In a cot with basketwork sides sat a little boy of about four, listening nervously. There were no grownups in the room; they had obviously all run out of the apartment.

"Windows breaking," said the little boy and cried, "Mummy!"

Nobody answered and he said, "Mummy, I'm frightened."

Margarita pushed aside the blind and flew in at the window.

"I'm frightened," said the little boy again, shivering.

"Don't be frightened, darling," said Margarita, trying to soften her now raucous, harsh voice. "It's only some boys breaking windows."

"With a slingshot?" asked the boy, as he stopped shivering.

"Yes, with a slingshot," agreed Margarita. "Go to sleep now."

"That's Fedya," said the boy. "He's got a slingshot."

"Of course, it must be Fedya."

The boy glanced slyly to one side and asked, "Where are you, auntie?"

"I'm nowhere," replied Margarita. "You're dreaming about me."

"I thought so," said the little boy.

"Now you lie down," said Margarita, "put your hand under your cheek, and I'll send you to sleep."

"All right," agreed the boy and lay down at once with his cheek on his palm.

"I'll tell you a story," Margarita began, laying her hot hand on the child's cropped head. "Once upon a time there was a lady . . . she had no children and she was never happy. At first she just used to cry, then one day she felt very naughty. . . ." Margarita stopped and took away her hand. The little boy was asleep.

Margarita gently put the hammer on the window sill and flew out of the window. Below, disorder reigned. People were shouting and running up and down the glass-strewn pavement, policemen among them. Suddenly a bell started clanging, and around the corner from the Arbat drove a red fire engine with an extension ladder.

Margarita had already lost interest. Steering her way past cables, she clutched the broom harder and in a moment was flying high above Dramlit House. The street veered sideways and vanished. Beneath her now was only an expanse of roofs, crisscrossed with brilliantly lit roads. Suddenly it all slipped sideways; the strings of light grew blurred and vanished.

Margarita gave another jerk, at which the sea of roofs disappeared, replaced below her by a sea of shimmering electric lights. Suddenly the sea of light swung round to the vertical and appeared over Margarita's head while the moon shone under her legs. Realizing that she had looped the loop, Margarita righted herself, turned around and saw that the sea had vanished; behind her there was now only a pink glow on the horizon. In a second that, too, had disappeared, and Margarita saw that she was alone with the moon, sailing along above her and to the left. Margarita's hair streamed out behind her in wisps as the moonlight swished past her body. From the two lines of widely spaced lights meeting at a point in the distance and from the rate at which they were vanishing behind her Margarita guessed that she was flying at prodigious speed and was surprised to discover that it did not take her breath away.

After a few seconds' travel, far below in the earthbound blackness an electric sunrise flared up and rolled beneath Margarita's feet, then twisted round and vanished. Another few seconds, another burst of light.

"Towns! Towns!" shouted Margarita.

Two or three times she saw beneath her what looked like dully glinting bands of steel ribbon, which were rivers.

Glancing upward and to the left, she stared at the moon as it flew past her, rushing backward to Moscow, yet strangely appearing to stand still. In the moon she could clearly see a mysterious dark shape—not exactly a dragon, not quite a little humpbacked horse, its sharp muzzle pointed toward the city she was leaving.

The thought then came to Margarita that there was really no reason for her to drive her broom at such a speed. She was missing a unique chance to see the world from a new viewpoint and savor the thrill of flight. Something told her that wherever her destination might be, her hosts would wait for her.

There was no hurry, no reason to make herself dizzy with speed or to fly at such a height, so she tilted the head of her broom downward and floated, at a greatly reduced speed, almost at ground level. This headlong dive, as though on an aerial toboggan, gave her the utmost pleasure. The earth rose up to her, and the moonlit landscape, until then an indistinguishable blur, was revealed in exquisite detail. Margarita flew just above the veil of mist over meadow and pond; through the wisps of vapor she could hear the croaking of frogs, from the distance came the heart-stopping moan of a train. Soon Margarita caught sight of it. It was moving slowly, like a caterpillar blowing sparks from the top of its head. She overtook it, crossed another lake in which a reflected moon swam beneath her legs, then flew still lower, nearly brushing the tops of the giant pines with her feet.

Suddenly Margarita caught the sound of heavy, snorting breath behind her, and it seemed to be slowly catching up with her. Gradually another noise like a flying bullet and a woman's raucous laughter could be heard. Margarita looked around and saw that she was being followed by a dark object of curious shape. As it drew nearer, it began to look like someone flying astraddle, until, as it slowed down to draw alongside her, Margarita saw clearly that it was Natasha.

Completely naked too, her hair streaming behind her, she was flying along mounted on a fat pig, clutching a briefcase in its front legs and furiously pounding the air with its hind feet. A pince-nez, which occasionally flashed in the moonlight, had fallen off its nose and was dangling on a ribbon, while the pig's hat kept falling forward over its eyes. After a careful look Margarita recognized the pig as Nikolai Ivanovich, and her laughter rang out, mingled with Natasha's, over the forest below.

"Natasha!" shrieked Margarita. "Did you rub the cream on yourself?"

"Darling!" answered Natasha, waking the sleeping pine forests with her screech. "Yes, and I smeared it on his bald head too!"

"My princess!" grunted the pig miserably.

"Darling Margarita Nikolayevna!" shouted Natasha as she galloped alongside her. "I confess—I took the rest of the cream. Why shouldn't I fly away and live, too? Forgive me, but I could never come back to you now—not for anything. This is the life for me! . . . He made me a proposition." Natasha poked her finger into the back of the pig's neck. "The old lecher—I didn't think he had it in him, did you? What did you call me?" she yelled, leaning down toward the pig's ear.

"Goddess!" howled the animal. "Slow down, Natasha, please! There are important papers in my briefcase and I may lose them!"

"To hell with your papers," shouted Natasha, laughing.

"Oh, please don't shout like that, somebody may hear us!" squealed the pig imploringly.

As she flew alongside Margarita, Natasha laughingly told her what had happened in the house after Margarita Nikolayevna had flown away over the gate.

Natasha confessed that without touching any more of the things she had been given she had torn her clothes off, rushed to the cream and started to anoint herself. The same transformation took place. Laughing with delight, she was standing in front of the mirror admiring her magical beauty when the door opened and in walked Nikolai Ivanovich. He was highly excited and was holding Margarita Nikolayevna's slip, his briefcase and his hat. At first he was riveted to the spot with horror, then announced, as red as a lobster, that he had thought he should return the garment. . . .

"The things he said, the beast!" screamed Natasha, roaring with laughter. "The things he suggested! The money he offered me! Said his wife would never find out. It's true, isn't it?" Natasha shouted to the pig, which could do nothing but wriggle its snout in embarrassment.

As they had romped about in the bedroom, Natasha smeared some of the cream on Nikolai Ivanovich, and then it was her turn to freeze with astonishment. The face of her respectable neighbor shrank and grew a snout, while his arms and legs sprouted pig's feet. Looking at himself in the mirror, Nikolai Ivanovich gave a wild, despairing squeal, but it was too late. A few seconds later, with Natasha astride him, he was flying through the air away from Moscow, sobbing with chagrin.

"I demand to be turned back into my usual shape!" the pig suddenly grunted, half angry, half begging. "I refuse to take part in an illegal assembly! Margarita Nikolayevna, kindly take your maid off my back."

"Oh, so I'm a maid now, am I? What d'you mean, maid!" cried Natasha, tweaking the pig's ear. "I was a goddess just now! What did you call me?"

"Venus!" replied the pig miserably, brushing a hazel bush with its feet as they flew low over a chattering, fast-flowing stream.

"Venus! Venus!" screamed Natasha triumphantly, slapping her mount on the ribs with one hand and waving the other toward the moon. "Margarita! Queen Margarita! Ask them to let me stay a witch! You have the power to ask for whatever you like and they'll do it for you."

Margarita replied, "Very well, I promise."

"Thanks!" screamed Natasha, raising her voice still higher to shout, "Hey, go on—faster, faster! Faster than that!"

She dug her heels into the pig's thin flanks, sending it flying forward. In a moment Natasha was nothing but a dark spot far ahead, and as she vanished altogether the swish of her passage through the air died away.

Margarita flew on slowly through the unknown, deserted countryside, over hills strewn with occasional rocks and sparsely grown with giant fir trees. She was no longer flying over their tops, but between their trunks, silvered on one side by the moonlight. Her faint shadow flitted ahead of her, as the moon was now at her back.

Sensing that she was approaching water, Margarita guessed that her goal was near. The fir trees parted and Margarita floated gently through the air toward a chalky hillside. Below it lay a river. A mist was swirling round the bushes growing on the cliff face, while the opposite bank was low and flat. There under a lone clump of trees was the flicker of a campfire, surrounded by moving figures, and Margarita seemed to hear the insistent beat of music. Beyond, as far as the eye could see, there was not a sign of life.

Margarita bounded down the hillside to the water, which looked tempting after her chase through the air. Throwing aside the broom, she took a run and dived head first into the water. As her body, as light as air, plunged in, it threw up a column of spray almost to the moon. The water was as warm as a bath, and as she glided upward from the bottom Margarita reveled in the freedom of swimming alone in a river at night.

There was no one near Margarita in the water, but farther away, near some bushes by the shore, she could hear splashing and snorting. Someone else was having a swim.

Margarita swam ashore and ran up the bank. Her body tingled. She felt no fatigue after her long flight and gave a little dance of pure joy on the damp grass. Suddenly she stopped and listened. The snorting was moving closer, and from a clump of reeds there emerged a fat man, naked except for a dented top hat perched on the back of his head. He had been plodding his way through sticky mud, which made him seem to be wearing black boots. To judge from his breath and his hiccups he had had a great deal to drink, which was confirmed by a smell of brandy rising from the water around him.

Catching sight of Margarita the fat man stared at her, then cried with a roar of joy, "Surely it can't be! It is—Claudine, the merry widow! What brings you here?" He waddled forward to greet her.

Margarita retreated and replied in a dignified voice, "Go to hell! What d'you mean—Claudine? Who d'you think you're talking to?" After a moment's reflection she rounded off her retort with a long, satisfying and unprintable obscenity. Its effect on the fat man was instantly sobering.

"Oh, dear," he exclaimed, flinching. "Forgive me—I didn't see you, Your Majesty, Queen Margot. It's the fault of the brandy." The fat man dropped onto one knee, took off his top hat, bowed and in a mixture of Russian and French jabbered some nonsense about having just come from a wedding in Paris, about brandy and about how deeply he apologized for his terrible mistake.

"You might have put your trousers on, you big fool," said Margarita, relenting though still pretending to be angry.

The fat man grinned with delight as he realized that Margarita had forgiven him, and he announced cheerfully that he just happened to be without his trousers at the moment because he had absent-mindedly left them on the bank of the River Yenisei where he had been bathing just before flying here, but would go back for them at once. With an effusive volley of farewells he began bowing and walking backward, until he slipped and fell headlong into the water. Even as he fell, however, his side-whiskered face kept its smile of cheerful devotion.

Margarita gave a piercing whistle, mounted the obedient broomstick and flew across to the far bank, which lay in the full moonlight beyond the shadow cast by the chalk cliff.

As soon as she touched the wet grass, the music coming from the clump of willows grew louder and a stream of sparks blazed upward with furious gaiety. Under the willow branches, hung with thick catkins, sat two rows of fat-cheeked frogs, puffed up as if they were made of rubber and playing a march on wooden pipes. Glowworms hung on the willow twigs in front of the musicians to light their sheets of music while a flickering glow from the campfire played over the frogs' faces.

The march was being played in Margarita's honor as part of a solemn ceremony of welcome. Translucent water sprites stopped their dance to wave fronds at her as their cries of welcome floated across the broad water meadow. Naked witches jumped down from the willows and curtsied to her. A goat-legged creature ran up, kissed her hand and, as he spread out a silken sheet on the grass, inquired if she had enjoyed her swim and whether she would like to lie down and rest.

As Margarita lay down, the goat-legged man brought her a goblet of champagne, which at once warmed her heart. Asking where Natasha was, she was told that Natasha had already bathed. She was already flying back to Moscow on her pig to warn them that Margarita would soon be coming and to assist in preparing a gown for her.

Margarita's short stay in the willow grove was marked by a curious event: a whistle split the air and a dark body, obviously missing its intended target, sailed through the air and landed in the water. A few moments later Margarita was faced by the same fat man with side whiskers who had so clumsily introduced himself earlier. He had obviously managed to fly back to the Yenisei because, although soaking wet from head to foot, he now wore full evening dress. He had been at the brandy again, which had caused him to land in the water, but as before his smile was indestructible and in his bedraggled state he was permitted to kiss Margarita's hand.

Now everyone prepared to depart. The water sprites ended

their dance and vanished. The goat-man politely asked how she had arrived at the river, and on hearing that she had ridden there on a broom he cried; "Oh, how uncomfortable!" In a moment he had twisted two branches into the shape of a telephone and ordered someone to send a car at once, which was done in a trice.

A brown open-topped car flew down to the island. Instead of a driver, the chauffeur's seat was occupied by a black, long-beaked crow in a check cap and gauntlets. The island emptied as the witches flew away in the moonlight, the fire burned out and the glowing embers turned to gray ash.

The goat-man opened the door for Margarita, who sprawled on the car's wide back seat. The car gave a roar, took off and climbed almost to the moon. The island fell away, the river disappeared, and Margarita was on her way to Moscow.

CHAPTER 22

BY CANDLELIGHT

The steady hum of the car as it flew high above the earth lulled Margarita to sleep and the moonlight felt pleasantly warm. Closing her eyes, she let the wind play on her face and thought wistfully of that strange river bank which she would probably never see again. After so much magic and sorcery that evening she had already guessed who her host was to be, but she felt quite unafraid. The hope that she might regain her happiness made her fearless. In any case she was not given much time to loll in the car and dream of future happiness. The crow was a good driver and the car a fast one. When Margarita opened her eyes, she no longer saw dark forests beneath her but the shimmering jewels of the lights of Moscow. The bird-chauffeur unscrewed the right-hand front wheel as they flew along, then landed the car in a deserted cemetery in the Dorogomilov district.

Opening the door to allow Margarita and her broom to alight on a gravestone, the crow gave the car a push and sent it rolling toward the ravine beyond the far edge of the cemetery. It crashed over the side and was shattered to pieces. The crow saluted politely, mounted the wheel and flew away on it.

At that moment a black cloak appeared from behind a headstone. A walleye glistened in the moonlight, and Margarita recognized Azazello. He gestured to Margarita to mount her broomstick and leaped astride his own long rapier. They both took off and landed soon afterward, unnoticed by a soul, near No. 302A Sadovaya Street.

As the two companions passed under the gateway into the courtyard, Margarita noticed a man in cap and high boots, apparently waiting for somebody. Light as their footsteps were, the lonely man heard them and shifted uneasily, unable to see who was there.

At the entrance to staircase 6 they encountered a second man, astonishingly similar in appearance to the first, and the same performance was repeated. Hearing footsteps, the man turned around uneasily and frowned. When the door opened and closed he hurled himself in pursuit of the invisible intruders and peered up the staircase but failed, of course, to see anything. A third man, an exact copy of the other two, was lurking on the third-floor landing. He was smoking a strong cigarette and Margarita coughed as she walked past him. The smoker leaped up from his bench as though stung, stared anxiously around, walked over to the banisters and glanced down. Meanwhile Margarita and her companion had reached apartment No. 50.

They did not ring, but Azazello silently opened the door with his key. Margarita's first surprise on walking in was the darkness. It was as dark as a cellar, so that she involuntarily clutched Azazello's cloak from fear of an accident, but soon from high up and far away a lighted lamp flickered and came closer. As they moved forward, Azazello took away Margarita's broom and it vanished soundlessly into the darkness.

They then began to mount a broad staircase, so vast that to Margarita it seemed endless. She was surprised that the hallway of an ordinary Moscow apartment could hold such an enormous, invisible but undeniably real and apparently unending staircase. They reached a landing and stopped. The light drew close, and Margarita saw the face of a tall man in black holding the lamp. Anybody unlucky enough to have crossed his path in those last few days would have recognized him at once. It was Koroviev, alias Faggot.

His appearance, it is true, had greatly changed. The guttering flame was reflected no longer in a shaky pince-nez long overdue for the trash can, but in an equally unsteady monocle. The mustaches on his insolent face were curled and waxed. He appeared black for the simple reason that he was wearing tails and black trousers. Only his shirt front was white.

Magician, choirmaster, wizard, or the devil knows what, Koroviev bowed and with a broad sweep of his lamp invited Margarita to follow him. Azazello vanished.

"How strange everything is this evening!" thought Margarita. "I was ready for anything except this. Are they trying to save current, or what? The oddest thing of all is the size of this place—how on earth can it fit into a Moscow apartment? It's simply impossible!"

Despite the feebleness of the light from Koroviev's lamp, Margarita realized that she was in a vast, colonnaded hall, dark and apparently endless. Stopping beside a small couch, Koroviev put his lamp on a pedestal, gestured to Margarita to sit down and then placed himself beside her in an artistic pose, one elbow leaned elegantly on the pedestal.

"Allow me to introduce myself," said Koroviev in a grating voice. "My name is Koroviev. Are you surprised that there's no light? Economy, I suppose you were thinking? Never! May the first murderer to fall at your feet this evening cut my throat if that's the reason. It is simply because Messire doesn't care for electric light, and we keep it turned off until the last possible moment. Then, believe me, there will be no lack of it. It might even be better if there were not quite so much."

Margarita liked Koroviev, and she found his flow of light-hearted nonsense reassuring.

"No," replied Margarita, "what really puzzles me is where you have found the space for all this." With a wave of her hand Margarita indicated the vastness of the hall they were in.

Koroviev smiled sweetly, wrinkling his nose.

"Easy!" he replied. "For anyone who knows how to handle the fifth dimension it's no problem to expand any place to whatever size you please. No, dear lady, I will say more— to the devil knows what size. However, I have known people," Koroviev burbled on, "who though quite ignorant have done wonders in enlarging their accommodations. One man in this town, so I've been told, was given a three-roomed apartment on the Zemlyanoi Rampart and in a flash, without using the fifth dimension or anything like that, he had turned it into four rooms by dividing one of the rooms in half with a partition. Then he exchanged it for two separate apartments in different parts of Moscow, one with three rooms and the other with two. That, you will agree, adds up to five rooms. He exchanged the three-roomed one for two separate two-roomers and thus became the owner, as you will have noticed, of six rooms altogether, though admittedly scattered all over Moscow. He was just about to pull off his last and most brilliant coup by putting an advertisement in the newspaper offering six rooms in various districts of Moscow in exchange for one five-roomed apartment on the Zemlyanoi Rampart, when his activities were suddenly and inexplicably curtailed. He may have a room somewhere now, but not, I can assure you, in Moscow. There's a smooth operator for you —and you talk of the fifth dimension!"

Although it was Koroviev and not Margarita who had been talking about the fifth dimension, she could not help laughing at the way he told his story of the ingenious property tycoon. Koroviev went on: "But to come to the point, Margarita Nikolayevna. You are a very intelligent woman and have naturally guessed who our host is."

Margarita's heart beat faster and she nodded..

"Very well, then," said Koroviev. "I will tell you more. We dislike all mystery and ambiguity. Every year Messire gives a ball. It is known as the springtime ball of the full moon, or the ball of the hundred kings. Ah, the people who come!" Here Koroviev clutched his cheek as if he had a toothache. "However, you will shortly be able to see for yourself. Messire is a bachelor, as you will realize, but there has to be a hostess." Koroviev spread his hands: "You must agree that without a hostess . . ."

Margarita listened to Koroviev, trying not to miss a word. Her heart felt cold with expectancy, the thought of happiness made her dizzy. "First, it has become a tradition," Koroviev went on, "that the hostess of the ball must be called Margarita and, second, she must be a native of the place where the ball is held. We, as you know, are always on the move and happen to be in Moscow at present. We have found a hundred and twenty-one Margaritas in Moscow, and would you believe it—" Koroviev slapped his thigh in exasperation—"not one of them was suitable! Then at last, by a lucky chance . . ."

Koroviev grinned expressively, bowing from the waist, and again Margarita's heart contracted.

"Now to the point!" exclaimed Koroviev. "To be brief— you won't decline this responsibility, will you?"

"I will not," replied Margarita firmly.

"Of course," said Koroviev, raising his lamp, and added, "please follow me."

They passed a row of columns and finally emerged into another hall which for some reason smelled strongly of lemons. A rustling noise was heard and something landed on Margarita's head. She gave a start.

"Don't be afraid," Koroviev reassured her, taking her arm. "Just some stunt that Behemoth has dreamed up to amuse the guests tonight, that's all. Incidentally, if I may be so bold, Margarita Nikolayevna, my advice to you is to be afraid of nothing you may see. There's no cause for fear. The ball will be extravagantly luxurious, I warn you. We shall see people who in their time wielded enormous power. But when one recalls how microscopic their influence really was in comparison with the powers of the one in whose retinue I have the honor to serve, they become quite laughable, even pathetic. . . . You too, of course, are of royal blood."

"How can I be of royal blood?" whispered Margarita, terrified, pressing herself against Koroviev.

"Ah, your majesty," Koroviev teased her, "the question of blood is the most complicated problem in the world! If you were to ask certain of your great-great-great-grandmothers, especially those who had a reputation for meekness, they might tell you some remarkable secrets, my dear Margarita Nikolayevna! To draw a parallel—the most amazing combinations can result if you shuffle the pack enough. There are some matters in which even class barriers and frontiers are powerless. I rather think that a certain king of France of the sixteenth century would be most astonished if somebody told him that after all these years I would have the pleasure of walking arm in arm round a ballroom in Moscow with his great-great-great-great-great-granddaughter. Ah—here we are!"

Koroviev blew out his lamp, it vanished from his hand, and Margarita noticed a patch of light on the floor in front of a black doorway. Koroviev knocked gently. Margarita grew so excited that her teeth started chattering and a shiver ran up her spine.

The door opened into a small room. Margarita saw a wide oak bed covered with dirty, rumpled bedclothes and pillows. In front of the bed stood a table with carved oaken legs bearing a candelabrum whose sockets were made in the shape of birds' claws. Seven fat wax candles burned in their grasp. On the table there was also a large chessboard set with elaborately carved pieces. A low bench stood on the small, worn carpet. There was one more table, laden with golden beakers and another candelabrum with arms fashioned like snakes. The room smelled of damp and tar. Shadows thrown by the candlelight crisscrossed the floor.

Among the people in the room Margarita at once recognized Azazello, now also wearing tails and standing near the bed head. Now that Azazello was smartly dressed he no longer looked like the ruffian who had appeared to Margarita in the Alexander Gardens, and he gave her a most gallant bow.

The naked witch, Hella, who had so upset the respectable bartender from the Variety Theater and who, luckily for Rimsky, had been driven away at cockcrow, was sitting on the floor by the bed and stirring some concoction in a saucepan which gave off a sulphurous vapor. Besides these, there was an enormous black cat sitting on a stool in front of the chessboard and holding a knight in its right paw.

Hella stood up and bowed to Margarita. The cat jumped down from its stool and did likewise, but in making its flourish it dropped the knight and had to crawl under the bed after it.

Faint with terror, Margarita blinked at this candlelit pantomime. Her glance was drawn to the bed, on which sat the man whom the wretched Bezdomny had recently assured at Patriarch's Ponds that he did not exist.

Two eyes bored into Margarita's face. In the depths of the right eye was a golden spark that could pierce any soul to its core; the left eye was as empty and black as a small black diamond, as the mouth of a bottomless well of darkness and shadow. Woland's face was tilted to one side, the right-hand corner of his mouth pulled downward, and deep furrows marked his forehead running parallel to his eyebrows. The skin of his face seemed burned by timeless sunshine.

Woland was lying sprawled on the bed, dressed only in a long, dirty, black nightshirt, patched on the left shoulder. One bare leg was tucked up beneath him, the other stretched out on the bench. Hella was massaging his knees with a steaming ointment.

On Woland's bare, hairless chest Margarita noticed a scarab on a gold chain, intricately carved out of black stone and engraved with an arcane script. Near Woland was a strange globe, lit from one side, which seemed almost alive.

The silence lasted for several seconds. "He is studying me," thought Margarita and by an effort of will tried to stop her legs from trembling.

At last Woland spoke. He smiled, causing his one sparkling eye to flash.

"Greetings, my queen. Please excuse my homely garb."

Woland's voice was so low-pitched that on certain syllables it faded into a mere growl.

Woland picked up a long sword from the bed, bent over, poked it under the bed and said, "Come out now. The game's over. Our guest has arrived."

"Please . . ." Koroviev whispered anxiously into Margarita's ear like a prompter.

"Please . . ." began Margarita.

"Messire . . ." breathed Koroviev.

"Please, Messire," Margarita went on quietly but firmly, "I beg you not to interrupt your game. I am sure the chess journals would pay a fortune to be allowed to print it."

Azazello gave a slight croak of approval, and Woland, staring intently at Margarita, murmured to himself, "Yes, Koroviev was right. The result can be amazing when you shuffle the pack. Blood will tell."

He stretched out his arm and beckoned Margarita. She walked up to him, feeling no floor under her bare feet. Woland placed his hand—as heavy as stone and as hot as fire—on Margarita's shoulder, pulled her toward him and sat her down on the bed by his side.

"Since you are so charming and kind," he said, "which was no more than I expected, we shan't stand on ceremony." He leaned over the edge of the bed again and shouted, "How much longer is this performance under the bed going to last? Come on out!"

"I can't find the knight," replied the cat in a muffled falsetto from beneath the bed. "It's galloped off somewhere and there's a frog here instead."

"Where do you think you are—on a fairground?" asked Woland, pretending to be angry. "There's no frog under the bed! Save those cheap tricks for the Variety! If you don't come out at once, we'll begin to think you've gone over to the enemy, you deserter!"

"Never, Messire!" howled the cat, crawling out with the knight in its paw.

"Allow me to introduce to you," Woland began, then interrupted himself. "No, really, he looks too ridiculous! Just look what he's done to himself while he was under the bed!"

The cat, covered in dust and standing on its hind legs, bowed to Margarita. Round its neck it was now wearing a made-up white bow tie on an elastic band, with a pair of ladies' mother-of-pearl binoculars hanging on a cord. It had also gilded its whiskers.

"What have you done?" exclaimed Woland. "Why have you gilded your whiskers? And what on earth do you want with a white tie when you haven't even got any trousers?"

"Trousers don't suit cats, Messire," replied the cat with great dignity. "Why don't you tell me to wear boots? Cats always wear boots in fairy tales. But have you ever seen a cat going to a ball without a tie? I don't want to make myself look ridiculous. One likes to look as smart as one can. And that also applies to my opera glasses, Messire!"

"But your whiskers?"

"I don't see why," the cat objected coldly, "Azazello and Koroviev are allowed to cover themselves with powder and why powder is better than gilt. I just gilded my whiskers, that's all. It would be a different matter if I'd shaved myself! A clean-shaven cat is something monstrous, that I agree. But I see—" here the cat's voice trembled with pique—"that this is a conspiracy to be rude about my appearance. Clearly I am faced with a problem—shall I go to the ball or not? What do you say, Messire?"

Outraged, the cat had so inflated itself that it looked about to explode at any second.

"Ah, the rogue, the sly rogue," said Woland, shaking his head. "Whenever he's losing a game he starts a spiel like a quack doctor at a fair. Sit down and stop all this hot air."

"Very well," replied the cat, sitting down, "but I must object. My remarks are by no means all hot air, as you so vulgarly put it, but a series of highly apposite syllogisms which would be appreciated by such connoisseurs as Sextus Empiricus, Martian Capella, even—who knows?—Aristotle himself."

"Check," said Woland.

"Check it is," rejoined the cat, surveying the chessboard through his lorgnette.

"So," Woland turned to Margarita, "let me introduce my retinue. That creature who has been playing the fool is the cat Behemoth. Azazello and Koroviev you have already met; this is my maid, Hella. She's prompt, clever, and there's no service she cannot perform for you."

The beautiful Hella turned her green eyes on Margarita and smiled, continuing to scoop out the ointment in the palm of her hand and to rub it on Woland's knee.

"Well, there they are," concluded Woland, wincing as Hella massaged his knee rather too hard. "A charming and select little band." He stopped and began turning his globe, so cleverly made that the blue sea within it shimmered in waves and the polar cap was of real ice and snow.

On the chessboard, meanwhile, confusion reigned. Distraught, the white king was stamping about on his square and waving his arms in desperation. Three white pawns, armed with halberds, were staring in bewilderment at a bishop who was waving his crozier and pointing to where Woland's black knights sat mounted on two hot-blooded horses, one pawing the ground of a white square, the other on a black square.

Margarita was fascinated by the game and amazed to see that the chessmen were alive.

Dropping its lorgnette, the cat gently nudged his king in the back, at which the wretched king covered his face in despair.

"You're in trouble, my dear Behemoth," said Koroviev in a voice of quiet malice.

"The position is serious but far from hopeless," retorted Behemoth. "What is more, I am confident of ultimate victory. All that is needed is a careful analysis of the situation."

His method of analysis took the peculiar form of making faces and winking at his king.

"That won't do you any good," said Koroviev.

"Oh!" cried Behemoth, "all the parrots have flown away, as I said they would."

From far off came the sound of innumerable wings. Koroviev and Azazello rushed out of the room.

"You're nothing but a pest with all your arrangements for the ball," grumbled Woland, preoccupied with his globe.

As soon as Koroviev and Azazello had gone, Behemoth's winking increased until at last the white king caught on to what was required of him. He suddenly pulled off his cloak, dropped it on his square and walked off the board. The bishop picked up the royal cloak, threw it around his shoulders and took the king's place.

Koroviev and Azazello returned. "False alarm, as usual," growled Azazello.

"Well, I thought I heard something," said the cat.

"Come on, how much longer do you need?" asked Woland. "Check."

"I must have misheard you, *mon maître*," replied the cat. "My king is not in check and cannot be."

"I repeat—check."

"Messire," rejoined the cat in a voice of mock anxiety, "you must be suffering from overstrain. I am not in check!"

"The king is on square K2," said Woland, without looking at the board.

"Messire, you amaze me," wailed the cat, putting on an amazed face. "There is no king on that square."

"What?" asked Woland, with a puzzled look at the board. The bishop, standing in the king's square, turned his head away and covered his face with his hand.

"Aha, you rogue!" said Woland reflectively.

"Messire! I appeal to the laws of logic!" said the cat, clasping its paws to its chest, "if a player says check and there is no king on the board, then the king is not in check!"

"Do you resign or not?" shouted Woland in a terrible voice.

"Give me time to consider, please," said the cat meekly. It put its elbows on the table, covered its ears with its paws and began to think. Finally, having considered, it said, "I resign."

"He needs murdering, the obstinate beast," whispered Azazello.

"Yes, I resign," said the cat, "but only because I find it impossible to play when I'm distracted by jealous, hostile spectators!" He stood up and the chessmen ran back into their box.

"It's time for you to go, Hella," said Woland and Hella left the room. "My leg has started hurting again and now there is this ball," he went on.

"Allow me," Margarita suggested gently.

Woland gave her a searching stare and moved his knee toward her. The ointment, hot as lava, burned her hands, but without flinching Margarita massaged it into Woland's knee, trying not to cause him pain.

"My friends maintain that it's rheumatism," said Woland, continuing to stare at Margarita, "but I strongly suspect that the pain is a souvenir of an encounter with a most beautiful witch that I had in 1571, on the Brocken in the Harz Mountains."

"Surely not!" said Margarita.

"Oh, give it another three hundred years or so and it will go. I've been prescribed all kinds of medicaments, but I prefer to stick to traditional old wives' remedies. I inherited some extraordinary herbal cures from my terrible old grandmother. Tell me, by the way—do you suffer from any complaint? Perhaps you have some sorrow which is weighing on your heart?"

"No, Messire, I have no such complaint," replied Margarita astutely. "In any case, since I have been with you I have never felt better."

"As I said, blood will tell," said Woland cheerfully to no one in particular, adding, "I see my globe interests you."

"I have never seen anything so ingenious."

"Yes, it is nice. I confess I never like listening to the news on the radio. It's always read out by some silly announcer who can't pronounce foreign names properly. Besides, at least one in three of the announcers is tongue-tied, as if they were chosen especially. My globe is much more convenient, especially as I need exact information. Do you see that little speck of land, for instance, washed by the sea on one side? Look, it's just bursting into flames. War has broken out there. If you look closer, you'll see it in detail."

Margarita leaned toward the globe and saw that the little square of land was growing bigger, emerging in natural colors and turning into a kind of relief map. Then she saw a river and a village beside it. A house the size of a pea grew until it was as large as a matchbox. Suddenly and noiselessly its roof flew upward in a puff of black smoke, the walls collapsed leaving nothing of the two-story matchbox except a few smoking heaps of rubble. Looking even closer, Margarita discerned a tiny female figure lying on the ground and beside her in a pool of blood a baby with outstretched arms.

"It's all over now," said Woland, smiling. "He was too young to have sinned. Abadonna has done his work impeccably."

"I wouldn't like to be on the side that is against Abadonna," said Margarita. "Whose side is he on?"

"The more I talk to you," said Woland kindly, "the more convinced I am that you are very intelligent. Let me reassure you. He is utterly impartial and is equally sympathetic to the people fighting on either side. Consequently the outcome is always the same for both sides. Abadonna!" Woland called softly, and from the wall appeared the figure of a man wearing dark glasses. These glasses made such a powerful impression on Margarita that she gave a low cry, turned away and struck her head on Woland's leg. "Stop it!" cried Woland. "How nervous people are nowadays!" He slapped Margarita on the back so hard that her whole body seemed to ring. "He's only wearing spectacles, that's all. There never has been and never will be a case when Abadonna comes to anyone too soon. In any case, I'm here—you're my guest. I just wanted to show him to you."

Abadonna stood motionless.

"Could he take off his glasses for a moment?" asked Margarita, pressing against Woland and shuddering, though now with curiosity.

"No, that is impossible," replied Woland in a grave tone. At a wave of his hand, Abadonna vanished. "What did you want to say, Azazello?"

"Messire," answered Azazello, "two strangers have arrived —a beautiful girl who is whining and begging to be allowed to stay with her mistress, and with her there is, if you'll forgive me, her pig."

"What odd behavior for a girl!" said· Woland.

"It's Natasha, my Natasha!" exclaimed Margarita.

"Very well, she may stay here with her mistress. Send the pig to the cooks."

"Are you going to kill it?" cried Margarita in fright. "Please, Messire, that's Nikolai Ivanovich, my neighbor. There was a mistake—she rubbed the cream on him—"

"Who said anything about killing him?" said Woland. "I merely want him to sit at the cooks' table, that's all. I can't allow a pig into the ballroom, can I?"

"No, of course not," said Azazello, then announced, "Midnight approaches, Messire."

"Ah, good." Woland turned to Margarita. "Now let me thank you in advance for your services tonight. Don't lose your head and don't be afraid of anything. Drink nothing except water, otherwise it will sap your energy and you will find yourself flagging. Time to go!"

As Margarita got up from the carpet Koroviev appeared in the doorway.

CHAPTER 23

SATAN'S ROUT

Midnight was approaching, it was time to hurry. Peering into the dim surroundings, Margarita discerned some candles and an empty pool carved out of onyx. As Margarita stood in the pool, Hella, assisted by Natasha, poured a thick, hot, red liquid all over her. Margarita tasted salt on her lips and realized that she was being washed in blood. The bath of blood was followed by another liquid—dense, translucent and pink—and Margarita's head swam with attar of roses. Next she was laid on a crystal couch and rubbed with large green leaves until she glowed.

The cat came in and began to help. It squatted on its haunches at Margarita's feet and began polishing her instep like a bootblack.

Margarita never remembered who it was who stitched her shoes out of pale rose petals or how those shoes fastened themselves of their own accord. A force lifted her up and placed her in front of a mirror; in her hair glittered a diamond crown. Koroviev appeared and hung on Margarita's breast a picture of a black poodle in a heavy oval frame with a massive chain. Queen Margarita found this ornament extremely burdensome, as the chain hurt her neck and the picture pulled her over forward. However, the respect with which Koroviev and Behemoth now treated her was some recompense for the discomfort.

"There's nothing you can do about it," murmured Koroviev at the door of the room with the pool. "You must wear it around your neck—you must. . . . Let me give you a last word of advice, your majesty. The guests at the ball will be mixed—oh, very mixed—but you must show no favoritism, Queen Margot! If you don't like anybody—I realize that you won't show it in your face, of course not—but you must not even let it cross your mind! If you do, the guest is bound to notice it instantly. You must be sweet and kind to them all, your majesty. For that, the hostess of the ball will be rewarded a hundredfold. And another thing—don't neglect anybody or fail to notice them. Just a smile if you haven't time to toss them a word, or just a little turn of your head! Anything you like except inattention—they can't bear that. . . ."

Escorted by Koroviev and Behemoth, Margarita stepped out of the bathing hall and into total darkness.

"Me, me," whispered the cat, "let me give the signal!"

"All right, give it," replied Koroviev from the dark.

"Let the ball commence!" shrieked the cat in a piercing voice. Margarita screamed and shut her eyes for several seconds. The ball burst upon her in an explosion of light, sound and scent. Arm in arm with Koroviev, Margarita found herself in a tropical forest. Scarlet-breasted parrots with green tails perched on lianas and, hopping from branch to branch, uttered deafening screeches of "Ecstasy! Ecstasy!" The forest soon came to an end, and its hot, steamy air gave way to the cool of a ballroom with columns made of a yellowish, iridescent stone. Like the forest the ballroom was completely empty except for some naked Negroes in silver turbans holding candelabra. Their faces paled with excitement when Margarita floated into the ballroom with her entourage, to which Azazello had now attached himself. Here Koroviev released Margarita's arm and whispered, "Walk straight toward the tulips!"

A low wall of white tulips rose up in front of Margarita. Beyond it she saw countless lights in globes and rows of men in tails and starched white shirts. Margarita saw then where the sound of ball music had been coming from. A roar of brass deafened her, and the soaring violins that broke through it poured over her body like blood. The members of the orchestra, all one hundred and fifty of them, were playing a polonaise.

Seeing Margarita the tail-coated conductor turned pale, smiled and suddenly raised the whole orchestra to its feet with a wave of his arm. Without a moment's break in the music the orchestra stood and engulfed Margarita in sound. The conductor turned away from the players and gave a low bow. Smiling, Margarita waved to him.

"No, no, that won't do," whispered Koroviev. "He won't sleep all night. Shout to him, 'Bravo, king of the waltz!' "

Margarita shouted as she was told, amazed that her voice, full as a bell, rang out over the noise of the orchestra. The conductor gave a start of pleasure, placed his left hand on his heart and with his right went on waving his white baton at the orchestra.

"Not enough," whispered Koroviev. "Look over there at the first violins and nod to them so that every one of them thinks you recognize him personally. They are all world-famous. Look, there . . . on the first desk—that's Joachim! That's right! Very good . . . Now—on we go."

"Who is the conductor?" asked Margarita as she floated away.

"Johann Strauss!" cried the cat. "May I be hung from a liana in the tropical forest if any ball has ever had an orchestra like this! I arranged it! And not one of them was ill or refused to come!"

There were no columns in the next hall, but instead it was flanked by walls of red, pink, and milky-white roses on one side and on the other by banks of Japanese double camellias. Fountains played between the walls of flowers and champagne bubbled in three ornamental basins, the first of which was a translucent violet in color, the second ruby, the third crystal. Negroes in scarlet turbans were busy with silver scoops filling shallow goblets with champagne from the basins. In a gap in the wall of roses a man in a red swallow-tail coat bounced up and down on a stage, conducting an unbearably loud jazz band. As soon as he saw Margarita, he bent down in front of her until his hands touched the floor, then straightened up and cried in a piercing yell, "Alleluia!"

He slapped himself once on one knee, then twice on the other, snatched a cymbal from the hands of a nearby musician and struck it against a pillar.

As she floated away, Margarita caught a glimpse of the virtuoso bandleader, struggling against the polonaise that she could still hear behind her, hitting the bandsmen on the head with his cymbal while they crouched in comic terror.

At last they regained the platform where Koroviev had first

met Margarita with the lamp. Now her eyes were blinded with the light streaming from innumerable bunches of crystal grapes. Margarita stopped and a little amethyst pillar appeared under her left hand.

You can rest your hand on it if you find it becomes too tiring," whispered Koroviev.

A black-skinned boy put a cushion embroidered with a golden poodle under Margarita's feet. Obeying the pressure of an invisible hand, she bent her knee and placed her right foot on the cushion.

Margarita glanced around. Koroviev and Azazello were standing in formal attitudes. Beside Azazello were three young men, who vaguely reminded Margarita of Abadonna. A cold wind blew at her back. Looking around, Margarita saw that wine was foaming out of the marble wall into a basin made of ice. She felt something warm and velvety by her left leg. It was Behemoth.

Margarita was standing at the head of a vast carpeted staircase stretching downward away from her. At the bottom, so far away that she seemed to be looking at it through the wrong end of a telescope, she could see a vast hall with an absolutely immense fireplace, into whose cold, black maw one could easily have driven a five-ton truck. The hall and the staircase, bathed in painfully bright light, were empty. Then Margarita heard the sound of distant trumpets. For some minutes they all stood motionless.

"Where are the guests?" Margarita asked Koroviev.

"They will be here at any moment, your majesty. There will be no lack of them. I confess I'd rather be sawing logs than receiving them here on this platform."

"Sawing logs!" said the garrulous cat. "I'd rather be a street-car conductor, and there's no job worse than that."

"Everything must be prepared in advance, your majesty," explained Koroviev, his eye glittering behind the broken lens of his monocle. "There can be nothing more embarrassing than for the first guest to wait around uncomfortably, not knowing what to do, while his lawful consort curses him in a whisper for arriving too early. We cannot allow that at our ball, Queen Margot."

"I should think not," said the cat.

"Ten seconds to midnight," said Koroviev. "It will begin in a moment."

Those ten seconds seemed unusually long to Margarita. They

had obviously passed, but absolutely nothing seemed to be happening. Then there was a crash from below in the enormous fireplace, and out of it sprang a gallows with a half-decayed corpse bouncing on its arm. The corpse jerked itself loose from the rope, fell to the ground and stood up, a dark handsome man in tail coat and lacquered pumps. A small, rotting coffin then slithered out of the fireplace, its lid flew off and another corpse jumped out. The handsome man stepped gallantly toward it and offered his bent arm. The second corpse turned into a nimble little woman in black slippers and black feathers on her head, and then man and woman together hurried up the staircase.

"The first guests," exclaimed Koroviev. "Monsieur Jacques and his wife. Allow me to introduce to you, your majesty, a most interesting man. A confirmed forger, a traitor to his country, but no mean alchemist. He was famous," Koroviev whispered into Margarita's ear, "for having poisoned the king's mistress. Not everybody can boast of that, can they? See how good-looking he is!"

Turning pale and open-mouthed with shock, Margarita looked down and saw gallows and coffin disappear through a side door in the hall.

"We are delighted!" the cat roared to Monsieur Jacques as he mounted the steps.

Just then a headless, armless skeleton appeared in the fireplace below, fell down and turned into yet another man in a tail coat.

Monsieur Jacques's wife had by now reached the head of the staircase, where she knelt down, pale with excitement, and kissed Margarita's foot.

"Your majesty . . ." murmured Madame Jacques.

"Her majesty is charmed!" shouted Koroviev.

"Your majesty . . ." said Monsieur Jacques in a low voice.

"We are charmed!" intoned the cat. The young men beside Azazello, smiling lifeless but welcoming smiles, were showing Monsieur and Madame Jacques to one side, where they were offered goblets of champagne by the Negro attendants. The single man in tails came up the staircase at a run.

"Count Robert," Koroviev whispered to Margarita. "An equally interesting character. Rather amusing, your majesty— the case is reversed: he was the queen's lover and poisoned his own wife."

"We are delighted, Count," cried Behemoth.

One after another three coffins bounced out of the fireplace, splitting and breaking open as they fell, then someone in a black cloak who was immediately stabbed in the back by the next person to come down the chimney. There was a muffled shriek. When an almost totally decomposed corpse emerged from the fireplace, Margarita frowned, and a hand, which seemed to be Natasha's, offered her a flacon of sal volatile.

The staircase began to fill up. Now on almost every step there were men in tailcoats accompanied by naked women who differed only in the color of their shoes and the feathers on their heads.

Approaching her, Margarita noticed a woman with the downcast gaze of a nun hobbling toward her, thin, shy, hampered by a strange wooden boot on her left leg and with a broad green kerchief around her neck.

"Who's that woman in green?" Margarita inquired.

"A most charming and respectable lady," whispered Koroviev. "Let me introduce you—Signora Toffana. She was extremely popular among the young and attractive ladies of Naples and Palermo, especially among those who were tired of their husbands. Women do get bored with their husbands, your majesty."

"Yes," replied Margarita dully, smiling at two men in evening dress who were bowing to kiss her knee and her foot.

"Well," Koroviev managed to whisper to Margarita as he simultaneously cried, "Duke! A glass of champagne? We are charmed! . . . Well, Signora Toffana sympathized with those poor Neapolitan women and sold them some liquid in a bladder. The woman would pour the liquid into her husband's soup. He would eat it, thank her for it and feel splendid. However, after a few hours he would begin to feel a terrible thirst, then lie down on his bed, and a day later another beautiful Neapolitan lady was as free as air."

"What's that on her leg?" asked Margarita, without ceasing to offer her hand to the guests who had overtaken Signora Toffana on the way up. "And why is she wearing green around her neck? Has she a withered neck?"

"Charmed, Prince!" shouted Koroviev as he whispered to Margarita, "She has a beautiful neck, but something unpleasant happened to her in prison. The thing on her leg, your majesty, is a Spanish boot, and she wears a scarf because when her jailers found out that about five hundred ill-matched husbands had been dispatched from Naples and Palermo forever, they strangled Signora Toffana in a rage."

"How happy I am, your majesty, that I have the great honor . . ." whispered Signora Toffana in a nunlike voice, trying to fall on one knee but hindered by the Spanish boot. Koroviev and Behemoth helped Signora Toffana to rise.

"I am delighted," Margarita answered her as she gave her hand to the next arrival.

People were now mounting the staircase in a flood. Margarita ceased to notice the arrivals in the hall. Mechanically she raised and lowered her hand, bared her teeth in a smile for each new guest. The landing behind her was buzzing with voices, and music like the waves of the sea floated out from the ballrooms.

"Now this woman is a terrible bore," Koroviev no longer bothered to whisper but shouted it aloud, certain that no one could hear his voice over the hubbub. "She loves coming to a ball because it gives her a chance to complain about her handkerchief."

Among the approaching crowd Margarita's glance picked out the woman at whom Koroviev was pointing. She was young, about twenty, with a remarkably beautiful figure but with a look of nagging reproach.

"What handkerchief?" asked Margarita.

"A maid has been assigned to her," Koroviev explained, "who for thirty years has been putting a handkerchief on her bedside table. It is there every morning when she wakes up. She burns it in the stove or throws it in the river, but every morning it appears again beside her."

"What handkerchief?" whispered Margarita, continuing to lower and raise her hand to the guests.

"A handkerchief with a blue border. One day when she was a waitress in a café the owner enticed her into the storeroom and nine months later she gave birth to a boy, carried him into the woods, stuffed a handkerchief into his mouth and then buried him. At the trial she said she couldn't afford to feed the child."

"And where is the café owner?" asked Margarita.

"But, your majesty," the cat suddenly growled, "what has the café owner got to do with it? It wasn't he who stifled the baby in the forest, was it?"

Without ceasing to smile and to shake hands with her right hand, she dug the sharp nails of her left hand into Behemoth's ear and whispered to the cat, "If you butt into the conversation once more, you little horror . . ."

Behemoth gave a distinctly unfestive squeak and croaked, "Your majesty . . . you'll make my ear swell. . . . Why spoil the ball with a swollen ear? I was speaking from the legal point of view. . . . I'll be quiet, I promise. Pretend I'm not a cat, pretend I'm a fish if you like, but please let go of my ear!"

Margarita released his ear.

The grim, importunate eyes looked into Margarita's.

"I am so happy, your majesty, to be invited to the great ball of the full moon."

"And I am delighted to see you," Margarita answered her, "quite delighted. Do you like champagne?"

"Hurry up, your majesty!" hissed Koroviev quietly but desperately. "You're causing a traffic jam on the staircase."

"Yes, I like champagne," said the woman imploringly and began to repeat mechanically, "Frieda, Frieda, Frieda! My name is Frieda, your majesty!"

"Today you may get drunk, Frieda, and forget about everything," said Margarita.

Frieda stretched out both her arms to Margarita, but Koroviev and Behemoth deftly took an arm each and whisked her off into the crowd.

By now people were advancing from below like a phalanx bent on assaulting the landing where Margarita stood. The naked women mounting the staircase between the tail-coated and white-tied men floated up in a spectrum of colored bodies that ranged from white through olive, copper and coffee to quite black. In hair that was red, black, chestnut or flaxen, sparks flashed from precious stones. Diamond-studded orders glittered on the jackets and shirt fronts of the men. Incessantly Margarita felt the touch of lips to her knee; incessantly she offered her hand to be kissed, her face stretched into a rigid mask of welcome.

"Charmed," Koroviev would monotonously intone, "we are charmed . . . her majesty is charmed."

"Her majesty is charmed," came a nasal echo from Azazello, standing behind her.

"I am charmed!" squeaked the cat.

"Madame la marquise," murmured Koroviev, "poisoned her father, her two brothers and two sisters for the sake of an inheritance. . . . Her majesty is delighted, Madame Minkin! . . . Ah, how pretty she is! A trifle nervous, though. Why *did* she have to burn her maid with a pair of curling irons? Of course, in the way she used them it was bound to be fatal. Her majesty is charmed! . . . Look, your majesty—the Emperor Rudolf, magician and alchemist . . . Another alchemist—he was hanged. . . . Ah, there she is! What a magnificent brothel she used to keep in Strasbourg! . . . We are delighted, madame! . . . That woman over there was a Moscow dressmaker who had the brilliantly funny idea of boring two peepholes in the wall of her fitting room . . .

"And didn't her lady clients know?" inquired Margarita.

"Of course, they all knew, your majesty," replied Koroviev. "Charmed! . . . That young man over there was a dreamer and an eccentric from childhood. A girl fell in love with him and he sold her to a brothel keeper. . . ."

On and on poured the stream from below. Its source—the huge fireplace—showed no sign of drying up. An hour passed, then another. Margarita felt her chain weighing more and more. Something odd was happening to her hand: she found she could not lift it without wincing. Koroviev's remarks ceased to interest her. She could no longer distinguish between slant-eyed Mongol faces, white faces and black faces. They all merged into a blur, and the air between them seemed to be quivering. A sudden sharp pain like a needle stabbed at Margarita's right hand, and clenching her teeth she leaned her elbow on the little pedestal. A sound like the rustling of wings came from the rooms behind her as the horde of guests danced, and Margarita could feel the massive floors of marble, crystal and mosaic pulsating rhythmically.

Margarita showed as little interest in the Emperor Caius Caligula and Messalina as she did in the rest of the procession of kings, dukes, knights, suicides, poisoners, gallows birds, procuresses, jailers, card sharpers, hangmen, informers, traitors, madmen, detectives and seducers. Her head swam with their names, their faces merged into a great blur, and only one face remained fixed in her memory—that of Malyuta Skuratov with his fiery beard. Margarita's legs were buckling, and she was afraid that she might burst into tears at any moment. The worst pain came from her right knee, which all the guests had kissed. It was swollen, and the skin had turned blue in spite of Natasha's constant attention to it with a sponge soaked in fragrant ointment. By the end of the third hour Margarita glanced wearily down and saw with a start of joy that the flood of guests was thinning out.

"Every ball is the same, your majesty," whispered Koroviev. "At about this time the arrivals begin to decrease. I promise you that this torture will not last more than a few minutes longer. Here comes a party of witches from the Brocken—they're always the last to arrive. Yes, there they are. And a couple of drunken vampires . . . Is that all? Oh, no, there's one more— no, two more."

The two last guests mounted the staircase. "Now this is someone new," said Koroviev, peering through his monocle. "Oh, yes, now I remember. Azazello called on him once and advised him, over a glass of brandy, how to get rid of a man who was threatening to denounce him. So he made a friend, who was under an obligation to him, spray the other man's office walls with poison."

"What's his name?" asked Margarita.

"I'm afraid I don't know," said Koroviev. "You'd better ask Azazello."

"And who's that with him?"

"That's his friend who did the job. Delighted to welcome you!" cried Koroviev to the last two guests.

The staircase was empty, and although the reception committee waited a little longer to make sure, no one else appeared from the fireplace.

A second later, half-fainting, Margarita found herself beside the pool again, where, bursting into tears from the pain in her arm and leg, she collapsed to the floor. Hella and Natasha comforted her, doused her in blood and massaged her body until she revived again.

"Once more, Queen Margot," whispered Koroviev. "You must make the round of the ballrooms just once more to show our guests that they are not being neglected."

Again Margarita floated away from the pool. In place of Johann Strauss's orchestra the stage behind the wall of tulips had been taken over by a jazz band of frenetic apes. An enormous gorilla with shaggy sideburns and holding a trumpet was leaping clumsily up and down as he conducted. Orangutan trumpeters sat in the front row, each with a chimpanzee accordionist on his shoulders. Two baboons with manes like lions' were playing the piano, their efforts completely drowned out by the roaring, squeaking and banging of the saxophones, violins and drums played by troops of gibbons, mandrills and marmosets. Innumerable couples circled round the glassy floor with amazing dexterity, a mass of bodies moving lightly and gracefully as one. Live butterflies fluttered over the dancing horde, flowers drifted down from the ceiling. The electric lights had been turned out, the capitals of the pillars were now lit by myriads of glowworms, and will-o'-the-wisps danced through the air.

Then Margarita found herself by the side of another pool, this time of vast dimensions and ringed by a colonnade. A gigantic black Neptune was pouring a broad pink stream from his great mouth. Intoxicating fumes of champagne rose from the pool. Joy reigned untrammeled. Women, laughing, handed their bags to their escorts or to the Negroes who ran along the edges holding towels and dived shrieking into the pool. Spray rose in showers. The crystal bottom of the pool glowed with a faint light which shone through the sparkling wine to light up the silvery bodies of the swimmers, who climbed out of the pool again completely drunk. Laughter rang out beneath the pillars until it drowned even the jazz band.

In all this debauch Margarita distinctly saw one totally drunken woman's face with eyes that were wild with intoxication yet still imploring—Frieda.

Margarita's head began to spin with the fumes of the wine, and she was just about to move on when the cat staged one of his tricks in the swimming pool. Behemoth made a few magic passes in front of Neptune's mouth; immediately all the champagne drained out of the pool, and Neptune began spewing forth a stream of brown liquid. Shrieking with delight the women screamed, "Brandy!" In a few seconds the pool was full.

Spinning around three times like a top, the cat leaped into the air and dived into the turbulent sea of brandy. It crawled out, spluttering, its tie soaked, the gilding gone from its whiskers, and minus its lorgnette. Only one woman dared follow Behemoth's example—the dressmaker-procuress and her escort, a handsome young mulatto. They both dived into the brandy, but before she had time to see any more Margarita was led away by Koroviev.

They seemed to take wing, and in their flight Margarita first saw great stone tanks full of oysters, then a row of hellish furnaces blazing away beneath the glass floor and attended by a frantic crew of diabolical chefs. In the confusion she remembered a glimpse of dark caverns lit by candles where girls were serving meat that sizzled on glowing coals and revelers drank Margarita's health from vast mugs of beer. Then came polar bears playing accordions and dancing a Russian dance on a stage, a salamander doing conjuring tricks unharmed by the flames around it. . . . And for a second time Margarita felt her strength beginning to flag.

"The last round," whispered Koroviev anxiously, "and then we're free."

Escorted by Koroviev, Margarita returned to the ballroom, but now the dance had stopped and the guests were crowded between the pillars, leaving an open space in the middle of the room. Margarita could not remember who helped her up to a platform which appeared in the empty space. When she had mounted it, to her amazement she heard a bell strike midnight, although by her reckoning midnight was long past. At the last chime of the invisible clock silence fell on the crowd of guests.

Then Margarita saw Woland. He approached surrounded by Abadonna, Azazello and several young men in black resembling Abadonna. She now noticed another platform beside her own, prepared for Woland. But he did not make use of it. Margarita was particularly surprised to notice that Woland appeared at the ball in exactly the same state in which he had been in the bedroom. The same dirty, patched nightshirt hung from his shoulders and his feet were in darned bedroom slippers. Woland was armed with his sword, but he leaned on the naked weapon as though it were a walking stick.

Limping, Woland stopped beside his platform. At once Azazello appeared in front of him bearing a dish. On that dish Margarita saw the severed head of a man with most of its front teeth missing. The absolute silence was broken only by the distant sound, puzzling under the circumstances, of a door-bell ringing.

"Mikhail Alexandrovich," said Woland quietly to the head, at which its eyelids opened. With a shudder Margarita saw that the eyes in that dead face were alive, fully conscious and tortured with pain.

"It all came true, didn't it?" said Woland, staring at the eyes of the head. "Your head was cut off by a woman, the meeting didn't take place and I am living in your apartment. That is a fact. And a fact is the most obdurate thing in the world. But what interests us now is the future, not the facts of the past. You have always been a fervent proponent of the theory that when a man's head is cut off his life stops, he turns to dust and he ceases to exist. I am glad to be able to tell you in front of all my guests—despite the fact that their presence here is proof to the contrary—that your theory is intelligent and sound. Now, one theory deserves another. Among them there is one which maintains that a man will receive his desserts in accordance with his beliefs. So be it! You shall depart into the void, and from the goblet into which your skull is about to be transformed I shall have the pleasure of drinking to life eternal!"

Woland raised his sword. Immediately the skin of the head darkened and shrank, then fell away in shreds, the eyes disappeared, and in a second Margarita saw on the dish a yellowed skull, with emerald eyes and pearl teeth, mounted on a golden stand. The top of the skull opened with a hinge.

"In a second, Messire," said Koroviev, noticing Woland's inquiring glance, "he will stand before you. I can hear the creak of his shoes and the tinkle as he puts down the last glass of champagne of his lifetime. Here he is."

A new guest, quite alone, entered the ballroom. Outwardly he was no different from the thousands of other male guests, except in one thing—he was literally staggering with fright. Blotches glowed on his cheeks, and his eyes were swiveling with alarm. The guest was stunned. Everything that he saw shocked him, above all the way Woland was dressed.

Yet he was greeted with marked courtesy.

"Ah, my dear Baron Maigel," Woland said with a welcoming smile to his guest, whose eyes were starting out of his head. "I am happy to introduce to you"— Woland turned toward his guests—"Baron Maigel, who works for the Entertainments Commission as a guide to the sights of the capital for foreign visitors."

Then Margarita went numb. She recognized this man Maigel. She had noticed him several times in Moscow theaters and restaurants. "Has he died, too?" Margarita wondered. But the matter was soon explained.

"The dear baron," Woland continued with a broad smile, "was charming enough to ring me up as soon as I arrived in Moscow and to offer me his expert services as a guide to the sights of the city. Naturally I was happy to invite him to come and see me."

Here Margarita noticed that Azazello handed the dish with the skull to Koroviev.

"By the way, Baron," said Woland, suddenly lowering his voice confidentially, "rumors have been going round that you have an unquenchable curiosity. This characteristic, people say, together with your rather less developed conversational gifts, has begun to attract general attention. What is more, evil tongues have let slip the words 'eavesdropper' and 'spy.' There is a suggestion that this may bring you to an unhappy end in less than a month from now. So in order to save you from the agonizing suspense of waiting we have decided to come to your help, making use of the fact that you invited yourself to see me with the intention of spying and eavesdropping as much as you could."

The baron turned paler than the pallid Abadonna, and then something terrible happened. Abadonna stepped in front of the baron and snatched off his glasses. At that moment there was a flash and a crack from Azazello's hand, and the baron staggered, crimson blood spurting from his chest and drenching his starched shirt front and waistcoat. Koroviev placed the skull under the pulsating stream of blood and when the goblet was full handed it to Woland. The baron's lifeless body had meanwhile crumpled to the floor.

"Your health, ladies and gentlemen," said Woland and raised the goblet to his lips.

An instant metamorphosis took place. The nightshirt and darned slippers vanished. Woland was wearing a black robe with a sword at his hip. He strode over to Margarita, offered her the goblet and said in a commanding voice, "Drink!"

Margarita felt dizzy, but the cup was already at her lips and a voice was whispering in her ears, "Don't be afraid, your majesty . . . don't be afraid, your majesty, the blood has long since drained away into the earth and grapes have grown on the spot."

Her eyes shut, Margarita took a sip and the sweet juice ran through her veins, her ears rang. She was deafened by cocks crowing, a distant band played a march. The crowd of guests faded—the tail-coated men and the women withered to dust, and before her eyes the bodies began to rot, the stench of the tomb filled the air. The columns dissolved, the lights went out, the fountains dried up and vanished with the camellias and the tulips. All that remained was what had been before: poor Berlioz' drawing room, with a shaft of light falling through its half-open door. Margarita opened it wide and went in.

CHAPTER 24

THE MASTER IS RELEASED

Everything in Woland's bedroom was as it had been before the ball. Woland was sitting in his nightshirt on the bed, only this time Hella was not rubbing his knee and a meal was laid on the table in place of the chessboard. Koroviev and Azazello had removed their tail coats and were sitting at the table, alongside them the cat, who still refused to be parted from his bow tie even though it was by now reduced to a grubby shred. Tottering, Margarita walked up to the table and leaned on it. Woland beckoned her, as before, to sit beside him on the bed.

"Well, was it very exhausting?" inquired Woland.

"Oh, no, Messire," replied Margarita in a scarcely audible voice.

"*Noblesse oblige,*" remarked the cat, pouring out a glassful of clear liquid for Margarita.

"Is that vodka?" Margarita asked weakly.

The cat jumped up from its chair in indignation. "Excuse me, your majesty," he squeaked, "do you think I would give vodka to a lady? That is pure spirits!"

Margarita smiled and tried to push away the glass.

"Drink it up," said Woland, and Margarita at once picked up the glass.

"Sit down, Hella," ordered Woland and explained to Margarita. "The night of the full moon is a night of celebration, and

I dine in the company of my close friends and my servants. Well, how do you feel? How did you find that exhausting ball?"

"Shattering!" quavered Koroviev. "They were all charmed, they all fell in love with her, they were all smitten! Such tact, such *savoir-faire*, such fascination, such charm!"

Woland silently raised his glass and clinked it with Margarita's. She drank obediently, expecting the spirits to knock her out. They had no ill effect, however. The reviving warmth flowed through her body, she felt a mild shock in the back of her neck, her strength returned as if she had just waked from a long refreshing sleep, and she felt ravenously hungry. As she remembered that she had not eaten since the morning of the day before, her hunger increased and she began wolfing down caviar.

Behemoth cut himself a slice of pineapple, salted and peppered it, ate it and chased it down with a second glass of spirits with a flourish that earned a round of applause.

After Margarita's second glassful the light in the candelabra burned brighter and the coals in the fireplace glowed hotter, yet she did not feel the least drunk. As her white teeth bit into the meat, Margarita savored the delicious juice that poured from it and watched Behemoth smearing an oyster with mustard.

"If I were you I should put a grape on top of it, too," said Hella, digging the cat in the ribs.

"Kindly don't teach your grandmother to suck eggs," Behemoth replied. "I know how to behave at table, so mind your own business."

"Oh, how nice it is to dine like this, at home," tinkled Koroviev's voice, "just among friends."

"No, Faggot," said the cat. "I like the ball—it's so grand and exciting."

"It's not in the least exciting and not very grand either, and those idiotic bears and the tigers in the bar—they nearly gave me migraine with their roaring," said Woland.

"Of course, Messire," said the cat. "If you think it wasn't very grand, I immediately find myself agreeing with you."

"And so I should think," replied Woland.

"I was joking," said the cat meekly, "and as for those tigers, I'll have them roasted."

"You can't eat tiger meat," said Hella.

"Think so? Well, let me tell you a story," retorted the cat. Screwing up its eyes with pleasure, it told a story of how it had once spent nineteen days wandering in the desert and its only food had been the meat of a tiger it had killed. They all listened with fascination, and when Behemoth came to the end of his story they all chorused in unison: "Liar!"

"The most interesting thing about that farrago," said Woland, "was that it was a lie from first to last."

"Oh, you think so, do you?" exclaimed the cat, and everybody thought that it was about to protest again, but it only said quietly, "History will be my judge."

"Tell me—" revived by the vodka, Margarita turned to Azazello—"did you shoot that ex-baron?"

"Of course," replied Azazello, "why not? He needed shooting."

"I had such a shock!" exclaimed Margarita, "it happened so unexpectedly!"

"There was nothing unexpected about it," Azazello objected, and Koroviev whined, "Of course she was shocked. Why, even I was shaking in my shoes! Bang! Crash! Down went the baron!"

"I nearly had hysterics," added the cat, licking a caviar-smeared spoon.

"But there's something I can't understand," said Margarita, her eyes sparkling with curiosity. "Couldn't the music and general noise of the ball be heard outside?"

"Of course not, your majesty," said Koroviev. "We saw to that. These things must be done discreetly."

"Yes, I see . . . but what about that man on the staircase when Azazello and I came up . . . and the other one at the foot of the staircase? I had the impression that they were keeping watch on your apartment."

"You're right, you're right," cried Koroviev, "you're right, my dear Margarita Nikolayevna! You have confirmed my suspicions. Yes, he was watching our apartment. For a while I thought he was some absent-minded professor or a lover mooning about on the staircase. But no! I had an uncomfortable feeling he might be watching the apartment. And there was another one at the bottom of the stairs, too. And the one at the main entrance—did he look the same?"

"Suppose they come and arrest you?" asked Margarita.

"Oh, they'll come all right, fairest one, they'll come!" answered Koroviev. "I feel it in my bones. Not now, of course, but they'll come when they're ready. But I don't think they'll have much luck."

"Oh, what a shock I had when the baron fell!" repeated Margarita, obviously still feeling the effects of seeing her first murder. "I suppose you're a good shot?"

"Fair," answered Azazello.

"At how many paces?"

"As many as you like," replied Azazello. "It's one thing to hit Latunsky's windows with a hammer, but it's quite another to hit him in the heart."

"In the heart!" exclaimed Margarita, clutching at her own heart. "In the heart!" she repeated grimly.

"What's this about Latunsky?" inquired Woland, frowning at Margarita.

Azazello, Koroviev and Behemoth looked down in embarrassment, and Margarita replied, blushing, "He's a critic. I wrecked his apartment this evening."

"Did you now! Why?"

"Because, Messire," Margarita explained, "he destroyed a certain master."

"But why did you put yourself to such trouble?" asked Woland.

"Let me do it, Messire!" cried the cat joyfully, jumping to its feet.

"You sit down," growled Azazello, rising. "I'll go at once."

"No!" cried Margarita. "No, I beg you, Messire, you mustn't!"

"As you wish, as you wish," replied Woland. Azazello sat down again.

"Where were we, precious Queen Margot?" said Koroviev. "Ah, yes, his heart . . . He can hit a man's heart all right." Koroviev pointed a long finger at Azazello. "Anywhere you like. Just name the auricle—or the ventricle."

For a moment Margarita did not grasp the implication of this, then she exclaimed in amazement, "But they're inside the body—you can't see them!"

"My dear," burbled Koroviev, "that's the whole point—you can't see them! That's the joke! Any fool can hit something you can see!"

Koroviev took the seven of spades out of a box, showed it to Margarita and asked her to point at one of the spots. Margarita chose the one in the upper right-hand corner. Hella hid the card under a pillow and shouted, "Ready!"

Azazello, who was sitting with his back to the pillow, took a black automatic out of his trouser pocket, aimed the muzzle over his shoulder and, without turning round toward the bed, fired, giving Margarita an enjoyable shock. The seven of spades was removed from under the pillow. The upper right-hand spot had been shot through.

"I wouldn't like to meet you when you've got a revolver," said Margarita with a coquettish look at Azazello. She had a passion for people who did things well.

"My precious queen," squeaked Koroviev, "I don't recommend anybody to meet him even without his revolver! I give you my word of honor as an ex-choirmaster that anybody who did would regret it."

During the trial of marksmanship the cat had sat scowling. Suddenly it announced, "I bet I can shoot better than that."

Azazello snorted, but Behemoth was insistent and demanded not one but two revolvers. Azazello drew another pistol from his left hip pocket and with a sarcastic grin handed them both to the cat. Two spots on the card were selected. The cat took a long time to prepare, then turned its back on the cushion. Margarita sat down with her fingers in her ears and stared at the owl dozing on the mantelpiece. Behemoth fired from both revolvers, at which there came a yelp from Hella, the owl fell off the mantelpiece dead and the clock stopped from a bullet in its vitals. Hella, one finger bleeding, sank her nails into the cat's fur. Behemoth in retaliation clawed at her hair, and the pair of them rolled on the floor in a struggling heap. A glass fell off the table and broke.

"Somebody pull this she-devil off me!" wailed the cat, lashing out at Hella, who had thrown the animal on its back and was sitting astride it. The combatants were separated and Koroviev healed Hella's wounded finger by blowing on it.

"I can't shoot properly when people are whispering about me behind my back!" shouted Behemoth, trying to stick back into place a large handful of fur that had been torn off his back.

"I bet you," said Woland with a smile at Margarita, "that he did that on purpose. He can shoot perfectly well."

Hella and the cat made friends again and sealed their reconciliation with a kiss. Someone removed the card from under the cushion and examined it. Not a single spot, except the one shot through by Azazello, had been touched.

"I don't believe it," said the cat, staring through the hole in the card at the light of the candelabra.

Supper went gaily on. The candles began to gutter, a warm dry heat suffused the room from the fireplace. Having eaten her fill, a feeling of well-being came over Margarita. She watched as Azazello blew smoke rings at the fireplace and the cat spiked them on the end of his sword. She felt no desire to go, although by her timing it was late—probably, she thought, about six o'clock in the morning.

During a pause Margarita turned to Woland and said timidly, "Excuse me, but it's time for me to go . . . it's getting late."

"Where are you going in such a hurry!" inquired Woland politely but a little coldly. The others said nothing, pretending to be watching the game with the smoke rings.

"Yes, it's time," said Margarita uneasily and turned round as if looking for a cloak or something else to wear. Her nakedness was beginning to embarrass her. She got up from the table. In silence Woland picked up his greasy dressing gown from the bed and Koroviev threw it over Margarita's shoulders.

"Thank you, Messire," whispered Margarita with a questioning glance at Woland. In reply he gave her a polite but apathetic smile. Black depression at once swelled up in Margarita's heart. She felt herself cheated. No one appeared to be going to offer her any reward for her services at the ball and nobody made a move to prevent her going. Yet she realized quite well that she had nowhere to go. A passing thought that she might have to go back home brought on an inner convulsion of despair. Dared she ask about the master, as Azazello had so temptingly suggested in the Alexander Gardens? "No, never!" she said to herself.

"Good-bye, Messire," she said aloud, thinking, "If only I can get out of here, I'll make straight for the river and drown myself!"

"Sit down," Woland suddenly commanded her.

A change came over Margarita's face and she sat down.

"Perhaps you'd like to say something in farewell?"

"Nothing, Messire," replied Margarita proudly. "However, if you still need me, I am ready to do anything you wish. I am not at all tired and I enjoyed the ball. If it had lasted longer I would have been glad to continue offering my knee to be kissed by thousands more gallows birds and murderers."

Margarita felt she was looking at Woland through a veil; her eyes had filled with tears.

"Well said!" boomed Woland in a terrifying voice. "That was the right answer!"

"The right answer!" echoed Woland's retinue in unison.

"We have put you to the test," said Woland. "You should

never ask anyone for anything. Never—and especially from those who are more powerful than yourself. They will make the offer and they will give of their own accord. Sit down, proud woman!" Woland pulled the heavy dressing gown from Margarita's back, and she again found herself sitting beside him on the bed. "So, Margot," Woland went on, his voice softening, "what do you want for having been my hostess tonight? What reward do you want for having spent the night naked? What price do you set on your bruised knee? What damages did you suffer at the hands of my guests, whom just now you called gallows birds? Tell me! You can speak without constraint now, because it was I who made the offer."

Margarita's heart began to knock, she sighed deeply and tried to think of something.

"Come now, be brave!" said Woland encouragingly. "Use your imagination! The mere fact of having watched the murder of that worn-out old rogue of a baron is worth a reward, especially for a woman. Well?"

Margarita caught her breath. She was about to utter her secret wish when she suddenly turned pale, opened her mouth and stared. "Frieda! Frieda! Frieda!" a sobbing, imploring voice cried in her ear. "My name is Frieda!" And Margarita said, stuttering, "Can I ask . . . for one thing?"

"Demand, don't ask, *madonna mia*," replied Woland with an understanding smile. "You may demand one thing." With careful emphasis Woland repeated Margarita's own words: "one thing."

Margarita sighed again and said, "I want them to stop giving Frieda back the handkerchief she used to stifle her baby."

The cat looked up at the ceiling and sighed noisily, but said nothing, obviously remembering the damage done to his ear.

"In view of the fact," said Woland, smiling, "that the possibility of your having taken a bribe from that idiot Frieda is, of course, excluded—it would in any case have been unfitting to your queenly rank—I don't know what to do. So there remains only one thing—to find yourself some rags and use them to block up all the cracks in my bedroom."

"What do you mean, Messire?" said Margarita, puzzled.

"I quite agree, Messire," interrupted the cat. "Rags—that's it!" And the cat banged its paw on the table in exasperation.

"I was speaking of compassion," explained Woland, the gaze of his fiery eye fixed on Margarita. "Sometimes it creeps in through the narrowest cracks. That is why I suggested using rags to block them up."

"That's what I meant, too!" exclaimed the cat, for safety's sake edging away from Margarita and covering its pointed ears with paws smeared in pink cream.

"Get out," Woland said to the cat.

"I haven't had my coffee," replied Behemoth. "How can you expect me to go yet? Surely you don't divide your guests into two grades on a festive night like this—first-grade- and second-grade-fresh, in the words of that miserable cheese-paring bartender?"

"Shut up," said Woland, then turning to Margarita inquired, "To judge from everything about you, you seem to be a good person. Am I right?"

"No," replied Margarita forcefully. "I know that I can only be frank with you and I tell you frankly—I am headstrong. I only asked you about Frieda because I was rash enough to give her a firm hope. She's waiting, Messire, she believes in my power. And if she's cheated, I shall be in a terrible position. I shall have no peace for the rest of my life. I can't help it—it just happened."

"That's quite understandable," said Woland.

"So will you do it?" Margarita asked quietly.

"Out of the question," replied Woland. "The fact is, my dear queen, there has been a slight misunderstanding. Each department must stick to its own business. I admit that our scope is fairly wide, in fact it is much wider than a number of very sharp-eyed people imagine—"

"Yes, much wider," said the cat, unable to restrain itself and obviously proud of its interjections.

"Shut up, damn you!" said Woland, and he turned and went on to Margarita. "But what sense is there, I ask you, in doing something which is the business of another department, as I call it? So you see I can't do it; you must do it yourself."

"But can I do it?"

Azazello squinted at Margarita, gave an imperceptible flick of his red mop and sneered.

"That's just the trouble—doing it," murmured Woland. He had been turning the globe, staring at some detail on it, apparently absorbed in something else while Margarita had been talking.

"Well, as to Frieda—" Koroviev prompted her.

"Frieda!" cried Margarita in a piercing voice.

The door burst open and a naked, disheveled but completely sober woman with ecstatic eyes ran into the room and stretched out her arms toward Margarita, who said majestically, "You are forgiven. You will never be given the handkerchief again."

Frieda gave a cry and fell spread-eagled, face downward on the floor in front of Margarita. Woland waved his hand and Frieda vanished.

"Thank you. Good-bye," said Margarita and rose to go.

"Now, Behemoth," said Woland, "as tonight is a holiday we shan't take advantage of her for being so impractical, shall we?" He turned to Margarita. "All right, that didn't count, because I did nothing. What do you want for yourself?"

There was silence, broken by Koroviev whispering to Margarita, *"Madonna bellissima,* this time I advise you to be more sensible. Or your luck may run out."

"I want you to give me back instantly, this minute, my beloved—the master," said Margarita, her face contorted.

A gust of wind burst into the room, flattening the candle flames. The heavy curtain billowed out, the window was flung open and high above appeared a full moon—not a setting moon, but the midnight moon. A dark green cloth stretched from the window sill to the floor, and down it walked Ivan's night visitor, the man who called himself the master. He was wearing his hospital clothes—dressing gown, slippers and the black cap from which he was never parted. His unshaven face twitched in a grimace, he squinted with fear at the candle flames, and a flood of moonlight boiled around him.

Margarita recognized him at once, groaned, clasped her hands and ran toward him. She kissed him on the forehead, the lips, pressed her face to his prickly cheek, and her long-suppressed tears streamed down her face. She could only say, repeating it like a senseless refrain, "It's you . . . it's you . . . it's you. . . ."

The master pushed her away and said huskily, "Don't cry, Margot, don't torment me, I'm very ill," and he grasped the window sill as though preparing to jump out and run away again. Staring round at the figures seated in the room, he cried, "I'm frightened, Margot! I'm having hallucinations again."

Stifling her sobs, Margarita whispered, "No, no, don't be afraid . . . I'm here . . . I'm here. . . ."

Deftly and unobtrusively Koroviev slipped a chair behind the master. He collapsed into it, and Margarita fell on her knees at his side, where she grew calmer. In her excitement she had not noticed that she was no longer naked but that she was now wearing a black silk gown. The master's head nodded forward and he stared gloomily at the floor.

"Yes," said Woland after a pause, "they have almost broken him." He gave an order to Koroviev: "Now, sir, give this man something to drink."

In a trembling voice Margarita begged the master, "Drink it, drink it! Are you afraid? No, no, believe me, they want to help you!"

The sick man took the glass and drank it, but his hand trembled, he dropped the glass and it shattered on the floor.

"Mazel tov!" Koroviev whispered to Margarita. "Look, he's coming to himself already."

It was true. The patient's stare was less wild and distraught.

"Is it really you, Margot?" asked the midnight visitor.

"Yes, it really is," replied Margarita.

"More!" ordered Woland.

When the master had drained the second glass, his eyes were fully alive and conscious.

"That's better," said Woland with a slight frown. "Now we can talk. Who are you?"

"I am no one," replied the master with a lopsided smile.

"Where have you just come from?"

"From the madhouse. I am a mental patient," replied the visitor.

Margarita could not bear to hear this and burst into tears again. Then she wiped her eyes and cried, "It's terrible—terrible! He is a master, Messire, I assure you! Cure him—he's worth it!"

"You realize who I am, don't you?" Woland asked. "Do you know where you are?"

"I know," answered the master. "My next-door neighbor in the madhouse is that boy, Ivan Bezdomny. He told me about you."

"Did he now!" replied Woland. "I had the pleasure of meeting that young man at Patriarch's Ponds. He nearly drove *me* mad, trying to prove that I didn't exist. But you believe in me, I hope?"

"I must," said the visitor, "although I would much prefer it if I could regard you as a figment of my own hallucination. Forgive me," added the master, recollecting himself.

"By all means regard me as such if that makes you any happier," replied Woland politely.

"No, no!" said Margarita with anxiety, shaking the master by the shoulder. "Think again! It really is him!"

"But I really am like a hallucination. Look at my profile in the moonlight." The cat moved into a shaft of moonlight and was going to say something more, but was told to shut up and only said, "All right, all right, I'll be quiet. I'll be a silent hallucination."

"Tell me, why does Margarita call you the master?" inquired Woland.

The man laughed and said, "An understandable weakness of hers. She has too high an opinion of a novel that I've written."

"What novel?"

"A novel about Pontius Pilate."

Again the candle flames flickered and jumped and the dishes rattled on the table as Woland gave a laugh like a clap of thunder. Yet no one was frightened or shocked by the laughter; Behemoth even applauded.

"About what? About whom?" said Woland, ceasing to laugh. "But that's extraordinary! In this day and age? Couldn't you have chosen another subject? Let me have a look." Woland stretched out his hand palm upward.

"Unfortunately I cannot show it to you," replied the master, "because I burned it in my stove."

"I'm sorry but I don't believe you," said Woland. "You can't have. Manuscripts don't burn." He turned to Behemoth and said, "Come on, Behemoth, give me the novel."

The cat jumped down from its chair, and where he had been sitting was a pile of manuscripts. With a bow the cat handed the top copy to Woland. Margarita shuddered and cried out, moved to tears. "There's the manuscript! There it is!" She flung herself at Woland's feet and cried ecstatically, "You are all-powerful!"

Woland took it, turned it over, put it aside and turned, unsmiling, to stare at the master. Without apparent cause the master had suddenly lapsed into uneasy gloom, rose from his chair, wrung his hands and, turning toward the distant moon, he started to tremble, muttering, "Even by moonlight there's no peace for me at night. . . . Why do they torment me? Oh, ye gods . . ."

Margarita clutched his hospital dressing gown, embraced him and moaned tearfully, "Oh, God, why didn't that medicine do you any good?"

"Don't be upset," whispered Koroviev, edging up to the master. "Another little glassful and I'll have one myself to keep you company."

A glass winked in the moonlight. It began to work. The master sat down again and his expression grew calmer.

"Well, that makes everything quite clear," said Woland, tapping the manuscript with his long finger.

"Quite clear," agreed the cat, forgetting its promise to be a silent hallucination. "I see the gist of this great opus quite plainly now. What do you say, Azazello?"

"I say," drawled Azazello, "that you ought to be drowned."

"Be merciful, Azazello," the cat replied, "and don't put such thoughts into my master's head. I'd come and haunt you every night and beckon you to follow me. How would you like that, Azazello?"

"Now, Margarita," said Woland, "say whatever you wish to say."

Margarita's eyes shone and she said imploringly to Woland, "May I whisper to him?"

Woland nodded, and Margarita leaned over the master's ear and whispered something into it. Aloud, he replied, "No, it's too late. I want nothing more out of life except to see you. But take my advice and leave me, otherwise you will be destroyed with me."

"No, I won't leave you," replied Margarita, and to Woland she said, "Please send us back to his basement in that street near the Arbat, light the lamp again and make everything as it was before."

The master laughed and clasping Margarita's disheveled head he said, "Don't listen to this poor woman, Messire! Somebody else is living in that basement now, and no one can turn back the clock." He laid his cheek on his mistress' head, embraced Margarita and murmured, "My poor darling . . ."

"No one can turn the clock back, did you say?" said Woland. "That's true. But we can always try. Azazello!"

Immediately a bewildered man in his underclothes crashed through the ceiling to the floor, with a suitcase in his hand and wearing a cap. Shaking with fear, the man bowed.

"Is your name Mogarych?" Azazello asked him.

"Aloysius Mogarych," said the new arrival, trembling.

"Are you the man who lodged a complaint against this man—" pointing to the master—"after you had read an article about him by Latunsky and denounced him for harboring illegal literature?" asked Azazello.

The man turned blue and burst into tears of penitence.

"You did it because you wanted to get his apartment, didn't you?" said Azazello in a confiding, nasal whine.

The cat gave a hiss of fury, and Margarita, with a howl of "I'll teach you to thwart a witch!" dug her nails into Aloysius Mogarych's face.

There was a brisk scuffle.

"Stop it!" cried the master in an agonized voice. "Shame on you, Margot!"

"I protest! There's nothing shameful in it!" squeaked the cat. Koroviev pulled Margarita away.

"I put in a bathroom," cried Mogarych, his face streaming blood. His teeth were chattering and he was babbling with fright. "I gave it a coat of whitewash—"

"What a good thing that you put in a bathroom," said Azazello approvingly. "He'll be able to have baths now." And he shouted at Mogarych: "Get out!"

The man turned head over heels and sailed out of the open window of Woland's bedroom.

His eyes starting from his head, the master whispered, "This beats Ivan's story!" He stared round in amazement, then said to the cat, "Excuse me, but are you . . ." he hesitated, not sure how one talked to a cat, "are you the same cat who boarded the streetcar?"

"I am," said the cat, flattered, and added, "It's nice to hear someone speak so politely to a cat. People usually address cats as 'pussy,' which I regard as an infernal liberty."

"It seems to me that you're not entirely a cat," replied the master hesitantly. "The hospital people are bound to catch me again, you know," he added to Woland resignedly.

"Why should they?" said Koroviev reassuringly. Some papers and books appeared in his hand. "Is this your case history?"

"Yes."

Koroviev threw the case history into the fire. "Remove the document and you remove the man," he said with satisfaction.

"And is this your landlord's rent book?"

"Yes."

"What is the tenant's name? Aloysius Mogarych?" Koroviev blew on the page. "Presto! He's gone and, please note, he was never there. If the landlord is surprised, tell him he was dreaming about Aloysius. Mogarych? What Mogarych? Never heard of him!" At this the rent book evaporated from Koroviev's hands. "Now it's back on the landlord's desk."

"You were right," said the master, amazed at Koroviev's efficiency, "when you said that once you remove the document, you remove the man as well. I no longer exist now—I have no papers."

"Oh, no, I beg your pardon," exclaimed Koroviev. "That is just another hallucination. Here are your papers!" He handed the master some documents, then said with a wink to Margarita, "And here is your property, Margarita Nikolayevna." Koroviev handed Margarita a manuscript with burnt edges, a dried rose, a photograph and, with special care, a savings bank book. "The ten thousand that you deposited, Margarita Nikolayevna. We have no use for other people's money."

"May my paws drop off before I touch other people's money," exclaimed the cat, bouncing up and down on a suitcase to flatten the copies of the ill-fated novel that were inside it.

"And a little document of yours," Koroviev went on, handing Margarita a piece of paper. Then turning to Woland he announced respectfully, "That is everything, Messire."

"No, it's not everything," answered Woland, turning away from the globe. "What would you like me to do with your retinue, madonna? I have no need of them myself."

Natasha, stark naked, flew in at the open window and cried to Margarita, "I hope you'll be very happy, Margarita Nikolayevna!" She nodded toward the master and went on: "You see, I knew about it all the time."

"Servants know everything," remarked the cat, wagging its paw sagely. "It's a mistake to think they're blind."

"What do you want, Natasha?" asked Margarita. "Go back home."

"Dear Margarita Nikolayevna," said Natasha imploringly and fell on her knees, "ask him—" she nodded toward Woland— "to let me stay a witch. I don't want to go back to that house! Last night at the ball Monsieur Jacques made me an offer." Natasha unclenched her fist and showed some gold coins.

Margarita looked inquiringly at Woland, who nodded. Natasha embraced Margarita, kissed her noisily and with a triumphant cry flew out of the window.

The next to appear was Nikolai Ivanovich. He had regained human form, but was extremely glum and rather cross.

"Now here's someone I shall be especially glad to release," said Woland, looking at Nikolai Ivanovich with repulsion. "I shall be delighted to see the last of him."

"Whatever you do, please give me a certificate," said Nikolai Ivanovich, anxiously but with great insistence, "to prove where I was last night."

"What for?" asked the cat sternly.

"To show my wife and to the police," said Nikolai Ivanovich firmly.

"We don't usually give certificates," replied the cat frowning, "but since it's for you we'll make an exception."

Before Nikolai Ivanovich knew what was happening, the naked Hella was sitting behind a typewriter and the cat was dictating to her:

" 'This is to certify that the bearer, Nikolai Ivanovich, spent the night in question at Satan's Ball, having been enticed there in a vehicular capacity.' Hella, put in brackets after that '[pig].' 'Signed—Behemoth.' "

"What about the date?" squeaked Nikolai Ivanovich.

"We don't mention the date, the document becomes invalid if it's dated," replied the cat, waving the piece of paper. Then the animal produced a rubber stamp, breathed on it in the approved fashion, stamped "Paid" on the paper and handed the document to Nikolai Ivanovich. He vanished without a trace, to be unexpectedly replaced by another man.

"Now who's this?" asked Woland contemptuously, shielding his eyes from the candlelight.

Varenukha hung his head, sighed and said in a low voice, "Send me back, I'm no good as a vampire. Hella and I nearly frightened Rimsky to death, but I'll never make a vampire— I'm just not bloodthirsty. Please let me go."

"What is he babbling about?" asked Woland, frowning. "Who is this Rimsky? What is all this nonsense?"

"Nothing to worry about, Messire," said Azazello, and he turned to Varenukha: "Don't play the fool or tell lies on the telephone any more. Understand? You're not going to, are you?"

Overcome with relief, Varenukha beamed and stammered, "Thank Go—I mean, your maj—as soon as I've had my supper . . ." He pressed his hand to his heart and gazed imploringly at Azazello.

"All right. Off you go home!" said Azazello, and Varenukha melted away.

"Now all of you leave me alone with these two," ordered Woland, pointing to the master and Margarita.

Woland's command was obeyed instantly. After a silence he said to the master, "So you're going back to your basement near the Arbat. How will you be able to write now? Where are your dreams, your inspiration?"

"I have no more dreams and my inspiration is dead," replied the master. "Nobody interests me any longer except her." He laid his hand again on Margarita's head. "I'm finished. My only wish is to return to that basement."

"And what about your novel? What about Pilate?"

"I hate that novel," replied the master. "I have been through too much because of it."

"Please," begged Margarita piteously, "don't talk like that. Why are you torturing me? You know I've put my whole life into your work," and she added, turning to Woland, "Don't listen to him, Messire. He has suffered too much."

"But won't you need to rewrite some of it?" asked Woland. "Or if you've exhausted your Procurator, why not write about somebody else—that Aloysius, for instance."

The master smiled. "Lapshennikova would never print it, and in any case that doesn't interest me."

"How will you earn your living then? Won't you mind being poor?"

"Not a bit," said the master, drawing Margarita to him. Embracing her shoulders, he added, "She'll leave me when she comes to her senses."

"I doubt it," said Woland, teeth clenched. He went on: "So the creator of Pontius Pilate proposes to go and starve in a basement?"

Margarita unlinked her arm from the master's and said passionately, "I've done all I can. I whispered to him the most tempting thing of all. And he refused."

"I know what you whispered to him," said Woland, "but that is not what tempts him most. Believe me—" he turned with a smile to the master—"your novel has some more surprises in store for you."

"What a grim prospect," answered the master.

"No, it is not grim at all," said Woland. "Nothing terrible will come of it, I assure you. Well now, Margarita Nikolayevna, everything is arranged. Have you any further claims on me?"

"How can I, Messire?"

"Then take this as a souvenir," said Woland and took a

small golden, diamond-studded horseshoe from under a cushion.

"No—I couldn't take it. Haven't you done enough for me?"

"Are you arguing with me?" asked Woland, smiling.

As Margarita had no pocket in her gown, she wrapped the horseshoe in a napkin and knotted it. Then something seemed to worry her. She looked out of the window at the moon and said, "One thing I don't understand—it still seems to be midnight. Shouldn't it be morning?"

"It's pleasant to stop the clock on a festive night such as this," replied Woland. "And now—good luck!"

Margarita stretched both hands to Woland in entreaty, but found she could come no nearer to him.

"Good-bye! Good-bye!"

"*Au revoir,*" said Woland.

Margarita in her black cloak and the master in his hospital dressing gown walked out into the corridor of Berlioz' apartment, where the light was burning and Woland's retinue was waiting for them. As they passed along the corridor, Hella, helped by the cat, carried the suitcase containing the novel and Margarita Nikolayevna's few belongings.

At the door of the apartment Koroviev bowed and vanished, while the others escorted them down the staircase. It was empty. As they passed the third-floor landing, a faint bump was heard, but no one paid it any attention. At the front door of staircase 6 Azazello blew into the air, and as they entered the dark courtyard they saw a man in boots and peaked cap sound asleep on the doorstep and a large, black car standing by the entrance with dimmed lights. Barely visible in the driver's seat was the outline of a crow.

Margarita was just about to sit down when she gave a stifled cry of despair: "Oh, God, I've lost the horseshoe."

"Get into the car," said Azazello, "and wait for me. I'll be back in a moment as soon as I've looked into this." He walked back through the doorway.

What had happened was this: shortly before Margarita, the master and their escort had left No. 50, a shriveled woman carrying a bag and a tin can had emerged from No. 48, the apartment immediately below. It was Anna—the same Anna who the previous Wednesday had spilt the sunflower-seed oil near the turnstile with such disastrous consequences for Berlioz.

Nobody knew, and probably never will know, what this woman was doing in Moscow or what she lived on. She was to be seen every day either with her tin can or her bag or both, sometimes at the oil shop, sometimes at the market, sometimes outside the block of apartments or on the staircase, but mostly in the kitchen of apartment No. 48, where she lived. She was notorious for being a harbinger of disaster wherever she went, and she was nicknamed "Anna the Plague."

Anna the Plague usually got up very early in the morning, but this morning something roused her long before dawn, soon after midnight. Her key turned in the door, her nose poked through and was followed by Anna herself, who slammed the door behind her. She was just about to set off on some errand when the door banged on the upstairs landing, a man came bounding downstairs, crashed into Anna and knocked her sideways so hard that she hit the back of her head against the wall.

"Where the hell do you think you're going like that—in your underwear?" whined Anna, rubbing the back of her head.

The man, who was wearing underclothes and a cap and carrying a suitcase, answered in a sleepy voice with his eyes closed, "Bath . . . whitewash . . . cost me a fortune . . ." and bursting into tears he bellowed, "I've been kicked out!"

Then he dashed off—not downstairs but upstairs again to where the windowpane had been broken by Popalevsky's foot, and through it he glided feet first out into the courtyard. Forgetting about her aching head, Anna gasped and rushed up to the broken window. She lay flat on the landing floor and stuck her head out into the courtyard, expecting to see the mortal remains of the man with the suitcase lit up by the courtyard lamp. But there was absolutely nothing to be seen on the courtyard pavement.

As far as Anna could tell, this weird sleepwalker had flown out of the house like a bird, leaving not a trace. She crossed herself and thought, "It's that No. 50! No wonder people say it's haunted."

The thought had hardly crossed her mind before the door upstairs slammed again and someone else came running down. Anna pressed herself to the wall and saw a respectable-looking gentleman with a little beard and, so it seemed to her, a slightly piggish face, who slipped past her and, like the first man, left the building through the window, also without hitting the ground below. Anna had long since forgotten her original reason for coming out and stayed on the staircase, crossing herself, moaning and talking to herself. After a short while a third man, with no beard but with a round clean-shaven face and wearing a shirt, emerged and shot through the window in turn.

To give Anna her due, she was of an inquiring turn of mind, and she decided to wait and see if there were to be any further marvels. The upstairs door opened again and a whole crowd started down the stairs, this time not running but walking like ordinary people. Anna ran from the window down to her own front door, quickly opened it, hid behind it and kept her eye, wild with curiosity, fixed to the crack which she had left open.

An odd sick-looking man, pale, with a stubbly beard, in a black cap and dressing gown, was walking unsteadily downstairs, carefully helped by a lady wearing what looked to Anna in the gloom like a black cassock. The lady was wearing some kind of transparent slippers, obviously foreign, but so torn and shredded that she was almost barefoot. It was indecent—bedroom slippers and quite obviously naked except for a black gown billowing out as she walked! "That No. 50!" Anna's mind was already savoring the story she was going to tell the neighbors tomorrow.

After this lady came a naked girl carrying a suitcase and helped by an enormous black cat. Rubbing her eyes, Anna could barely help bursting into a shriek of pure amazement. Last in the procession was a short, limping foreigner with a walleye, no jacket, a white evening-dress waistcoat and a bow tie. Just as the whole party had filed downstairs past Anna's door, something fell onto the landing with a gentle thump.

When the sound of footsteps had died away, Anna wriggled out of her doorway like a snake, put down her tin can, dropped onto her stomach and started groping about on the landing floor. Suddenly she found herself holding something heavy wrapped in a table napkin. Her eyes started from her head as she untied the napkin and lifted the jewel close to eyes that burned with a wolfish greed. A storm of thoughts whirled through her mind: "See no sights and tell no tales! Shall I take it to my nephew? Or split it up into pieces? I could pry the stones out and sell them one at a time. . . ."

Anna hid her find in the front of her blouse, picked up her tin can and was just about to abandon her errand and slip back indoors when she was suddenly confronted by the coatless man with the white shirt front, who whispered to her in a soft voice, "Give me that horseshoe wrapped in a serviette!"

"What serviette? What horseshoe?" said Anna, prevaricating

with great skill. "Never seen a serviette. What's the matter with you—drunk?"

Without another word but with fingers as hard and as cold as the handrail on a bus, the man in the white shirt front gripped Anna's throat so tightly that he prevented all air from entering her lungs. The tin can fell from her hand. Having stopped Anna from breathing for a while, the jacketless stranger removed his fingers from her neck. Gasping for breath, Anna smiled.

"Oh, you mean the little horseshoe?" she said. "Of course! Is it yours? I looked and there it was wrapped in a serviette. I picked it up on purpose in case anybody else might find it and vanish with it!"

With the horseshoe in his possession again, the stranger began bowing and scraping to Anna, shook her by the hand and thanked her warmly in a thick foreign accent: "I am most deeply grateful to you, madam. This horseshoe is dear to me as a memory. Please allow me to give you two hundred rubles for saving it."

At which he pulled the money from his waistcoat pocket and gave it to Anna, who could only exclaim with a bewildered grin, "Oh, thank you so much! *Merci!*"

In one leap the generous stranger had jumped down a whole flight of stairs, but before vanishing altogether he shouted up at her, this time without a trace of an accent, "Next time you find someone else's things, you old witch, hand it in to the police instead of stuffing it down your front!"

Utterly confused by events and by the singing in her ears, Anna could do nothing for a long time but stand on the staircase and croak, *"Merci! Merci!"* until long after the stranger had vanished.

Having returned Woland's present to Margarita, Azazello said good-bye to her, inquiring if she was comfortably seated; Hella gave her a smacking kiss, and the cat pressed itself affectionately against her hand. With a wave to the master as he lowered himself awkwardly into his seat and a wave to the crow, the party vanished into thin air, without bothering to return indoors and walk up the staircase. The crow switched on the headlights and drove out of the courtyard past the man asleep at the entrance. Finally the lights of the big black car were lost as they merged into the rows of street lights on silent, empty Sadovaya Street.

An hour later Margarita was sitting, softly weeping from

shock and happiness, in the basement of the little house in one
of the side streets off the Arbat. In the master's study all was
as it had been before that terrible autumn night of the year
before. On the table, covered with a velvet cloth, stood a vase
of lilies of the valley and a shaded lamp. The charred manuscript lay in front of her, beside it a pile of undamaged copies.
The house was silent. Next door on a couch, covered by his
hospital dressing gown, the master lay in a deep sleep, his
regular breathing inaudible in the adjoining room.

Drying her tears, Margarita picked up one of the unharmed
folios and found the place that she had been reading before
she had met Azazello beneath the Kremlin wall. She had no
wish to sleep. She smoothed the manuscript tenderly, as one
strokes a favorite cat and, turning it over in her hands, she
inspected it from every angle, pausing now on the title page,
now at the end. A fearful thought passed through her mind
that it was nothing more than a piece of wizardry, that the
folio might vanish from sight, that she would wake up and find
that she was in her bedroom at home and it was time to get
up and stoke the boiler. But this was only a last terrible
fantasy, the echo of long-borne suffering. Nothing vanished,
the all-powerful Woland really was all-powerful, and Margarita was able to leaf through the manuscript to her heart's
content, till dawn if she wanted to, stare at it, kiss it and
reread the words:

"The mist that came from the Mediterranean Sea blotted
out the city that Pilate so detested. . . ."

*How the Procurator Tried to Save
Judas of Karioth*

The mist that came from the Mediterranean Sea blotted out the city that Pilate so detested. The suspension bridges connecting the temple with the grim fortress of Antonia vanished, the murk descended from the sky and drowned the winged gods above the hippodrome, the crenelated Hasmonaean palace, the bazaars, the caravanserais, the alleyways, the pools. . . . Jerusalem, the great city, vanished as though it had never been. The mist devoured everything, frightening every living creature in Jerusalem and its surroundings. The city was engulfed by a strange cloud which had crept over it from the sea toward the end of that day, the fourteenth of the month of Nisan.

It had emptied its belly over Mount Golgotha, where the executioners had hurriedly dispatched their victims; it had flowed over the temple of Jerusalem, pouring down in smoky cascades from the mound of the temple and invading the Lower City. It had rolled through open windows and driven people indoors from the winding streets. At first it held back its rain and only spat lightning, the flame cleaving through the smoking black vapor, lighting up the great pile of the temple and its glittering, scaly roof. But the flash passed in a moment and the temple was plunged again into an abyss of darkness. Several times it loomed through the murk, to vanish again, and each time its disappearance was accompanied by a noise like the crack of doom.

Other shimmering flashes lit up the palace of Herod the Great facing the temple on the western hill; as they did so, the golden statues, eyeless and fearful, seemed to leap up into the black sky and stretch their arms toward it. Then the fire from heaven would be quenched again and a great thunderclap would banish the gilded idols into the mist.

The rainstorm burst suddenly and the storm turned into a hurricane. On the very spot near a marble bench in the garden where that morning the Procurator had spoken to the High Priest, a thunderbolt snapped the trunk of a cypress as though it were a twig. Along with the water vapor and the hail, the balcony under the arcade was swept with torn rose heads, magnolia leaves, small branches and sand as the hurricane scourged the garden.

At the moment when the storm broke only the Procurator was left beneath the arcade.

He was no longer sitting in a chair but lying on a couch beside a small low table laid with food and jugs of wine. Another, empty couch stood on the far side of the table. An untidy, blood-red puddle lay spread out at the Procurator's feet amid the shards of a broken jug. The servant who had laid the Procurator's table had been so terrified by his look and so nervous at his apparent displeasure that the Procurator had lost his temper with him and smashed the jug on the mosaic floor, saying, "Why don't you look me in the eyes when you serve me? Have you stolen something?"

The African's black face turned gray, mortal terror came into his eyes, and he trembled so much that he almost broke another jug, but the Procurator waved him away and the slave ran off, leaving the pool of spilt wine.

As the hurricane struck, the African hid himself in a niche with a statue of a white, naked woman with bowed head, afraid to show himself too soon, yet frightened of missing the call should the Procurator summon him.

Lying on his couch in the half-darkness of the storm, the Procurator poured out his own wine, drank it in long gulps, stretching out his arm for an occasional piece of bread, which he crumbled and ate in little pieces. Now and again he would swallow an oyster, chew a slice of lemon and drink again.

Without the roar of water, without the claps of thunder

which seemed to be about to smash the palace roof, without the crash of hail that hammered on the steps leading up to the balcony, a listener might have heard the Procurator muttering as he talked to himself. And if the momentary flashes of lightning had shone with a steady light, an observer might have noticed that the Procurator's face, the eyes inflamed with insomnia and wine, showed impatience; that the Procurator's glance was not only preoccupied with the two yellow roses drowning in the red puddle, but that he was constantly turning his face toward the garden, toward the water-lashed sand and mud; that he was expecting someone, waiting impatiently.

A little time passed, and the veil of water in front of the Procurator began to thin out. The storm, though still furious, was abating. No more branches creaked and fell. The lightning and thunder grew less frequent. The cloud hovering over Jerusalem was no longer violet edged with white but a normal gray, the rear guard of the storm that was now moving onward toward the Dead Sea.

Soon the sound of the rain could be distinguished from the noise of water running down the gutters and onto the staircase down which the Procurator had walked to the square to pronounce sentence. At last even the tinkle of the fountain, drowned out until now, could be heard. It grew louder. Windows of blue began to appear in the gray veil as it fled eastward.

Then from far away, above the weak patter of rain, the Procurator heard faint trumpet calls and the tattoo of several score of horses' hoofs. The sound caused the Procurator to stir and his expression to liven. The ala was returning from Mount Golgotha. To judge from the sound, they were just crossing the hippodrome square.

At last the Procurator heard the long-awaited footsteps and the slap of shoe leather on the staircase leading to the upper terrace of the garden in front of the balcony. The Procurator craned his neck and his eyes shone expectantly.

Between the two marble lions there appeared first the cowled head, then the figure of a man closely wrapped in his soaking-wet cloak. It was the same man with whom the Procurator, before pronouncing sentence, had held a whispered conference in a darkened room of the palace and who had watched the execution as he played with a stick seated on a three-legged stool.

Walking straight through the puddles, the cowled man

crossed the terrace, crossed the mosaic floor of the balcony and, raising his hand, said in a pleasant, high-pitched voice, "Hail, Procurator!" The visitor spoke in Latin.

"Gods!" exclaimed Pilate. "There's not a dry stitch on you! What a storm! Please go to my room at once and change."

The man pushed back his cowl, revealing a completely wet head with the hair plastered down over his forehead. With a polite smile on his clean-shaven face he declined the offer of a change of clothing, assuring the Procurator that a little rain would do him no harm.

"I won't hear of it," replied Pilate. He clapped his hands, summoning his cowering servant, and ordered him to help the visitor to change and then to bring him some hot food.

The Procurator's visitor needed only a short while to dry his hair, change his clothes and footgear, and tidy himself up, and he soon reappeared on the balcony in dry sandals, in a purple army cloak and with his hair combed.

At that moment the sun returned to Jerusalem, and before setting in the Mediterranean it sent its parting rays over the Procurator's hated city and gilded the balcony steps. The fountain was now playing again at full strength, pigeons had landed on the terrace, cooing and hopping between the broken twigs and pecking at the sand. The red puddle was mopped up, the pottery fragments were removed, and a steaming plateful of meat was set on the table.

"I await the Procurator's orders," said the visitor as he approached the table.

"Forget about my orders until you have sat down and drunk your wine," answered Pilate kindly, pointing to the other couch.

The man reclined, and the servant poured some thick red wine into his cup. Another servant, bending cautiously over Pilate's shoulder, filled the Procurator's cup, after which the latter dismissed them both with a gesture.

While the visitor ate and drank, Pilate sipped his wine and watched his guest through narrowed eyes. The man was middle-aged, with very pleasant, neat, round features and a fleshy nose. The color of his hair was vague, though its shade lightened as it dried out. His nationality was hard to guess. His main characteristic was a look of good nature, which was belied by his eyes—or rather not so much by his eyes as by a peculiar way of looking at the person facing him. Usually the man kept his small eyes shielded under eyelids that were curiously enlarged, even swollen. At these moments the chinks in his eyelids showed nothing but mild cunning, the look of a man with a sense of humor. But there were times when the man who was now the Procurator's guest opened his eyelids wide and gave a person a sudden, unwavering stare as though to search out an inconspicuous spot on his nose. It only lasted a moment, after which the lids dropped, the eyes narrowed again and shone with goodwill and sly intelligence.

The visitor accepted a second cup of wine, swallowed a few oysters with obvious relish, tasted the boiled vegetables and ate a piece of meat. When he had eaten his fill he praised the wine: "An excellent vintage, Procurator—but is it Falernian?"

"Cecuba—thirty years old," replied the Procurator amiably.

The visitor placed his hand on his heart and declined the offer of more to eat, saying that he had had enough. Pilate refilled his own cup, and his guest did the same. The two men each poured a libation into the dish of meat, and the Procurator, raising his cup, said in a loud voice, "To thee, O Caesar, father of thy people, best and most beloved of men."

Both drank their wine to its dregs, and the Africans cleared the dishes from the table, leaving fruit and jugs of wine. The Procurator dismissed the servants, leaving him alone with his visitor under the arcade.

"So," began Pilate quietly, "what have you to tell me of the mood of the city?" Involuntarily he turned his glance downward to where, past the terraces of the garden, the colonnades and flat roofs glowed in the golden rays of the setting sun.

"I believe, Procurator," said his visitor, "that the mood of Jerusalem can now be regarded as satisfactory."

"So I can rely on there being no further disorders?"

"One can only rely," Arthanius replied with a reassuring glance at the Procurator, "on one thing in this world—on the power of great Caesar."

"May the gods send him long life," Pilate said fervently, "and universal peace!" He was silent for a moment then went on: "What do you think—can we withdraw the troops now?"

"I think the cohort from the Lightning Legion can be sent away," replied the visitor, and added: "I think it would be a good idea if it were to parade through the city before leaving."

"A very good idea," said the Procurator approvingly. "I shall order it away the day after tomorrow. I shall also go myself and—I swear to you by the feast of the twelve gods,

I swear by the Lares—I would have given a lot to have been able to do so today!"

"Does the Procurator not like Jerusalem?" inquired the visitor amicably.

"Merciful heavens!" exclaimed the Procurator, smiling. "It's the most unsettling place on earth. It isn't only the climate—I'm ill every time I have to come here—that's only half the trouble. But these festivals! Magicians, sorcerers, wizards, the hordes of pilgrims. Fanatics—all of them. And what price this messiah of theirs, which they're expecting this year? Every moment there's likely to be some act of gratuitous bloodshed. I spend all my time shuffling the troops about or reading denunciations and complaints, half of which are directed at you. You must admit it's boring. Oh, if only I weren't in the imperial service!"

"Yes, the festivals here are trying times," agreed the visitor.

"I wish with all my heart that this one were over," said Pilate forcefully. "Then I can go back to Caesarea. Do you know, this lunatic building of Herod's"—the Procurator waved at the arcade, embracing the whole palace in a gesture—"is positively driving me out of my mind. I can't bear sleeping in it. It is the most extraordinary piece of architecture in the world. . . . However, to business. First of all, is that cursed Bar-Abba giving you any trouble?"

At this the visitor directed his peculiar stare at the Procurator, but Pilate was gazing wearily into the distance, frowning with distaste and contemplating the quarter of the city which lay at his feet, fading into the dusk. The visitor's glance also faded and his eyelids lowered again.

"I think that Bar is now as harmless as a lamb," said the visitor, his face wrinkling.

"He is hardly in a position to make trouble now."

"Too busy?" asked Pilate, smiling.

"The Procurator, as usual, has put the point with great finesse."

"But at all events," remarked the Procurator anxiously and raised a long, thin finger adorned with a black stone, "we must—"

"The Procurator may rest assured that as long as I am in Judea Bar will not move a step without my being on his heels."

"That is comforting. I am always comforted when you are here."

"The Procurator is too kind."

"Now tell me about the execution," said Pilate.

"What interests the Procurator in particular?"

"Chiefly, whether there were any attempts at insurrection from the mob?"

"None," answered the visitor.

"Good. Did you personally confirm that they were dead?"

"Of that the Procurator may be sure."

"And tell me—were they given a drink before being gibbeted?"

"Yes. But he—" the visitor closed his eyes—"refused to drink."

"Who did?" asked Pilate.

"I beg your pardon, hegemon!" exclaimed the visitor. "Didn't I say? Ha-Notsri!"

"Madman!" said Pilate, grimacing. A vein twitched under his left eye. "To die of sunstroke! Why refuse what the law provides for? How did he refuse?"

"He said," replied the guest, shutting his eyes again, "that he was grateful and blamed no one for taking his life."

"Whom did he thank?" asked Pilate in a low voice.

"He did not say, hegemon."

"He didn't try to preach to the soldiers, did he?"

"No, hegemon, he was not very loquacious on this occasion. His only words were that he regarded cowardice as one of the worst human sins."

"What made him say that?" The Procurator's voice suddenly trembled.

"I have no idea. His behavior was in any case strange, as it always has been."

"In what way strange?"

"He kept staring at individuals among the people standing around him, and always with that curiously vague smile on his face."

"Nothing more?" asked the husky voice.

"Nothing more."

The jug clattered against his cup as the Procurator poured himself some more wine. Having drained it, he said, "My conclusion is as follows: although we have not been able— at least not at present—to find any followers or disciples of his, we nevertheless cannot be certain that he had none."

The visitor nodded, listening intently.

"Therefore, to avoid any untoward consequences," the

Procurator went on, "please remove the three victims' bodies from the face of the earth, rapidly and without attracting attention. Bury them secretly and silently so that nothing more is heard of them."

"Very good, hegemon," said the visitor. He stood up and said, "As this matter is important and will present certain difficulties, may I have your permission to go at once?"

"No, sit down again," said Pilate, restraining his visitor with a gesture. "I have a couple more questions to ask you. First— your remarkable diligence in carrying out your task as chief of the secret service to the Procurator makes it my pleasant duty to mention it in a report to Rome."

The visitor blushed as he rose, bowed to the Procurator and said, "I am only doing my duty as a member of the imperial service."

"But," said the hegemon, "if you are offered promotion and transfer to another post, I should like to ask you to refuse it and stay here. I do not wish to be parted from you on any account. I shall see to it that you are rewarded in other ways."

"I am happy to serve under you, hegemon."

"I am very glad to hear it. Now for the second question. It concerns that man—what's his name?—Judas of Karioth."

At this the visitor again gave the Procurator his open-eyed glance, then, as was fitting, hooded his eyes again.

"They say," the Procurator went on, lowering his voice, "that he is supposed to have been paid for the way he took that idiot home and made him so welcome."

"Will be paid," corrected the visitor gently.

"How much?"

"No one can tell, hegemon."

"Not even you?" said the hegemon, praising the man by his surprise.

"Alas, not even I," replied the visitor calmly. "But I do know that he will be paid this evening. He has been summoned to Caiaphas' palace today."

"Ah, he must be greedy, that old man from Karioth!" said the Procurator with a smile. "I suppose he is an old man, isn't he?"

"The Procurator is never mistaken, but on this occasion he has been misinformed," replied the man kindly. "This man from Karioth is a young man."

"Really? Can you describe him? Is he a fanatic?"

"Oh, no, Procurator."

"I see. What else do you know about him?"

"He is very good-looking."

"What else? Has he perhaps a special passion?"

"It is hard to know so much with certainty in this huge city, Procurator."

"Come now, Arthanius! You underestimate yourself."

"He has one passion, Procurator." The visitor made a tiny pause. "He has a passion for money."

"What is his occupation?"

Arthanius looked up, reflected and answered, "He works for one of his relatives who has a money-changer's booth."

"I see, I see." The Procurator was silent, looked round to make sure that there was no one on the balcony and then said in a low voice, "The fact is—I have received information that he is to be murdered tonight."

At this the visitor not only turned his glance on the Procurator but held it for a while and then replied, "You have flattered me, Procurator, but I fear I have not earned your commendation. I have no such information."

"You deserve the highest possible praise," replied the Procurator, "but there is no doubting this information."

"May I ask its source?"

"You must allow me not to divulge that for the present, particularly as it is casual, vague and unreliable. But it is my duty to allow for every eventuality. I place great reliance on my instinct in these matters, because it has never failed me yet. The information is that one of Ha-Notsri's secret followers, revolted by this money-changer's monstrous treachery, has plotted with his confederates to kill the man tonight and to return his blood money to the High Priest with a note reading: 'Take back your accursed money!' "

The chief of the secret service gave the hegemon no more of his startling glances and listened, frowning, as Pilate continued: "Do you think the High Priest will be pleased at such a gift on Passover night?"

"Not only will he not be pleased," replied the visitor with a smile, "but I think, Procurator, that it will create a major scandal."

"I think so too. That is why I am asking you to look after the affair and take all possible steps to protect Judas of Karioth."

"The hegemon's orders will be carried out," said Arthanius, "but I can assure the hegemon that these villains have set themselves a very difficult task. After all, only think—" the visitor glanced round as he spoke—"they have to trace the man, kill him, then find out how much money he received and return it to Caiaphas by stealth. All that in one night? Today?"

"Nevertheless he will be murdered tonight," Pilate repeated firmly. "I have a presentiment, I tell you! And it has never yet played me false." A spasm crossed the Procurator's face, and he rubbed his hands.

"Very well," said the visitor obediently. He rose, straightened up and suddenly said coldly, "You say he will be murdered, hegemon?"

"Yes," answered Pilate, "and our only hope is your extreme efficiency."

The visitor adjusted the heavy belt under his cloak and said, "Hail and farewell, Procurator!"

"Ah, yes," cried Pilate, "I almost forgot. I owe you some money."

The visitor looked surprised. "I am sure you do not, Procurator."

"Don't you remember? When I arrived in Jerusalem, there was a crowd of beggars, I wanted to throw them some money, I had none and borrowed from you."

"But, Procurator, that was a trifle!"

"One should remember trifles." Pilate turned, lifted a cloak lying on a chair behind him, picked up a leather purse from beneath it and handed it to Arthanius. The man bowed, took the purse and put it under his cloak.

"I expect," said Pilate, "a report on the burial and on the matter of Judas of Karioth tonight—do you hear, Arthanius, tonight? The guards will be given orders to wake me as soon as you appear. I shall be waiting for you."

"Very well," said the chief of the secret service and walked out onto the balcony. For a while Pilate could hear the sound of wet sand under his feet, then the clatter of his sandals on the marble paving between the two stone lions. Then legs, torso and finally cowl disappeared. Only then did the Procurator notice that the sun had set and twilight had come.

The Burial

It may have been the twilight which seemed to cause such a sharp change in the Procurator's appearance. He appeared to have aged visibly, and he looked hunched and worried. Once he glanced round and shuddered, staring at the empty chair with his cloak thrown over its back. The night of the feast was approaching, the evening shadows were playing tricks, and the exhausted Procurator may have thought he had seen someone sitting in the chair. In a moment of superstitious fear the Procurator shook the cloak, then walked away and began pacing the balcony, occasionally rubbing his hands, drinking from the goblet on the table, or halting to stare unseeingly at the mosaic floor as though trying to decipher some writing in it.

For the second time that day a brooding depression overcame him. Wiping his brow, where he felt only a faintly nagging memory of the hellish pain from that morning, the Procurator racked his brain in an attempt to define the cause of his mental agony. He soon realized what it was, but, unable to face it, he tried to deceive himself. It was clear to him that this morning he had irretrievably lost something and now he was striving to compensate for that loss with a trivial substitute, which took the form of belated action. His self-deception consisted in trying to persuade himself that his actions this evening were no less significant than the sentence which he had passed earlier in the day. But in this attempt the Procurator had little success.

At one of his turns he stopped abruptly and whistled. In reply there came a low bark from the twilight shadows and a gigantic gray-coated dog with pointed ears bounded in from the garden, wearing a gold-studded collar.

"Banga, Banga," cried the Procurator weakly.

The dog stood up on its hind legs, put its forepaws on its master's shoulders, almost knocking him over, and licked his cheek. The Procurator sat down in a chair. Banga, his tongue hanging out and panting fast, lay down at Pilate's feet with an expression of delight that the thunderstorm was over, the only thing in the world that frightened this otherwise fearless animal; delighted, too, because it was back again with the man it loved, respected and regarded as the most powerful being on earth, the ruler of all men, thanks to whom the dog too felt itself a specially privileged and superior creature. But lying at his feet and gazing into the twilit garden without even looking at Pilate, the dog knew at once that its master was troubled. It moved, got up, went round to Pilate's side and laid its forepaws and head on the Procurator's knees, smearing the hem of his cloak with wet sand. Banga's action seemed to mean that he wanted to comfort his master and was prepared to face misfortune with him. This he tried to express in his eyes and in the forward set of his ears. These two, dog and man who loved each other, sat in vigil together on the balcony that night of the feast.

Meanwhile Arthanius was busy. Leaving the upper terrace of the garden, he walked down the steps to the next terrace and turned right toward the barracks inside the palace grounds. These quarters housed the two centuries who had accompanied the Procurator to Jerusalem for the feast days, together with the Procurator's secret bodyguard commanded by Arthanius. He spent a little while in the barracks, no longer than ten minutes, but immediately afterward three carts drove out of the barracks yard loaded with entrenching tools and a vat of water, and escorted by a detail of fifteen mounted men wearing gray cloaks. Carts and escort left the palace grounds by a side gate, set off westward, passed through a gateway in the city wall and first took the Bethlehem road northward; they reached the crossroads by the Hebron Gate and there turned onto the Jaffa road, along the route taken by the execution party that morning. By now it was dark and the moon had risen on the horizon.

Soon after the carts and their escort detail had set off, Arthanius also left the palace on horseback, having changed into a shabby black chiton, and rode into the city. Presently he could have been seen riding toward the fortress of Antonia, situated immediately north of the great temple. The visitor spent an equally short time in the fortress, after which his route took him to the winding, crooked streets of the Lower City. He had now changed his mount to a mule.

Thoroughly at home in the city, the man easily found the street he was looking for. It was known as the Street of the Greeks, as it contained a number of Greek shops, including one that sold carpets. There the man stopped his mule, dismounted and tethered it to a ring outside the gate. The shop was shut. The guest passed through a wicket gate in the wall beside the shop door and entered a small rectangular courtyard, fitted out as stables. Turning the corner of the yard, the visitor reached the ivy-grown veranda of the owner's house and looked round him. House and stables were dark, the lamps not yet lit. He called softly, "Niza!"

At the sound of his voice a door creaked and a young woman, her head uncovered, appeared on the veranda in the evening dusk. She leaned over the railing, looking anxiously to see who had arrived. Recognizing the visitor, she gave him a welcoming smile, nodded and waved.

"Are you alone?" asked Arthanius softly in Greek.

"Yes, I am," whispered the woman on the veranda. "My husband went to Caesarea this morning—" here the woman glanced at the door and added in a whisper—"but the servant is here." Then she beckoned him to come in.

Arthanius glanced round, mounted the stone steps and went indoors with the woman. Here he spent no more than five minutes, after which he left the house, pulled his cowl lower over his eyes and went out into the street. By now candles were being lit in all the houses, there was a large feast-day crowd in the streets, and Arthanius on his mule was lost in the stream of riders and people on foot. Where he went from there is unknown.

When Arthanius had left her, the woman called Niza began to change in a great hurry, though despite the difficulty of finding the things she needed in her dark room she lit no candle and did not call her servant. Only when she was ready, with a black shawl over her head, did she say, "If anybody asks for me, tell them that I've gone to see Enanta."

Out of the dark her old serving woman grumbled in reply, "Enanta? That woman! You know your husband's forbidden you to see her. She's nothing but a procuress, that Enanta of yours. I'll tell your husband—"

"Now, now, now, be quiet," retorted Niza and slipped out of doors like a shadow, her sandals clattering across the paved courtyard. Still grumbling, the servant shut the veranda door and Niza left her house.

At the same time a young man left a tumbledown little house with its blind side to the street and whose only windows gave onto the courtyard, and passed through the wicket into an unpaved alley that descended in steps to one of the city's pools. He wore a white kaffiyeh falling to his shoulders, a new dark-blue-fringed tallith for the feast day and creaking new sandals. Dressed up for the occasion, the handsome, hook-nosed young man set off boldly, overtaking passers-by as he hurried home to the solemn Passover-night table, watching the candles as they were lit in house after house. The young man took the road leading past the bazaar toward the palace of Caiaphas the High Priest at the foot of the temple hill.

After a while he entered the gates of Caiaphas' palace and left it a short time later.

Leaving the palace, already bright with candles and torches and festive bustle, the young man returned, with an even bolder and more cheerful step, to the Lower City. At the corner where the street joined the bazaar square, he was passed in the seething crowd by a woman walking with the hip-swinging gait of a prostitute and wearing a black shawl low over her eyes. As she overtook him, the woman raised her shawl slightly and flashed a glance in the young man's direction, but instead of slowing down she walked faster as though trying to run away from him.

The young man not only noticed the woman but recognized her. He gave a start, halted, stared perplexedly at her back and at once set off to catch up with her. Almost knocking over a man carrying a jug, the young man drew level with the woman and panting with agitation called out to her, "Niza!"

The woman turned, frowned with a look of chilling irritation and coldly replied in Greek, "Oh, it's you, Judas. I didn't recognize you. Still, it's lucky. We have a saying that if you don't recognize a person he's going to be rich."

So excited that his heart began to leap like a wild bird in a cage, Judas asked in a jerky whisper, afraid that the passers-by might hear, "Where are you going, Niza?"

"Why do you want to know?" answered Niza, slackening her pace and staring haughtily at Judas.

In a childish, pleading voice Judas whispered distractedly, "But, Niza . . . we agreed . . . I was to come to see you, you said you'd be at home all evening."

"Oh, no," replied Niza, pouting capriciously, which to Judas made her face, the most beautiful he had ever seen in the world, even more attractive. "I'm bored. It's a feast day for you, but what do you expect me to do? Sit and listen to you sighing on the veranda? And always frightened of the servant telling my husband? No, I've decided to go out of town and listen to the nightingales."

"Out of town?" asked Judas, bewildered. "What—alone?"

"Yes, of course," replied Niza.

"Let me go with you," whispered Judas with a sigh. His mind was confused, he had forgotten about everything, and he gazed pleadingly into Niza's blue eyes that now seemed black in the darkness.

Niza said nothing but walked faster.

"Why don't you say something, Niza?" asked Judas miserably, hastening to keep pace with her.

"Won't I be bored with you?" Niza asked suddenly and stopped. Judas now felt utterly helpless.

"All right," said Niza, relenting at last. "Come on."

"Where to?"

"Wait . . . let's go into this courtyard and arrange it, otherwise I'm afraid of someone seeing me and then telling my husband that I was out on the streets with my lover."

Niza and Judas vanished from the bazaar and began whispering under the gateway of a courtyard.

"Go to the olive grove," whispered Niza, pulling her shawl down over her eyes and turning away from a man who came into the courtyard carrying a bucket, "in Gethsemane, beyond Kedron—do you know where I mean?"

"Yes, yes . . ."

"I'll go first," Niza went on, "but don't follow close behind me, go separately. I'll go ahead. When you've crossed the stream—do you know where the grotto is?"

"Yes, I know, I know . . ."

"Go on through the olive grove on the hill and then turn right toward the grotto. I'll be there. But whatever you do, don't follow me at once, be patient, wait a while here." With these words Niza slipped out of the gateway as though she had never spoken to Judas.

Judas stood alone for some time, trying to collect his whirling thoughts. Among other things he tried to think how he would explain his absence from the Passover table to his parents. He stood and tried to work out some lie, but in his excitement his mind refused to function properly and still lacking an excuse he slowly walked out of the gateway.

Now he took another direction, and instead of making for the Lower City he turned back toward the palace of Caiaphas. The celebrations had already begun. From windows on all sides came the murmur of the Passover ceremony. Latecomers hastening home urged on their donkeys, whipping and shouting at them. On foot Judas hurried on, not noticing the menacing turrets of the fortress of Antonia, deaf to the call of trumpets from the fortress, oblivious of the Roman mounted patrol with their torches which threw an alarming glare across his path.

As he turned past the fortress Judas saw that two gigantic seven-branched candlesticks had been lit at a dizzy height above the temple. But he only saw them in a blur. They seemed like fourteen huge lamps that burned over Jerusalem in rivalry with the single lamp climbing high above the city—the moon.

Judas had no thought for anything now but his urgent haste to leave the city as quickly as possible by the Gethsemane Gate. Occasionally he thought he could make out, among the backs and faces of the people in front of him, a figure dancing along and drawing him after it. But it was an illusion. Judas realized that Niza must be well ahead of him. He passed a row of money-changers' shops and at last reached the Gethsemane Gate. Here, burning with impatience, he was forced to wait. A camel caravan was coming into the city, followed by a mounted Syrian patrol, which Judas mentally cursed.

But the delay was short, and the impatient Judas was soon outside the city wall. To his left was a small cemetery, beside it the striped tents of a band of pilgrims. Crossing the dusty, moonlit road, Judas hurried on toward the stream Kedron and crossed it, the water bubbling softly under his feet as he leaped from stone to stone. Finally he reached the Gethsemane bank and saw with joy that the road ahead was deserted. Not far away could be seen the half-ruined gateway to the olive grove.

After the stifling city Judas was struck by the intoxicating freshness of the spring night. Across a garden fence the scent of myrtles and acacia was blown from the fields of Gethsemane.

The gateway was unguarded, and a few minutes later Judas was far into the olive grove and running beneath the mysterious shadows of the great, branching olive trees. The way led uphill. Judas climbed, panting, occasionally emerging from darkness into checkered patches of moonlight which reminded him of the carpets in the shop kept by Niza's jealous husband.

Soon an oil press came in sight in a clearing to Judas' left, with its heavy stone crushing wheel and a pile of barrels. There was no one in the olive grove—work had stopped at sunset and choirs of nightingales were singing above Judas' head.

He was near his goal. He knew that in a moment from the darkness to his right he would hear the quiet whisper of running water from the grotto. There was the sound now and the air was cooler near the grotto. He checked his pace and called, "Niza!"

But instead of Niza slipping out from behind a thick olive trunk, the stocky figure of a man jumped out onto the path. Something glittered momentarily in his hand. With a faint cry Judas started running back, but a second man blocked his way.

The first man asked Judas, "How much did you get? Talk, if you want to save your life."

Hope welled up in Judas' heart and he cried desperately, "Thirty tetradrachms! Thirty tetradrachms! I have it all on me. There's the money! Take it, but don't kill me!"

The man snatched the purse from Judas' hand. At the same moment a knife was rammed into Judas' back under his shoulder blade. He pitched forward, throwing up his hands, fingers clutching. The man in front caught Judas on his knife and thrust it up to the hilt into Judas' heart.

"Na . . . za . . ." said Judas, in a low, reproachful growl quite unlike his own, youthful, high-pitched voice and made not another sound. His body hit the ground so hard that the air whistled as it was knocked out of his lungs.

Then a third figure stepped out onto the path, wearing a hooded cloak.

"Don't waste any time," he ordered. The cowled man gave the murderers a note, and they wrapped purse and note into a piece of leather which they bound crisscross with twine. The second man put the bundle down his shirt front, then the two assassins ran off the path and were swallowed by the darkness between the olive trees.

The third man squatted down beside the body and looked into his face. It seemed as white as chalk, with an expression not unlike spiritual beauty.

A few seconds later there was not a living soul on the path. The lifeless body lay with arms outstretched. Its left foot was in a patch of moonlight that showed up every strap and lace of the man's sandal. The whole of Gethsemane rang with the song of nightingales.

The man with the hood left the path and plunged deep through the olive grove, heading southward. He climbed over the wall at the southernmost corner of the olive grove where the upper course of masonry jutted out. Soon he reached the bank of the Kedron, where he waded in and waited in midstream until he saw the distant outlines of two horses and a man beside them, also standing in the stream. Water flowed past, washing their hoofs. The groom mounted one of the horses, the cowled man the other, and both set off down the bed of the stream, pebbles crunching beneath the horses' hoofs. The riders left the water, climbed up the bank and followed the line of the city wall at a walk. Then the groom galloped ahead and disappeared from sight, while the man in the cowl stopped his horse, dismounted on the empty road, took off his cloak, turned it inside out and, producing a flat-topped, uncrested helmet from the folds, put it on. The rider was now in military uniform with a short sword at his hip. He flicked the reins and the fiery cavalry charger broke into a trot. He had not far to go before he rode up to the southern gate of Jerusalem.

Torch flames danced and flickered restlessly under the arch of the gate, where the sentries from the second cohort of the Lightning Legion sat on stone benches playing dice. As the mounted officer approached, the soldiers jumped up; the officer waved to them and rode into the city.

The town was lit up for the festival. Candle flames played at every window, and from each came the sound of singsong incantations. Glancing occasionally into the windows that opened onto the street, the rider saw people at their tables set with kid's meat and cups of wine between dishes of bitter herbs. Whistling softly, the rider made his way at a leisurely trot through the deserted streets of the Lower City, heading toward the fortress of Antonia and looking up now and then at the vast seven-branched candlesticks flaring over the temples or at the moon above them.

The palace of Herod the Great had no part in the ceremonies of Passover night. Lights were burning in the outbuildings on the south side where the officers of the Roman cohort and the Legate of the Legion were quartered, and there were signs of movement and life. The frontal wings, with their one involuntary occupant—the Procurator—with their arcades and gilded statues, seemed blinded by the brilliance of the moonlight. Inside the palace was darkness and silence.

The Procurator, as he had told Arthanius, preferred not to go inside. He had ordered a bed to be prepared on the balcony where he had dined and where he had conducted the interrogation that morning. The Procurator lay down on the couch, but he could not sleep. The naked moon hung far up in the clear sky, and for several hours the Procurator lay staring at it.

Sleep at last took pity on the hegemon toward midnight. Yawning spasmodically, the Procurator unfastened his cloak and threw it off, took off the strap that belted his tunic with its steel sheath knife, placed it on the chair beside the bed, took off his sandals and stretched out. Banga at once jumped up beside him on the bed and lay down, head to head. Putting his arm round the dog's neck, the Procurator at last closed his eyes. Only then did the dog go to sleep.

The couch stood in half-darkness, shaded from the moon by a pillar, though a long ribbon of moonlight stretched from the staircase to the bed. As the Procurator drifted away from reality, he set off along that path of light, straight up toward the moon. In his sleep he even laughed from happiness at the unique beauty of that transparent blue pathway. He was walking with Banga and the vagrant philosopher beside him. They were arguing about a weighty and complex problem over which neither could gain the upper hand. They disagreed entirely, which made their argument the more absorbing and interminable. The execution, of course, had been a pure misunderstanding: after all this same man, with his ridiculous philosophy that all men were good, was walking beside him—consequently he was alive. Indeed the very thought of executing such a man was absurd. There had been no execution! It had never taken place! This thought comforted him as he strode along the moonlit pathway.

They had as much time to spare as they wanted, the storm would not break until evening. Cowardice was undoubtedly one of the most terrible sins. Thus spake Yeshua Ha-Notsri. No, philosopher, I disagree—it is the most terrible sin of all!

Had *he* not shown cowardice, the man who was now Procurator of Judea but who had once been a Tribune of the Legion on that day in the Valley of the Virgins when the wild Germans had so nearly clubbed Muribellum the Giant to death? Have pity on me, philosopher! Do you, a man of your intelligence, imagine that the Procurator of Judea would ruin his career for the sake of a man who has committed a crime against Caesar?

"Yes, yes . . ." Pilate groaned and sobbed in his sleep.

Of course he would risk ruining his career. This morning he had not been ready to, but now at night, having thoroughly weighed the matter, he was prepared to ruin himself if need be. He would do anything to save this crazy, innocent dreamer, this miraculous healer, from execution.

"You and I will always be together," said the ragged tramp-philosopher who had so mysteriously become the traveling companion of the Knight of the Golden Lance. "Where one of us goes, the other shall go too. Whenever people think of me, they will think of you—me, an orphan child of unknown parents and you the son of an astrologer-king and a miller's daughter, the beautiful Pila!"

"Remember to pray for me, the astrologer's son," begged Pilate in his dream. And reassured by a nod from the pauper from Ein-Sarid who was his companion, the cruel Procurator of Judea wept with joy and laughed in his sleep.

The hegemon's awakening was all the more fearful after the euphoria of his dream. Banga started to growl at the moon, and the blue pathway, slippery as butter, collapsed in front of the Procurator. He opened his eyes and the first thing he remembered was that the execution had taken place. Then the Procurator groped automatically for Banga's collar, then turned his aching eyes in search of the moon and noticed that it had moved slightly to one side and was silver in color. Competing with its light was another, more unpleasant and disturbing light that flickered in front of him. Holding a flaming, crackling torch, Muribellum scowled with fear and dislike at the dangerous beast, poised to spring.

"Lie down, Banga," said the Procurator in an anguished voice, coughing. Shielding his eyes from the torch flame, he went on: "Even by moonlight there's no peace for me at night. . . . Oh, ye gods! You too have a harsh duty, Mark. You have to cripple men."

Startled, Mark stared at the Procurator, who composed himself. To excuse his pointless remark, spoken while still half-dreaming, the Procurator said, "Don't be offended, centurion. My duty is even worse, I assure you. What do you want?"

"The chief of the secret service has come to see you," said Mark calmly.

"Send him in, send him in," said the Procurator clearing his throat and fumbling for his sandals with bare feet. The flame danced along the arcade, the centurion's caligae rang out on the mosaic as he went out into the garden.

"Even by moonlight there's no peace for me," said the Procurator to himself, clenching his teeth.

The centurion was replaced by the man in the cowl.

"Lie down, Banga," said the Procurator quietly, pressing down on the dog's head.

Before speaking Arthanius gave his habitual glance around and moved into a shadow. Having made sure that apart from Banga there were no strangers on the balcony, he said, "You may charge me with negligence, Procurator. You were right. I could not save Judas of Karioth from being murdered. I deserve to be court-martialed and discharged."

Arthanius felt that of the two pairs of eyes watching him, one was a dog's, the other a wolf's. From under his tunic he took out a bloodstained purse that was sealed with two seals.

"The murderers threw this purseful of money into the house of the High Priest. There is blood on it—Judas of Karioth's blood."

"How much money is there in it?" asked Pilate, nodding toward the purse.

"Thirty tetradrachms."

The Procurator smiled and said, "Not much."

Arthanius did not reply.

"Where is the body?"

"I do not know," replied the cowled man with dignity. "This morning we will start the investigation."

The Procurator shuddered and gave up trying to lace his sandal, which refused to tie.

"But you are certain he was killed?"

To this the Procurator received the cool reply: "I have been working in Judea for fifteen years, Procurator. I began my service under Valerius Gratus. I don't have to see a body to be able to say that a man is dead, and I am stating that the man called Judas of Karioth was murdered several hours ago."

"Forgive me, Arthanius," replied Pilate. "I made that remark because I haven't quite waked up yet. I sleep badly." The Procurator smiled. "I was dreaming of a moonbeam. It was funny, because I seemed to be walking along it. . . . Now, I want your suggestions for dealing with this affair. Where are you going to look for him? Sit down."

Arthanius bowed, moved a chair closer to the bed and sat down, his sword clanking.

"I shall look for him not far from the oil press in the Gethsemane olive grove."

"I see. Why there?"

"I believe, hegemon, that Judas was killed neither in Jerusalem itself nor far from the city, but somewhere in its vicinity."

"You are an expert at your job. I don't know about Rome itself, but in the colonies there's not a man to touch you. Why do you think that?"

"I cannot believe for one moment," said Arthanius in a low voice, "that Judas would have allowed himself to be caught by any ruffians within the city limits. The street is no place for a clandestine murder. Therefore he must have been enticed into some cellar or courtyard. But the secret service has already made a thorough search of the Lower City, and if he were there they would have found him by now. They have not found him, and I am therefore convinced that he is not in the city. If he had been killed a long way from Jerusalem, then the packet of money could not have been thrown into the High Priest's palace so soon. He was murdered near the city after they had lured him out."

"How did they manage to do that?"

"That, Procurator, is the most difficult problem of all, and I am not even sure that I shall ever be able to solve it."

"Most puzzling, I agree. A believing Jew leaves the city to go heaven knows where on the eve of Passover and is killed. Who could have enticed him and how? Might it have been done by a woman?" inquired the Procurator, making a sudden inspired guess.

Arthanius replied gravely: "Impossible, Procurator. Out of the question. Consider it logically: who wanted Judas done away with? A band of vagrant cranks, a group of visionaries which, above all, contains no women. To marry and start a family needs money, Procurator. But to kill a man with a woman as decoy or accomplice needs a very great deal of money indeed, and these men are tramps—homeless and destitute. There was no woman involved in this affair, Procurator. What is more, to theorize along these lines may even throw us off the scent and hinder the investigation."

"I see, Arthanius, that you are quite right," said Pilate.

"I was merely putting forward a hypothesis."

"It is, alas, a faulty one, Procurator."

"Well then—what is your theory?" exclaimed the Procurator, staring at Arthanius with avid curiosity.

"I still think that the bait was money."

"Remarkable! Who, might I ask, would be likely to entice him out of the city limits in the middle of the night to offer him money?"

"No one, of course, Procurator. No, I can only make one guess, and if it is wrong, then I confess I am at a loss." Arthanius leaned closer to Pilate and whispered, "Judas intended to hide his money in a safe place known only to himself."

"A very shrewd explanation. That must be the answer. I see it now: he was not lured out of town—he went of his own accord. Yes, yes, that must be it."

"Precisely. Judas trusted nobody. He wanted to hide his money."

"You said Gethsemane. . . . Why there? That, I confess, I don't understand."

"That, Procurator, is the simplest deduction of all. No one is going to hide money in the road or out in the open. Therefore Judas did not take the road to Hebron or to Bethany. He will have gone to somewhere hidden, somewhere where there are trees. It's obvious—there is no place in the vicinity of Jerusalem that answers to that description except Gethsemane. He cannot have gone far."

"You have completely convinced me. What is your next move?"

"I shall immediately start searching for the murderers who followed Judas out of the city, and meanwhile, as I have already proposed to you, I shall submit myself to be court-martialed."

"What for?"

"My men lost track of Judas this evening in the bazaar after he had left Caiaphas' palace. How it occurred, I don't know.

It has never happened to me before. He was put under observation immediately after our talk, but somewhere in the bazaar area he gave us the slip and disappeared without a trace."

"I see. You will be glad to hear that I do not consider it necessary for you to be court-martialed. You did all you could and no one in the world—" the Procurator smiled—"could possibly have done more. Reprimand the men who lost Judas. But let me warn you that I do not wish your reprimand to be a severe one. After all, we did our best to protect the scoundrel. Oh, yes—I forgot to ask—" the Procurator wiped his forehead—"how did they manage to return the money to Caiaphas?"

"That was not particularly difficult, Procurator. The avengers went behind Caiaphas' palace, where that back street overlooks the rear courtyard. Then they threw the packet over the fence."

"With a note?"

"Yes, just as you said they would, Procurator." Oh, by the way . . ." Arthanius broke the seals on the packet and showed its contents to Pilate.

"Arthanius! Take care what you're doing. Those are temple seals."

"The Procurator need have no fear on that score," replied Arthanius as he wrapped up the bag of money.

"Do you mean to say that you have copies of all their seals?" asked Pilate, laughing.

"Naturally, Procurator," was Arthanius' curt, unsmiling reply.

"I can just imagine how Caiaphas must have felt!"

"Yes, Procurator, it caused a great stir. They sent for me at once."

Even in the dark Pilate's eyes could be seen glittering. "Interesting . . ."

"If you'll forgive my contradicting you, Procurator, it was most uninteresting. A boring and time-wasting case. When I inquired whether anybody in Caiaphas' palace had paid out this money, I was told categorically that no one had."

"Really? Well, if they say so, I suppose they didn't. That will make it all the harder to find the murderers."

"Quite so, Procurator."

"Arthanius, it has just occurred to me—might he not have killed himself?"

"Oh no, Procurator," replied Arthanius, leaning back in his

chair and staring in astonishment. "That, if you will forgive me, is most unlikely!"

"Ah, in this city anything is likely. I am prepared to bet that before long the city will be full of rumors about his suicide."

Here Arthanius gave Pilate his peculiar stare, thought a moment and answered, "That may be, Procurator."

Pilate was obviously obsessed with the problem of the murder of Judas of Karioth, although it had been fully explained. He said reflectively, "I should have liked to have seen how they killed him."

"He was killed with great artistry, Procurator," replied Arthanius, giving Pilate an ironic look.

"How do you know?"

"If you will kindly inspect the bag, Procurator," Arthanius replied, "I can guarantee from its condition that Judas' blood flowed freely. I have seen some murdered men in my time."

"So he will not rise again?"

"He will rise again, Procurator," answered Arthanius, smiling philosophically, "when the trumpet call of their messiah sounds for him. But not before."

"All right, Arthanius, that case is dealt with. Now what about the burial?"

"The executed prisoners have been buried, Procurator."

"Arthanius, it would be a crime to court-martial you. You deserve the highest praise. What happened?"

While Arthanius had been engaged on the Judas case, a secret service squad under the command of Arthanius' deputy had reached the hill shortly before dark. On the hilltop one body was missing. Pilate shuddered and said hoarsely, "Ah, now why didn't I foresee that?"

"There is no cause for worry, Procurator," said Arthanius and went on: "The bodies of Dismas and Hestas, their eyes picked out by carrion crows, were loaded onto a cart. The men at once set off to look for the third body. It was soon found. A man called—"

"Matthew the Levite," said Pilate. It was not a question but an affirmation.

"Yes, Procurator . . . Matthew the Levite was hidden in a cave on the northern slope of Mount Golgotha, waiting for darkness. With him was Ha-Notsri's naked body. When the guard entered the cave with a torch, the Levite fell into a fit. He shouted that he had committed no crime and that according to the law every man had a right to bury the body of an executed criminal if he wished to. Matthew the Levite refused to leave the body. He was excited, almost delirious, begging, threatening, cursing—"

"Did they have to arrest him?" asked Pilate glumly.

"No, Procurator," replied Arthanius reassuringly. "They managed to humor the lunatic by telling him that the body would be buried. The Levite calmed down but announced that he still refused to leave the body and wanted to assist in the burial. He said he refused to go even if they threatened to kill him and even offered them a bread knife to kill him with."

"Did they send him away?" inquired Pilate in a stifled voice.

"No, Procurator. My deputy allowed him to take part in the burial."

"Which of your assistants was in charge of this detail?"

"Tolmai," replied Arthanius, adding anxiously, "Did I do wrong?"

"Go on," replied Pilate. "You did right. I am beginning to think, Arthanius, that I am dealing with a man who never makes a mistake—I mean you."

"Matthew the Levite was taken away by cart, together with the bodies, and about two hours later they reached a deserted cave to the north of Jerusalem. After an hour working in shifts the squad had dug a deep pit in which they buried the bodies of the three victims."

"Naked?"

"No, Procurator, the squad had taken chitons with them for the purpose. Rings were put on the bodies' fingers: Yeshua's ring had one engraved stroke, Dismas' two and Hestas' three. The pit was filled and covered with stones. Tolmai knows the identification mark."

"Ah, if only I could have known!" said Pilate, frowning. "I wanted to see that man Matthew the Levite."

"He is here, Procurator."

Pilate stared at Arthanius for a moment with wide-open eyes, then said, "Thank you for everything you have done on this case. Tomorrow please send Tolmai to see me and before he comes tell him that I am pleased with him. And you, Arthanius—" the Procurator took out a ring from the pocket of his belt and handed it to the chief of the secret service—"please accept this as a token of my gratitude."

With a bow Arthanius said, "You do me a great honor, Procurator."

"Please give my commendation to the squad that carried out the burial and a reprimand to the men who failed to protect Judas. And send Matthew the Levite to me at once. I need certain details from him on the case of Yeshua."

"Very good, Procurator," replied Arthanius and bowed himself out.

The Procurator clapped his hands and shouted, "Bring me candles in the arcade!"

Arthanius had not even reached the garden when servants began to appear bearing lights. Three candlesticks were placed on the table in front of the Procurator, and instantly the moonlit night retreated to the garden as though Arthanius had taken it with him. In his place a small, thin stranger mounted to the balcony accompanied by the giant centurion. At a nod from the Procurator, Muribellum turned and marched out.

Pilate studied the new arrival with an eager, slightly fearful look, in the way people look at someone of whom they have heard a great deal, who has been in their thoughts and whom they finally meet.

The man was about forty, dark, ragged, covered in dried mud, with a suspicious, wolfish stare. In a word he was extremely unsightly and looked very much like one of the city beggars who were to be found in crowds on the terraces of the temple or in the bazaars of the noisy and dirty Lower City.

The silence was long and made awkward by the man's strange behavior. His face worked, he staggered and he would have fallen if he had not put out a dirty hand to grasp the edge of the table.

"What's the matter with you?" Pilate asked him.

"Nothing," replied Matthew the Levite, making a movement as though he were swallowing something. His thin, bare, gray neck bulged and subsided again.

"What is it? Answer me," Pilate repeated.

"I am tired," answered the Levite and stared dully at the floor.

"Sit down," said Pilate, pointing to a chair.

Matthew gazed mistrustfully at the Procurator, took a step toward the chair, gave a frightened look at its gilded armrests and sat down on the floor beside it.

"Why didn't you sit in the chair?" asked Pilate.

"I'm dirty, I would make it dirty too," said the Levite, staring at the floor.

"You will be given something to eat shortly."

"I don't want to eat."

"Why tell lies?" Pilate asked quietly. "You haven't eaten all day and probably longer. All right, don't eat. I called you here to show me your knife."

"The soldiers took it away from me when they brought me here," replied the Levite and added dismally, "You must give it back to me, because I have to return it to its owner. I stole it."

"Why?"

"To cut the ropes."

"Mark!" shouted the Procurator and the centurion stepped into the arcade. "Give me his knife."

The centurion pulled a dirty bread knife out of one of the two leather sheaths on his belt, handed it to the Procurator and withdrew.

"Where did you steal the knife?"

"In a baker's shop just inside the Hebron Gate, on the left."

Pilate inspected the wide blade and tested the edge with his finger. Then he said, "Don't worry about the knife, it will be returned to the shop. Now I want something else—show me the parchment you carry with you on which you have written what Yeshua has said."

The Levite looked at Pilate with hatred and smiled a smile of such ill will that his face was completely distorted.

"Are you going to take it away from me—the last thing I possess?"

"I didn't say 'give it,' " answered Pilate. "I said 'show it to me.' "

The Levite fumbled in his shirt front and pulled out a roll of parchment. Pilate took it, unrolled it, spread it out in the light of two candles and with a frown began to study the barely decipherable script. The uneven strokes were hard to understand, and Pilate frowned and bent over the parchment, tracing the lines with his finger. He nevertheless managed to discern that the writings were a disjointed sequence of sayings, dates, household notes and snatches of poetry. Pilate managed to read: "There is no death. . . . Yesterday we ate sweet cakes. . . ."

Grimacing with strain, Pilate squinted and read: "We shall see the pure river of the water of life. . . . Mankind will look at the sun through transparent crystal. . . ."

Pilate shuddered. In the last few lines of the parchment he deciphered the words: ". . . greatest sin . . . cowardice . . ."

Pilate rolled up the parchment and with a brusque movement handed it back to the Levite.

"There, take it," he said, and after a short silence he added, "I see you are a man of learning, and there is no need for you, living alone, to walk around in such wretched clothes and without a home. I have a large library at Caesarea, I am very rich, and I would like you to come and work for me. You would catalogue and look after the papyri, you would be fed and clothed."

The Levite stood up and replied, "No, I don't want to."

"Why not?" asked the Procurator, his expression darkening. "You don't like me . . . are you afraid of me?"

The same evil smile twisted Matthew's face and he said, "No, because you would be afraid of me. You would not find it very easy to look me in the face after having killed him."

"Silence," Pilate cut him off. "Take this money."

The Levite shook his head, and the Procurator went on: "You, I know, consider yourself a disciple of Yeshua, but I tell you that you have acquired nothing of what he taught you. For if you had, you would have certainly accepted something from me. Remember—before he died he said that he blamed no one—" Pilate raised his finger significantly and his face twitched—"and I know that he would have accepted something. You are hard. He was not a hard man. Where will you go?"

Matthew suddenly walked over to Pilate's table, leaned on it with both hands and, staring at the Procurator with burning eyes, he whispered to him, "Know, hegemon, that there is one man in Jerusalem whom I shall kill. I want to tell you this so that you are warned—there will be more blood."

"I know that there will be more blood," answered Pilate. "What you have said does not surprise me. You want to murder me, I suppose?"

"I shall not be able to murder you," replied the Levite, baring his teeth in a smile. "I am not so stupid as to hope for that. But I shall kill Judas of Karioth if it takes the rest of my life."

At this the Procurator's eyes gleamed with pleasure. Beckoning Matthew the Levite closer, he said, "You will not succeed, but it will not be necessary. Judas was murdered tonight."

The Levite jumped back from the table, stared wildly round and cried, "Who did it?"

"You must not be jealous," said Pilate, baring his teeth

mirthlessly and rubbing his hands, "but I'm afraid he had other admirers beside yourself."

"Who did it?" repeated the Levite in a whisper.

Pilate answered him, "I did it."

Matthew opened his mouth and stared at the Procurator, who said quietly, "It is not much, but I did it." And he added: "Now you will accept something?"

The Levite thought for a moment, relented and finally said, "Order them to give me a clean piece of parchment."

An hour had passed since the Levite had left the palace. The dawn silence was only disturbed by the quiet tread of the sentries in the garden. The moon was fading, and on the other edge of heaven there appeared the whitish speck of the morning star. The candles had long been put out. The Procurator lay on his couch. He was sleeping with his hand under his cheek and breathing noiselessly. Beside him slept Banga.

Thus Pontius Pilate, fifth Procurator of Judea, met the dawn of the fifteenth of Nisan.

CHAPTER 27

THE LAST OF
APARTMENT NO. 50

Day was breaking as Margarita read the last words of the chapter: ". . . Thus Pontius Pilate, fifth Procurator of Judea, met the dawn of the fifteenth of Nisan."

From the yard she could hear the lively, cheerful, early-morning chatter of sparrows in the branches of the willow and the lime tree.

Margarita got up from her chair, stretched and only then realized how physically exhausted she felt and how much she wanted to sleep. Mentally, though, Margarita was in fine fettle. Her mind was clear, and she was completely unmoved by the fact that she had spent a night in the world of the supernatural. It caused her no distress to think that she had been at Satan's ball, that by some miracle the master had been restored to her, that the novel had risen from the ashes, that everything was back in its place in the basement apartment after the expulsion of the wretched Aloysius Mogarych. In a word, her encounter with Woland had done her no psychological harm. Everything was as it should be.

She went into the next room, made sure that the master was sound asleep, put out the unnecessary light on the bedside table and stretched out on the other little couch, covering herself with an old, torn blanket. A minute later she was in a dreamless sleep. Silence reigned in the basement rooms and in the whole house, silence filled the little street.

But on that early Saturday morning there was no sleep for a whole floor of a certain Moscow office. Its windows, looking out onto a large asphalted square which was being cleaned by slow, whirring vehicles with revolving brushes, competed with the rising sun in brightness.

The whole floor was busy investigating the Woland case; in nine offices the lights had been burning all night. Although the outlines of the case had been quite clear since the day before, when they had closed the Variety as a result of the disappearance of its management and the scandalous performance of black magic, everything was complicated by the incessant flow of new evidence.

The department in charge of this strange case now had the task of drawing together all the strands of the varied and confusing events, occurring all over Moscow, which included an apparent mixture of sheer devilry, hypnotic conjuring tricks and barefaced crime.

The first person summoned to the glaring electric light of that unsleeping floor was Arkady Apollonovich Sempleyarov, the chairman of the Acoustics Commission.

On Friday evening after dinner, the telephone rang in his flat on Kamenny Most, and a man's voice asked to speak to Arkady Apollonovich. His wife, who had answered the call, announced grimly that Arkady Apollonovich was unwell, had gone to lie down and could not come to the telephone. Nevertheless Arkady Apollonovich was obliged to come when the voice said who was calling.

"Of course . . . at once . . . right away," stammered Arkady's usually arrogant spouse, and she flew like an arrow to rouse Arkady Appollonovich from the couch where he had lain down to recover from the horrific scenes caused by the theater incident and the stormy expulsion from their apartment of his young cousin from Saratov. In a quarter of a minute, in underclothes and one slipper, Arkady Appolonovich was babbling into the telephone, "Yes, it's me. Yes, I will. . . ."

His wife, all thought of Arkady Apollonovich's infidelity instantly forgotten, put her terrified face around the door, waving a slipper in the air and whispering, "Put your other slipper on—you'll catch cold."

At this Arkady Apollonovich, waving his wife away with a bare leg and rolling his eyes at her, muttered into the receiver,

"Yes, yes, yes, of course . . . I understand. . . . I'll come at once."

Arkady Apollonovich spent the rest of the evening with the investigators.

The ensuing conversation was painful and unpleasant in the extreme; he was not only made to give a completely frank account of that odious show and the fight in the box, but was obliged to tell everything about Militsa Andreyevna Pokobatko, the actress from Yelokhovskaya Street, as well as all about his cousin from Saratov and much more besides, the telling of which caused Arkady Apollonovich inexpressible pain.

Naturally the evidence given by Arkady Apollonovich—an intelligent and cultured man who had been an eyewitness of the show and who as an articulate and informed observer was not only able to give an excellent description of the mysterious masked magician and his two rascally assistants but who actually remembered that the magician's name was Woland— helped considerably to advance the inquiry. When Arkady Apollonovich's evidence was compared with the evidence of the others, among them several of the ladies who had suffered such embarrassment after the show (including the woman in violet panties who had so shocked Rimsky) and Karpov the usher, who had been sent to apartment No. 50 at 302A Sadovaya Street, it became immediately obvious where the culprit was to be found.

They went to No. 50 more than once and not only searched it with extreme thoroughness but tapped on the walls, examined the chimney flues and looked for secret doors. None of this, however, produced any results, and nothing was found during the visits to the apartment. Yet someone was living in the apartment, despite the fact that every official body in Moscow concerned with visiting foreigners stated firmly and categorically that there was not and could not be a magician called Woland in Moscow.

He had definitely not registered on entry, he had shown no one his passport or any other documents, contracts or agreements, and no one had so much as heard of him. Kitaitsev, the director of the programs department of the Theatrical Commission swore by all the saints that the missing Stepa Likhodeyev had never sent him a program schedule for anyone called Woland for confirmation and had never telephoned Kitaitsev a word about Woland's arrival. Therefore he, Kitaitsev, failed completely to understand how Stepa could have allowed a show of this sort to be put on at the Variety. When he was told that Arkady Apollonovich had seen the performance with his own eyes, Kitaitsev could only spread his hands and raise his eyes to heaven. From those eyes alone it was obvious that Kitaitsev was as purse as crystal.

Prokhor Petrovich, the chairman of the Entertainment Commission, incidentally, had re-entered his suit as soon as the police reached his office, to the ecstatic joy of Anna Richardovna and to the great annoyance of the police, who had been alerted for nothing. As soon as he was back at his post and wearing his striped gray suit, Prokhor Petrovich fully approved all the minutes that his suit had drafted during his short absence.

So Prokhor Petrovich obviously knew nothing about Woland either.

The sum total of their inquiries amounted to a conclusion which was little short of farcical: thousands of spectators, plus the Variety Theater staff, plus, finally, Arkady Apollonovich, that highly intelligent man, had seen this magician and his thrice cursed assistants, yet in the meantime all four had completely vanished. What could it mean? Had Woland been swallowed up by the earth or had he, as some claimed, never come to Moscow at all? If one accepted the first alternative, then he had apparently spirited away the entire Variety management with him; if you believed the second alternative, it meant that the theater management itself, having first indulged in a minor orgy of destruction had decamped from Moscow leaving no trace.

The officer in charge of the case was, to give him his due, a man who knew his job. Rimsky, for instance, was tracked down with astonishing speed. Merely by linking the Ace of Diamond's behavior at the taxi rank near the movie theater with certain timings, such as the time of the end of the show and the time at which Rimsky apparently vanished, they were able to send an immediate telegram to Leningrad. An hour later (on Friday evening) the reply came back that Rimsky had been found in room 412 at the Astoria Hotel, on the fourth floor next to the room containing the repertory manager of one of the Moscow theaters then on tour in Leningrad, in that famous room with the blue-gray furniture and the luxurious bathroom.

Rimsky, found hiding in the wardrobe of his room at the Astoria, was interrogated in Leningrad, after which a telegram reached Moscow stating that treasurer Rimsky was an irresponsible witness who had proved unwilling or incapable of replying coherently to questions and had done nothing but beg to be put into an armor-plated strong room under armed guard. An order was telegraphed to Leningrad for Rimsky to be escorted back to Moscow, and he returned under guard by the Friday evening train.

But Friday evening, too, they were on the track of Likhodeyev. Telegrams asking for information on him had been sent to every major Russian town, and a reply came from Yalta that Likhodeyev was there but about to leave for Moscow by airplane.

The only person whose trail they failed to pick up was Varenukha. This man, known to the entire theatrical world of Moscow, seemed to have vanished without a trace.

Meanwhile investigations were under way concerning related incidents in other parts of Moscow. An explanation was needed, for instance, of the baffling case of the office staff who had sung the "Volga Boatmen" song (Stravinsky, incidentally, cured them all within two hours by subcutaneous injections) and of the cases of people (and their victims) who had passed various pieces of rubbish under the illusion that they were banknotes. The nastiest, the most scandalous and the most insoluble of all the episodes was, of course, the theft, in broad daylight, of Berlioz' head from the open coffin at Griboyedov.

The job of the team of twelve men assigned to the case was rather like that of someone with a knitting needle trying to pick up stitches dropped all over Moscow.

One of the detectives called at Professor Stravinsky's clinic and began by asking for a list of all patients admitted during the past three days. By this means they discovered Nikanor Ivanovich Bosoi and the unfortunate M.C. whose head had been wrenched off, although they were not greatly interested in these two. It was obvious now that they had both merely been victimized by the gang headed by this weird magician. In Ivan Nikolayich Bezdomny, however, the detective showed the very greatest interest.

Early on Friday evening the door of Ivan's room opened to admit a polite, fresh-faced young man. He looked quite unlike a detective, yet he was one of the best in the Moscow force. He saw lying in bed a pale, pinched-looking young man with lackluster, wandering eyes. The detective, a man of considerable charm and tact, said that he had come to see Ivan for a talk about the incident at Patriarch's Ponds two days previously.

The poet would have felt triumphant if the detective had called earlier, on Thursday, for instance, when Ivan had been trying so loudly and passionately to induce someone to listen to his story about Patriarch's Ponds. Now people were at last coming to listen to his version of the affair—just when his urge to help capture Professor Woland had completely evaporated.

For Ivan, alas, had altogether changed since the night of Berlioz' death. He was quite prepared to answer the detective's questions politely, but his voice and his expression betrayed his utter disinterest. The poet no longer cared about Berlioz' fate.

While Ivan had been dozing before the detective's arrival, a succession of images had passed before his mind's eye. He saw a strange, unreal, vanished city with great arcaded marble piles; with roofs that flashed in the sunlight; with the grim, black and pitiless tower of Antonia; with a palace on the western hill buried almost to roof level in a garden of tropical greenery and above the garden bronze statues that glowed in the setting sun; with Roman legionaries clad in armor marching beneath the city walls.

In his half-waking dream Ivan saw a man sitting motionless in a chair, a clean-shaven man with taut, yellowing skin who wore a white cloak lined with red, who sat and stared with loathing at this alien, luxuriant garden. Ivan saw, too, a treeless ocher-colored hill with three empty crossbarred gibbets.

The events at Patriarch's Ponds no longer interested Ivan Bezdomny the poet.

"Tell me, Ivan Nikolayich, how far were you from the turnstile when Berlioz fell under the streetcar?"

A barely detectable smile of irony crossed Ivan's lips as he replied, "I was far away."

"And was the man in check standing beside the turnstile?"

"No, he was on a bench nearby."

"You distinctly remember, do you, that he did not approach the turnstile at the moment when Berlioz fell?"

"I do remember. He didn't move. He was on the bench and he stayed there."

These were the detective's last questions. He got up, shook hands with Ivan, wished him a speedy recovery and said that he soon hoped to read some new poetry of his.

"No," said Ivan quietly. "I shall not write any more poetry."

The detective smiled politely and assured the poet that, although he might be in a slight state of depression at the moment, it would soon pass.

"No," said Ivan, staring not at the detective but at the distant twilit horizon, "it will never pass. The poetry I wrote was bad poetry. I see that now."

The detective left Ivan, having gathered some extremely important evidence. Following the thread of events backward from end to beginning, they could now pinpoint the source of the whole episode. The detective had no doubt that the events in question had all begun with the murder at Patriarch's Ponds. Neither Ivan, of course, nor the man in the check suit had pushed the unfortunate chairman of MASSOLIT under the streetcar; no one had physically caused him to fall under the wheels, but the detective was convinced that Berlioz had thrown himself (or had fallen) beneath the car while under hypnosis.

Although there was plenty of evidence and it was obvious whom they should arrest and where, it proved impossible to lay hands on them. There was no doubt that someone was in apartment No. 50. Occasionally the telephone was answered by a quavering or a nasal voice, occasionally someone in the apartment opened a window and the sound of a phonograph could be heard floating out. Yet whenever they went there the place was completely empty. They searched it at various hours of the day, each time going over it with a fine-tooth comb. The apartment had been under suspicion for some time and a watch had been placed on both the main stairs and the back stairs; men were even posted on the roof among the chimney pots. The apartment was playing tricks, and there was nothing that anyone could do about it.

The case dragged on in this way until midnight on Friday, when Baron Maigel, wearing evening dress and patent-leather pumps, entered apartment No. 50 as a guest. He was heard being let in. Exactly ten minutes later the authorities entered the apartment without a sound. It was not only empty of tenants, but, worse, there was not even a trace of Baron Maigel.

There things rested until dawn on Saturday, when some new and valuable information came to light as a six-seater passenger plane landed at Moscow airport from the Crimea. Among its passengers was one extremely odd young man. He had heavy stubble on his face, had not washed for three days, his eyes were red with exhaustion and fright, he had no luggage and was somewhat eccentrically dressed. He wore a sheepskin hat, a felt cloak over a nightshirt and brand-new blue leather bedroom slippers. As he stepped off the gangway from the aircraft cabin, a group of expectant men approached him. A short while later the one and only manager of the Variety Theater, Stepan Bogdanovich Likhodeyev, was facing the detectives. He contributed some new information. They were now able to establish that Woland had tricked his way into the Variety after hypnotizing Stepa Likhodeyev and had then spirited Stepa God knows how many miles away from Moscow. This gave the authorities more evidence, but far from making their job any easier it made it if anything rather harder, because it was obviously not going to be so simple to arrest a person capable of the kind of sleight-of-hand to which Stepan Bogdanovich had fallen victim. Likhodeyev, at his own request, was locked up in a strong room.

The next witness was Varenukha, arrested at home, where he had returned after an unexplained absence lasting nearly forty-eight hours. In spite of his promise to Azazello, the house manager began by lying. He should not, however, be judged too harshly for this—Azazello had, after all, only forbidden him to lie on the telephone and in this instance Varenukho was talking without the help of a telephone. With a shifty look Ivan Savyelich announced that on Thursday he had shut himself up in his office and had got drunk, after which he had gone somewhere—he couldn't remember where; then somewhere else and drunk some 100-proof vodka; had collapsed under a hedge—again he couldn't remember where. He was then told that his stupid and irrational behavior was prejudicial to the course of justice and that he would be held responsible for it. At this Varenukha broke down, sobbing, and whispered in a trembling voice, glancing round fearfully, that he was only telling lies out of fear of Woland's gang, who had already roughed him up once, and that he begged, prayed, longed to be locked up in an armored cell.

"There soon won't be room for them all in that strong room!" growled one of the investigators.

"These villains have certainly put the fear of God into them," said the detective who had questioned Ivan.

They calmed Varenukha as well as they could, assuring him that he would be given protection without having to resort to a strong room. He then admitted that he had never drunk any 100-proof vodka but had been beaten up by two characters, one with a walleye and the other a stout man—

"Who looked like a cat?"

"Yes, yes," whispered Varenukha, almost swooning with fear and glancing furtively around, adding further details of how he had spent nearly two days in apartment No. 50 as a vampire's decoy and had nearly caused Rimsky's death. . . .

Just then Rimsky himself was brought in from the Leningrad train, but this gray-haired, terror-stricken, psychologically disturbed old man, scarcely recognizable as the treasurer of the Variety Theater, stubbornly refused to speak the truth. Rimsky claimed that he had never seen Hella at his office window that night, nor had he seen Varenukha; he had simply felt ill and had taken the train to Leningrad in a fit of amnesia. Needless to say, the ailing treasurer concluded his evidence by begging to be locked up in a strong room.

Anna was arrested while trying to pay a store cashier with a ten-dollar bill. Her story about people flying out of the stair-landing window and the horseshoe, which she claimed to have picked up in order to hand it over to the police, was listened to attentively.

"Was the horseshoe really gold and studded with diamonds?" they asked Anna.

"You think I don't know diamonds when I see them?" replied Anna.

"And did he really give you ten-ruble notes?"

"You think I don't know a tenner when I see one?"

"When did they turn into dollars?"

"I don't know what dollars are and I never saw any!" whined Anna. "I know my rights! I was given the money as a reward and went to buy some material with it." Then she started raving about the whole thing being the fault of the house management committee, which had allowed evil forces to move in on the fifth floor and made life impossible for everybody else.

Here a detective waved a pen at Anna to shut up because she was boring them, and signed her release on a green form with which, to the general satisfaction, she left the building.

There followed a succession of others, among them Nikolai Ivanovich, who had been arrested thanks to the stupidity of his jealous wife in telling the police that her husband was missing. The detectives were not particularly surprised when Nikolai Ivanovich produced the joke certificate testifying that he had spent his time at Satan's ball. Nikolai Ivanovich departed slightly from the truth, however, when he described how he had carried Margarita Nikolayevna's naked maid through the air to bathe in the river at some unknown spot and how Margarita Nikolayevna herself had appeared naked at the window. He thought it unnecessary to recall, for instance, that he had appeared in the bedroom carrying Margarita's abandoned slip. According to him, Natasha had flown out of the window, mounted him and made him fly away from Moscow. . . .

"I was forced to obey under duress," said Nikolai Ivanovich, finishing his tale with a request not to tell a word of it to his wife, which was granted.

Nikolai Ivanovich's evidence established the fact that both Margarita Nikolayevna and her maid Natasha had vanished without a trace. Steps were taken to find them.

So the investigation progressed without a moment's break until Saturday morning. Meanwhile the city was seething with the most incredible rumors, in which tiny grains of truth were embellished with a luxuriant growth of fantasy. People were saying that after the show at the Variety all two thousand spectators had rushed out into the street as naked as the day they were born; that the police had uncovered a magic printing press for counterfeiting money on Sandovaya Street; that a gang had kidnaped the five leading impresarios in Moscow but that the police had found them all again; and much more that was unrepeatable.

As it grew near lunchtime, a telephone bell rang in the investigators' office. It was a report from Sadovaya Street that the haunted apartment was showing signs of life again. Someone inside had apparently opened the windows, sounds of piano music and singing had been heard coming from it and a black cat had been observed sunning itself on a window sill.

At about four o'clock on that warm afternoon a large squad of men in plain clothes climbed out of three cars that had stopped a short distance from No. 302A Sadovaya Street. Here the large squad divided into two smaller ones, one of which entered the courtyard through the main gateway and headed straight for staircase 6, while the other opened a small door, normally locked, leading to the back staircase, and both began converging on apartment No. 50 by different stairways.

While this was going on, Koroviev and Azazello, in their normal clothes instead of festive tail coats, were sitting in the dining room finishing their lunch. Woland, as was his habit, was in the bedroom, and no one knew where the cat was, but to judge from the clatter of saucepans coming from the kitchen Behemoth was presumably there, playing the fool as usual.

"What are those footsteps on the staircase?" asked Koroviev, twiddling his spoon in a cup of black coffee.

"They're coming to arrest us," replied Azazello and drained a glass of brandy.

"Well, well . . ." was Koroviev's answer.

The men coming up the front staircase had by then reached the third-floor landing, where a couple of plumbers were fiddling with the radiator. The party exchanged meaningful looks with the plumbers.

"They're all at home," whispered one of the plumbers, tapping the pipe with his hammer.

At this the leader of the squad drew a black Mauser from under his overcoat, and the man beside him produced a skeleton key. All the men were suitably armed. Two of them had thin, easily unfurled silk nets in their packets, another had a lasso, and the sixth man was equipped with gauze masks and an ampoule of chloroform.

In a second the front door of No. 50 swung open and the party was in the hall, while the knocking on the door from the kitchen to the back staircase showed that the second squad had also arrived on time.

This time at least partial success seemed to be in their grasp. Men at once fanned out to all the rooms and found no one, but on the dining room table were the remains of an obviously recently finished meal and in the drawing room, a huge black cat was perched on the mantelpiece beside a crystal jug, holding a kerosene burner in its front paws.

There was a long pause as the men gazed at the cat.

"Hm, yes . . . that's him," whispered one of them.

"I'm doing no harm—I'm not playing games, I'm mending the kerosene burner," said the cat with a hostile scowl, "and I'd better warn you that a cat is an ancient and inviolable animal."

"Brilliant performance," whispered a man, and another said loudly and firmly, "All right, you inviolable ventriloquist's dummy, come here!"

The net whistled across the room, but the man missed his target and only caught the crystal jug, which broke with a loud crash.

"Missed!" howled the cat. "Hurrah!" Setting down the kerosene burner, the cat whipped a Browning automatic from behind its back. In a flash it took aim at the nearest man, but the detective beat the cat to the draw and fired first. The cat flopped headfirst from the mantelpiece, dropping the Browning and upsetting the kerosene burner.

"It's all over," said the cat in a weak voice, stretched out in a pool of blood. "Leave me for a moment, let me say good-bye. Oh, my friend Azazello," groaned the cat, streaming blood, "where are you?" The animal turned its expiring gaze toward the door into the dining room. "You didn't come to my help when I was outnumbered . . . you left poor Behemoth, betraying him for a glass of brandy—though it was very good brandy! Well, my death will be on your conscience, but I'll bequeath you my Browning."

"The net, the net," whispered the men urgently around the cat. But the second net had somehow got tangled up in the man's pocket and would not come out.

"The only thing that can save a mortally wounded cat," said Behemoth, "is a drink of kerosene." Taking advantage of the confusion, it puts its mouth to the round filler hole of the burner and drank some kerosene. At once the blood stopped pouring from above its left forepaw. The cat jumped up bold and full of life, tucked the kerosene burner under its foreleg, leaped back with it onto the mantelpiece and from there, tearing the wallpaper, crawled along the wall and in two seconds it was high above the invaders, sitting on a metal curtain valance.

In a moment hands were grabbing the curtains and pulling them down together with the valance, bringing the sunlight flooding into the darkened room. But neither the cat nor the kerosene burner fell. Without dropping the burner the cat managed to leap through the air and jump onto the chandelier hanging in the middle of the room.

"Stepladder!" came the cry from below.

"I challenge you to a duel!" screamed the cat, sailing over their heads on the swinging chandelier. The Browning appeared in its paw again and it wedged the kerosene burner between the arms of the chandelier. The cat took aim and, as it swung like a pendulum over the detectives' heads, opened fire on them. The sound of gunfire rocked the apartment. Fragments of crystal strewed the floor, the mirror over the fireplace was starred with bullet holes, plaster dust flew everywhere, ejected cartridge cases clattered to the floor, window panes shattered and kerosene began to leak from the punctured tank of the burner. There was now no question of taking the cat alive and the men were aiming hard at its head, stomach, breast and back. The sound of the fusillade started a panic in the courtyard below.

But this fusillade did not last long and soon died down. It had not, in fact, caused either the men or the cat any harm. There were no dead and no wounded. No one, including the cat, had been hit. As a final test one man fired five rounds into the beastly animal's stomach, and the cat retaliated with a whole volley that had the same result—not a scratch. As it swung on the chandelier, whose pendulum motion was gradually slowing down, it blew into the muzzle of the Browning and spat on its paw.

The faces of the silent men below showed total bewilderment. This was the only case, or one of the only cases, in their experience in which gunfire had proved to be completely ineffectual. Of course the cat's Browning might have been a toy, but this was certainly not true of the detectives' Mausers. The cat's first wound, which had undoubtedly been inflicted, had been nothing but a trick and a villainous piece of deception, as was its kerosene-drinking act.

One more attempt was made to seize the cat. The lasso was thrown, it looped itself round one of the candles and the whole chandelier crashed to the floor. Its fall shook the whole building, but it did not help matters. The men were showered with splinters of glass, while the cat flew through the air and landed high up under the ceiling on the gilded frame of the mirror above the mantelpiece. It made no attempt to bolt, but from its relatively safe perch announced, "I completely fail to understand the reason for this rough treatment—"

Here the cat's speech was interrupted by a low rumbling voice that seemed to come from nowhere: "What's happening in this flat? It's disturbing my work."

Another voice, ugly and nasal, cried, "It's Behemoth, of course, damn him!"

A third, quavering voice said, "Messire! Saturday. The sun is setting. We must go."

"Excuse me, I've no more time to spare talking," said the cat from the mirror. "We must go." It threw away its Browning, smashing two windowpanes, then poured the kerosene onto the floor where it burst spontaneously into a great flame as high as the ceiling.

It burned fast and hard, with even more violence than is usual with kerosene. At once the wallpaper started to smoke, the torn curtain caught fire and the frames of the broken windowpanes began to smolder. The cat crouched, gave a miaow, jumped from the mirror to the window sill and disappeared, still clutching the kerosene burner. Shots were heard from outside. A man sitting on an iron fire escape on a level with No. 50's windows fired at the cat as it sprang from window sill to window sill, heading for the drainpipe at the corner of the building. The cat scrambled up the drainpipe to the roof. There it came under equally ineffectual fire from the men covering the chimney pots, and the cat faded into the westering sunlight that flooded the city.

Inside the flat the parquet flooring was already crackling under the men's feet, and in the fireplace, where the cat had shammed dead, there gradually materialized the corpse of Baron Maigel, his little beard jutting upward, his eyes glassy. The body was impossible to move.

Hopping across the burning squares of parquet, beating out their smoldering clothes, the men in the drawing room retreated to the study and the hall. Those who had waited in the dining room and bedroom ran out into the passage. The drawing room was already full of smoke and fire. Someone managed to dial the fire department and barked into the receiver: "Sadovaya, three hundred and two A!"

They could stay no longer. Flame was lashing into the hallway, and it was becoming difficult to breathe.

As soon as the first wisps of smoke appeared through the shattered windows of the haunted apartment, desperate cries were heard from the courtyard: "Fire! Fire! Help! We're on fire!"

In several apartments people were shouting into the telephone: "Sadovaya! Sadovaya, three hundred and two A!"

Just as the heart-stopping sound of bells was heard from the long red fire engines racing toward Sadovaya Street from all over the city, the crowd in the courtyard saw three dark figures, apparently men, and one naked woman, float out of the smoking windows on the fifth floor.

THE FINAL ADVENTURE
OF KOROVIEV AND BEHEMOTH

No one, of course, can say for certain whether those figures were real or merely imagined by the frightened inhabitants of that ill-fated block on Sadovaya Street. If they were real, no one knows exactly where they were going; but we do know that about a quarter of an hour after the outbreak of fire on Sadovaya Street a tall man in a check suit and a large black cat appeared outside the glass doors of the Torgsin Store in Smolensk Market.

Slipping dexterously through the passers-by, the man opened the outer door of the store only to be met by a small, bony and extremely hostile porter who barred his way and said disagreeably, "No cats allowed!"

"I beg your pardon," quavered the tall man, cupping his knotty hand to his ear as though he were hard of hearing, "no cats, did you say? What cats?"

The doorman's eyes bulged, and with reason: there was no cat by the man's side, but instead a large fat man in a tattered cap, with vaguely feline looks and holding a kerosene burner, was pushing his way into the shop.

For some reason the misanthropic doorman did not care for the look of this couple. "You can only buy with foreign currency here," he croaked, glaring at them from beneath ragged, moth-eaten eyebrows.

"My dear fellow," warbled the tall man, one eye glinting through his broken pince-nez, "how do you know that I haven't got any? Are you judging by my suit? Never do that, my good man. You may make a terrible mistake. Read the story of the famous caliph Haroun-al-Raschid and you'll see what I mean. But for the present, leaving history aside for a moment, I warn you I shall complain to the manager and I shall tell him such tales about you that you'll wish you had never opened your mouth."

"This burner of mine may be full of foreign currency for all you know," said the stout catlike figure. An angry crowd was forming behind them. With a look of hatred and suspicion at the dubious pair, the doorman stepped aside and our friends Koroviev and Behemoth found themselves in the store. First they looked around and then Koroviev announced in a penetrating voice, audible everywhere, "What a splendid store! A very, very good store indeed!"

The customers turned round from the counters to stare at Koroviev in amazement, although there was every reason to praise the store. Hundreds of bolts of richly colored poplins stood in holders on the floor, while behind them the shelves were piled with calico, chiffon and worsted. Racks full of shoes stretched into the distance, near which several women were sitting on low chairs, a worn old shoe on their right foot, a gleaming new one on their left. From somewhere out of sight came the sound of singing and phonograph music.

Spurning all these delights, Koroviev and Behemoth went straight to the delicatessen and confectionary departments. These were spaciously laid out and full of women in head scarves and berets. A short, completely square, blue-jowled little man wearing horn-rims, a pristine hat with unstained ribbon, a fawn overcoat and tan kid gloves, was standing at a counter and booming away in an authoritative voice at a salesclerk in a clean white coverall and blue cap. With a long sharp knife very like the knife Matthew the Levite stole, he was easing the snakelike skin away from the fat, juicy flesh of a pink salmon.

"This department is excellent, too," Koroviev solemnly pronounced, "and that foreigner looks like a nice man." He pointed approvingly at the fawn coat.

"No, Faggot, no," answered Behemoth thoughtfully. "You're wrong. I think there is something missing in that gentleman's face."

The fawn back quivered, but it was probably coincidence, because he was after all a foreigner and could not have understood what Koroviev and his companion had been saying in Russian.

"Is goot?" inquired the fawn customer in a stern voice.

"First class!" replied the clerk, showing off his bladework with a flourish that lifted a whole side of skin from the salmon.

"Is goot, I like; is bad, I not like," added the foreigner.

"But of course!" rejoined the salesman.

At this point our friends left the foreigner to his salmon and moved over to the cakes and pastries.

"Hot today," said Koroviev to a pretty, red-cheeked young salesgirl, to which he got no reply. "How much are the tangerines?" Koroviev then asked her.

"Fifteen kopeks a pound," replied the salesgirl.

"They look delicious," said Koroviev with a sigh. "Oh, dear!" He thought for a while longer, then turned to his friend. "Try one, Behemoth."

The stout cat-person tucked his burner under his arm, took the uppermost tangerine off the pyramid, ate it whole, skin and all, and then took another.

The salesgirl was appalled. "Hey, are you crazy?" she screamed, the color vanishing from her cheeks. "Where are your traveler's checks or foreign currency?" She threw down her pastry tongs.

"My dear, sweet girl," cooed Koroviev, leaning across the counter and winking at the salesman, "I can't help it, but we're just out of currency today. I promise you I'll pay you it all, cash down, definitely not later than Monday! We live nearby on Sadovaya, where the house caught fire."

Having demolished a third tangerine, Behemoth thrust his paw into an ingenious structure built of chocolate bars, pulled out the bottom one, which brought the whole thing down with a crash, and swallowed the chocolate complete with its gold wrapper.

The salesman at the fish counter stood petrified, knife in hand. The fawn-colored foreigner turned round toward the looters, revealing that Behemoth was wrong: far from his face lacking something, it was if anything overendowed—huge, pendulous cheeks and bright, shifty eyes.

The salesgirl, now pale yellow, wailed miserably. "Palosich! Palosich!"

The sound brought customers running from the drapery department. Meanwhile Behemoth had wandered away from the temptations of the confectionary counter and thrust his paw into a barrel labeled "Selected Kerch-Salted Herring," pulled out a couple of herrings, gulped them both down and spat out the tails.

"Palosich!" came another despairing shriek from the confectionary counter, and the man at the fish counter, his goatee wagging in fury, barked, "Hey, you—what d'you think you're doing?"

Pavel Yosifovich (reduced to "Palosich" in the excitement) was already hurrying to the scene of action. He was an imposing man, dressed in a clean white coverall like a surgeon, with a pencil sticking out of his breast pocket. He was clearly a man of great experience. Catching sight of a herring's tail protruding from Behemoth's mouth, he summed up the situation in a moment and, refusing to join in a shouting match with the two villains, waved his arm and gave the order: "Whistle!"

The doorman shot out into Smolensk Market and relieved his feelings with a furious whistle blast. As customers began edging up to the rogues and surrounding them, Koroviev went into action.

"Citizens!" he cried in a vibrant ringing voice, "what's going on here, eh? I appeal to you! This poor man—" Koroviev put a tremor into his voice and pointed at Behemoth who had immediately assumed a pathetic expression—"this poor man has been mending a kerosene burner all day. He's hungry. Where could he get any foreign currency?"

Pavel Yosifovich, usually calm and reserved, shouted grimly, "Shut up, you!" and gave another impatient wave of his arm. Just then the automatic bell on the door gave a cheerful tinkle.

Koroviev, quite undisturbed by the manager's remark, went on: "I ask you—where? He's racked with hunger and thirst, he's hot. So the poor fellow tried a tangerine. It's only worth three kopecks at the most, but they have to start whistling like nightingales in springtime, bothering the police and stopping them from doing their proper job. But it's all right for *him*, isn't it?"

Koroviev pointed at the fat man in the fawn coat, who exhibited violent alarm. "Who is he? H'm? Where's he from? Why is he here? Were we dying of boredom without him? Did we invite him? Of course not!" roared the ex-choirmaster, his mouth twisted into a sarcastic leer. "Look at him—in his smart fawn coat, bloated with good Russian salmon, pockets bulging with currency—and what about our poor comrade here? What about him, I ask you?" wailed Koroviev, completely overcome by his own oratory.

This ridiculous, tactless and doubtless politically dangerous speech made Pavel Yosifovich shake with rage, but strangely enough it was clear from the looks of the customers that many of them approved of it. And when Behemoth, wiping his eyes with a ragged cuff, cried tragically, "Thank you, friend, for speaking up for a poor man," a miracle happened.

A quiet, dignified, little old man, shabbily but neatly dressed, who had been buying three macaroons at the pastry counter, was suddenly transformed. His eyes flashed fire, he turned purple, threw his bagful of macaroons onto the floor and shouted in a thin, childish voice, "He's right!" Then he picked up a tray, threw away the remains of the chocolate-bar Eiffel Tower that Behemoth had ruined, waved it about, pulled off the foreigner's hat with his left hand, swung the tray with his right and brought it down with a crash on the fawn man's balding head. There was a noise like that of sheet steel being thrown from a truck. Turning pale, the fat man staggered and fell backward into the barrel of salted herrings, sending up a fountain of brine and fish scales. This produced a second miracle.

As the fawn man fell into the barrel of fish he screamed in perfect Russian without a trace of an accent, "Help! Murder! They're trying to kill me!" The shock had obviously given him sudden command of a hitherto unknown language.

The doorman had by now stopped whistling, and through the crowd of excited customers could be seen the approach of two police helmets. But the cunning Behemoth poured kerosene from the burner onto the counter and it burst spontaneously into flame. It flared up and ran along the counter, devouring the beautiful paper ribbons decorating the baskets of fruit. The salesgirls leaped over the counter and ran away screaming as the flames ignited the window shades and more kerosene caught fire on the floor.

With a shriek of horror the customers shuffled out of the confectionary department, sweeping aside the helpless Pavel Yosifovich, while the fish salesmen galloped away toward the staff door, clutching their razor-sharp knives.

Heaving himself out of the barrel, the fawn man, covered with salt-herring juice, staggered past the salmon counter and followed the crowd. There was a tinkling and crashing of glass at the doorway as the public fought to get out, while the two villains, Koroviev and the gluttonous Behemoth, disappeared, no one knew where. Later, witnesses described having seen them float up to the ceiling and then burst like a couple of balloons. This story sounds too dubious for belief, and we shall probably never know what really happened.

We do know however that exactly a minute later Behemoth and Koroviev were seen on the boulevard pavement just outside Griboyedov House.

Koroviev stopped by the railing and said, "Look, there's the writers' club. You know, Behemoth, that house has a great reputation. Look at it, my friend. How lovely to think of so much talent ripening under that roof."

"Like pineapples in a hothouse," said Behemoth, climbing up onto the concrete base of the railings for a better look at the yellow, colonnaded house.

"Quite so," agreed his inseparable companion Koroviev, "and what a delicious thrill one gets, doesn't one, to think that at this moment in that house there may be the future author of a *Don Quixote* or a *Faust* or—who knows?—*Dead Souls?*"

"Frightening thought," said Behemoth.

"Yes," Koroviev went on, "think what astonishing growths may sprout from the seedbeds of that house and its thousands of devotees of Melpomene, Polyhymnia and Thalia. Just imagine the furor if one of them were to present the reading public with an *Inspector General* or at least a *Eugene Onegin!*"

"It could easily happen," said Behemoth.

"Yes," Koroviev went on, wagging a warning finger, "but—but, I say, and I repeat, *but!*—provided those hothouse growths are not attacked by some microorganism, provided they're not nipped in the bud, provided they don't rot! And it can happen with pineapples, you know! Ah, yes, it can happen!"

"By the way," inquired the cat, poking its round head through a gap in the fence, "what are they doing on the veranda?"

"Eating," explained Koroviev. "I should add that this place has a very decent, cheap restaurant. And now that I think of it, like any tourist starting on a long journey I wouldn't mind a snack and large mug of iced beer."

"Nor would I," said Behemoth, and the two rogues set off under the lime trees and up the asphalt path toward the unsuspecting restaurant.

A pale, bored woman in white ankle socks and a white-tasseled beret was sitting on a bentwood chair at the corner entrance to the veranda, where there was an opening in the creeper-grown trellis. In front of her on a plain kitchen table lay a large book like a ledger, in which for no known reason the woman wrote the names of the people entering the restaurant. She stopped Koroviev and Behemoth.

"Your membership cards?" she said, staring in surprise at Koroviev's pince-nez, at Behemoth's kerosene burner and scraped elbow.

"A thousand apologies, madam, but what membership cards?" asked Koroviev in astonishment.

"Are you writers?" asked the woman in return.

"Indubitably," replied Koroviev with dignity.

"Where are your membership cards?" the woman repeated.

"Dear lady . . ." Koroviev began tenderly.

"I'm not a dear lady," interrupted the woman.

"Oh, what a shame," said Koroviev in a disappointed voice and went on: "Well, if you don't want to be a dear lady, which would have been delightful, you have every right not to be. But look here—if you wanted to make sure that Dostoyevsky was a writer, would you really ask him for his membership card? Why, you only have to take any five pages of one of his novels and you won't need a membership card to convince you that the man's a writer. I don't suppose he ever had a membership card, anyway! What do you think?" said Koroviev, turning to Behemoth.

"I'll bet he never had one," replied the cat, putting the kerosene burner on the table and wiping the sweat from its brow with its paw.

"You're not Dostoyevsky," said the woman to Koroviev.

"How do you know?"

"Dostoyevsky's dead," said the woman, though not very confidently.

"I protest!" exclaimed Behemoth warmly. "Dostoyevsky is immortal!"

"Your membership cards, please," said the woman.

"This is really all rather funny!" said Koroviev, refusing to give up. "A writer isn't a writer because he has a membership card but because he writes. How do you know what bright ideas may not be swarming in my head? Or in his head?" And he pointed at Behemoth's head. The cat removed its cap to give the woman a better look at its head.

"Stand back, please," she said, irritated.

Koroviev and Behemoth stood aside and made way for a writer in a gray suit and a white summer shirt with the collar turned out over his jacket, no tie and a newspaper under his arm. The writer nodded to the woman and scribbled a flourish in the book as he passed through to the veranda.

"We can't," said Koroviev sadly, "but he can have that mug of cold beer which you and I, poor wanderers, were so longing for. We are in an unhappy position and I see no way out."

Behemoth only spread his paws bitterly and put his cap back on his thick head of hair that so resembled cat's fur.

At that moment a quiet but authoritative voice said to the woman, "Let them in, Sofia Pavlovna."

The woman with the ledger looked up in astonishment. From behind the trellis foliage emerged the maître d'hôtel's white shirtfront and wedge-shaped beard. He greeted the two ruffians with a welcoming look and even went so far as to beckon them in. Archibald Archibaldovich made his authority felt in this restaurant, and Sofia Pavlovna obediently asked Koroviev, "What is your name?"

"Panayev," was the polite reply. The woman wrote down the name and raised her questioning glance to Behemoth.

"Skabichevsky," squeaked the cat, for some reason pointing to his kerosene burner. Sofia Pavlovna inscribed this name too and pushed the ledger forward for the two visitors to sign. Koroviev wrote "Skabichevsky" opposite the name "Panayev" and Behemoth wrote "Panayev" opposite "Skabichevsky."

To Sofia Pavlovna's utter surprise Archibald Archibaldovich gave a seductive smile, led his guests to the best table on the far side of the veranda, where there was the most shade, where the sunlight dappled the table through a gap in the trellis. Blinking with perplexity, Sofia Pavlovna stared for a long time at the two curious signatures.

The waiters were no less surprised. Archibald Archibaldovich personally moved the chairs back from the table, invited Koroviev to be seated, winked at one and whispered to the other, while two waiters fussed around the new arrivals, one of whom put his kerosene burner on the floor beside his reddish-brown boot.

The old stained tablecloth vanished instantly from the table and another, whiter than a bedouin's burnoose, flashed through the air in a crackle of starch as Archibald Archibaldovich whispered, softly, but most expressively, into Koroviev's ear, "What can I offer you? I've a rather special fillet of smoked sturgeon. I managed to save it from the architectural congress banquet. . . ."

"Er . . . just bring us some hors d'oeuvres," boomed Koroviev patronizingly, sprawling in his chair.

"Of course," replied Archibald Archibaldovich, closing his eyes in exquisite comprehension.

Seeing how the maître d'hôtel was treating these two dubious guests, the waiters abandoned their suspicions and set about their work seriously. One offered a match to Behemoth, who had taken a butt-end out of his pocket and stuck it in his mouth; another advanced in a tinkle of green glass and laid out tumblers, claret glasses and those tall-stemmed white wine glasses which are so perfect for drinking a sparkling wine under the awning—or rather, moving on in time, which *used* to be so perfect for drinking sparkling wine under the veranda awning—at Griboyedov.

"A little breast of grouse, perhaps?" said Archibald Archibaldovich in a musical purr. The guest in the shaky pince-nez thoroughly approved the captain's suggestion and beamed at him through his one useless lens.

Petrakov-Sukhovei, the essayist, was dining at the next table with his wife and had just finished eating a pork chop. With typical writer's curiosity he had noticed the fuss that Archibald Archibaldovich was making and was extremely surprised. His wife, a most dignified lady, felt jealous of the ex-pirate's attention to Koroviev and tapped her glass with a spoon as a sign of impatience: Where's my ice cream? What's happened to the service?

With a flattering smile at Madame Petrakov, Archibald Archibaldovich sent a waiter to her and stayed with his two special customers. Archibald Archibaldovich was not only intelligent; he was at least as observant as any writer. He knew all about the show at the Variety and much else besides; he had heard, and unlike most people he had not forgotten, the words "checks" and "cat." Archibald Archibaldovich had immediately guessed who his clients were and, realizing this, he was not going to risk having an argument with them. And Sofia Pavlovna had tried to stop them coming onto the veranda! Still, what else could you expect from her? . . .

Haughtily spooning up her melting ice cream, Madame Petrakov watched disagreeably as the table, occupied by what appeared to be a couple of scarecrows, was loaded with food as if by magic. A bowl of fresh caviar, garnished with sparkling lettuce leaves . . . a moment later, and a silver ice bucket appeared on a special little side table.

Only when he had made sure that all was properly in hand and when the waiters had brought a simmering chafing dish, did Archibald Archibaldovich allow himself to leave his two mysterious guests and then only after whispering to them, "Please excuse me—I must go and attend to the grouse!"

He fled from the table and disappeared inside the restaurant. If anyone had observed what Archibald Archibaldovich did next, they might have thought it rather strange.

The maître d'hôtel did not make for the kitchen to attend to the grouse, but instead went straight to the larder. Opening it with his key, he locked himself in, lifted two heavy fillets of smoked sturgeon out of the icebox, taking care not to dirty his shirt cuffs, wrapped them in newspaper, carefully tied them up with string and put them to one side. Then he went next door to check whether his silk-lined overcoat and hat were there, and only then did he pass on to the kitchen, where the chef was carefully slicing the breast of grouse.

Odd though Archibald Archibaldovich's movements may have seemed, they were not, and would have seemed so only to a superficial observer. His actions were really quite logical. His knowledge of recent events and above all his phenomenal sixth sense told the Griboyedov maître d'hôtel that although his two guests' meal would be plentiful and delicious, it would be extremely short. And this ex-buccaneer's sixth sense, which had never yet played him false, did not let him down this time either.

Just as Koroviev and Behemoth were clinking their second glass of delicious, chilled, double-filtered Moscow vodka, a journalist called Boba Kandalupsky, famous in Moscow for knowing everything that was going on, arrived on the veranda sweating with excitement and immediately sat down at the Petrakovs' table. Dropping his bulging briefcase on the table, Boba put his lips to Petrakov's ear and whispered some obviously fascinating piece of news. Dying with curiosity, Madame Petrakov leaned her ear toward Boba's thick, fleshy lips. With furtive glances the journalist whispered on and on, just loud enough for occasional words to be heard:

"I swear! . . . Here, on Sadovaya Street . . . !" Boba lowered his voice again. ". . . the bullets couldn't hit it . . . bullets . . . kerosene . . . fire . . . bullets . . ."

"Well, as for liars who spread rumors like that," came Madame Petrakov's contralto boom, a shade too loud for Boba's liking, "they're the ones who should be shot! And they would be if I had my way. What a lot of dangerous gossip!"

"It's not gossip, Antonia Porfiryevna," exclaimed Boba, piqued at her disbelief. He began hissing again: "I tell you, bullets couldn't touch it! . . . And now the building's on fire. They floated out through the air . . . through the air!" whispered Boba, never suspecting that the people he was talking about were sitting alongside him and thoroughly enjoying the situation.

However, their enjoyment was soon cut short. Three men, tightly belted, booted and armed with revolvers, dashed out of the indoor restaurant and onto the veranda. The man in front roared, "Don't move!" and instantly all three opened fire at the heads of Koroviev and Behemoth.

The two victims melted into the air and a sheet of flame leaped up from the kerosene burner to the awning. A gaping mouth with burning edges appeared in the awning and began spreading in all directions. The fire raced across it and reached the roof of Griboyedov House. Some bundles of paper lying on the second-floor window sill of the editor's office burst into flame, which spread to a window shade, and then, as though someone had blown on it, the fire was sucked, roaring, into the house.

A few seconds later the writers, their suppers abandoned, were streaming along the asphalted paths leading to the iron railing along the boulevard, where on Wednesday evening Ivan had climbed over to bring the first incomprehensible news of disaster.

Having left in good time by a side door, without running and in no hurry, like a captain forced to be the last to leave his flaming brig, Archibald Archibaldovich calmly stood and watch it all. He wore his silk-lined overcoat and two fillets of smoked sturgeon were tucked under his arm.

CHAPTER 29

THE FATE OF THE MASTER
AND MARGARITA IS DECIDED

At sunset, high above the town, on the stone roof of one of the most beautiful buildings in Moscow, built about a century and a half ago, stood two figures—Woland and Azazello. They were invisible from the street below, hidden from the vulgar gaze by a balustrade adorned with stucco flowers in stucco urns, although they could see almost to the limits of the city.

Woland was sitting on a folding stool, dressed in his black soutane. His long, broad-bladed sword had been rammed vertically into the cleft between two flagstones, making a sundial. Slowly and inexorably the shadow of the sword was lengthening, creeping toward Satan's black slippers. Resting his sharp chin on his fist, hunched on the stool with one leg crossed over the other, Woland stared unwaveringly at the vast panorama of palaces, huge blocks of apartments and condemned slum dwellings.

Azazello, without his usual garb of jacket, bowler and patent-leather shoes and dressed instead like Woland in black, stood motionless at a short distance from his master, also staring at the city.

Woland remarked, "An interesting city, Moscow, don't you think?"

Azazello stirred and answered respectfully, "I prefer Rome, Messire."

"Yes, it's a matter of taste," replied Woland. After a while his voice rang out again: "What is that smoke over there—on the boulevard?"

"That is Griboyedov burning," said Azazello.

"I suppose that inseparable couple, Koroviev and Behemoth, have been there?"

"Without a doubt, Messire."

There was silence again, and both figures on the roof stood watching the setting sun reflected in all the westward-facing windows. Woland's eyes shone with the same fire, even though he sat with his back to the sunset.

Then something made Woland turn his attention to a round tower behind him on the roof. From its walls appeared a grim, ragged, mud-spattered man with a beard, dressed in a chiton and homemade sandals.

"Ha!" exclaimed Woland, with a sneer at the approaching figure. "You are the last person I expected to see here. What brings you here, of all people?"

"I have come to see you, spirit of evil and lord of the shadows," the man replied with a hostile glare at Woland.

"Well, tax collector, if you've come to see me, why don't you wish me well?"

"Because I have no wish to see you well," said the man impudently.

"Then I am afraid you will have to reconcile yourself to my good health," retorted Woland, his mouth twisted into a grin. "As soon as you appeared on this roof, you made yourself ridiculous. It was your tone of voice. You spoke your words as though you denied the very existence of shadows or of evil. Think, now: where would your good be if there were no evil, and what would the world look like without shadow? Shadows are thrown by people and things. There's the shadow of my sword, for instance. But shadows are also cast by trees and living beings. Do you want to strip the whole globe by removing every tree and every creature to satisfy your fantasy of a bare world? You're stupid."

"I won't argue with you, old sophist," replied Matthew the Levite.

"You are incapable of arguing with me for the reason I have just mentioned—you are too stupid," answered Woland and inquired, "Now tell me briefly and without boring me why you are here?"

"He has sent me."

"What message did he give you, slave?"

"I am not a slave," replied Matthew the Levite, growing angrier, "I am his disciple."

"You and I are speaking different languages, as always," said Woland, "but that does not alter the things we are talking about. Well?"

"He has read the master's writings," said Matthew the Levite, "and asks you to take the master with you and reward him by granting him peace. Would that be hard for you to do, spirit of evil?"

"Nothing is hard for me to do," replied Woland, "as you well know." He paused for a while and then added, "Why don't you take him yourself to the light?"

"He has not earned light, he has earned rest," said the Levite sadly.

"Tell him it shall be done," said Woland, adding with a flash in his eye, "And leave me this instant."

"He asks you also to take the woman who loved him and who has suffered for him," Matthew said to Woland, a note of entreaty in his voice for the first time.

"Do you think that we needed you to make us think of that? Go away."

Matthew the Levite vanished and Woland called to Azazello, "Go see them and arrange it."

Azazello flew off, leaving Woland alone.

He was not, however, alone for long. The sound of footsteps and animated voices was heard along the roof and Koroviev and Behemoth appeared. This time the cat had no kerosene lamp but was loaded with other things. It was carrying a small, gold-framed landscape under one arm, a half-burned cook's apron in its paw, and under its other arm was a whole salmon complete with skin and tail. Both Koroviev and Behemoth smelled of burning, Behemoth's face was covered with soot and his cap was badly burned.

"Greetings, Messire," cried the tireless pair, and Behemoth waved his salmon.

"You're a fine couple," said Woland.

"Imagine, Messire!" cried Behemoth excitedly. "They thought I was looting!"

"Judging by that stuff," replied Woland with a glance at the painting, "they were right."

"Believe me, Messire—" the cat began in an urgently sincere voice.

"No, I don't believe you," was Woland's short answer.

"Messire, I swear I made heroic efforts to save everything I could, but this was all that was left."

"It would be more interesting if you were to explain why Griboyedov caught fire in the first place."

Simultaneously Koroviev and Behemoth spread their hands and raised their eyes to heaven. Behemoth exclaimed, "It's a complete mystery! There we were, harming no one, sitting quietly having a drink and a bite to eat when—"

"—suddenly—bang, bang, bang! We were being shot at! Crazed with fright, Behemoth and I started running for the street, our pursuers behind us, and we made for Timiryazev!"

"But a sense of duty," put in Behemoth, "overcame our cowardice and we went back."

"Ah, you went back, did you?" said Woland. "By then, of course, the whole house was burnt to a cinder."

"To a cinder!" Koroviev nodded sadly. "Literally to a cinder, as you so accurately put it. Nothing but smoldering ashes."

"I rushed into the assembly hall," said Behemoth, "the colonnaded room, Messire—in case I could save something valuable. Ah, Messire, if I had a wife, she would have been nearly widowed at least twenty times! Luckily I'm not married, and believe me I'm glad. Who'd exchange a bachelor's life for a yoke around his neck?!"

"More of his nonsense," muttered Woland with a resigned glance upward.

"Messire, I promise to keep to the point," said the cat. "As I was saying, I could only save this little landscape. There was no time to salvage anything else, the flames were singeing my fur. I ran to the larder and rescued this salmon, and into the kitchen where I found this chef's coverall. I consider that I did everything I could, Messire, and I fail to understand the skeptical expression on your face."

"And what was Koroviev doing while you were looting?" inquired Woland.

"I was helping the fire brigade, Messire," answered Koroviev, pointing to his torn trousers.

"In that case I suppose it was totally destroyed and they will have to put up a new building."

"It will be built, Messire," said Koroviev. "I can assure you of that."

"Well, let us hope it will be better than the old one," remarked Woland.

"It will, Messire," said Koroviev.

"Believe me, it will," added the cat. "My sixth sense tells me so."

"Well, here we are, Messire," Koroviev reported, "and we await your instructions."

Woland rose from his stool, walked over to the balustrade and, turning his back on his retinue, stared for a long time over the city in lonely silence. Then he turned back, sat down on his stool again and said, "I have no instructions. You have done all you could, and for the time being I no longer require your services. You may rest. A thunderstorm is coming and then we must be on our way."

"Very good, Messire," replied the two buffoons and vanished behind the round tower in the center of the roof.

The thunderstorm that Woland had predicted was already gathering on the horizon. A black cloud was rising in the west; first half and then all of the sun was blotted out. The wind on the terrace freshened. Soon it was quite dark.

The cloud from the west enveloped the vast city. Bridges and buildings were all swallowed up. Everything vanished as though it had never been. A single whiplash of fire cracked across the sky, then the city rocked to a clap of thunder. There came another; the storm had begun. In the driving rain Woland was no more to be seen.

CHAPTER 30

TIME TO GO

"Do you know," said Margarita, "that just as you were going to sleep last night I was reading about the mist that came in from the Mediterranean . . . and those idols, ah, those golden idols! Somehow I couldn't get them out of my mind. I think it's going to rain soon. Can you feel how the air's growing fresher?"

"That's all very fine," replied the master, smoking and fanning the smoke away with his hand. "Let's forget about the idols . . . but what's to become of us now, I'd like to know?"

This conversation took place at sunset, just about the time Matthew the Levite appeared to Woland on the roof. The basement window was open, and if anybody had looked into it, he would have been struck by the odd appearance of the two people. Margarita had a plain black gown over her naked body and the master was in his hospital pajamas. Margarita had nothing else to wear. She had left all her clothes at home and, although her top-floor apartment was not far away, there was, of course, no question of her going there to collect her belongings. As for the master, all of whose suits were back in the wardrobe as though he had never left, he simply did not feel like getting dressed because, as he explained to Margarita, he had a premonition that some more nonsense might be on the way. He had, however, had his first proper shave since that autumn night, because the hospital staff had done no more than trim his beard with electric clippers.

The room, too, looked strange and it was hard to discern any order beneath the chaos. Manuscripts lay all over the floor and couch. A book was lying, spine upward, on the armchair. The round table was laid for supper, several bottles standing among the plates of food. Margarita and the master had no idea where all this food and drink had come from—it had simply been there on the table when they woke up.

Having slept until Saturday evening, both the master and his love felt completely revived, and only one symptom reminded them of their adventures of the night before—both of them felt a slight ache in the left temple. Psychologically they had both changed considerably, as anyone who overheard their conversation would have realized. But there was no one to overhear them. The advantage of the little yard was that it was always empty. The lime tree and the maple, turning greener with each day, exhaled the perfume of spring and the rising breeze carried it into the basement.

"The devil!" the master suddenly exclaimed. "Just think of it." He stubbed out his cigarette in the ashtray and clasped his head in his hands. "Listen—you're intelligent and you haven't been in the madhouse as I have—do you seriously believe that we spent last night with Satan?"

"Quite seriously, I do."

"Oh, of course, of course," said the master ironically. "There are obviously two lunatics in the family now—husband and wife!" He raised his arms toward heaven and shouted, "No, the devil knows what it was!"

Instead of replying, Margarita collapsed onto the divan, burst into laughter, waved her bare legs in the air and practically shouted, "Oh, I can't help it . . . I can't help it. . . . If you could only see yourself!"

When the master, embarrassed, had buttoned up his hospital pants, Margarita grew serious. "Just now you unwittingly spoke the truth," she said. "The devil *does* know what it was and the devil, believe me, will arrange everything!" Her eyes suddenly flashed; she jumped up, danced for joy and shouted, "I'm so happy, so happy, happy that I made that bargain with him! Hurrah for the devil! I'm afraid, my dear, that you're doomed to live with a witch!"

She flung herself at the master, clasped him round the neck and began kissing his lips, his nose, his cheeks. Floods of unkempt black hair caressed the master's neck and shoulders while his face burned with kisses.

"You really are like a witch."

"I don't deny it," replied Margarita. "I'm a witch and I'm very glad of it."

"All right," said the master, "so you're a witch. Fine, splendid. They've abducted me from the hospital—equally splendid. And they've brought us back here—let us grant them that, too. Let's even assume that neither of us will be caught. But what, in the name of all that's holy, are we supposed to live on? Tell me that, will you? You seem to care so little about the problem that it really worries me."

Just then a pair of blunt-toed boots and the lower part of a pair of trousers appeared in the little basement window. Then the trousers bent at the knee and the daylight was shut out by a man's ample bottom.

"Aloysius, are you there, Aloysius?" asked a voice from slightly above the trousers.

"It's beginning," said the master.

"Aloysius?" asked Margarita, moving closer to the window. "He was arrested yesterday. Who wants him? What's your name?"

Instantly the knees and bottom vanished, there came the click of the gate and everything returned to normal. Again, Margarita collapsed onto the divan and laughed until tears started from her eyes. When the fit was over, her expression changed completely, she grew serious, slid down from the divan and crawled over to the master's knees. Staring him in the eyes, she began to stroke his head.

"How you've suffered, my poor love! I'm the only one who knows how much you've suffered. Look, there are gray and white threads in your hair and hard lines around your mouth. My sweetest love, forget everything and stop worrying. You've had to do too much thinking; now I'm going to think for you. I swear to you that everything is going to be perfect!"

"I'm not afraid of anything, Margot," the master suddenly replied, raising his head and looking just as he had when he had created that world he had never seen yet knew to be true. "I'm not afraid, simply because I have been through everything that a man can go through. I've been so frightened that nothing frightens me any longer. But I feel sorry for you, Margot— that's the point, that's why I keep coming back to the same question. Think, Margarita—why ruin your life for a sick pauper? Go back home. I feel sorry for you, that's why I say this."

"My dear, dear, dear," whispered Margarita, shaking her tousled head, "you weak, faithless, stupid man! Why do you think I spent the whole of last night prancing about naked, why do you think I sold my human nature and became a witch, why do you think I spent months in this dim, damp little hole thinking of nothing but the storm over Jerusalem, why do you think I cried my eyes out when you vanished? You know why, yet when happiness suddenly descends on us and gives us everything, you want to get rid of me! All right, I'll go. But you're a cruel, cruel man. You've become completely heartless."

Bitter tenderness filled the master's heart, and without knowing why he burst into tears as he fondled Margarita's hair.

Crying too, she whispered to him as her fingers caressed his temple, "There are more than just threads—your head is turning white under my eyes . . . my poor suffering head. Look at your eyes! Empty . . . And your shoulders, bent with the weight they've borne . . . They've crippled you." Her voice was lost in helpless sobbing.

Then the master dried his eyes, raised Margarita from her knees, stood up himself and said firmly, "That will do. You've made me utterly ashamed. I'll never mention it again, I promise. I know that we are both suffering from some mental sickness which you have probably caught from me. Well, we must see it through together."

Margarita put her lips close to the master's ear and whispered, "I swear by your life, I swear by the astrologer's son you created that all will be well!"

"All right, I'll believe you," answered the master with a smile, adding, "Where else can such wrecks as you and I find help except from the supernatural? So let's see what we can find in the other world."

"There, now you're like you used to be—you're laughing," said Margarita. "To hell with all your long words! Supernatural or not supernatural, what do I care? I'm hungry!" And she dragged the master toward the table.

"I can't feel quite sure that this food isn't going to disappear through the floor in a puff of smoke or fly out of the window," said the master.

"I promise you it won't."

At that moment a nasal voice was heard at the window: "Peace be with you."

The master was startled, but Margarita, accustomed to the unfamiliar, cried, "It's Azazello! Oh, how nice!" And whispering to the master, "You see—they haven't abandoned us!" she ran to open the door.

"You should at least fasten the front of your dress," the master shouted after her.

"I don't care," replied Margarita from the passage.

His blind eye glistening, Azazello came in, bowed and greeted the master. Margarita cried, "Oh, how glad I am! I've never been so happy in my life! Forgive me, Azazello, for meeting you naked like this."

Azazello begged her not to let it worry her, assuring Margarita that he had not only seen plenty of naked women in his time but even women who had been skinned alive. First putting down a bundle wrapped in dark cloth, he took a seat at the table.

Margarita poured Azazello a brandy, which he drank with relish. The master, without staring at him, gently scratched his left wrist under the table, but it had no effect. Azazello did not vanish into thin air, and there was no reason why he should. There was nothing terrifying about this stocky little demon with red hair, except perhaps his walleye, but that afflicts plenty of quite unmagical people, and except for his slightly unusual dress—a kind of cassock or cape—but ordinary people sometimes wear clothes like that too. He drank his brandy like all good men do, a whole glassful at a time and on an empty stomach.

The same brandy was already beginning to make the master's head buzz, and he said to himself, "No, Margarita's right . . . of course this creature is an emissary of the devil. After all only the day before yesterday I was proving to Ivan that he had met Satan at Patriarch's Ponds, yet now the thought seems to frighten me and I'm inventing excuses like hypnosis and hallucinations. . . . Hypnotism—hell!"

He studied Azazello's face and was convinced that there was a certain constraint in his look, some thought which he was holding back. "He's not just here on a visit, he has been sent here for a purpose," thought the master.

His powers of observation had not betrayed him. After his third glass of brandy, which had no apparent effect on him, Azazello said, "I must say it's comfortable, this little basement of yours, isn't it? The only question is, what on earth are you going to do with yourselves, now that you're here?"

"That is just what I have been wondering," said the master with a smile.

"Why do you make me feel uneasy, Azazello?" asked Margarita.

"Oh, come now!" exclaimed Azazello, "I wouldn't dream of doing anything to upset you. Oh, yes! I nearly forgot . . . Messire sends his greetings and asks me to invite you to take a little trip with him—if you'd like to, of course. What do you say to that?"

Margarita gently kicked the master's foot under the table.

"With great pleasure," replied the master, studying Azazello, who went on: "We hope Margarita Nikolayevna won't refuse?"

"Of course not," said Margarita, again brushing the master's foot with her own.

"Splendid!" cried Azazello. "That's what I like to see—one, two and away! Not like the other day in the Alexander Gardens!"

"Oh, don't remind me of that, Azazello, I was so stupid then. But you can't really blame me—one doesn't meet the devil every day!"

"More's the pity," said Azazello. "Think what fun it would be if you did!"

"I love the speed," said Margarita excitedly, "I love the speed, and I love being naked—just like a bullet from a gun— bang! Ah, how he can shoot!" cried Margarita, turning to the master. "He can hit any spot on a card—under a cushion, too!" Margarita was beginning to get drunk and her eyes were sparkling.

"Oh, I nearly forgot something else, too," exclaimed Azazello, slapping himself on the forehead. "What a fool I am! Messire has sent you a present—" here he spoke to the master —"a bottle of wine. Please note that it is the same wine that the Procurator of Judea drank. Falernian."

This rarity aroused great interest in both Margarita and the master. Azazello drew a sealed wine jar, completely covered with mildew, out of a piece of an old winding sheet. They sniffed the wine, then poured it into glasses and looked through it toward the window. The light was already fading with the approach of the storm. Filtered through the glass, it turned everything to the color of blood.

"To Woland!" exclaimed Margarita, raising her glass.

All three put their lips to the glasses and drank a large mouthful. Immediately the light began to fade before the master's eyes, his breath came in gasps and he felt the end coming. He could just see Margarita, deathly pale, helplessly stretch out her arms toward him, drop her head onto the table and then slide to the floor.

"Poisoner . . ." the master managed to gasp. He tried to snatch the knife from the table to stab Azazello, but his hand slithered lifelessly from the tablecloth, everything in the basement seemed to turn black and then vanished altogether. He collapsed sideways, grazing his forehead on the edge of the bureau as he fell.

When he was certain that the poison had taken effect, Azazello started to act. First he flew out of the window and in a few moments he was in Margarita's flat. Precise and efficient as ever, Azazello wanted to check that everything necessary had been done. It had. Azazello saw a depressed-looking woman, waiting for her husband to return, come out of her bedroom and suddenly turn pale, clutch her heart and gasp helplessly, "Natasha . . . somebody . . . help . . ." She fell to the drawing-room floor before she had time to reach the study.

"All in order," said Azazello. A moment later he was back with the murdered lovers. Margarita lay face downward on the carpet. With his iron hands Azazello turned her over like a doll and looked at her. The woman's face changed before his eyes. Even in the twilight of the oncoming storm he could see how her temporary witch's squint and her look of cruelty and violence disappeared. Her expression relaxed and softened, her mouth lost its predatory sneer and simply became the mouth of a woman in her last agony. Then Azazello forced her white teeth apart and poured into her mouth a few drops of the same wine that had poisoned her.

Margarita sighed, rose without Azazello's help, sat down and asked weakly, "Why, Azazello, why? What have you done to me?"

She saw the master lying on the floor, shuddered and whispered, "I didn't expect this . . . murderer!"

"Don't worry," replied Azazello. "He'll get up again in a minute. Why must you be so nervous?"

He sounded so convincing that Margarita believed him at once. She jumped up, alive and strong, and helped to give the master some of the wine. Opening his eyes, he gave a stare of grim hatred and repeated his last word, "Poisoner . . ."

"Oh, well, insults are the usual reward for a job well done!" said Azazello. "Are you blind? You'll soon see sense."

The master got up, looked around briskly and asked, "Now what does all this mean?"

"It means," replied Azazello, "that it's time for us to go. The thunderstorm has already begun—can you hear? It's getting dark. The horses are pawing the ground and making your little garden shudder. You must say good-bye, quickly."

"Ah, I understand," said the master, gazing round, "you have killed us. We are dead. How clever—and how timely! Now I see it all."

"Oh, come," replied Azazello, "what did I hear you say? Your beloved calls you the master, you're an intelligent being —how can you be dead? It's ridiculous."

"I understand what you mean," cried the master, "don't go on! You're right—a thousand times right!"

"The great Woland!" Margarita said to him urgently, "the great Woland! His solution was much better than mine! But the novel, the novel!" she shouted at the master. "Take the novel with you, wherever you may be going!"

"No need," replied the master, "I can remember it all by heart."

"But you . . . you won't forget a word?" asked Margarita, embracing her lover and wiping the blood from his bruised forehead.

"Don't worry. I shall never forget anything again," he answered.

"Then the fire!" cried Azazello. "The fire—where it all began and where we shall end it!"

"The fire!" Margarita cried in a terrible voice. The basement windows were banging, the blind was flapping in the wind. There was a short, cheerful clap of thunder. Azazello thrust his bony hand into the stove, pulled out a smoldering log and used is to light the tablecloth. Then he set fire to a pile of old newspapers on the divan, then the manuscript and the curtains.

The master, intoxicated in advance by the thought of the ride to come, threw a book from the bookcase onto the table, thrust its leaves into the burning tablecloth, and the book burst merrily into flame.

"Burn away, past!"

"Burn, suffering," cried Margarita.

Crimson pillars of fire were swaying all over the room,

when the three ran out of the smoking door, up the stone steps and out into the courtyard. The first thing they saw was the landlord's cook sitting on the ground surrounded by potato peelings and bunches of onions. Her position was hardly surprising—three black horses were standing in the yard, snorting, quivering and kicking up the ground in fountains of dust. Margarita mounted the first, then Azazello, and the master last. Groaning, the cook was about to raise her hand to make the sign of the cross when Azazello shouted threateningly from the saddle, "If you do, I'll cut off your arm!" He whistled and the horses, smashing the branches of the lime tree, whinnied and plunged upward into a low black cloud. From below came the cook's faint, pathetic cry: "Fire . . ."

The horses were already galloping over the roofs of Moscow.

"I want to say good-bye to someone," shouted the master to Azazello, who was cantering along in front of him. Thunder drowned the end of the master's sentence. Azazello nodded and urged his horse into a gallop. A cloud was rushing toward them, though it had not yet begun to spatter rain.

They flew over the boulevard, watching as the little figures ran in all directions for shelter from the rain. The first drops were falling. They flew over a pillar of smoke—all that was left of Griboyedov. On they flew over the city in the gathering darkness. Lightning flashed above them. Then the roofs changed to treetops. Only then did the rain begin to lash them and turned them into three great bubbles in the midst of endless water.

Margarita was already used to the sensation of flight, but the master was not, and he was amazed how quickly they reached their destination, where he wished to say good-bye to the only other person who meant anything to him. Through the veil of rain he immediately recognized Stravinsky's clinic, the river and the pine forest on the far bank that he had stared at for so long. They landed among a clump of trees in a meadow not far from the clinic.

"I'll wait for you here," shouted Azazello, folding his arms. For a moment he was lit up by a flash of lightning, then vanished again in the gray pall. "You can say good-bye, but hurry!"

The master and Margarita dismounted and flew, like watery shadows, through the clinic garden. A moment later the master was pushing aside the balcony grille of No. 117 with a practiced hand. Margarita followed him. They walked into Ivan's room, invisible and unnoticed, as the storm howled and thundered. The master stopped by the bed.

Ivan was lying motionless, as he had been when he had first watched the storm from his enforced rest home. This time, however, he was not crying. After staring for a while at the dark shape that entered his room from the balcony, he sat up, stretched out his arms and said joyfully, "Oh, it's you! I've been waiting for you! It's you, my neighbor!"

To this the master answered, "Yes, it's me, but I'm afraid I shan't be your neighbor any longer. I am flying away forever and I've only come to say good-bye."

"I knew, I guessed," replied Ivan quietly, then asked, "Did you meet him?"

"Yes," said the master, "I have come to say good-bye to you because you're the only person I have been able to talk to in these last days."

Ivan beamed and said, "I'm so glad you came. You see, I'm going to keep my word, I shan't write any more stupid poetry. Something else interests me now—" Ivan smiled and stared crazily past the figure of the master—"I want to write something quite different. I have come to understand a lot of things since I've been lying here."

The master grew excited at this and said as he sat down on the edge of Ivan's bed, "That's good, that's good. You must write the sequel to it."

Ivan's eyes sparkled. "But won't you be writing it?" Then he looked down and added thoughtfully, "Oh, yes, of course . . . what am I saying?" Ivan stared at the ground, frightened.

"No," said the master, and his voice seemed to Ivan unfamiliar and hollow, "I won't write about him any more. I shall be busy with other things."

The roar of the storm was pierced by a distant whistle.

"Do you hear?" asked the master.

"The noise of the storm . . ."

"No, they're calling me, it's time for me to go," explained the master and got up from the bed.

"Wait! One more thing," begged Ivan. "Did you find her? Had she been faithful to you?"

"Here she is," replied the master, pointing to the wall. The dark figure of Margarita materialized from the wall and moved over to the bed. She looked at the young man in the bed and her eyes filled with sorrow.

"Poor, poor boy," she whispered silently and bent over the bed.

"How beautiful she is," said Ivan, without envy but sadly and touchingly. "Everything has worked out wonderfully for you, you lucky fellow. And here am I, sick. . . ." He thought for a moment, then added thoughtfully, "Or perhaps I'm not so sick after all."

"That's right," whispered Margarita, bending right down to Ivan. "I'll kiss you and everything will be as it should be. Believe me, I know."

Ivan put his arms around her neck and she kissed him.

"Farewell, disciple," said the master gently and began to melt into the air. He vanished, as did Margarita. The grille closed.

Ivan felt uneasy. He sat up in bed, gazing round anxiously, groaned, talked to himself, got up. The storm was raging with increasing violence, and it was obviously upsetting him. It upset him so much that his hearing, lulled by the permanent silence, caught the sound of anxious footsteps, murmured voices outside his door. Trembling, he called out irritably, "Praskovya Fyodorovna!"

As the nurse came into the room, she gave Ivan a worried, inquiring look.

"What's the matter?" she asked. "Is the storm frightening you? Don't worry—I'll bring you something in a moment. I'll call the doctor right away."

"No, Praskovya Fyodorovna, you needn't call the doctor," said Ivan, staring anxiously not at her but at the wall. "There's nothing particularly wrong with me. I'm in my right mind now, don't be afraid. But you might tell me," asked Ivan confidentially, "what has just happened next door in No. 118?"

"In 118?" Praskovya Fyodorovna repeated hesitantly. Her eyes flickered in embarrassment. "Nothing has happened there." But her voice betrayed her.

Ivan noticed this at once and said, "Oh, Praskovya Fyodorovna! You're such a truthful person. Are you afraid I'll get violent? No, Praskovya Fyodorovna, I won't. You had better tell me, you see I can sense it all through that wall."

"Your neighbor has just died," whispered Praskovya Fyodorovna, unable to overcome her natural truthfulness and goodness, and she gave a frightened glance at Ivan, who was suddenly clothed in lightning.

But nothing terrible happened. He only raised his finger and said, "I knew it! I am telling you, Praskovya Fyodorovna, that another person has just died in Moscow, too. I even know who." Here Ivan smiled mysteriously. "It is a woman!"

CHAPTER 31

ON SPARROW HILLS

The storm had passed and a rainbow had arched itself across the sky, its foot in the Moscow River. On top of a hill between two clumps of trees could be seen three dark silhouettes. Woland, Koroviev and Behemoth sat mounted on black horses, looking at the city spread out beyond the river with fragments of sun glittering from thousands of west-facing windows, and at the onion domes of the Novodevichy monastery.

There was a rustling in the air and Azazello, followed in a black cavalcade by the master and Margarita, landed by the group of waiting figures.

"I'm afraid we had to frighten you a little, Margarita Nikolayevna, and you, master," said Woland after a pause. "But I don't think you will have cause to complain to me about it or regret it. Now—" he turned to the master—"say good-bye to this city. It's time for us to go." Woland pointed his hand in its black gauntlet toward where countless glass suns glittered beyond the river, where above those suns the city exhaled the haze, smoke and vapor of the day.

The master leaped from his saddle, left his companions and ran to the hillside, black cloak flapping above the ground behind him. He looked at the city. For a few moments a tremor of sadness crept over his heart, but it soon changed to a delicious excitement, the gypsy's thrill of the open road.

"Forever . . . I must think what that means," whispered the master and licked his dry, cracked lips. He began to listen to what was happening in his heart. His excitement, it seemed to him, had given way to a profound and grievous sense of hurt. But it was only momentary and gave place to one of proud indifference and finally to a presentiment of eternal peace.

The party of riders waited for the master in silence. They watched the tall, black figure on the hillside gesticulate, then raise his head as though trying to cast his glance over the whole city and to see beyond its limits; then he hung his head as if he were studying the sparse, trampled grass under his feet.

Behemoth, who was getting bored, broke the silence: "Please, *mon maître,*" he said, "let me give a farewell whistle call."

"You might frighten the lady," replied Woland. "Besides, don't forget that you have done enough fooling about for one visit. Behave yourself now."

"Oh, no, Messire," cried Margarita, sitting her mount like an Amazon, one arm akimbo, her long black train reaching to the ground. "Please let him whistle. I feel sad at the thought of the journey. It's quite a natural feeling, even when you know it will end in happiness. If you won't let him make us laugh, I shall cry, and the journey will be ruined before we start."

Woland nodded to Behemoth. Delighted, the cat leaped to the ground, put its paws in its mouth, filled its cheeks and whistled.

Margarita's ears sang. Her horse roared, twigs snapped off nearby trees, a flock of rooks and crows flew up, a cloud of dust billowed toward the river and several passengers on a river steamer below had their hats blown off.

The whistle blast made the master flinch; he did not turn around, but began gesticulating even more violently, raising his fist skyward as though threatening the city. Behemoth looked proudly around.

"You whistled, I grant you," said Koroviev condescendingly. "But frankly it was a very mediocre whistle."

"I'm not a choirmaster, however," said Behemoth with dignity, puffing out his chest and suddenly winking at Margarita.

"Let me have a try, just for old times' sake," said Koroviev. He rubbed his hands and blew on his fingers.

"Very well," said Woland sternly, "but without endangering life or limb, please."

"Purely for fun, I promise you, Messire," Koroviev assured him, hand on heart. He suddenly straightened up, seemed to stretch as though he were made of rubber, waved the fingers of his right hand, wound himself up like a spring and then, suddenly uncoiling, he whistled.

Margarita did not hear this whistle, but she felt it, as she and her horse were picked up and thrown twenty yards sideways. Near her the bark was ripped off an oak tree and cracks opened in the ground as far as the river. The water in it boiled and heaved, and the river steamer, with all its passengers unharmed, was grounded on the far bank by the blast. A jackdaw, killed by Faggot's whistle, fell at the feet of Margarita's snorting horse.

This time the master was thoroughly frightened and ran back to his waiting companions.

"Well," said Woland to him from the saddle, "have you made your farewell?"

"Yes, I have," said the master and boldly returned Woland's stare.

Then like the blast of a trumpet the terrible voice of Woland rang out over the hills: "It is time!"

Like an echo came a piercing laugh and a whistle from Behemoth. The horses leaped into the air, and the riders rose with them as they galloped upward. Margarita could feel her fierce horse biting and tugging at the bit. Woland's cloak billowed out over the heads of the cavalcade, and as evening drew on, his cloak began to cover the whole vault of the sky. When the black veil blew aside for a moment, Margarita turned round in flight and saw that not only the many-colored towers but the whole city had long since vanished from sight, swallowed by the earth, leaving only mist and smoke where it had been.

CHAPTER 32

ABSOLUTION AND
ETERNAL REFUGE

How sad, O gods, how sad is the world at evening, how mysterious the mists over the swamps. You will know it when you have wandered astray in those mists, when you have suffered greatly before dying, when you have walked through the world carrying an unbearable burden. You know it, too, when you are weary and ready to leave this earth without regret—its mists, its swamps and its rivers—ready to give yourself into the arms of death with a light heart, knowing that death alone can comfort you.

The magic black horses were growing tired, carrying their riders more slowly as inexorable night began to overtake them. Sensing it behind him, even the irrepressible Behemoth was hushed, and digging his claws into the saddle he flew on in silence, his tail streaming behind him.

Night laid its black cloth over forest and meadow, night lit a scattering of sad little lights far away below, lights that for Margarita and the master were now meaningless and alien. Night overtook the cavalcade, spread itself over them from above and began to seed the lowering sky with white specks of stars.

Night thickened, flew alongside, seized the riders' cloaks and, pulling them from their shoulders, unmasked their disguises.

When Margarita opened her eyes in the freshening wind, she saw the features of all the galloping riders change, and when a full, purple moon rose toward them over the edge of a forest, all deception vanished and fell away into the marsh beneath as their magical, trumpery clothing faded into the mist.

It would have been hard now to recognize Koroviev-Faggot, self-styled interpreter to the mysterious professor who needed none, in the figure who now rode immediately alongside Woland at Margarita's right hand. In place of the person who had left Sparrow Hills in shabby circus clothes under the name of Koroviev-Faggot, there now galloped, the gold chain of his bridle clinking softly, a knight clad in dark violet with a grim and unsmiling face. He leaned his chin on his chest, looked neither at the moon nor at the earth, thinking his own thoughts as he flew along beside Woland.

"Why has he changed so?" Margarita asked Woland above the hiss of the wind.

"That knight once made an ill-timed joke," replied Woland, turning his fiery eye on Margarita. "Once when we were talking of darkness and light, he made a somewhat unfortunate pun. As a penance he was condemned to spend rather more time as a practical joker than he had bargained for. But tonight is one of those moments when accounts are settled. Our knight has paid his score and the account is closed."

Night stripped away, too, Behemoth's fluffy tail and his fur and scattered it in handfuls. The creature who had been the pet cat of the prince of darkness was revealed as a slim youth, a page demon, the greatest jester that there has ever been. He, too, was now silent and flew without a sound, holding up his young face toward the light that poured from the moon.

On the flank, gleaming in steel armor, rode Azazello, his face transformed by the moon. Gone was the idiotic walleye, gone was his false squint. Both Azazello's eyes were alike, empty and black, his face white and cold. Azazello was now in his real guise, the demon of the waterless desert, the murderer demon.

Margarita could not see herself, but she could see the change that had come over the master. His hair had whitened in the moonlight and had gathered behind him into a mane that flew in the wind. Whenever the wind blew the master's cloak away from his legs, Margarita could see the spurs that winked at the heels of his jackboots. Like the page demon the master rode staring at the moon, though smiling at it as though it were a dear, familiar friend and—a habit acquired in room No. 118—talking to himself.

Woland, too, rode in his true aspect. Margarita could not say what the reins of his horse were made of; she thought that they might be strings of moonlight and the horse itself only a blob of darkness, its mane a cloud and its rider's spurs glinting stars.

They rode for a long time in silence until the country beneath began to change. The grim forests slipped away into the gloom below, drawing with them the dull curved blades of rivers. The moonlight was now reflected from scattered boulders with dark gulleys among them.

Woland reined in his horse on the flat, grim top of a hill, and the riders followed him at a walk, hearing the crunch of flints and pebbles under the horses' shoes. The moon flooded the ground with a harsh green light, and soon Margarita noticed on the bare expanse a chair, with the vague figure of a man seated on it, apparently deaf or lost in thought. He seemed not to hear the stony ground shuddering beneath the weight of the horses, and he remained unmoved as the riders approached.

In the brilliant moonlight, brighter than an arc light, Margarita could see the seemingly blind man wringing his hands and staring at the moon with unseeing eyes. Then she saw that beside the massive stone chair, which sparkled fitfully in the moonlight, there lay a huge, gray dog with pointed ears, gazing like his master at the moon. At the man's feet were the fragments of a jug and a reddish-black pool of liquid.

The riders halted.

"We have read your novel," said Woland, turning to the master, "and we can only say that unfortunately it is not finished. I would like to show you your hero. He has been sitting here and sleeping for nearly two thousand years, but when the full moon comes he is tortured, as you see, with insomnia. It plagues not only him, but his faithful guardian, his dog. If it is true that cowardice is the worst sin of all, then the dog at least is not guilty of it. The only thing that frightened this brave animal was a thunderstorm. But one who loves must share the fate of his loved one."

"What is he saying?" asked Margarita, and her calm face was veiled with compassion.

"He always says," said Woland, "the same thing. He is saying that there is no peace for him by moonlight and that his duty is a hard one. He says it always, whether he is asleep or awake, and he always sees the same thing—a path of moonlight. He longs to walk along it and talk to his prisoner, Ha-Notsri, because he claims he had more to say to him on that distant fourteenth day of Nisan. But he never succeeds in reaching that path and no one ever comes near him. So it is not surprising that he talks to himself. For an occasional change he adds that most of all he detests his immortality and his incredible fame. He claims that he would gladly change places with that vagrant, Matthew the Levite."

"Twenty-four thousand moons in penance for one moon long ago, isn't that too much?" asked Margarita.

"Are you going to repeat the business with Frieda again?" said Woland. "But you needn't distress yourself, Margarita. All will be as it should; that is how the world is made."

"Let him go!" Margarita suddenly shouted in a piercing voice, as she had shouted when she was a witch. Her cry shattered a rock on the mountainside, sending it bouncing down into the abyss with a deafening crash, but Margarita could not tell whether what she heard was the falling rock or the sound of satanic laughter.

Whatever it was, Woland laughed and said to Margarita, "Shouting at the mountains will do no good. Landslides are common here, and he is used to them by now. There is no need for you to plead for him, Margarita, because his cause has already been pleaded by the man he longs to join." Woland turned round to the master and went on: "Now is your chance to complete your novel with a single sentence."

The master seemed to be expecting this while he had been standing motionless, watching the seated Procurator. He cupped his hands into a trumpet and shouted with such force that the echo sprang back at him from the bare, treeless hills: "You are free! Free! He is waiting for you!"

The mountains turned the master's voice to thunder and the thunder destroyed them. The grim cliffsides crumbled and fell. Only the platform with the stone chair remained. Above the black abyss into which the mountains had vanished glowed a great city topped by glittering idols above a garden overgrown with the luxuriance of two thousand years. Into the garden stretched the Procurator's long-awaited path of moonlight, and the first to bound along it was the dog with pointed ears. The man in the white cloak with the blood-red lining rose from his chair and shouted something in a hoarse, uneven voice. It was impossible to tell whether he was laughing or crying, or what he was shouting. He could only be seen hurrying along the moonlight path after his faithful watchdog.

"Am I to follow him?" the master inquired uneasily, with a touch on his reins.

"No," answered Woland, "why try to pursue what is completed?"

"That way, then?" asked the master, turning and pointing back to where rose the city they had just left, with its onion-domed monasteries, fragmented sunlight reflected in its windows.

"No, not that way either," replied Woland, his voice rolling down the hillsides like a thick torrent. "You are a romantic, master! Your novel has been read by the man your hero, whom you have just released, so longs to see." Here Woland turned to Margarita: "Margarita Nikolayevna! I am convinced that you have done your utmost to devise the best possible future for the master, but believe me, what I am offering you and what Yeshua has begged to be given to you is even better! Let us leave them alone with each other," said Woland, leaning out of his saddle toward the master and pointing to the departing Procurator. "Let's not disturb them. Who knows, perhaps they may agree on something."

At this Woland waved his hand toward Jerusalem, which vanished.

"And there too," Woland pointed backward. "What good is your little basement now?" The reflected sun faded from the windows. "Why go back?" Woland continued, quietly and persuasively. "Oh, thrice romantic master, wouldn't you like to stroll under the cherry blossom with your love in the daytime and listen to Schubert in the evening? Won't you enjoy writing by candlelight with a goose quill? Don't you want, like Faust, to sit over a retort in the hope of fashioning a new homunculus? That's where you must go—where a house and an old servant are already waiting for you and the candles are lit—although they are soon to be put out because you will arrive at dawn. That is your way, master, that way! Farewell—I must go!"

"Farewell!" cried Margarita and the master together. Then the black Woland, taking none of the paths, dived into the abyss, followed with a roar by his retinue. The mountains, the platform, the moonbeam pathway, Jerusalem—all were gone. The black horses, too, had vanished. The master and Margarita saw the promised dawn, which now rose in succession to the midnight moon. In the first rays of the morning the master and his beloved crossed a little moss-grown stone bridge. They left the stream behind them and followed a sandy path.

"Listen to the silence," said Margarita to the master, the sand whispering under her bare feet. "Listen to the silence and enjoy it. Here is the peace that you never knew in your lifetime. Look, there is your home for eternity, which is your reward. I can already see a Venetian window and a climbing vine which grows right up to the roof. It's your home, your home forever. In the evenings people will come to see you, people who interest you, people who will never upset you. They will play to you and sing to you, and you will see how beautiful the room is by candlelight. You shall go to sleep with your dirty old cap on, you shall go to sleep with a smile on your lips. Sleep will give you strength and make you wise. And you can never send me away—I shall watch over your sleep."

Thus spoke Margarita as she walked with the master toward their everlasting home, and Margarita's words seemed to him to flow like the whispering stream behind them, and the master's memory, his accursed, needling memory, began to fade. He had been freed, just as he had set free the character he had created. His hero had now vanished irretrievably into the abyss; on the night of Sunday, the day of the Resurrection, pardon had been granted to the astrologer's son, fifth Procurator of Judea, the cruel Pontius Pilate.

EPILOGUE

But what happened in Moscow after sunset on that Saturday evening when Woland and his followers left the capital and vanished from Sparrow Hills?

There is no need to mention the flood of incredible rumors which buzzed around Moscow for a long afterward and even spread to the dimmest and most distant reaches of the provinces. The rumors are, in any case, too nauseating to repeat.

On a train journey to Theodosia, the honest narrator himself heard a story of how in Moscow two thousand people had rushed literally naked out of a theater and were driven home in taxis.

The whispered words "evil spirits" could be heard in milk lines and streetcar lines, in shops, apartments and kitchens, in commuter trains and long-distance expresses, at station stops, in weekend cottages and on beaches.

Educated and cultured people, of course, took no part in all this gossip about evil spirits descending on Moscow, and even laughed at those who did and tried to bring them to reason. But facts, as they say, are facts, and they could not be brushed aside without some explanation: someone had come to Moscow. The few charred cinders which were all that was left of

Griboyedov, and much more besides, were eloquent proof of it.

Educated people took the viewpoint of the police: a gang of brilliantly skillful hypnotists and ventriloquists had been at work.

Immediate and energetic steps to arrest them in Moscow and beyond were naturally taken, but unfortunately without the least result. The man calling himself Woland and all his followers had vanished from Moscow, never to return there or anywhere else. He was of course suspected of having escaped abroad, but there was no evidence of his being there either.

The investigation of his case lasted for a long time. It was certainly one of the strangest on record. Besides four gutted buildings and hundreds of people driven out of their minds, several people had been killed. At least two of them were definitely known to have been killed: Berlioz and that wretched guide to the sights of Moscow, ex-Baron Maigel. His charred bones were found in apartment No. 50 after the fire had been put out. Violence had been done and violence could not go unchecked.

There were victims who suffered as a result of Woland's stay in Moscow, and these were, sad to say, black cats.

A good hundred of these peaceful, devoted and useful animals were shot or otherwise destroyed in various parts of the country. Thirty-odd cats, some in cruelly mutilated condition, were handed in to police stations in various towns. In Armavir, for instance, one of these innocent creatures was brought to the police station with its forelegs tied up.

The man had ambushed the cat just as the animal, wearing a very furtive expression (how can cats help looking furtive? It is not because they are depraved but because they are afraid of being hurt by creatures stronger than they are, such as dogs and people. It is easy enough to hurt them, but it is not something that anyone need be proud of) was about to jump into some bushes.

Pouncing on the cat and pulling off his tie to pinion it, the man snarled threateningly, "Aha! So you've decided to come to Armavir, have you, you hypnotist? No good pretending to be dumb! We know all about you!"

The man took the cat to the police station, dragging the wretched beast along by its front legs, which were bound with a green tie so that it was forced to walk on its hind legs.

"Stop playing the fool!" shouted the man, surrounded by a

crowd of hooting boys. "No good trying that trick—walk properly!"

The black cat could only suffer in silence. Deprived by nature of the gift of speech, it had no means of justifying itself. The poor creature owed its salvation largely to the police and to its mistress, an old widow. As soon as the cat was delivered to the police station, it was found that the man smelled violently of spirits, which made him a dubious witness. Meanwhile the old woman, hearing from her neighbor that her cat had been abducted, ran to the police station and arrived in time. She gave the cat a glowing reference, saying that she had had it for five years, since it was a kitten in fact, would vouch for it as she would for herself, proved that it had not been caught in any mischief and had never been to Moscow. It had been born in Armavir, had grown up there and learned to catch mice there.

The cat was untied and returned to its owner, though having learned by bitter experience the consequences of error and slander.

A few other people besides cats suffered minor inconveniences. Several arrests were made. Among those arrested for a short time were: in Leningrad one man called Wollman and one called Wolper, three Woldemars in Saratov, Kiev and Kharkov, a Wallach in Kazan and for some obscure reason a druggist in Penza by the name of Vetchinkevich. He was, it is true, a very tall man with a dark complexion and black hair.

Apart from that, nine Korovins, four Korovkins and two Karavaevs were picked up in various places. One man was taken off the Sevastopol train in handcuffs at Belgorod station for having tried to amuse his fellow passengers with card tricks.

One lunchtime at Yaroslavl a man walked into a restaurant carrying a kerosene burner, which he had just had repaired. As soon as they caught sight of him, the two cloakroom attendants abandoned their post and ran, followed by all the customers and staff. Afterward the cashier found that all her day's takings had been stolen.

There was more, much more than anyone can remember. A shock wave of disgust ran through the country.

It cannot be said too often that the police did an admirable job, given the circumstances. Everything possible was done, not only to catch the criminals but to provide explanations for what they had done. A reason was found for everything, and one must admit that the explanations were undeniably sensible.

Spokesmen for the police and a number of experienced psychiatrists established that the members of the gang, or perhaps one of them (suspicion fell chiefly on Koroviev), were hypnotists of incredible skill, capable of appearing to be in two or more places at once. Furthermore, they were frequently able to persuade people that things or people were where they weren't, or, vice versa, they could remove objects or people from someone's field of vision that were really there all the time.

In the light of this information everything was explicable, even the extraordinary incident of the bulletproof cat in apartment No. 50. There had, of course, been no cat on the chandelier, no one had fired back at the detectives, they had been firing at nothing, while Koroviev, who had made them believe that there was a cat going berserk on the chandelier, had obviously been standing behind the detectives' backs and deploying his colossal though criminally misused powers of suggestion. It was he, of course, who had poured kerosene all over the room and set fire to it.

Stepa Likhodeyev, of course, had never been to Yalta at all (a trick like that was beyond even Koroviev) and had sent no telegram from Yalta. After fainting in the doorway of his bedroom, frightened by Koroviev's trick of producing a cat eating a pickled mushroom on a fork, he had lain there until Koroviev had rammed a sheepskin hat on his head and sent him to Moscow airport, suggesting to the reception committee of detectives that Stepa was really climbing out of an airplane that had flown from the Crimea.

It is true that the Yalta police claimed to have seen Stepa and to have sent telegrams about him to Moscow, but not a single copy of these telegrams was to be found, which led to the sad but incontrovertible conclusion that the band of hypnotists had the power of hypnotizing people at vast distances, and then not only individuals but whole groups.

This being the case, the criminals were obviously capable of sending even the sanest people mad, so that trivia like packs of cards in a man's pocket or vanishing ladies' dresses or a beret that turned into a cat and suchlike were scarcely worth mentioning. Tricks like that could be done by any mediocre hypnotist on any stage, including the old dodge of wrenching off the M.C.'s head. The talking cat was child's play, too. To show people a talking cat one only had to know the first principles of ventriloquism, and clearly Koroviev's abilities went far beyond such basic principles.

No, packs of cards and false letters in Nikanor Ivanovich's briefcase were mere trifles. It was he, Koroviev, who had pushed Berlioz to certain death under the streetcar. It was he who had driven the wretched poet Ivan Bezdomny out of his mind, he who had given him nightmares about ancient Jerusalem and parched, sun-baked Mount Golgotha with the three crucified men. It was he and his gang who had spirited Margarita Nikolayevna and her maid away from Moscow. The police, incidentally, paid special attention to this aspect of the case, trying to discover whether these women had been kidnaped by this gang of murderers and arsonists or whether they had voluntarily run away with the criminals. Basing their findings on the ridiculous and confused evidence provided by Nikolai Ivanovich, taking into account the preposterous note that Margarita Nikolayevna had left for her husband to say that she was becoming a witch, and considering the fact that Natasha had vanished leaving all her movables at home, the investigators came to the conclusion that both maid and mistress had been hypnotized like so many others and then kidnaped by the gang. There was always, of course, the likely consideration that the crooks had been attracted by two such pretty women.

However, one thing baffled the police completely: what could have been the gang's motives for abducting a mental patient, who called himself the master, from a psychiatric clinic? This completely eluded them, as did the abducted patient's real name. He was therefore filed away forever under the pseudonym of "No. 118, Block 1."

Thus nearly everything was explained away, and the investigation, as all good things must, came to an end.

Years passed and people began to forget about Woland, Koroviev and the rest. Many things changed in the lives of those who had suffered at the hands of Woland and his associates, and however minor these changes may have been, they are still worth following up.

George Bengalsky, for example, after three months in the hospital, recovered and was sent home, but he had to give up his job at the Variety at the busiest time of the season, when

the public was storming the theater for tickets; the memory of
the black magic and its revelations was too unbearable. Bengalsky gave up the Variety because he realized that he could
not stand the agony of standing up in front of two thousand
people every evening, being inevitably recognized and endlessly
subjected to jeering questions about how he preferred to be—
with or without his head? Apart from that, the master of
ceremonies had lost a lot of the cheerfulness which is essential
in his job. He developed a nasty, compulsive habit of falling
into a depression every spring at the full moon, of suddenly grabbing his neck, staring round in terror and bursting
into tears. These attacks did not last for long, but nevertheless
since he did have them he could hardly go on doing his old
job, and the M.C. retired and began living on his savings,
which, by his modest reckoning, were enough to keep him for
fifty years.

He left and never again saw Varenukha, who had won
universal love and popularity for his incredible charm and
politeness, remarkable even for a theater manager. The free-
ticket hounds, for instance, regarded him as their patron saint.
At whatever hour they rang the Variety, through the receiver
would always come his soft, sad "Hello," and if the caller
asked for Varenukha to be brought to the telephone, the same
voice hastened to reply: "Speaking—at your service." But
how Ivan Savyelich had suffered for his politeness!

You can no longer speak to Stepa Likhodeyev if you telephone the Variety. Immediately after his week's stay in the
hospital, Stepa was transferred to Rostov, where he was made
the manager of a large delicatessen store. There are rumors that
he never touches port these days, that he only drinks vodka
distilled from black currants and is much healthier for it.
They say, too, that he is very silent and avoids women.

Stepan Bogdanovich's removal from the Variety did not bring
Rimsky the joy he had dreamed of for so many years. After
the hospital and a cure at Kislovodsk the treasurer, now an old,
old man with a shaking head, tendered his resignation. It was
Rimsky's wife who brought his letter of resignation to the
theater; Grigory Danilovich himself could not find the strength,
even in daytime, to revisit the building where he had seen the
moonlit windowpane rattling and the long arm reaching down
to grasp the catch.

Having retired from the Variety, Rimsky got a job at the

children's marionette theater on the far side of the Moscow River. Here he never had to deal with Arkady Apollonovich Sempleyarov on the subject of acoustics, because he in turn had been transferred to Bryansk and put in charge of a mushroom-canning plant. Now Muscovites eat his salted chanterelles and his pickled button mushrooms, and they are so delicious that everybody is delighted with Arkady Apollonovich's change of job. It is all so long ago now that there is no harm in saying that Arkady Apollonovich never had much success at improving the acoustics of Moscow's theaters, and the situation remains much the same today.

Apart from Arkady Apollonovich, several other people have given up the theater for good, among them Nikanor Ivanovich Bosoi, even though his only link with the theater was a fondness for free tickets. Nowadays Nikanor Ivanovich not only refuses to accept free tickets; he wouldn't set foot inside a theater if you paid him, and he even turns pale if the subject crops up in conversation. More than the theater he now loathes both Pushkin and that gifted artiste, Savva Potapovich Kurolesov; in fact, he detests that actor to such a degree that last year, catching sight of a black-bordered announcement in the newspaper that Savva Potapovich had been struck down in the prime of life by a heart attack, Nikanor Ivanovich turned such a violent shade of purple that he almost joined Savva Potapovich, and he roared; "Served him right!"

What is more, the actor's death stirred so many painful memories for Nikanor Ivanovich that he went out and, with the full moon for company, got blind drunk. With every glass that he drank, the row of hated figures lengthened in front of him: there stood Sergei Gerardovich Dunchill, there stood the beautiful Ida Herkulanovna, there stood the red-bearded man and his herd of fearsome geese.

And what happened to them? Nothing. Nothing could happen to them because they never existed, just as the master of ceremonies, the theater itself, the miserly old aunt hoarding currency in her cellar and the rude cooks never existed either. Nikanor Ivanovich had dreamed it all under the evil influence of the beastly Koroviev. The only real person in his dream was Savva Potapovich the actor, who got involved merely because Nikanor Ivanovich had so often heard him on the radio. Unlike all the others, he was real.

So perhaps Aloysius Mogarych did not exist either? On the

contrary. Aloysius Mogarych is still with us, in the very job that Rimsky gave up—treasurer of the Variety Theater.

About twenty-four hours after his call on Woland, Aloysius had regained consciousness in a train somewhere near Vyatka. Finding that he had absent-mindedly left Moscow without his trousers but had somehow brought his landlord's rent book with him, Aloysius had given the conductor a colossal tip, borrowed a pair of filthy old trousers from him and turned back to Moscow from Vyatka. But he failed to find his landlord's house. The ancient pile had been burnt to the ground. Aloysius, however, was extremely ingenious. Within a fortnight he had moved into an excellent room in Bryusov Street, and a few months later he was installed in Rimsky's office. Just as Rimsky had suffered under Stepa, Varenukha's life was now made a misery by Aloysius. Ivan Savyelich's one and only wish is for Aloysius to be removed as far away from the Variety as possible because, as Varenukha sometimes whispers among his close friends, "he has never met such a swine in his life as that Aloysius and he wouldn't be surprised at anything Aloysius might do."

The house manager is perhaps biased. Aloysius is not known to have done anything suspicious—indeed, he does not appear to have done anything at all, except of course to appoint another bartender in place of Sokov. Andrei Fokich died of cancer of the liver nine months after Woland's visit to Moscow. . . .

More years passed, and the events described in this truthful account have faded from most people's memories—with a few exceptions.

Every year, at the approach of the vernal full moon, a man of about thirty or a little more can be seen walking toward the lime trees at Patriarch's Ponds. A reddish-haired, green-eyed, modestly dressed man. He is Professor Ivan Nikolayich Poniryov of the Institute of History and Philosophy.

When he reaches the lime trees, he always sits down on the same bench on which he sat that evening when Berlioz, now long forgotten by everybody, saw the moon shatter to fragments for the last time in his life. Now that moon, whole and in one piece, white in the early evening and later golden with its outline of a dragon-horse, floats over the erstwhile poet Ivan Nikolayich though seeming to stand still.

Ivan Nikolayich now knows and understands everything. He

knows that as a young man he fell victim to some crooked hypnotists, went to the hospital and was cured. But he knows that there is still something that is beyond his control. He cannot control what happens at the springtime full moon. As soon as it draws near, as soon as that heavenly body begins to reach that fullness it once had when it hung in the sky high above the two seven-branched candlesticks, Ivan Nikolayich grows uneasy and irritable, loses his appetite, cannot sleep and waits for the moon to wax. When full moon comes, nothing can keep Ivan Nikolayich at home. Toward evening he leaves home and goes to Patriarch's Ponds.

As he sits on the bench, Ivan Nikolayich openly talks to himself, smokes and peers at the moon or at the familiar turnstile.

Ivan Nikolayich spends an hour or two there, then gets up and walks, always following the same route, across Spiridonovka Street with unseeing eyes toward the side streets near the Arbat.

He passes an oil shop, turns by a crooked old gas lamp and creeps up to a fence, through which he can see a garden that is splendid, though not yet in flower, and in it—lit on one side by moonlight, dark on the other, with an attic that has a triple-casement window—a house in the Gothic style.

The professor never knows what draws him to that fence or who lives in that house, but he knows that it is useless to fight his instinct at full moon. He knows, too, that in the garden beyond the fence he will inevitably see the same thing every time.

He sees a stout, elderly man sitting on a bench, a man with a beard, a pince-nez and very, very slightly piggish features. Ivan Nikolayich always finds that tenant of the Gothic house in the same dreamy attitude, his gaze turned toward the moon. Ivan Nikolayich knows that having stared at the moon the seated man will turn and look hard at the attic windows, as though expecting them to be flung open and something unusual to appear on the window sill.

The rest, too, Ivan Nikolayich knows by heart. At this point he has to duck down behind the fence, because the man on the bench begins to twist his head anxiously, his wandering eyes seeking something in the air. He smiles in triumph, then suddenly clasps his hands in delicious agony and mutters quite distinctly, "Venus! Venus! Oh, what a fool I was . . . !"

"Oh, God," Ivan Nikolayich starts to whisper as he hides behind the fence with his burning gaze fixed on the mysterious stranger. "Another victim of the moon . . . another one like me . . ."

And the man goes on talking: "Oh, what a fool I was! Why, why didn't I fly away with her? What was I afraid of, stupid old ass that I am? I had to ask for that document! . . . Well, you must just put up with it, you old cretin!"

So it goes on until a window opens on the dark side of the house, something white appears in it and an unpleasant female voice rings out: "Where are you, Nikolai Ivanovich? What the hell are you doing out there? Do you want to catch malaria? Come and drink your tea!"

At this the man blinks and says in a lying voice, "I'm just having a breath of fresh air, my dear! The air out here is so nice!"

Then he gets up from his bench, furtively shakes his fist at the window which has just closed and stumps indoors.

"He's lying, he's lying! Oh, God, how he's lying!" mumbles Ivan Nikolayich as he walks away from the fence. "He doesn't come down to the garden for the fresh air—he sees something in that springtime sky, something high above the garden! What wouldn't I give to find out his secret, to know who the Venus is that he lost and now tries vainly to catch by waving his arms in the air."

The professor returns home a sick man. His wife pretends not to notice it and hurries him into bed, but she stays up and sits by the lamp with a book, watching the sleeping man with a bitter look. She knows that toward dawn Ivan Nikolayich will wake up with an agonized cry, will start to weep and rave. That is why she keeps in front of her on the tablecloth a hypodermic syringe ready in a dish of spirit and an ampoule of liquid the color of strong tea.

Later the poor woman is free to go to sleep without misgiving. After his injection Ivan Nikolayich will sleep until morning with a calm expression, and he will dream, unknown to her, dreams that are sublimely happy.

It is always the same thing that wakens the scholar and wrings that pitiful cry from him. He sees a strange, noseless executioner who, jumping up and uttering a grunt as he does so, pierces the heart of the maddened Hestas, lashed to a gibbet. But what makes the dream so horrible is not so much the executioner as the lurid, unnatural light that comes from a cloud, seething and drenching the earth, of the kind that only accompanies natural disasters.

After his injection the sleeper's vision changes. From the bed to the moon stretches a broad path of moonlight and up it is climbing a man in a white cloak with a blood-red lining. Beside him walks a young man in a torn chiton and with a disfigured face. The two are talking heatedly, arguing, trying to agree about something.

"Ye gods!" says the man in the cloak, turning his proud face to his companion. "What a disgusting method of execution! But please, tell me—" here the pride in his face turns to supplication—"it did not take place, did it? I beg you—tell me that it never took place?"

"No, of course it never took place," answers his companion in a husky voice. "It was merely your imagination."

"Can you swear to that?" begs the man in the cloak.

"I swear it!" answers his companion, his eyes smiling.

"That is all I need to know!" gasps the man in the cloak as he strides on toward the moon, beckoning his companion on. Behind them walks a magnificently calm, gigantic dog with pointed ears.

Then the moonbeam begins to shake, a river of moonlight floods out of it and pours in all directions. From the flood materializes a woman of incomparable beauty and leads toward Ivan a man with a stubble-grown face, gazing fearfully around him. Ivan Nikolayich recognizes him at once. It is No. 118, his nocturnal visitor. In his dream Ivan stretches out his arms toward him and asks greedily, "So was that how it ended?"

"That is how it ended, disciple," replies No. 118 as the woman approaches Ivan and says, "Of course. It has ended, and everything has an end. . . . I'll kiss you on the forehead and everything will be as it should be. . . ."

She leans over Ivan and kisses him on the forehead, and Ivan strains toward her to look into her eyes, but she draws back, draws back and walks away toward the moon with her companion. . . .

Then the moon goes mad, deluges Ivan with streams of light, sprays light everywhere, a moonlight flood invades the room, the light sways, rises, drowns the bed. It is then that Ivan sleeps with a look of happiness on his face.

In the morning he wakes silent, but quite calm and well. His bruised memory has subsided again, and until the next full moon no one will trouble the professor—neither the noseless man who killed Hestas nor the cruel Procurator of Judea, fifth in that office, the knight Pontius Pilate.